OTHER BOOKS BY JESSAMYN WEST

The Friendly Persuasion
A Mirror for the Sky
The Witch Diggers
Cress Delahanty
Love, Death, and the Ladies' Drill Team
To See the Dream
Love Is Not What You Think
South of the Angels
A Matter of Time
Leafy Rivers
Except for Me and Thee
Crimson Ramblers of the World, Farewell
Hide and Seek
The Secret Look
The Massacre at Fall Creek
The Woman Said Yes

THE LIFE
I REALLY
LIVED:
a novel by
JESSAMYN
WEST

HARCOURT BRACE JOVANOVICH
NEW YORK AND LONDON

Printed in the United States of America

LIBRARY OF CONGRESS CATALOGING IN PUBLICATION DATA
West, Jessamyn.
The life I really lived.
I. Title.
PZ3.W51903Li   [PS3545.E8315]   813′.5′4   79-1853
ISBN 0-15-151562-X

A limited first edition has been privately printed.

B C D E

For my husband with love

A man sets himself the task of portraying
the world. Through the years he peoples
a space with images of provinces, king-
doms, mountains, boys, ships, islands,
fishes, rooms, instruments, stars, horses,
peoples. Shortly before his death he dis-
covers that the patient labyrinth of lives
traces the image of his face.

—JORGE LUIS BORGES

One's real life is the life one does not
lead.

—OSCAR WILDE

I
MORNING

1

Once my mother phoned me and said, "Oh, why did the mother in your story have to be so slangy?"

"It's not you, Mama."

"But why the mother? Since it's all fiction anyway, the mother didn't have to be the slipshod speaker, did she?"

No, she didn't. It *was* all fiction. I wanted, when I began to write, to forget the life I had lived and the people I had lived among. I imagined and painted a world not only different from, but better than, the one I grew up in. It wasn't difficult. Judge for yourself after you read what follows.

Why tell the truth now? The urge to confess is an old one: to come clean; to cease sailing under false colors; to end the belief that I wrote of joy and courage and faith because I had never known anything else. Oh, I knew. I knew.

I made a choice when I first wrote. I created a landscape more familiar to me than the hills I had climbed, the branches I had waded, the corn I had hoed. I pictured in those early novels the landscapes of my heart.

I can speak freely now. Mama is no longer here to care how mothers speak. Actually, only three of the people I'll rightly name (four, counting myself) are still alive.

Perhaps I do wrong to decry those first pious stories. Perhaps joy has been the true story of my life. Perhaps the events I witnessed, and sometimes participated in, were no more a part of me than the wind that blows through the forest is a part of the forest.

Barn-burning, dog-poisoning, incest, rape, suicide, murder: these events of my girlhood will be briefly told. I have my need to confess. You may not have a like need to suffer.

So, after almost forty years of writing and eighteen novels, I am determined to look inward: not for the purpose, in today's cliché, of "discovering my identity." I take it that what I did is who I am.

In remembering these happenings, I will at least escape what Socrates called "the greatest tragedy," that is, "an unexamined life."

My mother, Myra Chase, named me Orpha after Orpheus, the legendary Greek poet. She valued writing, and Joe, her first born, in her own words, "never still for a moment, body or tongue," was not good material for so silent and sedentary an occupation. Perhaps the name affected me. I think names can. In any case, though the language of my story, let alone the events, remembered and reported, would probably not have my mother's approval, still she, by her naming, put a pen in my hand.

Where did these events take place? In that part of Kentucky so far north it might as well have been Indiana. Border country. Where a man hadn't the settled values of a long-established community to bolster him up. He was on his own there, and his own quite often wasn't enough.

The landscape? Beautiful. Nothing more beautiful in the United States.

Streams, creeks, branches, rivers: Rush Branch, Salt Lick, Rattatack River, Otter Creek, Little Sandy, Big Sandy.

Trees: beech, black walnut, sycamore, maple.

Farmland, marginal: corn, tobacco, timothy, apples, hogs.

This story begins "back east." The story—not my life—ends, like many stories with such a beginning, in California. Endings are not California's fault. If there were a little more to the continent, if the Pacific could be postponed for another thousand miles, California would be as blameless as Iowa or Kansas. But there it is—land's end— a natural place for endings. Thousands have been heading there for a hundred years, I one of them; we have made California what it is. Meanwhile, those left behind point their fingers westward and say accusingly, "L.A., L.A." As if Los Angeles were too obscene a word to be said syllable by syllable.

L.A.! V.D., S.O.B., T.B. That's the category.

When? This story starts at the turn of the century. My parents' dates are a little earlier; mine a little later. It is being concluded now.

Everything in the beginning happened in the thirty square miles surrounding the small country town of Amesville, a settlement named for Amos Ames, who pushed through the Cumberland Gap with a wife and six sons in 1793.

4

I'll begin as gently as I can, which isn't very gentle. There is no other way I can tell the truth, either about the backwoods in which I grew up or my reason for having written fiction far distant in miles and mood from that dark and bloody ground.

2

I started school at Fairmont and stayed there until I had graduated from the eighth grade. When I was ten or eleven I had a classmate named Wilbur Ott. Ott was not the name of the family Wilbur lived with. Wilbur was an orphanage boy, given a home by old Mr. and Mrs. Eli Reese in return for the work he could do.

Mr. and Mrs. Reese (her name was Almira) were both as white as bleached bones. Eli had plenty of hair and a long white beard. Almira's hair was so scanty that when it was skinned back the effect was of a percale with stripes: big stripes of pinkish scalp, narrow stripes of white hair. I thought then that the Reeses were eighty or ninety. They were probably in their sixties.

Wilbur was their hired hand and their only one. He was up before daylight milking cows, slopping hogs, starting fires. When he got home from school Wilbur started work again.

"Mr. Reese says," Wilbur told me, "don't stop hoeing until it gets so dark you can see the sparks fly when your hoe hits a stone."

Mrs. Reese kept their little two-story frame house as tidy as her husband did the farm. Wilbur helped her. She sold eggs: Wilbur gathered them. She sold butter: Wilbur churned it. The churn was bigger around than Wilbur and the dasher was higher than his head. When churning gave him a backache, Mrs. Reese said, "Cure it the way you got it. Churn."

Wilbur looked so much like the Reeses he might have been their own son. He was bone white like them, thinner, if anything, stoop-shouldered, and he couldn't run any more than they could.

He sat in front of me at school and was always falling asleep. I tried to keep him out of trouble. When I saw that the teacher was going to call on him, I would poke him awake.

I had a ten-year-old's wisdom. "You ought to sleep more at night so you can stay awake in school."

"Mrs. Reese says I can sleep when I'm dead."

The Reeses' house burned down one night, the second year

Wilbur lived with them. Burned up the Reeses, too. Wilbur, who slept in the attic, escaped by sliding down the drainpipe that carried the rain off the roof to the water barrel below.

People wondered why the old couple downstairs hadn't run outside. They *had* made it as far as the door; their bodies were found there. Confused and dizzy with smoke, perhaps.

People, before Wilbur went back to the orphanage, sympathized with him on the loss of his benefactors. Wilbur was philosophical. "Mr. Reese was a hard worker. He can sleep now," he said.

The three children of Clint and Elsie Burden were also schoolmates of mine. The two boys, Ben and Brock, were my age; the daughter, Ina, was two or three years older.

Clint was black-haired with a sooty pitted skin. He was thickheaded and so were the boys. Ina was like her mother, put together, it appeared, with spun-gold wires covered with the least possible amount of skin.

Ina was as quick-witted as the boys were slow. She knew the answer before the teacher had finished asking the question. She was easy to please. Any joke made her laugh. The trouble was, she laughed till she cried.

One Sunday afternoon at three o'clock Ina and her mother, Elsie, appeared at our house. They had walked three miles from their farm the other side of Rush Branch.

"I know you folks have strawberries and I got so hungry for strawberries and cream for supper that Ina and I just walked over for a treat."

That was a strange thing to do: invite yourself to neighbors you hardly knew for supper and tell them what the menu will be.

There were no strawberries in the house; Mama and I had to go out and pick a mess. Then Mama cooked a company supper. What else could she do?

It got dark, bedtime really, and still Elsie and Ina lingered.

Joseph, my brother—we called him Joey—offered to hitch up a horse and drive them home. They wouldn't hear of it. "The dark's the least thing we're afraid of," Elsie said, and they set off finally under a setting quarter-moon for Rush Branch.

Ina wasn't at school the next day. Ben and Brock were. They told me Ina was poorly and wanted to see me. Would I walk home with them? I did.

What I saw I'll never forget. People see scenes like this on TV and in the movies nowadays and never turn a hair. So I could describe it and no one would be shocked. But I was a child and I saw the *real* thing, not a picture. The blood was blood, not catsup. The brains on the floor were brains, not corn-meal mush. The white that showed through the flesh was bones, not papier-mâché.

Elsie was the battered one. Someone had banged her around like a rag doll, and when she came to pieces, it wasn't sawdust that had poured out.

Clint was the one with very little head. The gun he had used to kill himself with was by his side.

Ina was in one piece, completely unharmed, but she was the one I remember best. She was naked, seated in a rocking chair and rocking. That seemed an odd thing to be doing, naked. Her body was more grown up than I had supposed. She had breasts and that spun-gold wire was at her fork. I had never seen anyone naked before; not even myself. I stared more at her than I did at the spilled blood and the shattered head.

She told us—as if we had asked her "Why?" (I don't think we did)—"She wouldn't let him do it."

We didn't ask her what. But she repeated those words over and over again, rocking in time to them as if they were a verse. "She wouldn't let him do it." Alive, she scared me more than her father and mother dead.

The boys and I ran off, leaving poor Ina there in the rocker, as fast as we could go. We went to my home. There we reported what we had seen. I didn't mention the nakedness. Murder and suicide seemed more decent subjects to talk about before your own mother and father.

3

Ina's nakedness shocked me because I had been taught never to be completely naked—even when taking a bath.

All that is necessary for a bath, I was instructed, is a towel, a rag, a piece of soap, a basin of water, and five minutes. There is no need to strip bare.

You take off your outer clothes, of course. Then you take off your drawers, but you leave on your petticoat, which is fastened at the waist, and your shimmy, which has elbow-length sleeves and reaches halfway to the knees. Before you begin washing, you take your arms out of your shimmy, so that it hangs around your neck like a cape. Then you start: rag wet and well soaped. Left side of shimmy held away from body while that side is washed; right side exposed next and washed. Old shimmy off and clean shimmy on: quickly.

Now the petticoat can be removed. The shimmy will cover the body below the waist. The body can then be easily washed (the shimmy is full), without undue exposure. Feet and legs, one at a time, are next washed in the basin; drawers and stockings are put on last of all. Five minutes and the job is done! The body has been washed, the clothes are fresh, and nothing has occurred that you would be ashamed to have a neighbor see.

Brought up this way, the sight of Ina naked and rocking was a shock I've never forgotten. When I went to work at the Poor House (my mother's father was the superintendent), Ina was there. Her brothers had been taken in by relatives in Kansas, but no one wanted Ina. She wore clothes now and had stopped rocking, but still all she would say was, "She wouldn't let him do it." This was better than what some of the people at the Poor House said, as I soon found out. I could tell that she recognized me; but even to me all she would say was, "She wouldn't let him do it."

I was at the Poor House less to do work myself than to see that the inmates got their work done. Many were willing enough, but their minds wandered.

I went to the Poor House in early winter and one of my tasks was to see that Darkey Bob, thirty years old, a man's body but a child's mind, kept the three big wood boxes filled: one in the kitchen, and one in each living room, the family's and the inmates'. Bob was perfectly willing to work, only he had to be reminded to keep at it. If not reminded, he started gathering butternuts or making corrals for sow bugs.

One night, after a day when *my* mind had wandered, too, dark came and the wood boxes were still empty. My grandfather, a harsh Scotch-Irishman, made me, not Darkey Bob, fill all three boxes myself. I was strong enough for the job, but not courageous enough. To get to the woodshed I had to go through a gate into the barnyard; then, once in the woodshed, I had to feel around in the dark for the logs and chunks of wood that were needed.

8

After each armload, Grandpa would say, "Go back and get some more. Maybe you will remember tomorrow night to have Bob bring in the wood."

While I went back and forth with my loads of wood, Grandma sat and crocheted, hard and fast. I knew she was suffering with me, but she was afraid to cross her husband.

Grandpa, like many others who are harsh and even cruel to their own families, had a soft spot for one particular person. This person was Toss Courtney, the only man I ever heard of who was named for his dog. Usually it's the other way around. Toss the dog was a little black spaniel, and Toss the man, while not little, had curly black hair and big dark Spanish eyes. People spoke of "Toss the cur" and "Toss the sir" to differentiate between them.

Toss never wore suspenders, and his pants always hung precariously on his hipbones, apparently due at any minute to slide off completely. Toss spent a lot of time hoisting his pants up, getting them too tight in the crotch, then having to do a lot of wriggling to make himself comfortable there.

He was twenty-five or twenty-six years old, and at fourteen I thought he was an old man. But Grandpa doted on him. He *was* a hard worker and he had a smooth tongue. He knew better than anyone else how to rub Grandpa's fur the right way. Grandpa was in charge of the Poor Farm, kept the accounts, ordered supplies, admitted inmates, put those who misbehaved into the Poor House jail. But Toss did the outside work while Grandpa stayed in his office.

Toss went into Amesville each week to buy supplies, groceries mostly, but medicines, food for the animals, even a little whiskey and tobacco for special occasions and emergencies. He made the trip in a miniature covered wagon, an ordinary spring wagon really, but with a covering of canvas stretched over steel hoops.

On one trip I went with him. Grandma wanted some things for herself—crochet thread, outing flannel for nightgowns, some female medicine.

Grandpa said that Toss had his hands full taking care of the buying for the county, so if Grandma wanted shopping done for herself she should send me. Grandma objected. Maybe she knew something about Toss that Grandpa didn't. More likely he knew and didn't think I was of an age or aspect to kindle Toss.

9

He kindled. No sooner were we out of town after finishing our buying than he ran his fingers around the ear nearest him and told me it was as pretty as a pink shell. I didn't care to have an old man fondling my ears; I thought the pink-shell bit was just a sample of the soft soap I'd heard him ladle out so often to Grandpa. I wasn't much bothered.

But when he said, "I bet I know something else that's pink, too," and started to look for it, I resisted. I was strong and big; and besides, I didn't have to drive a horse. I could take his hands off me faster than he could put them on. Also, I wasn't afraid to bite, scratch, and claw, and he, whatever he had in mind for me, didn't want to take me home to Grandpa mussed up and bleeding. Toss thought he might get me over into the back of the spring wagon. But besides not wanting his hands on me, I didn't care about being mixed up with the coal oil, corn meal, and sorghum molasses back there.

Old Fox, Grandpa's horse, a dapple-gray mare, was on my side. First she wouldn't stand still, so Toss couldn't use both hands to shove me over into the back under the canvas top.

Then, when we got to the Rattatack, a real river, no little branch or creek, she lay right down in the middle. She had never done such a thing before.

Toss had to jump out to keep Fox from thrashing around and upsetting the wagon. I jumped, too, and made for the far bank. The water was only waist deep. I was more curious than afraid, so I turned around to see how Toss was making out with Fox. He didn't have any trouble getting her up. A dip, it seemed, was all she wanted.

I didn't run, and when Toss caught up with me and asked me to get back on the wagon, I did. I figured he'd had all the excitement he needed for one drive to town. He had. He spent the rest of the trip to the Farm pleading with me not to tell Grandpa.

"All I had in mind was a little frolic. Lots of girls are complimented when a man wants to frolic with them."

"You could've asked me."

"When I seen you wasn't, I stopped, didn't I?"

"You stopped when Fox laid down."

"Don't tell your grandfather."

"It's my duty."

"I'll lose my job."

"You should've thought of that before you started frolicking."

10

He cried real tears. But I wouldn't make any promises. I wouldn't have told Grandpa for anything. Crusty to his family as he was and with his soft spot for Toss, he would have accused me of leading Toss on. Lead him on? You can't lead anyone who is already all over you any direction except off, can you?

When he drove into the yard, Toss gave me a dollar bill; at least he said it was that. I couldn't see in the dark.

"Here's a dollar. It's a thank-you for not telling your grandfather."

I threw the bill, whatever it was, out into the dark. "Keep your dirty money," I said.

It was gone next morning, so I guess he did.

Toss caused me no more trouble. Instead, he tried to be complimentary to me, to bribe me with praise. When he did, I would say to *him*, "Toss, you've got real pretty pink ears."

The minute I said that, Toss's pink ears would get flaming red. I didn't say that, of course, when Grandpa was around. It wasn't nice for a girl to make comments to a man about anything as personal as his ears.

When I went home at Christmastime, I told my father, not about Toss Courtney, but about Grandpa's making me carry in load after load of wood in the dark. That was the end of my working at the Poor House.

"You are never to work there again," said Papa. There had never been any love lost between him and his father-in-law. Papa was a steady, quiet man; Grandpa was an impatient, hotheaded fireball.

I never did work there again. They got Lucy Cahill to take my place as Grandma's hired girl. Lucy was a good girl, about sixteen, one of the twelve children of Emmett Cahill and his wife, who lived high on a hill above the Rattatack. The Cahills, except for Lucy, who was sweet and biddable, were a shiftless lot. Em drank too much and his wife had too many children too fast to do much but start weaning the last one before morning sickness for the next one set in.

In February, Lucy made the same trip and for the same reason I had to town with Toss. On the way home, with no Old Fox to save her, Lucy was raped by Toss in the back of the wagon.

I knew of this because Toss told my brother all about it. Toss told a lot of people all about it. Lucy was too humiliated and ashamed to talk about it at all. So when a young man would say, "Give me

11

what you gave Toss or I'll tell everyone," she gave. Finally she moved to Indianapolis: "A regular little whore." I guess you know who told me that and who helped make her one.

4

Abel and Mabel Fetters lived below the Cahills on the bottom lands of the Rattatack; good land except when spring freshets made it a swamp, not a farm. They had no children, though Abel had a hobby. People accounted for the hobby by saying, "With Mabel, Fetters ain't able." Abel was a dog poisoner. It sometimes works out that way. A man wants to have some direct connection with life. If he can't bring life into being, he'll put an end to it. In that way he's not completely powerless. Some men can start it. Others can end it.

You see this in hunters. The most avid hunters are grizzled old bucks who are past the age of creating. Their substitute for the thrill they've lost is another thrill; for the life they can't make, they substitute the life they can take. They can still get a gun up and put a bullet into something warm and living and see it crumple.

Joey and I had two small run-ins with the Fetters before Joey had his big run-in with old Abel.

One day when he and I had been fishing in the Rattatack, we caught more catfish than we wanted to carry home, so we decided to leave a mess with the Fetters'.

The Fetters didn't have more than four rooms, and Mrs. Fetters, when we knocked, was just finishing sweeping the sitting room. She had been doing it right, with torn-up pieces of damp paper spread over the rag carpet to keep the dust down. She gathered up two or three dustpanfuls of dirt and damp paper before she was ready to talk to us.

Then she said, "That's an awful lot of dirt to get out of one room, ain't it?"

It did seem like an awful lot and we agreed. We weren't old enough yet to know that when people say things like that, they do so to be contradicted.

Someone says, "I'll never see fifty again."

Disagree. "You mean thirty, don't you?"

Someone says, "I made a botch of that pie."

Disagree. "Tastiest bit of pastry I've had in a month of Sundays."

Someone says, "You shouldn't have gone to the trouble of coming over."

Disagree. "No trouble at all. A great pleasure."

The next day Mrs. Fetters came to our house to complain to Mama about the rudeness of her children in commenting on the amount of dirt in her house. While there she took occasion to look at my bare feet; stare at them is what she did. Finally she said, "That's the queerest-looking pair of feet I ever saw on a human being."

After she left, Mama reassured me. "Your feet are exactly like everyone else's."

They weren't, exactly. My second toe was, and is, a lot longer than my big toe. After that, when I was barefooted, I tried to spread my skirts over my misshapen feet when I sat down. It wasn't until I saw pictures of Greek statues that I learned that a long second toe is the sign of a "classical" foot. It was too late to tell Mrs. Fetters. Though if I had said to her that summer afternoon, "I have a classical foot," she would have thought I was queer in the head as well as the feet.

Abel Fetters poisoned our Old Pedro. I don't think that what Joey and I said to his wife had anything to do with it.

Dogs are like humans in their characteristics. Some are kids all of their lives, never grow up; teeth go, ears lose their starch, and still they are gamboling. Some are born grandfathers, sour and bossy. Old Pedro was an uncle, dignified, but jovial and ready to accept you as an equal. He was a big dog, with black curly hair, a plume of a tail, and a red-tongued smile. He looked like the dogs woven into the patterns of Axminster rugs made to put in front of grates. And Old Pedro would lie as still as a rug if you wanted him to act as a pillow for your head when you stretched out in front of the fire. Old Pedro wasn't really old. Seven or eight, which is prime time for a dog. "Old" is a way of saying "darling" by people too shamefaced to say that even to a human, let alone a dog. We loved Old Pedro, his warm body, his silky curls, his red-tongued and white-toothed smile.

There are various ways of poisoning a dog. The commonest method is to put strychnine in a patty of meat. This disguise wasn't necessary with Old Pedro. He was trustful. So Abel Fetters did something worse: poured most of a big bottle of carbolic acid into his red-and-white grin before Pedro could clamp his trusting jaws shut or jerk free. He had his tongue, his throat, his stomach burned out. Old Pedro died bleeding and howling—howling as long as he had any throat to howl with. Then he was silent, still alive and suffering, but only able to talk with his eyes. Then he was dead.

Joey and his friend Lon Dudley, coming home from a rabbit hunt, caught Abel in the act of pouring liquid down Old Pedro's throat. They pinned Abel down, took the bottle, and poured the few spoonfuls of liquid in it down Abel's throat. Then they picked up the writhing dog and raced to the stream. Old Pedro never had a chance to survive.

Abel never talked again. He could make sounds: growls and grunts, whines and barks. His vocal cords had been burned out. No one blamed Joey and Lon for what they had done. Abel brought no charges against them. When Abel tried to talk, growling and whining, some said it was God's way of making him remember the pain he had caused dogs. What he remembered, I'm sure, was the pain Joey and Lon had caused him. Your own sufferings are always more memorable than any other person's, let alone a dog's.

We had a real burial for Old Pedro. Mama's hired girl, Mag Owens, put one of my outgrown dresses on him for a shroud. This was peculiar, but Mama allowed it because Mag said this would show Old Pedro that we considered him one of the family. What it showed the neighbors, I'm not sure. But then, Egyptians embalmed their cats, wound them up for burial in the same elaborate strands of cloth they used for human beings.

5

When I recall the events of my girlhood, I wonder that I didn't suffer more. The reason, I now believe, is that children and grownups did not inhabit the same world. In their sympathies, children feel nearer animals than adults. They frolic with animals, caress them, share with them feelings neither has words for. Have they ever stroked any adult with the love they bestow on a cat? Hugged any grownup with the ecstasy they feel when clasping a puppy?

For one thing, animals are nearer their own size—disregarding.

cows and horses, of course. I once had a pet hen more content to sit on my lap than any baby I ever tried to rock and fondle.

And animals are dependent on us, not the other way around. We love those we feed, not vice versa; in caring for others we nourish our own self-esteem. Children are dependent upon adults. It's a craven role for a child. It's very natural to want to bite the hand that feeds you.

So I sorrowed more for Old Pedro than for Abel Fetters.

And, sometime later, when my grandfather, my Poor House grandfather, that dour, bearded Scotch-Irishman, took *his* carbolic acid, I did not sorrow greatly, either; not because he had overworked me, or sent me to town with a rapist, but because he was a grownup. A grownup must know what he is doing. That's what we are all taught as children to believe, isn't it?

I have been a writer of fiction.

Fictional characters are made up. Now the writer who can create a character, describe his exterior, give him popeyes, sweaty hands, size twelve feet, is expected to know something about his interior as well. Or pretend to know. Why does he fall in love with fat women? Hate bees? Go to church only on the last Sunday of every month? The fiction writer can't just say that the character *does* such things and let it go at that. The reader wants to know *why* he does. And the fiction writer must be prepared to produce plausible motives.

The writer of a true tale does not and cannot provide such information. The minute he does so he becomes a fiction writer. How was a fifteen-year-old girl to know why a seventy-five-year-old man took deadly poison? Still less anything about the motives for the act, almost demented, that led to it? I didn't make up Grandpa and hence can't explain him.

In August, after my winter at the Poor House, both Grandma and Grandpa came down with typhoid. Grandpa began to mend, but Grandma, as her typhoid let up, developed the bloody flux and of that she died.

Grandpa was much too weak to attend her funeral. It was held in the United Brethren Church at Lick Skillet, with the Reverend Ezra Vawter officiating. The services were very largely attended.

Not only friends, neighbors, and relatives, but also all Poor House inmates with the exception of those too deranged to make a seemly appearance on so dignified an occasion.

Grandma was buried in the Old Grove Cemetery in a nice well-varnished coffin. The coffin was half covered by an anchor made of blossoms from the snowball bush in our own yard. Why an anchor instead of a cross? I don't know. It was a very warm day, and the snowballs, as if they were the real thing, not flowers, had melted into puddles of petals.

Except for the wilted state of all the flowers, the funeral was in every way stately and decorous. The Reverend Vawter in his sermon praised Grandma's virtues, consoled the mourners by assuring them that Grandma had "gone home," and stirred up the wayward by urging them to repent, since "the night cometh" when man can work no more.

At the conclusion of the Reverend Vawter's sermon, those at the graveside sang "We Shall Gather at the River." Then Grandma, with her tiny feet, her firm bosom, and her once-pink doll-baby cheeks, was lowered by means of a webbing of ropes into her final resting place.

Or so all supposed.

By October Grandpa was well again, and in possession of all his old hard-headedness. He planned another funeral, at which *he* could be present as chief mourner. Grandma would now be buried, not in the Old Grove Cemetery, but in a steel vault in the New Hope Burial Ground in Amesville. Everyone was to be present at this, the official, funeral.

The steel vault would protect Grandma from rain and now, from hard frost and spring thaws. She would be as cozy as in her own sitting room, the steel vault her weatherproof home for all eternity.

At this, her official, funeral, her casket would be again opened so that all, and especially Grandpa, who had been unable to bid her farewell when she had died might once again look upon the face of one they had loved and who had left them.

My father at first forbade us to attend this second funeral. We had said farewell once, he said, and Grandma would not be helped by our hearing a second sermon and watching a second entombment. Since it was his wife's father's wish, command, in fact, he relented. "We will go," he told Mama, "since your father wants it, but no looking into the open casket. You said good-bye once. That's enough."

I don't know whether my father knew what my grandfather should have known or not. This is not fiction. I didn't have access to the minds of either of the men. Grandfather was no fool. He was able to run an institution like the county Poor House in a businesslike way. The Louisville *Courier* came every day, two or three days late, of course, but he read it every day. Yet he evidently believed that his wife, after more than two months in the grave, would appear to him as she always had. Or at least as she had in her final sickness.

Why he should think this, I don't know, unless the undertaker (he sold hay, grain, and furniture as well as coffins and steel vaults) had told him that Grandma had been embalmed in some such way as would preserve her. The undertaker may really have believed in his embalming process. Perhaps what he believed in was the extra money he was going to receive from a second funeral for the same person—a second that would outdo the first.

Nothing went amiss until the coffin was opened. We were—Papa, Mama, Joey, and I—as Papa had ordered, far back in the church. We never saw inside the coffin. What we did see was Grandpa bending to kiss, I suppose, then stepping back, back, and finally collapsing, crumbling, it was really, to the floor.

That ended a funeral for which no one except Grandpa had had any heart. Someone closed the casket lid. Others tried to revive Grandpa, and failed.

He was carried to the Claybank, the only hotel in town, where he lay unconscious for three days. At the end of that time he came to, dressed, went out, bought a bottle of carbolic acid, returned to his room, and drank the bottle down to the last drop. It took him three days to die. My mother was with him. He died, she said, like a snake, wordless and writhing.

6

Why was I so little affected by these tragic and sordid happenings? Was it because they were so common in that time and place that I took them for granted, like the killing of flies and the butchering of hogs?

Was it because they happened to grownups, people of another world, a world no child ever expects to enter?

Was I cold and without feeling?

The last, at least, was not true. True, I remember these happenings and can recount them; but in the same way we know and report famines, tortures, catastrophes in distant lands. They were happening, these miseries, to a race to which I did not belong: grownups. Should I have understood that I, too, would soon be subject to the same pains and sorrows? But this is what makes youth youth. It is able to walk among the signposts pointing to its own decay and final destruction and still believe that it will never be so foolish as to tread *that* path. We think when young that the stiff-kneed, humped-shouldered, chop-fallen walk and look that way because they choose to. They *could* straighten up, step out, look better if only they wanted to. They simply don't care. Youth cares. It will always be ramrod straight, limber-legged, and firm-faced.

That, I believe, is what permitted me to live among so much pain without much suffering of my own. Kill, rape, poison, die by your own hand! I was a traveler observing the peculiar ugly rites of another race. It wasn't my idea of fun: but live and let live.

My ability to live undaunted in the midst of such happenings didn't mean that I was unfeeling. I had my own raptures and tears; but for small things, child-size happenings.

That comment about my feet was a small thing; it has kept me shod all my life. I still avoid open-toed shoes, still wear sandals even when I go in the water.

I gave Alice Matthews—my own age and one of the nine Matthews children—who came to school with her braids tied with dirty cord string, my second-best hair ribbons. They were Alice blue. I thought she should have them. I tied the ribbons, one to each of her long hard braids, myself. She seemed pleased. I was pleased. I had made a real sacrifice. Where dull dirtiness had been, there was now bright cleanness.

Next morning Alice came into the schoolroom after we were all seated at our desks. She carried the sheared-off bottom half of each of her long stiff braids, with the ribbons still attached. She placed them on my desk. "Mama says to tell you that I have a father and mother who will look after me." Her own braids were tied again with cord string—clean now, though.

I was too humiliated and hurt to march the severed braids up to a wastepaper basket. They lay on my desk all morning. At noon my teacher, a young woman as downy-faced as a peach, took pity on me.

"Do you want to keep these?"

"No," I whispered.

She carried the braids by the ribbons, not touching the hair, and dropped them into the big wastepaper basket by her desk.

Alice, except for her mother, would, I think, have enjoyed the ribbons and not have held them against me. It was as if Mrs. Crit Matthews had been able somehow to look forward into the entanglement of our future lives and had begun early to pay me for the pain that would later come to her—through me, she would believe.

We played at school, when there was a heavy fall of wet snow that would pack easily into balls, a game called "ante-over." We used a snowball instead of the baseball of spring and autumn. I have forgotten the rules of the game, but the person who was "it" could be "caught," "imprisoned," and with luck "saved." It was a childhood allegory of war, of fate and salvation. We didn't know this, of course.

For me the joy was in the movement, the coldness of the air, the sight of the round white ball sailing up against the hard blue sky and clearing the ridgepole of the schoolhouse. This was followed by the mad run to reach the other side of the building before the enemy—that's the way we thought of them—reached our side. I was good at this. I delighted in it. Not only in the jubilant response of muscles, lungs, and heart, but in the appealing spectacle I thought I made for spectators.

Boy spectators, that is. I had reached the age—I was fourteen—when I cared about the boys. I wanted them to think me attractive. I was a thinker, if not a very rational one, and I thought boys would be drawn to someone who had the qualities they admired in each other: speed, strength, courage, daring. Examples of the compulsion of sex had been taking place all around me, its miseries and fatalities. Of its pleasures, I knew nothing.

Boys, I believed, would like a girl who was boyish, and I was equipped to be so. Horses are drawn to their own kind, aren't they? Cows are gentler, but no horse is ever seen rubbing his nose to a cow. Cats are more graceful than dogs. Dogs nevertheless like dogs; and any cat who wants a dog's attention will do well to learn to bark and pee with one leg up.

19

This was my reasoning; so out of love of boys I was as boyish as possible and could, because of my build and strength, out-boy some boys. Simon Wycoff was one such. He was smart as a whip in the schoolroom and slow as molasses outside. He was spindly and smart and I doted on him. Nothing I could do in class deserved his attention. But when it came to games outside, Simon, I thought, could not but admire me. I was not only better than Simon. I could rescue him.

In ante-over, I did. Released him from captivity by the other side. When I did so and was leading him to safety, he said, "You army mule, you."

It is bad enough to be called a "mule." An army mule, I supposed, was the worst kind, one selected because of its pugnacious qualities.

Words, they say, can do no harm. But sticks and stones can break your bones.

Not altogether true. A broken bone can heal, but the wound a word opens can fester forever. Army mule. Because of these two words I have all my life pretended to an amiable spiritlessness not truly mine.

So I was capable of feeling about what happened to me, but my feelings were for the most part truly ones of joy.

I never meet anyone nowadays who admits to having had a happy childhood. Everyone appears to think happiness betokens a lack of sensitivity. They were not loved enough, they say, by mother or father. Or they were loved too much. They were enmeshed in the trauma of "discovering their own identity." They suffered from sibling rivalry. They felt guilty about sex. They go now to consciousness-raising sessions and sensitivity-training seminars to understand and so heal their childhood wounds.

As a child, I was happy as a lark. I was loved as much as I wanted to be loved by my parents. I cannot remember ever being kissed by them or of suffering from the lack. I did suffer once because I wanted to kiss my father good-bye, when he was going off to Ohio to the funeral of his mother; I didn't dare to, because I knew my mother wouldn't approve. I didn't know why then; I know why now, and I don't blame her. In those dark backwoods days, couplings took place between male and female without much regard to blood relationship. Incest was common. It was a sexy neighborhood. The

20

advice "Keep your pecker up" was never needed there. It was the common state.

So I never kissed or was kissed by my father. My mother, either, for that matter. But I never missed it. You have to stand still to be kissed, and what child wants to stand still?

I had a cat called "Pumpkin" because it was pumpkin-colored. It was a female, barren by some fortunate (as far as I was concerned) natural defect. When it comes to humans, I prefer males. With cats, I was a lesbian. Tomcats, to the hand, are a network of ropes. The tabby can spring as high as a tom, but her mechanism is less exposed. To the hand she is warm live flesh, responsive as only the living can be.

Pumpkin would lie flat on my chest, her nose an inch from mine. She rose and fell with my breathing. Her heartbeat was a counterpoint to mine. Her golden eyes altered in size and focus like a sunflower following the sun. Could a mother's kisses surpass this eye touch? Perhaps. Perhaps this is a pitiful confession.

In the fall when I was young, turkey buzzards held flying circuses above the sycamores and catalpas. It was all done for me, I thought, that drift of black snow across the sky. The snow that never fell. It lived, it was movement, it was the joy of soaring, no destination in mind, no food being sought. I was brought up to believe in God and I thanked Him when the buzzards danced their airborne autumn ballet above my head.

I named the stars myself. I noted the difference between planets and stars. They kept clock time. I said "Thank you" when at the appointed hour Venus (I called her Lamplighter because she came at dusk) lit her lantern in the west. I was happy as a shepherd in the desert to have their company. We were companions.

When I was about six, a boy named Tommy Fitzgerald gave me a wad of sweet gum, pried loose from a tree. Tommy had black hair and red cheeks. I chewed the gum until it melted away in spit. I was too proud to ask for more. Tommy chose me first when he was team captain. He did not think I was an army mule.

I liked to eat, and my mother set a good table. I never went hungry. I didn't have that to be sad about. There is as much variety in flavors as in the looks of birds. I relished them all: musky yams, sweet pork tenderloin, sauerkraut so crisp it had to be well chewed and, after greasy gravies and buttered potatoes, was a throat cleanser.

Joey was my friend. He didn't look down on me because I was a girl and younger. If I had been his brother, it might have been different. He grew up wild, but he was a gentle brother. He was a tall, lanky, black-haired rascal, but he was a sweet big brother to me and he made me happy. He pitied me because I *was* a girl, and I think girls deserve pity. They have to wait to be asked: or did in my day. He played the French harp and taught me the words of songs. I was no more musical than a muskrat, but I could memorize. I sang "Skip to My Lou" and "Over the Water to Charlie" and "Home at Last the Harbor Past" when Joey played loud.

He showed me how boys were made and asked me to touch him, but I wouldn't. I'd as lief have grabbed hold of his tongue. Girls have tongues, too, but down at the crotch they are neater than boys.

Joey was a Christian. He saw Jesus in the stars on Christmas night, His face in glory, not suffering, on the cross.

Girls besieged him, and he gave in now and then. But no girl took her downfall from him. If she'd already fallen, and had nothing to lose, he was willing to stand in line.

Some children are mirrors, reflecting the unhappiness of their parents. Many who say they had an unhappy childhood are really saying their parents were unhappy. If your parents are happy, you can be an unmusical army mule, freckled as a turkey egg, and a pain in the neck to your peers, determined and able to outtalk, outrun, and outsmart them—and still be happy. If your parents are happy, the center holds. Mine were. I don't, or at least didn't, know why. Papa was a quiet, ruminative nurseryman. Mama was an ex-school-teacher with a switchblade tongue and a father who drank poison. Papa made plants grow and Mama made words jump. They admired each other. He was big and blond, like the sun on snow. She was small and black, a clinker still glowing. They let me alone, but they were there for me to come home to.

All around me, fornication and suicide; children mistreated and hired girls knocked up; cancer treated with poultices of dock leaves boiled in urine. And I didn't care a whit about the pain and the tears and the yelps of agony. Because what happened, happened to grownups. They were a race apart. Is your happiness spoiled now because cats starve in alleys, foxes die in traps while trying to chew their legs off, and old hens lose their cherished heads on chopping blocks? Animals are a race apart. You couldn't care less. They don't really feel. You'll never be a fox, a hen, or a cat. You can't put yourself in their shoes.

It was the same with grownups. I had only to look at a grownup to know I'd never be one. They had *permitted* what happened to them to happen: dewlaps swinging, eyelids fold on fold, chin whiskers for women, bald heads for men. How feel pity for people who have no regard for themselves?

Yet, I was verging on being one, though I didn't guess it. So the moments of bliss continued.

When I say bliss, I'm not talking about a full stomach or running fast or being best in a spelling match or waking up to the whisper of snow. They're good. But what I'm talking about now is—bliss. Bliss is a feeling unsought, almost indescribable. It comes when the body, which is flesh with definite boundaries, escapes those boundaries and is a part of sunlight or wind, of starshine, or of the known and loved order of the pieces of wood called "furniture" in a building called "home."

Once, when I was nearly six, I was in the furrow of a field Papa was plowing, his plow pulled by Polly. Polly was white. White horses are not generally credited with the brains or stamina or speed of roans or claybanks or bays. But Polly had all the sense that was needed on that day of plowing. I was flat in the furrow watching a dung beetle dig deeper. Papa had his eyes on the earth he was turning up. Only Polly was paying attention to what was at least as important as beetles or furrows—me. She stopped in her tracks, put her head down to mine; her long-lashed eyes (one eye was what is called "glass," colorless) looked right into mine with love. Papa slapped her with the reins, yelled, "Gitty up," but Polly stood rock still, big as a fortress behind me. Then I knew bliss. Then I broke out of the boundaries of skin and was neither child nor horse nor the beetle I had been watching, but had the sensation of being all of them—and safe, to boot.

I was sorry when Papa came round to Polly's head to see what

23

ailed her. What he discovered took away my bliss and made me merely lucky.

Once I visited Grandma and was homesick. Between my parents' home and my grandparents', separated by only a mile, my grandfather (not my Poor House grandfather) had rigged up a homemade telephone. It worked only between the two houses, but between them it did work. I phoned my own home, and it was not my mother's voice, but the sound of the clock striking there that canceled miles, dissolved walls, and put me in a state where everything was everywhere. Distant sounds rang in my ears, the rooms they housed rose up around me, home was in my heart, and I knew bliss.

On a gloomy day, an in-between time—winter over, spring late —I walked through a woods lot, trees not yet leafed out, the ground thawed and muddy. I was walking to get somewhere, blind as I could make myself to what was colorless and ugly when suddenly about the stone foundation of an old, burned-out homestead, I saw the massed yellow bloom of what we called "China lilies," flowers that were either jonquils or narcissus. It was beautiful, as unexpected as a rainbow and more durable. I knew bliss.

I knew a way to reach bliss, but I often forgot the way, so that I came to it with surprise each time. I had only to be alone, usually in the sitting room at home, the room orderly, dusk already arrived, darkness near, a fire in the grate, and a lamp lit by my own hand on a stand-table across the room. It helped if the door into either the parlor or the dining room was at least partially opened showing, in a room unlighted, the dim outlines of half-guessed objects.

Then, lamp lighted, I sat on the sofa, waiting, I thought, for the folks to come home, or for Joey to stamp in from chores. I watched the pendulum of the clock toss reflected light from left to right, watched the lampwick burn higher on an angled corner, so the surfaces of dusted furniture gleamed like moons. I heard the wind go round the corner of the house, listened as a piece of firewood settled in the grate, heard ashes falling more silent than snow. I smelled the pine or oak that was burning, and the coal oil which I myself had used as furniture polish when dusting.

Then, what I saw and smelled and heard absorbed me. All blended, so that what I saw had order; and what I heard was visible; and what I smelled had form; and all, fusing, touched me with warmth and light. I became the center of a universe without boundaries. Then I knew bliss.

I write this for two reasons. First, to exonerate myself from my occasional suspicion that I may have been an unfeeling child. I explain this (to myself) by my early belief that grownups were of another world—a world connected to mine, but not yet a part of it. I was moved by the things of my world.

Second, I want to convince myself that I was not, because of the cruelty and violence around me, a child who moped and gnawed her nails; who said when grown, "I am a mess, but what can you expect, considering what I went through?" The truth is, I not only had a happy childhood, I also knew bliss.

But without being aware of it, I was about to move into the world of suffering. There were forewarnings, but I didn't recognize them. Only afterward can one look back at an event, meaningless at the time, and say, "It was an early warning signal, but at the time the code had never been explained to me."

II
ORMAND

1

After graduating from the eighth grade at Fairmont, the only other schooling available to me was at the "Normal" in Amesville. It ran for six weeks in the summer, and graduates were certificated as schoolteachers. Amesville was nine miles from our home, a two-hour trip for a schoolgirl on a horse chosen for safety, not speed. The Rattatack had to be forded. In rainstorms the horse would be hitched to a buggy. Papa, a careful man, preferred a daughter alive and without a higher education to one smart as a whip but dead in a runaway or drowned in an overturned buggy. And I was happy at home: a runner, a jumper, a cake baker, an animal lover. I had no longing for desks and inkwells. I worked at home, helped neighbors at harvest time or when there was sickness. Sometimes the help was neighborly and unpaid for; sometimes I was a hired girl with a weekly salary of a dollar.

I was a hired girl at the Bakers', because when Victoria Cinderella Baker asked Mama if I could help, she knew she was asking for weeks of labor, perhaps months. Her husband, Hiram, had had a stroke. His body was not paralyzed, but his brain had been damaged. His memory was gone. He didn't know who he was. Each morning he asked me, "Who am I?" He kept a suitcase packed because he expected to be going home soon. In his own mind he was a very young man, visiting some elderly lady, his wife, Victoria Cinderella. He had been a farmer, but he could work no more. He was unable to remember what he had done five minutes ago. He could hitch up a horse, but no sooner was this done than he believed he had just come in from work, and started unhitching.

He would eat a meal, see his clean plate, and ask, "When will dinner be ready?" "Oh, please pass the gravy," he pleaded politely, because the stroke that had ruined his mind hadn't changed his disposition, which was sweet. "I am starving," he would say.

I was his caretaker, a young woman of about his own age, he

believed. A relative? The hired girl? A kindly disposed neighbor? Sometimes he thought I was the Victoria Cinderella he had wooed. But that was a memory only. The part of his mind that set in motion a wooer's machinery had also been destroyed.

I did not think that Victoria Cinderella and I could ever have looked alike. She was still a doll-baby lady at forty-five. At sixteen, when her corn-tassel hair was still silky and yellow, and her doll-baby cheeks were still pink as paint without the streaking of a single broken vein, Hiram, then thirty, must have wanted to cuddle the sawdust out of her. In his damaged brain, his wife's early image still remained. He remembered youth, which she had had, and I had, and he, with thirty years of his life erased in the stroke, believed he still had. So Victoria Cinderella was "that old lady."

"She's not right in her mind," he told me. "Women at that age get fancies. She thinks she's my wife. What in the world would I want with a woman her age? Even if she's a hired girl, she's old for the job, though she does try. I wouldn't have the heart to fire her. Specially with her believing she's my wife. In her own mind she'd be a wife cast out, not a hired girl fired. It's my nature to befriend the elderly and addled."

The hired man at the Bakers' was neither elderly nor addled. His name was Ormand Slaughter, he was perhaps twenty-six, and he was what was then called "backward." I don't know exactly how backward he was—as far back as a slow ten, perhaps. He could count to twelve and could read "cat" and "rat" and "rug" and "bug." He did this reading and counting as a show-off stunt prompted by Victoria Cinderella. "Ormand," she said, "is getting smarter every day." Maybe he was, but he was never going to sit down with a book, or figure out how much a cord of wood at thirty cents a rick would fetch.

It was the time when a man, if he was youthfully good-looking, was called "pretty boy." Pretty Boy Floyd, who came later, is an example. There was a degree of feminine softness in the faces of such men, but not in their bodies. No pretty boy was ever anything but a solidly built fellow. The pretty boy was *boy* as well as *pretty*. Pretty alone was just sissy. Ormand was, except for Lon Dudley, the prettiest pretty boy I ever saw.

He was my early warning, though I didn't of course know this at the time. A rattlesnake that doesn't bite teaches you nothing; and

I don't know that Ormand would ever, even without Victoria Cinderella, have been able to prepare me for what was to come. After all, he was in his mind only ten; and I, in body and mind, an ignorant fifteen. Older, but in as much need of a leader as he.

In Victoria Cinderella, Ormand had a leader. He was a heart-thumper, and Victoria Cinderella understood the implications of that feeling. Heart-thumping and breathlessness were, as far as I was concerned, the whole of it. Who could ask for anything more? A sweet dizzy sensation when near him was enough. I didn't want to fall over in a swoon.

And besides, since he was ten in his mind and I was the nearest his age of anyone in that disordered household, we were each other's only companions when it came to riding the cows home from pasture or collecting tadpoles in the spring branch pools. There's more than one activity that coupling enhances. Sliding down a haystack, straddling the limber branch of a tree for a sky ride, racing like Jack and Jill up a hill, Jack never falling and Jill never tumbling after: those were breathless pleasures, doubled when two shared them.

Oh, it was, as far as our ages went, a strange household indeed. The sixty-year-old thought he was a youth; the twenty-six-year-old thought he was a boy. The fifteen-year-old hadn't reached any conclusions about age except that grownups were a race apart.

Victoria Cinderella thought she was twenty. She told me so. She was able to do this because I was another female and in some ways, she had decided, about as old as Ormand. I was way beyond cat and rat, of course, in reading; so lost in bookishness, she believed (it is now my opinion), that what cats did when they weren't eating rats had never occurred to me. She was not altogether wrong. Until my experience of breathlessness when Ormand was around, boys had existed for me to beat in foot races. Why the pleasure of a contest with a boy was greater than any experienced in a contest with a girl, I had not examined. I didn't have to win the race with a boy; though it always was close. But win or lose, we panted together at the finish line.

Victoria Cinderella told me in so many words that she had become a twenty-year-old. She had lost a quarter of a century, she said, when she began to love Ormand. Ormand needed to gain about the same amount to make a forty-five-year-old woman a suitable companion.

Or maybe not. A ten-year-old (most of them) likes to be hugged. Ten years old in the head and twenty years older in the body had changed the child some but not altogether.

"Is it not," Victoria Cinderella told me, "as if I were really married any more."

Well, it wasn't. Hiram didn't consider Victoria Cinderella his wife and even if he did he was incapable of doing anything about it. Cat and rat were as far as Ormand had been able to go in understanding relationships. Husband and wife he had heard of, but sweethearting was in a book he had never opened.

I took care of Hiram, repacked his going-home suitcase every morning, trimmed his beard, and reminded him that only babies wet the bed. Even Ormand, I told him, knew better than that. He doubted it, but he wasn't of a mind to be bested by the hired man.

Victoria knew exactly what she was going to do: take care of Hiram (have me do it) until he died, then marry Ormand. With her brain and Ormand's brawn the farm would prosper as it never had under Hiram's care. Everything went as planned. Hiram had another stroke and in six months was dead. In seven months Victoria and Ormand were married—and I was out of a job as a hired girl.

III
LON

1

Finally I was eighteen, an old maid. My hand had been asked for, but by no one who made my heart thump as Ormand had done. There is a process called "imprinting" nowadays. By it, for example, a duck who from the shell is mothered by a human cares for nothing but humans—wants to mate with humans, eat with humans, sleep with humans. I had a hen, as I have said, cuddled by me from the time she was a chick, who would sit in my lap like a pussycat, lay her cheek to mine, and take a crumb from my lips with as much assurance as if I also were beaked and feathered. She had been imprinted.

Ormand in turn had imprinted me. I did not feel inclined to marry anyone who did not have long heavy thighs, a thick lay-back thatch of ash-blond hair, and who did not make me breathless.

At eighteen, no such person having appeared, my father and mother decided that for me the life of an old-maid schoolteacher would be preferable to that of an old-maid hired girl. They then decided, and I was more than willing, that I should go to the Normal in Amesville for the summer term and get myself a teacher's certificate. I drove a two-seated cart each day, forded the Rattatack without mishap, and was the number-one student in my class. Not because I was the oldest. I was far from that. Pupils in that neck of the woods were graduating from grade school every day at that age. If they graduated at all.

The teacher was Alonzo T. Dudley, an Ormand in looks but his own age, twenty-eight, in the head. He was the boy who had helped Joey to punish Abel Fetters for poisoning Old Pedro. In the winter term Alonzo was principal of the Academy at Amesville, with two teachers, both female, on his staff. He owned the Dudley farm, located on the fertile flats south of the Sandusky. Alonzo had the farm, his principalship, and what he made giving lectures, for he did that, too. He wasn't a lazy man. Or a poor one.

The Academy principal, always called "Lon" or "Lonnie," was

good-looking and well set-up, a ladies' man in outward appearance, still unmarried, but with no reputation as a woman-chaser. Why hadn't he married? Boys back then married in their teens. True, Joe hadn't married, but he was five years younger than Lon and had started spitting blood in his teens. Joe had gone to live with an uncle in California for a while, chasing a cure that for a while he thought he had found.

The explanation for Lon Dudley was said to be that he was an eccentric: a bookworm, a teacher, a lecturer. Everyone knew that male teachers were a breed apart: men who would rather read than hunt, rather talk to a schoolhouse filled with old ladies than dance at a play-party with a buxom girl.

This was not true of Lon. He could read and hunt, dance and talk; but people will always seize upon the more unusual of two explanations as the true one. It does more to satisfy their hunger for the strange, which most lack in their own lives.

The fact that Lon, besides being a teacher, made a good living as a farmer and got, in addition to his income from these occupations, two dollars and fifty cents a night for just talking, *did* cut some ice with them. If Lon Dudley was crazy, he was crazy like a fox, able to turn his quirks into cash.

Lon had another quirk, if that is the name for it, that people accepted: he was an atheist. But an atheist with a difference. Otherwise he would scarcely have been hired as a teacher at that time and in that community.

He made no bones about being an unbeliever; but his chief lectures were on the Bible. It is difficult to explain the attraction any lecture had for people in backwoods neighborhoods fifty years ago. It was the time of the Chautauqua, but Amesville was not on any Chautauqua circuit. There were box suppers, spelling bees, play-parties, protracted meetings. But Lon was not only entertainment; he mixed entertainment with information like a modern novelist who not only gives you a lot of love-making, but also leaves you, when the lovers part, with a lot of information about running a hotel, avoiding sharks, or living in a kibbutz.

Lon knew the Bible backward and forward. He could lecture on Old Testament prophecies or New Testament miracles. All perfectly straightforward and reverent. No cynicism. Then, when he finished, he would say, "I am an unbeliever. God, help Thou my unbelief."

36

People accepted him, thought he was studying the Bible and talking about it in an effort to overcome his unbelief. They prayed for him. They listened to him more closely than to any camp-meeting spieler. Lon, they believed, was as much a seeker as they were. To refuse him a job because he had not yet broken through to conviction would be an un-Christian act. So he taught, farmed, lectured.

There were seventeen girls and four boys in the six-week Normal session I attended. I was certainly not the oldest girl, but I was the largest—tall, that is. I have never been fat. Nevertheless, I had to look up to my teacher, who was six inches taller than I.

I was well dressed. Frills and furbelows. Mama would not, if she could help it, have me condemned to the life of an old-maid schoolteacher. Men might choose to be bachelors—for whatever reason—but spinsterhood was hardly ever the *choice* of a girl. It was thrust upon her. There were no boys of a suitable age for me in that session of Normal. Mama may have had Lon himself in mind. She may have thought Lon a queer stick in some ways, but he was also solvent, male, and, God knows, handsome.

God knows. He was an Ormand in looks, yes, but even more beautiful because the thoughts of a ten-year-old can't fill the eyes and mold the lips as can those of twenty-eight-year-olds. Small ears; luminous gray eyes; straight hair, a lot of it, the color of hay in a straw stack that has been weathered—almost a touch of green in the gold; a mouth that liked words (that was all I knew then); a big Adam's apple plunging out of a muscular neck.

I didn't really know what falling in love meant. I had been cheek-kissed, but I had never kissed back. Now I knew I wanted to be near Lon, speak to him, smell him. The palms of my hands tingled when I was near him, but I didn't dare touch him.

2

A thought once occurred to me—it must have been ten, perhaps even twenty, years beyond the events I am just now recalling—and I wonder whether it has struck me alone or may have caught the speculation of other women also. It seemed to me that I had never loved or been drawn to a man who did not have the letter *o* or *u* in his name. Consider the prevalence of this vowel in almost all words that have to do with love or love-making. Take the word "love" itself. Change it to lave, or even live. Something of the subterranean depths and movements of sexual passion is subtracted. Change a word we all know to fick or fack and what do you have? Something funny, near to a bird's peck or a light's flick. Change another word to cant or cent, and it's done for, sexually.

I could go on, but the point for me is that unless a man's name had an *o* in it, I was not drawn to him. (True, Toss, the Poor House lecher, failed in spite of his name—with me. But he was successful elsewhere. Would my brother, Joey, have had the girls swarming around him if he had been an Art or an Al or a Ben?)

Whether or not this holds true about girls' names with men, I've never inquired. Are the Eloises, Rowenas, Olives more appealing than the Mabels, Graces, and Inas to men?

Look at the names Shakespeare gave his characters when he wanted to bear down hard on sex. Lear was not of the age, and Macbeth and Hamlet were not of the disposition to be much concerned with sex. The men who were—Othello, Romeo, Iago, Anthony, Troilus—carried the round, the heavy *o*, in their names. Cleopatra was probably Cleo to her boyfriends, and Portia's tongue expressed her passion.

I realize now that science, statistics, and my own ultimate experience would refute this once-startling discovery. But there are times when I've thought there might be some fragment of validity, some half-truth in it.

3

I was in love with Lon from the beginning, though I didn't use that word for it. In that time, which was my time, the phrase was "stuck on." A peculiar phrase, since you are stuck on what you touch and there certainly had been no touching between me and the principal. Unless eyes can touch. I never saw another human being into whose eyes there could ascend so strong and pure a statement of virility. The man Lon was, and what that man could do, rose up and darkened the clear gray of his eyes when he looked at me. It undoubtedly did so when he was with others; but at that time I didn't suspect this. While it was happening, it was happening to me, at me, in me—and for me alone.

There was nothing but that dark visual uprising. No word, no touch, no preferential treatment as a pupil.

Until finally there was a note attached to one of my compositions. We handed in compositions twice a week. This one I titled "A Brother." It was a description of Joe and contained a good deal of the admiration I felt for that swashbuckler. The composition, apart from what it had to say about Joey, was well written. I didn't have an ex-schoolmarm mother for nothing. No "ain'ts," "haints," "I seens," and "I dones" in our household. I had learned to spell with a ruler at hand to emphasize mistakes. Bible lectures were beyond me, but I read a chapter of the New Testament aloud each night after supper to my parents; I understood, as a result, though incapable of duplicating, the arrangement of words into noble sentences.

Lon's note read: "I never had a sister, but I can imagine nothing sweeter than a girl who would write of me in the way you have written of your brother. E."

The E stood for Excellent. I didn't care about my grade. What I cared about was the word "sweeter" and the word "girl." He could have used the word "better" or "kinder"; and instead of "girl" he could have used "pupil." The note was intimate. It spoke to me, a girl, not a pupil, and it said, "Be sweet to me." God knows I wanted to be. There was another phrase used in those parts years ago that meant the same as stuck on. It was "sweet on." I was sweet on Alonzo Dudley.

Lon's note on my composition inflamed me more than any touch. Touch, much as I wanted it, might have made me wary. Men touched, as well I knew after my tussle with Toss, because of the enjoyment it gave them. Who they were touching didn't cut much ice with them. I resisted; Toss, as a result, didn't mope, but found as soon as possible someone who didn't resist. But words are more discriminating than touch. You couldn't touch one person in a way that was very much different from the way you touched another. Words could be (there were so many thousands of them) chosen, if you knew a few thousand, and Lon did, just to fit the earhole of a particular listener. Words enter like personal messengers, selected to fit the unique spirals and curlicues of your individual hearing passages; and to go from there into the brain's storehouse, where they fire memories and imaginings that have long been waiting.

So Lon's note spoke to my storehouse of imaginings. There it said: "You have written tenderly of a young man. I can think of nothing sweeter than that you should use such words to me."

It said something else, too. It said, "You are capable of doing so." It asked for my words of love, for I had written of Joey with love; but it recognized something no one else, not I myself, had noted before. I enjoyed using words.

Nowadays it is a commonplace thing to say, "She is good in bed." Lon said, "You are good in a sentence." And in the long run, if there is to be a long run, good in the sentence beats good in bed because there is more conversation than carnal congress in the average coupling of any duration.

I treasured Lon's note, but he made no sign to me that he had intended it as anything more than a comment on a composition. He was surrounded by pupils. He rode horseback to school from his farm a couple of miles distant, punctual to arrive and to leave. I had no chance to talk to him, unless I pretended that I needed help with some problem, and I was never good at pretending.

He solved the problem, perhaps no problem for him, of arranging an opportunity for me to be near him. He walked to school one morning, told me that his riding mare had gone lame, and, since it wouldn't be much out of my way, asked would I give him a ride home. It was only a step for him, he said, and if it would be a chore for me, he could easily walk. Chore? It was a heaven-sent opportunity.

I half believed, wanted to believe, that his lame mare was a story he had made up in order to have an excuse to be with me. But when we got to his place, there was his white mare, Mouse, obviously favoring her right front foot.

I had to content myself by thinking that there were at least a dozen other girls he could have asked to give him a lift, but he had asked me.

The trip was less than a half-mile out of my way. I had to cross and recross the Sandusky, passing each time Crit Matthews' farm. Crit was the father of Alice, the girl to whom I had given my second-best hair ribbons, and who had brought them back to me still tied to her chopped-off braids. Alice, my own age, had long since married and gone to Louisville to live. But Crit Matthews, the best-hearted man in the world, though he was a poor hand at farming, produced children regularly. So there were plenty of children, most of them young people by now, who waved as I passed the Matthews' house— for Mouse stayed lame for over two weeks. Mrs. Crit, who still held the hair ribbons against me (I guess), never waved; but Leota, a daughter of fifteen or sixteen, did, and so did the three half-grown young men, her brothers.

Lon was a ready talker and, with him, so was I. But most of what was said those years ago, I don't remember. Except that we conversed like tennis players, back and forth, stroke for stroke. It was rally after rally, no points scored if a remark was placed beyond your fellow player's (opponent is the wrong word here) reach. And in the game of conversation I, at least, developed powers I didn't know I had. A part of learning is being asked the right questions. Understanding you didn't know you possessed emerges, like fish from a pond when the right bait is thrown in.

Once, Lon asked me if I had ever seen a hawk moth. I had never even heard of a hawk moth, but at that minute (we were driving up the lane to Lon's house, with its rows of flags along the driveway) I saw something like a bird, but not a bird, hovering over one of the flowers.

"Of course," I said. "Look there."

"Is that the first you ever saw?"

"Yes."

"Would you have noticed it if I hadn't asked you that question?"

"No."

"Did my question bring the moth?"

"No. My answer."

It was like that all along the way with Lon and me. I was, when with him, more than I had known I was or could be. Or have been since. Loving another is in part so satisfying because you, too, become lovable. Filled with unknown knowledge and intuitions, tender with desire to shield and protect. For the same reason it is hateful to hate. How can you like yourself, a person who would so gladly see harm come to another?

"How could you and Joe pour that carbolic acid down Mr. Fetters's throat?" I asked him once.

"I shouldn't have done it. I lose control of myself sometimes. I wanted to do nothing but punish him for the pain he had caused your dog."

"It didn't help the dog any."

"It helped me—for ten or fifteen minutes."

I had never been in Lon's house. I drove him home (Lon never offered to do the driving himself), up the lane between the purple flags. I then said, "Good-bye, Mr. Dudley" (for he was still Teacher to me, not Alonzo, and certainly not Lon), turned the cart around, recrossed the Sandusky, waved once again to the Matthews', and was home only a half an hour later than my usual time.

Lon's home had belonged to his parents. He was an only child, and both parents had died within a week, struck down by milk fever, when he was about twenty. The home was said to be nice in an unusual way for a farmhouse: ingrain carpets; a china closet with a curved glass front that showed off hand-painted plates to advantage; a coal-oil lamp with a china shade that hung over the dining-room table on a metal chain and could be raised and lowered at will.

One afternoon Lon asked me if I would come in and help him with the preparation of one of his speeches. I was flattered, of course. Besides being in love with him, he was Teacher. It is difficult to convey to readers today the respect a teacher commanded when I was young. He could, like Lon, be no more than the graduate of an academy of the kind he now headed, an institution of learning with teachers less well educated and a curriculum less advanced than that of a junior high school today.

Nevertheless, Teacher was then "Professor," a man who had put knowledge ahead of money and had the ability not only to ferret facts out of books, but also to implant them in the minds of the young.

So I went, on Lon's invitation, into the house I had never seen, with pride. I was going to "help Teacher." The house was just as pretty and orderly as had been reported. I was in love with Lon, yes, but at the minute very vain about being his assistant.

The help Lon wanted was simple. It was his practice first to write out, then memorize, his lectures. What he wanted me to do was to listen, with the completed speech before me, to his delivery, and, when his memory failed, to prompt him. This was a little less easy than it sounds, since it was a part of his speechmaking style to pretend that he was speaking spontaneously, and hence, on occasion, to grope for just the right word. I had to learn to recognize which

42

gropings were real and which pretended. He did not want those pauses that were assumed for rhetorical effect spoiled by my blurting out the word he would apparently come upon by sheer inspiration.

I helped him with more than one speech. I remember the subject of only the first. It was entitled "Biblical Suffering" and was an account of the sufferings of the men of the Bible, good men, who remained steadfast in spite of pain and torture. Lon began with Abraham and Isaac, went on to Job and Jonah, and wound up with the deaths of the New Testament martyrs.

Lon's descriptions of Biblical suffering were vivid—and horrible. People liked them, I suppose, for the same reason they like movies of torment and suffering today; though I understand the reason for that even less. Lon at least did something the movies can't, or don't, do. The shark in the movie chews up a man; but Lon told his audience what Jonah felt down amidst the whale's digestive juice en route to his intestines.

There was no hint in Lon's speech of criticism of God's treatment of the faithful. He told it Bible-straight and concluded as he always did, "I am an unbeliever. Lord, help Thou my unbelief."

After Lon's mare recovered, he continued to ask me to stop at his house after school to help him with his speeches, to grade papers, or to copy out questions for classes. That poor little Normal School didn't even own a hectograph. Because I was "helping Teacher" and expected someday to be a teacher myself, my parents were pleased that my pedagogical abilities were being recognized.

I was in love with Lon, and quivered each day with the suspense of wondering whether or not I would be asked to help him with some schoolwork after the day at Normal was over. Lon never courted me in any of the accepted ways of the time: never took me to an oyster supper or bought me a bottle of Florida Water. Nevertheless, because of a thing or two he said, and an act or two, and, above all of course, because by the time the Normal session was over he had asked me to marry him, I believed he loved me. And he must certainly have known long before he asked for my hand that I loved him.

Late one afternoon Lon and I were working at his round dining-room table. The day had been sultry, a thunderstorm was threatening, and both the front and back doors were open to let what air

43

there was flow through the house. Lon's mother had been a great gardener, and the perfume of her pinks and stocks filled the room.

Lon was preparing an examination (we were in the fifth week of Normal) that would test two areas of his pupils' learning at once. He had made a list of twelve uncommon, though not strange, words. Pupils were to use these words in describing a historical event chosen from five suggested by Lon. Thus two birds could be hit with one stone: Had any history been learned? And could the student use what he had learned in the composition class to report what his learning in history had been?

In the midst of selecting his historical happenings Lon's pencil stopped. I, aware of every breath he drew, of course noticed this and stopped my own work of copying. Into his gray eyes, for he was looking directly at me, came that darkening, a kind of smoke signal from deep inside that made words unnecessary. But Lon tried to put into words what it was he had just felt and that his eyes had, with their own language, told me. What he said was not what I had expected.

"This comes at the right time," he said.

I was bewildered. What "this" meant to him, I had no idea. Being in love with him, the time for me was certainly right, though five years earlier would have been a good time, too.

I couldn't ask him what he meant—and for a number of reasons. If I asked, I might be told that what he meant was, "This is certainly the right time for me to discover a capable helper." That wasn't what his eyes had said. But if they had said what I hoped, my question would rob the message of value anyway. What is the worth of anything asked for? Even if you get what you want, the transaction has then occurred across a shop counter. You get what you want, but you have been made to pay for it. I wouldn't do that, run after love like it was a bargain-counter commodity.

So I didn't ask. I didn't say a single word. But all night long I heard Lon's words again, over and over. "This comes at the right time."

If that *did* mean "being in love," why was this the right time? What had changed in his life to make this summer better than last year's summer?

If he had said, "*You* come at the right time," he might have meant, "Just at the time when I was thinking of marrying and settling down, you, the right girl, came along."

But he hadn't said "you." He had said "this." And I didn't know

44

what "this" was. Not me at all, perhaps; perhaps just falling in love, with anyone. And maybe not even love. And why now? His mother and father had been dead for eight years. The farm was his. He had been of a marriageable age for more than ten years.

What was "this"? And why "now"? I had no answer and I could ask for none. I could only wonder, and long, and wait.

I didn't have long to wait, though it seemed long then. The words I wanted to hear were "love" and "marriage." "I love you." "Will you marry me?"

It wasn't until the day before the Normal session closed that he said, "I should have married you." This also was ambiguous, I thought, when I heard it, but could not say so: "It's still not too late." Maybe it *was* too late for him. I didn't want to face that. But he *had* said the word "married."

"Should have" means "ought to." Why hadn't he, then? What had prevented his saying it earlier? I had been in the same neighborhood all of his life. I knew he had helped Joe punish Mr. Fetters. I was no newcomer. True, when he was nineteen, a ripe age for young men to marry then, I was a grade-school girl in pigtails.

Normal School, and especially Lon, had taught me something I didn't know about myself. I was quick at books. I had never, except in grade school, had books to be quick *at*, or slow at, for that matter. The Bible, yes. And McGuffey's *Readers*. And a book about Africa, with monkeys who, by holding each other's tails, made a bridge across a chasm for their traveling tribesmen. Books, perhaps, like other drugs, must be sampled a number of times before the habit takes hold. The habit took hold of me that summer in Normal. If it hadn't, I would never have been any kind of a companion for the principal of an academy. Or able to write this.

There was something else I had known all along, and wasn't very proud of—wasn't proud until I saw how much my ability pleased Lon. It had to do with my "army-mule" capabilities. There were no organized games for girls then, but a girl could, if she had a brother like Joey, play catch with him and his friends, run races with them, jump over bushel baskets set up to form hurdles with them. I was a better runner and jumper than Joey; Joey was a tall, handsome daredevil, but no athlete. There wasn't anyone I couldn't outrun. I was left-handed, and a born first baseman, if I'd been given a chance to play. I couldn't broad jump as far as some, but I was never more than half a dozen inches behind.

I could do something no boy even tried: kick a tin piepan held higher than my head twenty times in succession without missing once: bang, bang, bang. I did come to recognize finally that the boys were more interested in the sight of my drawers when I kicked than in my athletic ability; but I still held to my belief that like was drawn to like: runners admired runners; catchers liked catchers; high kickers envied higher kickers. I hadn't yet caught on to the real difference sex makes. And even if I had, I don't know that I would have been able to hide the pleasure I had in using my body strenuously: in running and jumping—and winning.

It was then, finally, when I was on the verge of spinsterhood and almost ready for schoolmarming, that Lon, another athlete, came along. He was as good as I, a faster runner; he would hold the piepan for me, encouraging me to higher kicks. "You're not really trying." He *liked* my running and jumping. He said so. His eyes said so. He said so by asking me to play catch and to run races with him. He was truly interested in the number and height of my kicks, not my drawers.

"You act like two boys together," Joey told me. Joey didn't care for girls who acted like boys—though he made an exception of his sister. But then, Joey, with his lungs always troubling him, didn't enjoy roughhousing with boys, either.

Lon, if he had lived where tennis racquets were known, would have been another Big Bill Tilden. He was built that way. Or a swimmer like Duke K. He had the height and reach and the long-muscled thighs of a swimmer or tennis player.

He voiced his approval of my athletic ability just as enigmatically as he had talked about "this comes at the right time" and "I should have married you."

"You," he said one afternoon after we had finished a long game of catch, "are a physical phenomenon."

A phenomenon, I knew, was something unusual. No one in Amesville but Lon would have used such a word; and I was about the only one who would have understood it. But he knew what it meant and so did I. I would have preferred being told that I was skillful or graceful or lithe. But if unusual was what he liked, I was glad that that was what I was.

On the next to the last day of Normal, I helped Lon, as usual, correct papers. The grades this time were especially important. Only

46

students receiving an average of eighty-five in all subjects would be licensed to teach. Lon was especially careful in grading my papers. Even so, he was unable to give me less than a ninety-four. So I was a licensed teacher.

When we had finished our work, I prepared as usual to go home. At the door Lon kissed me. I didn't know kissing could be like that. I knew what a kiss was, of course; I'd had some. But never the whole mouth, lips open, really taking possession of my mouth. It was stunningly pleasurable. That kiss traveled the entire length of my body. There was not a vein it did not enter. I didn't want it to stop—ever.

It stopped, of course. Even I needed to breathe. Then I kissed Lon, not as he had kissed me, but I presented my mouth for a repetition of what had happened before. It was better the second time because I knew what was coming. But the second kiss ended, too. And Lon then let me know that kissing was over for the evening. "You must go home now, dear. Your folks will be worried. Tomorrow is a big day. I'll see you here after the Commencement Exercises are over."

He had kissed me, he had called me "dear." I was, I thought, as good as engaged. And if kissing and being engaged were this inflammatory, marriage must burn clear to the bone. I wondered how flesh and blood could endure the ecstasy. How did married couples manage to look so calm and unexcited?

The Commencement Exercises *were* long. Speeches from everybody; diplomas and teaching certificates handed out; and finally, from the Principal himself, who elsewhere got paid for speaking, a free speech entitled "Life Is More Than Learning." I, who was finding personal meanings in every look and gesture of Lon's, believed that that speech was a direct declaration to me: "Do not think that a teacher's certificate and a grade of ninety-four is the only reward you have received from six weeks at Normal School. Life is more than learning. Life is loving and I love you."

He hadn't said so yet; but what other message could those lips, busy with nothing now but appropriate commencement-time wisdom, have meant when they took hold of mine? What lips do, I supposed, was like what men do, more important than what they say. If a man kills shouting "love," the jury judges him by his act, not by his word. I judged Lon by his act. His act was a kiss.

The Commencement Exercises, with relatives to greet and parents to congratulate, took forever, but finally they were over.

47

I had come to the exercises in the surrey with my father and mother. Joey, who had the excuse of a summer cold for missing what would have bored him anyway, was not there. I supposed that I would go home with my parents. But as the congratulating and handshaking wound up, Lon came to me and said, "I have told your folks that I will drive you home."

He didn't need to ask me if I would like that, and my parents didn't come over to tell me good-bye. They left at once, as if they feared that Lon, on second thought, might change his mind. Spinsterhood was failure. They would do all they could to make me a winner.

That was the first time I had ever been driven anyplace by Lon. His horse, his buggy, Lon driving. I was an entirely different person from the young woman who had driven her own cart to be Teacher's helper. I felt changed in every way: tender, frail, needing protection. I couldn't have won a foot race with a snail. Mules were animals I had never heard of. Piepans were for pies.

Lon and I talked about his mare Mouse some more. White horses, I knew, were thought to be less valuable than horses of other colors. They ran more slowly, had less endurance, their skin sunburned more easily, their feet were more often bruised. None of this, Lon said, was true. It was a part of the superstition about the powers of night and darkness. The animal world was strongest, it was said, when it shared the colors of the Prince of Darkness. The human world was at its best when it was white, sons of the Prince of Light. This, according to Lon, was tommyrot. It was one of the beliefs that kept him from being a Christian.

I had nothing to say about this. I wanted to be touched. I knew nothing about the Prince of Darkness and the Prince of Light; and I *had* always heard that on a long pull the white horse gives up. But arguing separates. I was no authority on white horses. If Lon believed in white horses, his belief was enough to convince me.

When I went inside Lon's house with him, I wondered what we would do. Always before there had been work: papers to correct, exercises to copy out, speeches to hear. I didn't know enough about horses to keep up an evening of that kind of talk. I could listen and agree, but that wouldn't really be a conversation; more like the preacher preaching and the congregation saying "Amen."

There couldn't be any running, catching, or kicking, either. I was dressed for the Commencement, in gray soisette with a high-necked lace guimpe, and, under that, corset, shimmy, drawers, petticoat. The Pope was better dressed for racing than I.

But neither conversation nor athletic competitions were what Lon had in mind. Nor anything else I could ever have dreamed of. He seated me in a rocking chair in the sitting room like a formal caller, not like someone he had so thoroughly kissed the evening before. He brought me a glass of lemonade from a pitcher he had made that morning. He didn't even ask me to take off my hat, but I did so anyway. It was big and heavy, pure Milan straw with half of a bird; only one wing, but an entire head with a flower in its beak holding up one side of the brim. I put my hat on the sofa, drank my lemonade, and rocked.

"Your speech was very good," I said.

Lon said, "I want you to see me."

I was looking directly at him. He was standing opposite me against the door to the dining room, which he had closed. I didn't understand how he could believe that I *didn't* see him, but I made my gaze more intent, stared at him as if he were the size of a flea the some color as the woodwork, and his outlines barely distinguishable from where I sat.

If Lon noticed what I was doing, he didn't show it. He was too busy doing what *he* was doing, and this did make me stare, made it impossible for me not to stare.

He was taking off his clothes; not hurriedly, not impetuously, but quietly, methodically—and completely. Tie, shirt, undershirt. The most exciting moment was when he took down his suspenders; that meant the pants were coming off.

He stood up straight, not sucking in his stomach or throwing out his chest, but as easily as though nakedness was as natural to him as clothes. To him, perhaps it was.

I wasn't accustomed to seeing naked men. Except for Joe, aged ten, and he hadn't really counted as a *man*, Lon was the first I had ever seen. I am surprised to remember my calmness. I had been told to look, so I looked. At Normal there was a book called *Classic Myths*. The myths were illustrated with pictures of Greek statues, so I had some idea of how a well-set-up man should look. I had also enough sense to avoid the cliché "You are as beautiful as a Greek god," or even "as a Greek statue." I did say, or breathe, "You are beautiful."

He was. Men don't often have the combination of a broad-shouldered, slim-hipped bone structure with just the right amount of muscled flesh to clothe the boniness with grace. Lon did. The statue called "Discobolus," which I had seen in *Classic Myths*, was not Lon's equal.

After the statues, one thing did surprise me: the hair. The statues weren't hairy, of course; and maybe, I thought, Greeks aren't. The hair on the chest I accepted as manly; elsewhere it seemed feminine. I was judging by scant knowledge, naturally, for I had seen only one woman, Ina, completely naked, and I had never seen a naked man. Taught to bathe without taking off all my clothes, I had scarcely seen myself.

Did Lon expect me to embrace him? Caress him? I don't think so; otherwise he would surely have made some move toward me. Said something. I think he expected me to do exactly what I did: look.

This, I know now, was peculiar wooing, if it was wooing. And I think it was, because later that evening, Lon proposed marriage. Usually a man wants to see the girl with *her* clothes off. But if Lon had any interest in what my dove-gray dress covered, he didn't show it. If I had been less ignorant, I might have wondered at Lon's disrobing. I didn't. I was so much in love with him that I was deeply grateful for this gift of himself that he made me. He didn't seem vain to me, just generous. It didn't occur to me that there was something odd about a man who wanted to give himself to a woman, not take her; to be seen, not see.

I was perfectly happy rocking, sipping my lemonade, and looking. When my glass was empty, Lon stopped being a Greek statue and refilled my glass. This made me laugh. A Greek statue was one thing, a naked waiter was another.

"What's funny?" Lon asked.

"I've never been served before by a naked waiter." (As a matter of fact, I had never been in a restaurant.)

"Marry me," said Lon, "and you may have a naked waiter as often as you like."

There was my proposal: "Marry me." But love was not mentioned and no kiss given. Very quickly I said, "I will marry you."

Lon then put his clothes back on and drove me home.

When we got there, he told my father, "I would like to marry your daughter before the fall term begins."

I was surprised at the speed: the fall term was only six weeks away, but I was pleased with Lon's eagerness.

"Is this what you want, Sis?" Papa asked.

"Yes, Papa," I said.

We were married on September 4, 1920.

IV
MARRIAGE

1

I know more about marriage now than I did then. I ought to. I've been married three times. My marriage to Alonzo T. Dudley lasted two years, two months, and seven days. Could I have been any happier? No, not at that time. There is no point in a cup that runneth over. You can't lap up the spillings. I had all the happiness I could manage. To make use of more happiness I would have needed a different upbringing, some experience of sex, a man whose every gesture and intonation were less enthralling to me than Lon's. I was married, wasn't I? Alonzo T. Dudley was my husband, wasn't he? We slept in the same bed, didn't we? I washed and ironed his shirts and mended his socks, didn't I? I was his helpmate.

I was more than that. I was his colleague.

Lon had suggested that since I had my teacher's certificate I should use it. He had foreseen what was true; I would be finished with housework by nine o'clock in the morning. A day teaching seventeen pupils at Fairmont, the school I had once attended, would pass faster than a day alone with twelve turkeys, eight guinea hens, and a varying number of Plymouth Rocks.

Oh, it was a wonder time! Lon and I bought a bookcase by mail order, and by mail order, too, began to buy books from Chicago. We bought one a month, good books. I still have them. One of the first was *Classic Myths*, bought for the sole reason, insofar as I was concerned, that there was in it a picture of Lon in marble.

I was getting bolder. We both were. I told Lon why I wanted the book. It was the first time I had ever spoken to him of that early disrobing except in love-making, where I often took the lead. Lon, especially in talking, was the leader. But we were beginning to be able to exchange roles. I could bring up a subject to talk about. Lon was finding touch easier.

Now, as I talked of Greek gods, Lon took my hand and put it where the Greek gods wore their fig leaves.

"Nothing like that on a Greek god," said Lon.

"Who knows, under the fig leaf?"

Then Lon asked me a question. "Is Joe very masculine?"

People had sometimes thought of me a tomboy, but no one had ever accused Joe of being a sissy.

"Joe? You know Joe," I said. "Why, Joe's fallen in love with more girls and had more fights with boys than anyone else in Bigger Township. If that's not masculine, what is?"

Maybe it was, but it wasn't what Lon was talking about.

"Being sick has made Joe skinny. But he does have a big heavy frame," Lon said.

Big heavy frame! What was the connection between masculinity and framework? Masculinity was how you acted, wasn't it?

"He would be better off if he were less masculine. He's got weak lungs. He needs to take it easy."

Lon said no more. He was asking me something else, something he couldn't put into words, and which, unless it was put in words, I couldn't understand. And wouldn't have understood even then, actually, in words or out.

2

Remember, I was still a teen-ager, a backwoods teen-ager. I thought I knew all the words for love and all the love there was to have words about. I was ignorant as a two-year-old.

Now I really do know all the words. You'd have to be blind, deaf, too, probably, to have reached my age in this century and lack the current vocabulary.

What I don't understand is why women who call themselves liberated (free of the domination of men, that is) feel impelled to demonstrate their liberation by taking over the vocabulary of men. Slaves, it is true, often aped their masters after their liberation. To do as old massa did was a sign of freedom. If old massa said "fuck," the slave, once he had thrown off his chains, used that word. But the enslaved woman, liberated, is not of the same sex as old massa. And the vocabulary she inherits, the fuck, the screw, the lay, the bang, implies an act of lesser charge and shorter duration than that she knows. These words are one with the valve grind the old massa gives his car, the oil change, the tune-up, the fast getaway, accelerator clear to the floorboard and rubber burning: mechanical terms for mechanical acts.

Linguists have gone pretty far in discerning inside its symmetrical structure the nature of the persons who fabricated language. But they have had nothing to say as to whether language is predominately a man-made tool. My guess would be yes, and particularly so when it comes to sex. And now liberated woman proves her liberation by declaring, "What a man can say, I can say." But does it convey *her* experience? That doesn't seem to matter to her.

If you were born middle class and went to college, you can use the once-forbidden vocabulary as a sign that you've come a long way, baby.

But if you were born down among the wild ones, the renters, the ranters, the sharecroppers, the men who went off to the factories; if you lived amid the tobacco fields, the corn rows, the woods lots, the stands of sassafras and hackberry, those words prove just one thing: you haven't moved an inch or learned a thing. You're still out there in the haymow with the hired man or riding home in the spring wagon with the Poor House handyman.

There's nothing wrong with the haymow or the spring wagon or with using that word; except that if you came from where I did, it is filled with echo chambers of encounters that men called "fuck"; and fuck didn't mean a thing more to them than a hearty sneeze. You can use that word if what you're trying to prove to old massa is that anything he could say you can say, too. I am not old massa's emancipated slave, however. I use my own words.

On the dark and bloody ground where I was born, early meanings were still just beneath the surface of those four letters. No one in my clearing went away to college, learned there a new vocabulary that later had to be discarded to show he hadn't been brainwashed. That present code word for female freedom was once the Old English word for foe. It went on to become *faege,* meaning "marked for death"; then *behida,* meaning "feud"; and finally, using its nearest modern equivalent, "Drop dead." There was hate and malice and scorn at the root of the word.

My Sandusky and Rattatack neighbors didn't have this knowledge in their minds when I grew up; but it was in their bodies and between their lips and on their tongues when they shaped that word and spat it out with a smile. "Foe," "fated to die," "feud," "drop dead." It was what was done to a woman, not with her. "Fuck you."

I can't write that way about Lon. I can't use him as an opportunity to show that I've come a long way, baby. I have and I haven't; and not always in the right direction, either. But I need a word with more letters, a phrase with more life than "drop dead"; something more like "live in splendor," or "burst into bloom."

What happened, because I loved Lon, was no stopwatch happening; I was transported without meditating into a transcendental state. Whether the flow was inward to me from the world, or outward from me to the world, I don't know; but a fusion took place. I and all creation were one. I breathed flowers, touched clouds, and warmed the dust about my bare toes. This state was not of short duration. I could teach without shattering the connection because I loved my kids. But the appearance of neighbors put me in an acid mood if they came wtih their chitchat before the glory had abated.

Lon was the perfect husband for me. Goodness should be lovable, but beauty turns me on. That's another automobile word, but, like it or not, we live in an internal-combustion world. When solar energy comes, there'll be new words.

3

In addition to the mail-order bookcase that we were filling with mail-order books, Lon had bought of a neighbor who had been a nurseryman, but had gone out of the business, a grafting table. This was a narrow pine table, six feet long, waxed, stained with and still scented by the sap of scions. Lon set this table at right angles to the south wall of the sitting room. We used it as a desk, Lon on one side, I on the other, face to face evening after evening. I could not have endured this with any other human being.

Marriage lies in the eye, unless it goes so deep looks don't count at all. The Elizabethans wrote of making babies in each other's eyes. They did this by seeing their own diminished image in the iris of a lover. Lon and I were never able to make any babies in bed, but evening after evening at that old waxed, stained grafting table, we did make babies in each other's eyes.

We'd each had a long day before we could seat ourselves across from each other at that table. Our work wasn't just teaching and correcting papers. We were up at 5:30 in the summer, 6:30 in the winter. Stock to feed, hogs to slop, cows to milk, milk to be strained and put in the springhouse.

The housework, as Lon had said, I could do with one hand tied behind my back. Outside I was responsible for the turkeys, damnable birds that die at a heavy fall of dew; guinea hens, handsome and hardy, natural burglar alarms, as friendly as dogs to their owners and as heartbreaking to kill; Plymouth Rock hens laying eggs as large as doorknobs and with yolks as gold as marigolds.

The first work at the table, once supper and the dishes were finished, was schoolwork; and after that, if Lon had a lecture engagement, work on a lecture. He was getting five dollars a lecture now, with invitations coming from as far south as Tennessee and as far north as Illinois. But finally we would be free for what was our private pleasure: learning. Lon, the teacher; I, the pupil.

Lon was a born teacher, and I may have been a born learner, late coming to it, perhaps, but I haven't stopped yet. Men and women are so made that finding each other as male and female is not much of a trick. Shape, smell, voice timbre, a light in the eye, lead man to woman (and vice versa) as unerringly as bees to flowers or lions to lambs. But teacher and learner aren't provided with any such identifying equipment.

So it was pure luck. I fell in love with a man's body, with his eyes and arms and mouth. I did not recognize, because I had never encountered one before, a mind so stored with knowledge. And I was, though I didn't know it, as hungry for knowledge as a dog for a bone.

A bride learns in bed. What she learns sometimes is, "Stay away from beds." But the bed *is* the accepted symbol of conjugal life, not a scarred pine table still smelling of the fruit scions grafted on it years ago.

But for me it is. True, in bed the body, never before touched, turns to the husband like a flower to the sun: Oh, make me bloom again, it says.

The mind, multifaceted, is just as responsive. It has multiple ecstasies, each just as transporting as those that touch brings to the body.

Lon lived as intensely in ideas and the expression of these as in the coupling of bodies. Not more so, I think, though he came to teaching earlier than to coupling.

Table time was never cut short for bedtime. But then, we never stayed up all night to study, either. We studied a set number of hours, covered an assigned (by Lon) number of subjects. Nothing was ever hit-or-miss with him.

Bible study came first, each evening. Lon was an atheist who wanted to believe. If there was anything in the Bible or anything written about the Bible that would convince him that God existed and had made man in His own image, Lon yearned to know it. He longed to know that he was a son of God.

I, a United Brethren, baptized in a stream still milky with melting ice, was a believer from childhood. If I had had to find God by reading in the Bible, I might have failed. I had an impulse to pray, to worship, to sing. I played burn-out in honor of God, and touched flower petals with praise for Him. Did I learn this in Sunday school and church? I don't know. In any case, "Praise God," "Thank God," "Help me, God" were as natural to me as breathing.

In the 1920s men all over the world were still suffering because Darwin had exploded the myth of Adam and Eve in the Garden of Eden.

Neither Lon nor I suffered because of Darwin. The Red Sea parting or not parting; the Ark, filled or empty; Lot's wife, salt or human flesh: true or false, these had nothing to do with the bubble of joy I had in my chest and that I called "the presence of God."

They had nothing to do with Lon, either. Long before Lon knew of Darwin, he had been convinced that God had been created by man, not vice versa. God was man's way of accounting for the unaccountable. Bad men prospered here on earth, but God promised that in the hereafter they would receive the punishment they deserved. This was reassuring to good men who hadn't prospered.

All this Lon's mind told him. But in his heart he longed, as he said in his lectures, to become a true believer. Every night at that pine table he hoped to find the key that would open the door that separated him from God.

A generation that searches for the perfect orgasm and attends seminars on mastering techniques of masturbation may find it hard to believe that someone who might be alive today was more concerned with finding God than developing sexual adequacy. Of course, Lon had the one and didn't have the other.

After the Bible study came English. Lon used as a textbook Bishop Trench's *Study of Words*.

He made long lists of words for me. First, I was to memorize their meaning, then to master their pronunciation, and finally to use the words in sentences. All came easy to me except the pronunciation. Lon laughed at my struggles. "Orpha," he said, "I wonder if I should split your tongue like a starling's. Pronunciation doesn't come natural to you."

It didn't. Not of words of the kind Lon gave me. Susurration, insufflation, amniotic, anamnois, widdershens, tombols.

I still know what these words mean, still have trouble pronouncing them, and until now have never used them when writing.

We had time for more than textbook study at night. Our evenings were long. Though we got up at 5:30 or 6:30 in the morning, we didn't go to bed until 11:30. Lon said that people out of habit slept more than was necessary. We had six or seven hours in bed and seventeen or eighteen out. And of the seventeen or eighteen only one was not given to work or study.

For an hour before we went to bed we had a party. We drank cider, ate apples, cracked nuts, and talked. Lon, like my Poor House grandfather, took the Louisville *Courier*, so we knew what was going on. True, we didn't always understand the importance of what was going on. Henry Ford was perfecting his Model T at that time. I don't remember our ever mentioning automobiles, let alone comprehending the importance of the Model T. We were the last of the horse-drawn generation and didn't know it. We drove Polly and Mouse without any farewell thoughts.

We talked about presidents, past and present. Lon had admired Roosevelt when he bolted the Republican party and became a Bull Mooser. I was for Teddy Roosevelt because he was a swashbuckler and a hero—a living legend. Imagine Taft, who followed Roosevelt as President, on horseback leading a charge up San Juan Hill. He would have broken the horse's back. They had to build an oversized bathtub for him in the White House.

I never forgave the government for refusing to let Teddy go to Europe during World War I.

We read novels and poetry in our party hour before bedtime. It didn't make sense to us to read them during our study hour at the table. They were our entertainment. They made me laugh and cry.

Lon liked to read aloud and I liked to hear him. Lon's voice was so resonant that my hand, if I put it on his back between his shoulder blades when he was talking, tingled as much as it did on an organ when bass chords were played.

Othello was Lon's favorite play of Shakespeare's. When Lon read "Put up your bright swords," his voice had the glitter of moonlight on burnished steel in it.

After Desdemona's strangling, my throat would ache all night. Like all great actors, Lon didn't seem to be acting. He seemed to be living. Desdemona was really dead when Lon finished with her.

"Could you do what Othello did, Lon?"

"He thought she was guilty."

"She was innocent. Iago hoodwinked him."

"I know that. That's why it's so tragic. Othello killed when it wasn't necessary."

"Is killing necessary sometimes?" The United Brethren didn't think so.

"The world would be better off with some men dead."

"That's what John Wilkes Booth thought."

"Booth was crazy."

Oh, we had much to talk about in those long evenings, much to learn, and body-love awaiting us when we left our table and talk and went to bed.

4

I had only one complaint and I was ashamed of it. Lon tutored the middle Matthews boy, Ebon, a seventeen-year-old. He was a born student, Lon said, like me; but without Lon's help he would never have known more than he had when he left school at the fifth grade. Lon spent one evening a week at the Matthews', without pay, of course, teaching Ebon. This didn't bother me, though I missed Lon on Ebon's evenings. What did upset me was when Ebon started coming over to our house once a week to sit at the table with Lon and me just as if he belonged there.

I certainly hadn't invited him. Lon said he hadn't. But Lon hadn't the heart to tell anyone so eager to learn to stay away. Ebon, it was true, studied just as hard as I did. And he didn't gobble down food when the cider and gingerbread came out.

If my foot and Lon's body came out of *Classic Myths*, Ebon's face could be found there. He had a Grecian nose—no hook, no button, no Irish turnip—a manly, somewhat fleshy prow with a bridge not much lower than his forehead. His upper lip was short and already downy. He had a full-lipped smiling mouth. He worked outdoors and was tanned, but underneath the tan there was an apricot-colored flush. His eyes were hazel, like the poet Keats's; viper eyes, they are called, with a threatening glitter.

The truth was, I was jealous; and jealous of a mild-mannered, polite schoolboy. I should have been as interested in his learning as Lon. He did kowtow to Lon, but he didn't ignore me. Was I still holding a grudge against the Matthews tribe because Ebon's mother ten years ago had thrown a gift of mine back in my face? Mrs. Matthews was hatchet-faced and sharp-tongued, but Crit Matthews had the sweet look of a farmer who has never loved anything more passionately than a clean well-cut furrow.

The boy learner! Why did my heart harden when he appeared? I lived, it was true, almost as passionately at the grafting table with Lon as I did in bed. Did I resent Ebon at the table as I would have in bed?

One night when Ebon lingered later than usual, talking surveying with Lon, a subject I didn't understand, I flounced off to bed, mad. I was still mad when Lon came to bed. I could hear him being quiet, trying not to awaken me. Shoes came off and onto the floor soft as snowflakes. Tiptoe to the closet for the nightshirt I had been too mad to put out as I usually did. Creep, creep, creep to the kitchen and the squawk of the pump as he got his bedtime glass of water.

When he came back I said, "I'm wide awake. You don't need to do so much tiptoeing."

"I thought you were asleep. I was trying not to wake you."

"How could I be asleep with you two downstairs jabbering away?"

"We tried to be quiet."

"It's more disturbing to hear and not quite understand than to have some talking right in your ear. If you can't bear to part with Ebon, bring him to bed. Then I could at least understand what's being said; and maybe learn something, too."

Lon, who was in bed when I said that, threw the covers straight back over the footboard, jumped out of bed, and pulled me out, too.

"Sit there," he said, pushing me into the one chair in the room. Then he lit the lamp and stood in front of me, a Lon I had never seen before. Not a man seeking God, but Jehovah himself, knowing

63

right from wrong. And I was wrong. "Orpha, what made you say a thing like that?"

"There isn't anything so bad about what I said. I didn't mean for Ebon to sleep next to me. You'd be next to me and Ebon would be on the outside rail, next to you, so if you had anything more to say, you could."

"Husbands and wives don't take boys to bed with them."

"I told you I wouldn't even know he was there unless you talked. You'd be between us."

"Men don't take boys to bed with them."

"I know that. I'm not an idiot. I was mad. It was our bedtime and I lay here waiting for you, and you stayed out there talking to Ebon. I thought you liked him more than you liked me."

"More than I liked you? You're my wife, Orpha."

Then Lon did something he had never done before, not even on our wedding night. He pulled me up from my chair, lifted my arms, and slipped my nightgown off over my head. I had never stood body-naked in front of Lon before. I had been in bed with him, my nightgown as good as off; but never before had he looked at me unclothed; or appeared to want to see me without any clothes on.

This had troubled me. Was there something wrong with me? If I had shrunk from seeing Lon naked, it would have meant I didn't truly love him; not as a husband, anyway. Lon had never been bashful about being naked himself. He was proud of his body and liked my praise. He took off his nightshirt now, raised his arms so that he was stretched out in front of me, taut and hard as a man carved in marble.

"You can see that I love you, Orpha."

I did see. And though I had often yearned to have Lon love me with his eyes as well as his hands, I was unaccustomed to nakedness. I felt shamefaced and was tongue-tied before him.

Not Lon. He was exhilarated. "Adam and Eve in the garden," he said.

Because we had been quarreling about Ebon, I almost said, "And Ebon is our snake." For Ebon, like the snake, had brought us together, naked. I didn't say it. I would not give Ebon the credit.

We never quarreled about Ebon again. He stopped coming to study with us. Lon told him, I suppose, to stay away. I blamed myself for having put an end to his visits, which, to a born teacher like Lon, were undoubtedly a pleasure; and were certainly a help to a would-be learner like Ebon. But I couldn't bring myself to say, "Let Ebon come back again." I didn't want him back. I didn't want to talk about him. Lon gave him one night a week. That was as generous as I could bring myself to be.

5

I still have the book we were reading the afternoon it happened. Lon had bought it on a lecture trip to Cincinnati, bought it especially for this anniversary. It was Masefield's *Gallipoli,* and Lon had been turning the pages at a pace that would let us finish it on Armistice Day. It is a fine book, a terrible book, forgotten now in the welter of accounts of a world war even longer and bloodier than the First.

Reading it was a part of Lon's conviction that since he had not been permitted because of his eyes to fight in the war, he should at least share in his imagination the hardships of the men who had fought and died for democracy.

What happened a quarter-century later at Omaha Beach was no more violent, perhaps even less so, than what had happened at Sedd el Bahr and Sulva. The average life on the boats was some three minutes. "The landing party was stranded and men from the battleship River Clyde leaped from her to bring water or succour to the wounded. . . . A hundred brave men gave their lives thus. Every man there earned the cross that day. A boy earned it by one of the bravest deeds of the war; leaping into the sea with a rope in his teeth to try to secure a drifting lighter."

Lon cried when he read those words. "Just a boy," he said.

I loved that in Lon. If he had been an undersized spindly man, he might have felt it necessary to hide his tears; or to pretend that he was tough and didn't care whether he found God or not. But a towering man like Lon could cry openly, seek God openly, and no one would think it a sign of softness.

We were within a few pages of the end of the book when Crit Matthews appeared. Lon had gone inside to get a pitcher of lemonade. I saw Crit on his switch-tailed claybank before he crossed the Sandusky and headed up the lane to our house.

Crit climbed the porch steps looking woebegone, which he always did, more or less, anyway. A rabble of children and a sour-faced wife accounted for that, I thought.

"Lon's gone inside for lemonade," I told Crit. "Sit down. He'll be right out with a pitcherful in a minute."

Crit sat himself down on the porch swing.

"I am here to see Lon. But you've both got to hear what I've come to say. I'm sorry to be the one to bring you such news. Though it won't be no news to Lon. Except for this one thing, you've both been good neighbors, even Lon."

Lon, because it was a holiday, brought out the lemonade in his mother's cut-glass pitcher.

"Have a glass, Crit."

"No, I don't think I will. I reckon you know why I'm here, Lon."

"I'm not a good guesser. You'll have to tell me, Crit."

"I'll have to tell your wife, too."

"I wouldn't do that, Crit."

"Do you want to tell her?"

"Come inside, Crit. We'll talk there."

"No. What I have to say she's got a right to hear. She'll hear it anyway, sooner or later. It's my duty to tell her."

"It's my duty to stop you."

I was still holding Masefield's book in my hands, open at the place where we had stopped reading.

"Put in something to mark the place, Orpha. You'll likely have to finish it alone," Lon told me. Then he went into the house.

I picked up one of the maple leaves that had blown onto the porch and put it between pages 174 and 175. I don't have to remember that. I have the book before me now. The maple leaf is still there, faded, but not crumpled. We were at the paragraph that begins "It was said by Dr. Johnson that, 'no man does anything, consciously for the last time, without a feeling of sadness.'"

That may seem a strange coincidence, considering what was about to happen. I've known stranger. Once, in a book that had the word "spider" in it, I found the body of a dead spider covering the word: as if the spider had chosen for itself a resting place marked with its name.

I have never, though I've kept the Masefield book all these years, looked into it again until this morning. If I had, I would have found, soon after Johnson's words, Masefield himself saying, "Many things are possible in this world, and the darkness is strange, and the heart of a fellow man is darkness to us."

Masefield was talking about the Turks, but the heart of my own husband was darkness to me, too.

When Lon came out of the house, he had his gun with him, his long-barreled squirrel rifle.

"She doesn't have to hear, Crit."

"She has to hear. You or me. Choose."

Lon shot Crit first, very cleanly in the head, so that Crit never knew what hit him.

Lon wasn't as lucky when he turned the gun on himself. A rifle is an unhandy weapon to shoot yourself with. With his first shot, Lon took off an ear. This never fazed him. He looked at me and said, "Good-bye, Orpha. Remember, you were my wife."

His third shot was as clean as his first. The two men, dead, neither moving, neither bleeding much, lay within inches of each other, their eyes wide open.

I don't know how long I sat where I was. I don't know why I had not leaped up and wrestled the gun, or tried to wrestle it, out of Lon's hands. I might have succeeded.

I had no inclination to scream, weep, clasp Lon. What had happened, I certainly saw. I heard the gun, and the strange plushy shuddering thump of falling bodies. My eyes saw, my ears heard, but I wasn't present. What happened took place far, far from me. I had never seen a movie then, but movies can make death more real than Lon's death was for me in the minute of his dying.

Motionless, speechless. But not without feeling, for I pressed the edges of the book I was holding so tightly against my chest that I had a speckling of red broken veins under my breasts next day.

Did I believe that if I didn't accept what had happened as real, it would not be real?

Was this proof of the conviction I had had all along: Lon's love for me was a dream? Our life together couldn't last? I had never expected this ending, but I had expected a time when I would go back to being alone: an old maid, a teacher, a hired girl. In fairy tales, Prince Charmings marry girls of my kind, but never in real life.

It was Crit's horse, nibbling his way along the frost-damaged asters toward the front porch, that aroused me.

67

I must take the Matthews' horse home. I must tell Mrs. Matthews that her husband is dead; it was this thought that roused me.

When I stood, I re-entered the world in which I had lived before Lon fired his gun. I was there with two dead men, and one was my husband. I sat on the porch floor beside Lon. I lifted his head to my lap. I closed his eyes and kissed them. "Crit could have told me anything," I said. "It wouldn't matter. Whatever it was, you didn't have to die for it."

I now think that I am able to remember Lon's face exactly. Perhaps not. No woman knows what the man she loves really looks like. She knows what she feels for him, and this feeling is what she calls his face.

Crit was certainly dead; and though my mind knew that Lon was also dead, my heart could not believe that life had left the long supple body, still warm against mine.

I went into the house and got a pillow for Lon's head. I had never seen him sleeping before. He had an alarm clock in his head. When it went off, he awakened me. "Wake up, Orpha, Wake up, my sleepyhead. The sun is up and shining. So must you."

"Wake up, Lon," I said under my breath. I half expected him to lift his head and say, "I've been dreaming I was hurt, Orpha." A small trickle of blood came from one nostril. Lon was dead. The alarm clock had run down.

Crit's horse had munched his way clear to the porch railing. He was mowing down tangle-headed dahlias and Lon's mother's bleeding hearts. He put his head through the railing, as if understanding that something was wrong with Crit. The dark was coming down fast. Mrs. Matthews had to be told.

Lon lay at his ease. He lay as if a struggle that had worn him out was finished. Perhaps it would be a pity to wake him up.

I got on Crit's horse, riding him bareback, as Crit had done. The claybank was a barner, a horse that rides out reluctantly but goes home to the barn with enthusiasm. I had no desire to go racing pell-mell across the Sandusky, then pound up the lane to the Matthews'. With the news I was bringing, a string-haltered gait would be more seemly. But I had no choice. There is no way to command a horse who has no bit in his mouth. His neck is ten times as strong as your arms, and a jerk on his halter is likely more a pleasure than anything else to him.

In the Matthews' yard was a collection of rigs, mostly horse-drawn, but a few automobiles, too. The Matthews' were celebrating Armistice Day with a pitch-in supper. Why Crit had chosen this day to come to our house, I don't know. Perhaps he thought he'd never be missed at home.

6

Why is it that faces that mean nothing to us are registered in living color on our brain plate and remain unfaded after decades? While faces loved beyond telling vanish? They vanish because we never saw them clearly in the first place. Emotion blinds. The eye films over. Emotion thickens the blood. Touch is stronger then than sight; flesh remembers what eyes can no longer see.

I had no feeling for the faces that looked up at me on that early evening when Crit's horse and I, both wet with Sandusky water, galloped into the Matthews' raggle-taggle yard.

Uncle Johnny Wilson grabbed the gelding's halter before he could gallop me clear on into the barn. Uncle Johnny was Irish, red-faced, with ginger side whiskers: he wore, even when working, a fancy vest with a heavy gold watch chain. He was descended, he said, from the Irish aristocracy.

His wife had one eye. She didn't miss anything with it. "Jump down, Sis," she told me, "and the horse will head straight for the barn without you."

I did and it did.

Mark Trickey was there. He had only one leg. He was a cobbler from Amesville, with a leathery face. He was a ladies' man, and he took my arm to steady me as if I might be worn out from my galloping bareback ride.

Belle Clarkin was there, red-headed, with red-brown eyes and a skin like the cream on a crock of milk.

Dick Willey, a fat sawmill man, was there. His wife was with him; she was built like a chicken, a plump big-breasted body ending in a beaky little hen's head.

The Matthews tribe was all there, of course: Ebon and the other two half-grown boys. Leota, almost a young woman. Opal, Crit's wife, pinch-faced and mean, looking as a woman would have to in order to chop off her daughter's hair braids to spite a schoolmate.

They gathered round me. Crit had ridden off on his horse and I had ridden back on it. What was the explanation? That was what I had come to give. But I could not speak. So long as I remained silent, I denied what had happened.

Opal Matthews took the flesh of my upper arm in her hard pinching fingers. "Where is Crit?"

I fainted, for the first and last time in my life.

"It is getting dark," I said and, without knowing it, fell.

The next thing I knew, I thought I was swimming.

"It won't help matters to drown her, Opal."

Jake Hesse, not a cobbler like Mark Trickey, but a shoe-store owner from up north, in Cincinnati, who came home now and then to live on his farm, was hauling me onto my feet.

When I stood up, I was dripping wet, but it was no longer dark.

"Where is Crit?" his wife asked.

"He is dead."

"Dead? I don't believe you. Crit never had a sick day in his life."

"Now he is dead."

"He didn't look well when he left," Jake said.

"I don't believe it," Opal said again.

"You can go see for yourself."

"Where is Lon? Why isn't he here?"

"Lon is dead, too."

"Two men don't suddenly die at the same time."

"They do if one shoots the other, then shoots himself."

"Lon? Lon did the shooting? Why?"

"I don't know why. I came to ask you why."

"Don't ask me why Lon killed Crit. The only reason could be he's crazy. He's always been crazy. You know that."

I didn't know that. "He was never crazy. He shot Crit because Crit was going to tell me something Lon didn't want me to hear."

"He was going to tell Lon about me."

Leota Matthews pulled her dress, a kind of wrapper called a Hoover apron, so tight around her middle that the bulge of her pregnancy was very visible.

Then Ebon turned his sister to face him. "You're a liar and you know it. Lon didn't do that."

"Alonzo Dudley believed it enough to shoot your daddy," Opal told her son. "Your daddy has died for Leota. You ought to be willing to keep your mouth shut while she tells her own story."

"I don't believe Leota, either," I said.

"What did you expect?" Opal asked. "You teaching school and running foot races. A man don't marry for high-kicking and book-reading. While you were reading books, what did you think Lon was doing?"

"He started me to reading. He liked me to read."

"There were things he liked even better."

Jake Hesse said, "It would make more sense, instead of arguing about something we can't know for sure, to go over to the Dudleys and see what's happened. Orpha's overwrought. She could be mistaken."

I was overwrought, but I wasn't mistaken. They were both dead. Everyone said so, when they came back.

7

Lon was an atheist, a murderer, and a suicide. And if this wasn't enough, he had got a girl in trouble. No church would claim him, no graveyard accept him. Even the United Brethren, my own people, less hidebound than most, and Lon the husband of a lifelong member, balked.

I didn't care because I knew Lon wouldn't. Though when the Reverend Kibbler said no, I reminded him that Christ on the cross had said to the thief on the cross, "Thou shalt dine with me this day in Paradise."

"Those weren't exactly His words, Orpha. And the man was only a thief. No one had died because of him. No girl had been wronged."

In my opinion, Leota Matthews had probably been wronged before Lon ever laid eyes on her. But that was not a suitable subject for debate with your minister while planning your husband's funeral.

"Lon will rest easier on his own land anyway than in the graveyard of some church he never believed in and that doesn't want him."

"I'll tell you what I can do, Orpha," the Reverend Kibbler told me. "What I'd like to do, in fact. Lon was a great reader of Scripture. Since the burial isn't to be in sanctified ground, no one will raise any objection if I read Scripture at the graveside."

A minister, I thought, should be concerned with what was right, not with people's possible objections.

The Reverend Kibbler was as round-headed as an otter, with hair more like fur than hair. He had otter eyes, too, round, shallow, and brimming with innocence.

"No," I said. "Lon was not a church member. He would rather die as he lived."

Joe, who was with me when I talked with the Reverend Kibbler, said, "I will read Scripture, Sis. Lon wouldn't object to that, would he?"

"He wouldn't. And I would like it."

We buried Lon on his own land, on acres that had belonged to the Dudley family for more than a hundred years. The burial site I chose was a plot of earth under a giant sycamore on the slope just above the house. Lon and I had stood there many an evening watching the setting sun turn the Sandusky waters red.

Not many came to the funeral. Even those who liked Lon and had been friends and neighbors of the Dudleys for years stayed away, afraid that their presence would appear to condone murder in general and Crit Matthews' killing in particular.

It was the season for Indian summer, but both summer and the Indians were absent. No color, no warmth. The dogwood leaves had faded, the maple leaves fallen. There was no sun to liven Sandusky waters. A heavy gray day and Lon dead in a pine box.

My mother and father were there, of course. Joe, spitting blood again, should have stayed home. But Lon had been Joe's friend before he became my husband. And nothing ever kept Joe away from what he wanted to do.

Ebon Matthews was there; at the back of the small crowd, always standing behind someone taller. Mourning whom? Lon? His father? Both? But mourning. His face looked deader than Lon's.

When all had assembled, and since there was no ceremony to postpone burial, the four men who had been chosen to handle the ropes that would lower Lon into his grave stepped to the sawhorses that supported the coffin.

Then Joe, black hair roached up thick and solid as a helmet and cheekbones aflame with his afternoon fever, came forward and said, "Wait a minute."

Joe had a carrying voice. There was a blare to it, there was the sound of metal behind it, the sound of a trumpet or a gun.

"My friend Alonzo Dudley," said Joe, "read in his lifetime more Scripture than all of us put together. He did not find in Scripture what he was seeking, but he never gave up the search. It would not be right to put him underground without reading in his memory words from the book he read more often than he read any other." Then Joe opened his Bible and said, "I will read to you Psalm Thirty-eight."

This is the Psalm that begins "O Lord, rebuke me not in thy wrath: neither chasten me in thy hot displeasure" and ends, "Forsake me not, O Lord: O my God, be not far from me. Make haste to help me, O Lord my salvation."

"This," said Joe when he had finished reading, "was Lon's constant prayer." Then, remembering some funeral service he had once heard, he concluded, "Earth to earth, ashes to ashes."

It was not until then that Lon really died for me. Up to that minute, he had been absent, silent, asleep. But not *dead*. Not an object to put underground like a poisoned dog, or a tomcat torn apart in a fight.

We live in our eyes. If Lon could have remained visible, intact, in his chair across from me at the table each night, not speaking, never touching me, but *there,* in all the ripe wheat of his cresting hair and the water-gray of his sometimes dark eyes, I wouldn't, I thought at the time, have asked for more.

At that minute, I understood Grandpa. He wasn't crazy after all. If Lon had died while I was sick, I would have dug him up with my own hands in order to once more see and touch him. We talk of spirit and soul and love and affection, but flesh and the sight of it is what we want. Touch, and smell, and sound, yes; but oh, to *see*. Then I understood the origin of mummies and why widows in the South Seas keep the skulls of their husbands with them as long as they live. Then I understood the potency of the finger bones of saints and of the locks of hair from the heads of dead husbands braided into breastpins.

The ceremony, which was only Joe's reading—no songs, no prayers —was soon over. Lon was put in a hole in the ground and the earth piled on top of him like a heavy coverlet; Lon, who could never sleep with his arms under the covers, let alone his shoulders! Here he was, buried, smothered. No one cared any more about Lon's preferences in sleeping.

I was not a widow who could throw herself into her husband's grave pit, or a woman who could walk into the blaze of a funeral pyre. But I was a woman bereaved, more broken-hearted than I knew. No more willing it than you will a tear or a sigh, I lay down on the mound above Lon's body. There had been no chance for any farewell words before he died. "Mark the place" in the book, he said, and "Remember, you were my wife." Nothing else. Now, on his first night alone under earth, in the dark and the cold, I thought I would stay with him, should stay with him, as I would with a child left alone in a dark and ugly place.

"Orpha," my mother called, "get up from there."

Everyone else had gone home. Only my mother, father, and Joe waited for me in the surrey.

"What good do you think you are doing Lon?" she asked.

I was doing him no good. I knew that. I was not even doing myself any good. A cold wind had come up. The night would be frosty. The gravel in the dirt that mounded the grave cut into my flesh. I inhaled dust.

"Orpha, don't make a spectacle of yourself."

To whom was I a spectacle? No one was there but Mama, Papa, and Joe. I dug my fingers more deeply into the earth. Lon had *died*. Compared with dying, what was the embarrassment of seeing a daughter make a spectacle of herself?

Then someone—with my eyes closed and nose in the dust I couldn't see who—said, "I'll spend the night here, Orpha. I wanted to, anyway. You go on home with your folks. It'll be all right with Lon if I stay the night instead of you."

I recognized Ebon's voice without looking up. I believed what he said. He reached down, took my hand, and pulled me to my feet.

"You go on home. Lon would rather you did."

I knew this was true. I got into the back seat of the surrey with Joe.

Ebon didn't stretch himself out on the grave, as I had done. He sat down like a man by a campfire, pulled his knees up, clasped them, then rested his chin on his knees and gazed at the grave. I watched him as long as he was in sight.

V

EBON

1

I awakened next morning in the room that had been mine for eighteen years of my life. I had lived there nine times longer than I had lived with Lon. Back where I had been a girl. I would be a girl again, I thought.

In that room nothing had changed: cherry bureau, washstand, blue bowl and pitcher, rag carpet, feather bed, pillow shams embroidered to say "Good morning" were just as they had been. Oh! things outlive people. Unchanged, my room told me how much I had changed. A girl left; a widow came back.

Downstairs at the breakfast table I heard again the story my room had told me. I was no longer a girl to my parents: the widow of a murderer, an unfaithful husband, a man who had preferred death to continuing to live with me. I was a failure.

I had not expected to be petted and hugged. If I had ever been kissed by either my father or my mother, I had forgotten it. Except for Joe, I felt myself to be an outsider. To Joe, I was still a young sister.

"Have some fried mush, Orphy," he said. "You need something that'll stick to your ribs. You look peaked."

"What do you expect?" Mama asked.

"I expected her to look peaked," Joe said, "and I advise eating to offset it."

Mama never crossed swords with Joe. She had her say, he had his, and the word-tussle ended before it started. Papa and I, less nimble-witted than Joe, would continue to argue with Mama, and would continue to be bested. And we would both continue to resent it. Or I would. Perhaps Papa wouldn't. He was proud of his wife, rejoiced in her being feisty, an ex-schoolteacher, a Sunday-school superintendent, a terror to lazy hired girls and to hired men who kept their knees under the table too long at mealtime. He liked Mama's looks, or so I judged. He would bring in a single white tuberose, and fasten it against the shiny black of her high-coiled hair.

"Sweets to the sweet," he would say.

"You old soft-soaper, you," Mama would answer. "You'll never need to kiss the Blarney stone."

Except for a lover, no one is as conscious of a woman's looks as a daughter. More conscious, for the mother is a prophecy to the daughter of what lies ahead for her.

I didn't want to look like my mother. And of course I didn't. She *was* handsome. But she also looked, in my opinion, like a schoolmarm and a Sunday-school superintendent and a woman who would begin clearing the table while the hired man was still eating. I didn't want to look like my mother. I didn't want to act like her.

This, psychologists now think, is a handicap for a girl. A girl learns to be a woman, they say, by imitating her mother. I wanted to imitate my father; the reason being, I suspect, that I was so much more like my mother. Hustling the hired man out of the kitchen and organizing Sunday-school classes is nothing to what I've found myself capable of doing.

Admiration hasn't made me look like Papa. Looks are changed by what we are inside, not what we admire outside. Feelings shape our faces as fingers shape clay. The flesh reveals what the heart has felt. Every heart thump leaves its mark: hollowed cheeks, sunken eye sockets, downturned lips. The admiring eye is powerless to shape the flesh that houses it.

Papa's face said "Love." Mama's said "Hurry." Joe's said "Endure." There was more hurry and endure in my face than love.

Lon had softened my face, but traces of the army mule and high-kicker still remained. When Lon drew me to him, I could feel my face soften and change. If I had spent my lifetime with Lon, I wouldn't have the face I have today.

After I had followed Joe's advice, had eaten some fried mush and sorghum, Mama said, "Now, Orpha, what are your plans?"

I had no plans. Live through one day, live through the next.

"Who's taking care of the stock?"

"Ebon Matthews."

"Looking after the place of the man who killed his father? It'll cause talk."

"He asked to do it."

"He'll likely slip some poison in the watering trough."

78

"He was Lon's friend. He wouldn't do a thing like that."

" 'An eye for an eye.' That's Biblical."

That was one of the ways in which I didn't want to be like my mother: suspect the worst of people. You suspect in others what you're capable of yourself.

Joe, who usually didn't come clear alive until afternoon, woke up at this.

"I didn't know you knew Ebon Matthews, Mama."

"I know human nature."

"You should've warned Orpha about the man she was marrying."

"I did. She'll bear me out in this."

She had. Much as she was pleased to have me engaged to be married, she had said, "Think twice about Alonzo Dudley, Orpha. There's a queer streak in the Dudley family."

"You'll bear me out in this. Won't you, Orpha?"

"You did, Mama. You said there was a queer streak in the Dudley family. After what Grandpa did, I might've said there was a queer streak in ours, too."

"Pa didn't kill anyone."

"What Lon did was wrong," Joe said. "He was out of his head. But you got to remember he was trying to protect Orpha."

Mama exploded. "Protect Orpha! That's a great way to protect a wife. Murder one man, then kill yourself. Trying to protect himself, more likely."

"From what?"

"Being sued by the Matthews' for getting·their daughter in trouble, for one thing. Having to support a woods colt. Losing his wife. At least, I hope Orpha would have left him."

"Ebon says his sister lied."

"Lon didn't think so. He shot Crit to keep him from spilling the news to Orpha. No. Lon took the easy way out. If a man wants to kill himself, that's his own business. It's not God's will, and it's cowardly. But murder is the worst crime there is. What Lon did doesn't make sense unless he had a good reason for wanting to shut up Crit."

Before Joe could agree or disagree, Papa said, "This isn't a jury trial for Lon. This is a welcome-home for a girl who has come home sorrowing. She's lost her husband, and lost him in a bad way. Let's not drag her back over the coals she's been trying to get away from."

That kindness made me cry, the first tear I had shed since Lon's death. Crying made me feel better. Tears melted the heavy rough stone in my chest. I put my hand in gratitude on top of Papa's and patted it.

"I suppose you miss your husband," Mama said coldly.

Perhaps she hadn't even seen me pet Papa's hand. But I took my hand away. I knew a daughter's place.

The weather had faired off from the funeral gray of the day before. The sun was silver on the haystack, gold on the corncrib, and bright enough to make the long morning shadows black.

A breeze that made the windmill clack as the blades went round, and the pump whine as it lifted the water, smelled of windfall apples in the orchard. Two Rhode Island Red roosters were having a crowing contest.

Anyone looking at our breakfast table, at the red-checkered tablecloth (no oilcloth or scrubbed pine wood for Mama), the four gathered round it, all gilded with the clear sunlight of a fall morning, would have thought, "There sit health and happiness."

There sat sickness and sorrow: Joe, with the lung trouble that had killed one in every generation of Mama's people since they left Ireland; I, a widow at twenty, the wife of a murderer and the cause, perhaps, of my husband's crime ("A man don't marry for high-kicking and book-reading").

Mama, with a disease worse than lung trouble, and less kind: jealousy. It never kills, but it never lets up, either. It gnaws at you till you draw your last breath. And no need, in Mama's case. No slightest need. Reason, not need, should perhaps be the word. Mama perhaps had need for some passionate emotion that Papa couldn't provide. He, steady as a pump bolt, faithful as the seasons, could provide her with none of the heart stoppage of doubt, the knife twist of fear she craved.

She, Sunday-school superintendent, United Brethren, baptized in creek water and born again, couldn't sin; though she was capable of it. But her life would have been infinitely enlivened if *somebody* would; somebody who meant a lot to her, who could cut her to the quick.

Her own husband, Wesley, was the one who could do that; and since Wesley wouldn't, she had to imagine the covert glances, the surreptitious touchings of females crowding closer to him than need be. There wasn't much of this, but where the imagination is already

80

inflamed and expectant, it was enough to cause the pain and uncertainty she wanted.

What did Papa think of all this? For Mama didn't for a minute try to hide her feelings. He could have stopped it, couldn't he? He could have said, "Myra, any more of this nonsense and I'll give you something to worry about."

Once, I praised Irma, the long-nosed hired girl, in Papa's hearing for the beautiful job she had done scouring the case knives.

"They were never so shiny before."

Mama treated me as a conspirator, in cahoots with Irma, trying to discredit her as housewife and case-knife cleaner in front of her husband.

When Mama berated Papa for carrying the bags of Cousin Estelle to her rig instead of letting the hired man do it, I thought, Mama, you keep that up and you'll put ideas in Papa's head.

She kept it up, but if she put any ideas in his head, he never acted on them.

Perhaps, though it is hard to believe, Papa relished being regarded as a man whose wife had to fight off predatory females. Did Papa, who wouldn't have pinched the bottom of a five-year-old, enjoy the flare-ups that only a real skirt-lifter merited? Have all the excitement, but none of the brutal finality of real-life entanglements?

Anyway, they lived happily (it seemed to me) inside this myth of Mama's making. At that breakfast table I saw who wasn't going to be happy there: me. There was no role for me, grown woman and widow, inside the myth. When there was no visiting cousin or Sunday-school organist on hand to play the part, who would I be but the other woman?

How could a devoted mother and loving wife have such ideas? By living in a neck of the woods where such ideas had been acted on. That's how. Mama didn't have to imagine *that*.

The tears that were making me feel better didn't help the appetites of anyone else.

Joe said, "I'm not hungry, either, Orpha. Come on up to my room. I want to talk to you."

Joe's room was at the head of the kitchen stairs. It had been planned for the hired man, but Joe had taken it over. It was about the size of a prison cell, with a sloping ceiling and a narrow window;

a window so close to the windmill that its blades cooled you like a dozen waving palm-leaf fans when they were turning. The room was prison-sized but not prison-colored. The Star of Bethlehem quilt on the bed was a shine of glory; the hooked rug, Mama's own design, was either a Roman candle blazing or a cockscomb blooming. (Mama had so much energy and imagination, the "other woman" was probably one of the mildest forms they might have taken. A little more of either and she might have become another Pope Joan or a second Lizzie Borden.)

Joe put me down on his bed like an invalid, propped me up against the headboard with pillows, and pulled the room's one chair close. He held my hand in both of his. Touch was as natural to Joe as talking or seeing. How had he learned it? Well, for one thing, no one had ever called him the "other man."

I thought Joe had brought me up to his room to talk about me and my trouble. Not at first, anyway. I had lost a husband. Joe was faced with losing his own life. No one's death, certainly not a brother-in-law's, is as important to you as your own.

"I am going back to California," he said. "It's my only chance. One more winter here will kill me."

"Are you worse, Joe?"

"Where have you been, Sis?"

"Not keeping track of your lungs, that's true."

Joe coughed so often you never noticed it. You train yourself not to notice what pains you. He coughed then, put his handkerchief to his lips, then showed me the stains.

"That's blood," he said. "If I stay here, I'll bleed to death. I'm going back to California. It stopped there."

"Where'll you get the money?"

"Mama. She's been saving it all her life. She planned a trip to Niagara for her and Papa."

"This is more important."

"Glad you think so, too."

Couldn't I give Mama credit for anything? "Will you stay with Uncle Charlie again?"

"No. A tent city on the desert, where it's even drier and warmer."

I thought, Who'll pay? I didn't say it.

"Don't worry about the costs. Let me tell you something, Sis. I am going to get well and I am going to make a name for myself. I know it. I can show you my handkerchief and you know what's in

82

my lungs. I've got some ideas here"—he tapped his forehead—"but there's no way of showing you yet. I can't spit ideas up on a handkerchief."

I believed him. He had a face that bred belief: the face of successful gamblers and great preachers, filled with the invitation to come in and share the power. It is a pleasure to be in their presence, even after the gambler has robbed you of your money, and the preacher of any satisfaction you've had in sin.

Joseph Raymond Chase, my brother, with his feet on that hooked rug of exploding stars or flowers, with his big plank-flat shoulders topping his ladder-back chair, was born to make a name for himself. His straight heavy eyebrows continued the promise of the sooty hair. The eyes, gray with dark irises, ordinary size maybe, but afloat in great blue-white lakes, sent you a dare you wanted to accept. His nose was strong enough to be a boat prow and cleave waves. The mouth had nothing to do with eating. Blood and words came out of it. And Joe promised he'd stanch the blood.

Was he masculine? In whatever way Lon meant it, yes. He was no beauty, like Lon. There was a threat in Joe's face: not of any specific evil—greed or sloth or double-dealing. It was the threat of power: power that would take charge like a strong wind or a big sea.

He took charge of me that very morning.

At the table Mama had asked, "What are your plans?" I would be a widow and mourn; beyond that, I had no plans.

Before Joe and I came downstairs, I had plans.

"You can't stay here," Joe told me.

"I supposed I would."

"What would you do?"

"Help Mama."

"She doesn't need help. You get on her nerves."

"I would try not to."

"That would get on her nerves, too. What're you going to do about the farm?"

"Lon's farm?"

"It's your farm now."

"I don't know. I can't farm."

"If I wasn't going to California, I'd help you. Not that pushing a plow is my long suit. But I know who'd be willing to help you. The Matthews boy."

"Ebon? Lon killed his father."

"That's past. He'd be willing."

"Ride over every morning and back every night?"

"No. He'd live there."

"With me?"

"Not *with* you. He don't want to live with you. You don't want to live with him, do you?"

"Of course not. He's a kid."

"Live there like a hired man."

"Like Victoria Cinderella and—"

"Don't be silly. Ebon's not feeble-minded, and you're not man-hungry, are you?"

"For Lon. I'm not hungry for anyone else."

"You'll go a long time before you find another Lon. No. Ebon would farm for you. He'd be glad to get away from his own home. You could go ahead with your teaching. Between the farm and your job, there'd be enough money to send me a little now and then. Mama's got the money for the fare. Uncle Charlie will help, but I'm not fool enough to expect any miracle cure. I'll be cured—I can tell you that—but it won't happen overnight. I'll pay you back later, but it'll be hard sledding at first. You could help."

I don't think Joe really felt the need of my help. He could use it, yes. What he was doing was giving me a purpose for living and a reason for leaving home, where he knew I'd never be happy. And maybe do Ebon a good turn, too. He knew Ebon better than I did.

Sitting there on Joe's bed, the midmorning sun gone over the top of the ridgepole, I saw a future that had not existed begin to take shape.

"You like to teach, don't you?" Joe asked.

I loved it, or at least I loved the kids. We had a day-long game to play. The game was called "learning": add numbers, define words, memorize dates, tell stories: Franklin with his kite; Washington with his dollar; Jackson saying, "Let us cross over the river"; and Thomas More at the chopping block taking care of his beard—"It has done no harm."

"I love teaching. Lon said I was a born teacher."

"Lon probably knew what he was talking about. Lon would like the idea of the land that had been his and his folks' staying in the family, wouldn't he?"

"In the family?"

"You're the only family he had."

Lon *had* said, "Remember, you were my wife."

"You don't have anything against Ebon, do you?"

I once had. But I was ashamed to tell Joe that I had been jealous of him—of the time and attention Lon gave him.

"No. He's a good boy."

"You're a lucky girl, Sis. A job and a farm to make money, a brother who needs money. Don't sit here at home and mope. There's a lot of people to think of besides yourself. Lon got you started teaching. Tell him he didn't do it for nothing."

"Tell him?"

"He's still alive to you, isn't he?"

"In heaven, you mean?"

"I mean in your heart."

"Yes, in my heart."

"Do something to prove it."

Joe and I didn't go downstairs until dinnertime. I could hardly swallow breakfast. Now I was hungry for food.

"Mama," I said, "you asked me what my plans were, and I told you I didn't have any. Now I have plans." I told her what Joe and I had worked out together.

She approved of everything but Ebon living at the farm. "People will talk," she said.

"He's a kid," I reminded her. "He was Lon's pupil."

"They'll talk even more."

Joe said, "We can't live our lives by what people say."

"We do," said Mama. "Lose your good name, and what's left?"

"Whatever you had before you lost it."

"Let's return thanks for what we've got now," Papa said, and we bowed our heads.

2

Ebon had already moved in when I went home at the end of the week. I don't know whether Joe had asked him to or not, but he was there with everything he owned in the parlor bedroom. The parlor bedroom was downstairs. Lon and I had slept in the south bedroom upstairs.

"I could sleep in the barn," he said.

A lot of hired men did, but with bedroom space going to waste, it seemed silly. It would probably say to the suspicious that we were guilty of what they suspected and were trying to hide our tracks. There was nothing to hide. Since I wasn't going to lead my life according to what people thought, I would try to lead it according to what was sensible and convenient.

Ebon not only had all the outside work done when I came home from school, but he also had a fire going both in the grate in the sitting room and in the cookstove in the kitchen. He had a supper cooked and waiting. Mama couldn't have done it better. Neither Lon nor Joe would starve to death if left alone in a house; but neither one would cook a real meal.

A bowl of bread and milk was what I had expected. Ebon had ham and sweet potatoes baked together, pickled beets, corn bread, and baked apples served with a thick dip.

I returned thanks. I always had.

"Lon never said a blessing," Ebon said.

"Did he eat at your house when he came over to teach you?"

"Not supper with the family. But I cooked him a snack before he went home."

"What did your mother think of that?"

"Nothing. I paid for extra groceries I used."

"What did Lon think of it?"

"He liked it. He thought I was a good cook. Not better than you, though. He would never have said that."

Ebon said this very earnestly, the way people do when they're lying.

"Lon always praised you. He said no one could equal your salt rising bread."

I had supposed that one of the pleasures of having Ebon on the place would be the chance it would give me to talk about Lon with someone who had known him. That first night it didn't. Everything he said brought the jealousy of which I had been ashamed to life again. It is bad to feel jealousy about a live husband; it is ghoulish to be jealous of a dead one.

The minute supper was over Ebon said, "I've got the books for study laid out on the study table. The Bible's there and the *Courier*s you missed while you were away."

He thought we'd take up right where Lon had left off. I couldn't do it.

"I'll take care of the supper things first."

86

"That'll be my job."

I was willing for him to do that, but sit down at Lon's table and take Lon's place a week after Lon's death? Not yet, anyway. Maybe never.

"I have to prepare for school tomorrow," I said.

Before I went upstairs I walked out onto the porch. It was a cold, clear night moving toward December's glitter. The chairs Lon and I had sat in ten days ago were where they had been. But someone, I could see, had been at pains to scrub the floorboards. There hadn't been much blood on the floor, but there had been some. I had planned to leave those stains there forever. They were the last visible sign I had of what had been as much a part of Lon as his flesh and bones. I had planned to kneel down and put my hand to blood that had run through Lon's veins. It was gone now, the floor scrubbed clean as a kitchen table, white as an iced-over pond when frost settles on it.

The boy had done it. He had meant well. I went up the front stairs to bed without saying good night. He had robbed me of all that was left of Lon.

But once I was in bed, the thought that someone else was in the house helped me to sleep.

3

Fairmont! Not any other of the many buildings I have now occupied are as clear in my mind. Why is that? Is happiness translucent, even illuminating? Does it light up the places where you know it?

Fairmont! One-room clapboard schoolhouse with a belfry holding the bell I rang at eight, at quarter to one (to call the kids back from Stone Hill, where they ran to eat their lunches), at four to tell the parents school was out and anyone home later than five was dawdling.

Oh, Fairmont! One door, a row of windows head-high opposite it; high enough so that pupils couldn't waste their time watching bumblebees in the clover or squirrels in the butternut trees.

No well; water in a five-gallon canteen. No clock: alarm clock in Teacher's basket. No steam heat; big baseburner started by

Teacher when she arrived and fueled by volunteers who'd rather carry in wood than study long division. No teeter-totters, tetherball poles, basketball baskets, volleyball nets, cinder tracks, tennis courts.

A baseball diamond. I pitched for both sides, which wasn't fair to would-be pitchers, but was fair to each side as a whole.

Two outhouses. A combined woodshed and stable for horses.

A flagpole. We saluted the flag each morning, pledged our allegiance to the nation for which it stood.

Then we marched inside. The marching was necessary. Otherwise there'd be a race, with first graders trampled on.

Once inside we prayed. Everybody believed in God in those days. Even Lon didn't *deny* that. He just questioned. The praying helped us. It reminded us that Jesus had wanted us to "do unto others as you would be done by."

After the flag and God came learning.

Oh, Fairmont, how I loved you. I think the children loved me, too. This contradicts what I've been saying about children and grownups. Perhaps I have been wrong to attribute to all children feelings similar to my own. I believe the Fairmont pupils thought that the only difference between them and Teacher was size; and there wasn't even that between me and Beth Perkins and Willis Van Cleave.

Was what they felt about me different from what they felt about other adults? If so, why?

Once, twenty-five years later, a woman at a conference asked to draw my picture. I was flattered. It was the nearest thing to a caress: pencil tracing cheeks and eyes and lips.

In the midst of the drawing she threw up her hands. "I can't do it. You don't have a woman's face."

I was too embarrassed to ask, "What kind of a face do I have? Inhuman? Unfeminine? Deformed?" Now, I think she meant childlike.

Men, great men, Churchill and Eisenhower, can have boyish, even babyish, faces, and it's no impediment to their careers. Is a "boyish man" less of a contradiction than a "girlish woman"? It's a great compliment to call a woman "motherly" in appearance. Who compliments a man by saying he looks "fatherly"? If at forty-five I still looked like a "big girl," how did I look at twenty to my pupils? One of them, but oversized?

Does writing have anything to do with it? Who tells stories? Children and writers. Is that one of the reasons my Fairmont kids, though I had not yet written a word, saw something in me that made me one of them? Childlike?

I don't know. At any rate, the morning I came back to school after Lon's death, they had all come early and were waiting for me. I could have been the child, they the mothers. They hugged me, they petted me. They unhitched Mouse and put her away. Someone had crawled in a window and started the fire. They hung up my coat. The woodbox was full. The erasers cleaned.

"We thought you might not come back."

"I brought you a piece of marble cake."

"I learned my twelves while you were away."

"He was a wicked man. You should be glad he is gone."

"Somebody else will marry you."

I began to cry.

"Shut up, everybody," said Nettie Mozier. "She doesn't want to marry anyone else. She's not a grass widow."

Nettie was the boss. Except for fractions, compound interest, and pitching, she was as good a teacher as I. Nettie had everyone programed that morning to behave as if the class had assembled in a funeral parlor. The blackboard was covered with arithmetic problems, silent-reading questions, and state capitals to be memorized. There was nothing for me to do but to sit at my desk. I appreciate Nettie's concern. Her mistake was her prescription for my recovery. The remedy I needed was participation, not exclusion.

At noon I pitched, as usual. The schoolroom, when we went back into it, was no longer a funeral parlor. Poor Nettie was demoted.

I still have a picture captioned "Fairmont 1923." On the back of the picture are the names and ages of all the pupils. Where are they now? Fourteen-year-old Nettie is now sixty-nine. I could pass her in the street without knowing her. Would she know me? Most teachers even at twenty-five look old to their pupils; at sixty-five they don't appear to have changed much. But the pupils! If you want proof of mortality, teach school; then see your pupils fifty years later. It's like going from May to December in one day. Try not to remember that the same changes, only worse, can be seen in you.

We may not have learned much at Fairmont, but we were happy.

Perhaps I run myself down. Perhaps we learned a lot, Teacher most of all. Teaching is the royal road to learning. The three R's are the least of it; though keeping up with Nettie Mozier did make me a whiz at mental arithmetic.

The pupil's ages ranged from four to fifteen. Neither four-year-old Bernard nor fifteen-year-old Alpha should have been in school. Bernard, the four-year-old, came because his mother was dead and he had a sister at Fairmont. We were, in some respects, an early day-care center. Bernard was brown-eyed, pink-cheeked, and plump; he was always smiling, and when he smiled he had dimples as deep as acorns. Everyone wanted to cuddle Bernard; at home, said his sister, he had been tickled as well as cuddled. This, she claimed, had caused him to stutter. Bernard didn't mind. He just stuttered away until what he was after came out. He seemed to like stuttering.

At the Christmas program, Bernard always recited "Gentle Jesus, meek and mild." It took him so long to get to the crib, everyone felt as tired as a shepherd or a wise man who had trudged a long way before arriving. No speedy sixth grader could have conveyed the journey so well. Everyone loved Bernard when, in spite of his terrible handicap, he made it.

Fifteen-year-old Alpha was stuck in the third grade. She had as well have been in the first or the eighth. Numbers were entirely beyond her. One and one did not make two for Alpha; or even two ones. Multiplying, dividing, and subtracting were too weird for her to even contemplate. They made her cry. But she had one strange gift.

Alpha's gift was in a way like Bernard's stutter. No one, I think, had ever tickled Alpha. As soon think of tickling Dobbin. But Alpha, like Bernard, repeated sounds. She was a rhymer. Every word she had ever heard was stored in her memory bank. Say cat to her and she would produce, at once, rat, mat, fat, sat, bat, ghat, and more. You had to be careful about what you started Alpha out on. She had heard a lot of nasty words in her life, and there are more rhymes to these words than you might think.

Everyone at Fairmont wrote poems. Poetry comes more naturally to children than prose. Most of these poems were rhymeless, haikus, or very free verse. I had them printed in a little paperbound book in Louisville. The book was called *Young Pegasus*, a title that came out of *Classic Myths*. Most of the poems were like this:

Spring Song
Does Spring sing a song?
Listen and you will hear
A gurgling, gurgling, gurgling.
This is Spring's song.

Tin Soldiers
Tin soldiers, what are you fighting about now?
Yesterday you killed your captain.
Who can you kill today?

But Alpha's poems were very different. They went rat-a-tat-tat, bang-bang-bang, boom-de-lay.

Soft Hay
I ran around the barn one day
I ran into some hay.
The hay was soft and I fell down.
I fell through the hay and hit the ground.

Crusty Rusty
We've got a cat, his name is Rusty.
We've teased him so much, his temper is crusty.
So this morning when I pulled his tail,
He scratched me with his hind toenail.

Some people see double. I seem to remember double. I remember stuttering, rhyming—and twins. There were twin boys at Fairmont —George Washington Harriman and his brother, Thomas Jefferson Harriman.

Mrs. Harriman came with them to school on their first day. She was big enough to have had quadruplets; twins must have been lonesome in that wide expanse of Mrs. Harriman.

"Mrs. Dudley," she said to me, "my boys were brought up pure and I want them to stay pure."

What did she expect? She talked like a mother at a modern school with sex-education classes illustrated with charts.

"No one in this schoolroom says an unclean word."

"I'm not talking about talk," she said. "I am talking about what goes on out in boys' privies."

"You know very well, Mrs. Harriman, I can't go out to the boys' privy."

"You don't have to. My boys won't go at noon or recess time. That's been drummed into them. They know how to hold their water. What I want you to do is to see that when one of my boys asks to be excused, you see to it that no one else goes out at the same time. And don't let them stay out there for more than five minutes. Five minutes is plenty long enough for any call of nature."

A warning about spending more time than was necessary in the outhouse made sense to me. When I was in school, my friends and I played flinch in the privy for half an hour at a time without ever being missed.

"I'll keep track of the time."

"Don't send any big boy out after him. Some can't be trusted. He'll start playing with him."

Flinch, I thought.

"You're a married woman. You know what I mean."

Well, if marriage had something to do with it, flinch wasn't the answer. Or what she was talking about, either. "Playing with each other." A dim-witted habit I'd heard of, about on the level of picking your nose or putting beans in your ears.

I was insulted. "Mrs. Harriman, school here is so interesting no one would miss a class for anything like that. And I'll make them even more interesting. I'll think of—"

Mrs. Harriman interrupted me. "How old are you, Mrs. Dudley?"

"Twenty."

"Your mother was a teacher?"

"Yes."

"Well, she knows, even if she didn't tell you, that the finest teaching in the world won't stop some things. You're likely teaching good enough. Don't strain yourself about that. Just do what I ask. Keep my boys out of the privy when anyone else is out there and don't let them stay for more than five minutes at a time."

"What about the others? What can I do about them?"

"Not a thing, likely. Don't worry about what you can't help. Boys have been playing with themselves since the beginning of time. You just do what I ask you about mine. Maybe your teaching is the magic that will cure the others the way you think it will."

92

She was making fun of me but she was kind about it. She put an arm around me and gave me something between a shake and a hug.

"Maybe you can," she said. "Maybe you're a kind of faith healer."

I wasn't. She knew it and I knew it.

I didn't have any trouble with George Washington or Thomas Jefferson, though. They were scared even to go near a privy. Out behind the woodshed maybe, or in a horse stall. Or maybe not at all until school was over. Scared not only of playing with themselves but actually afraid to pee any place except at home.

Ten thousand one-room schools were no doubt like my Fairmont: bright Netties, slow Alphas, sweet Bernards. A little poetry and more than I knew, perhaps, of what Mrs. Harriman was trying to stop.

4

Two weeks after Lon died, on a blustery afternoon, first sleet, then snow blurring the windows, Fairmont School had a visitation.

We were putting on a play. This was easy for us to do since neither teacher nor pupils had ever seen a play. The eighth graders had read some scenes from Shakespeare, and I had read whole plays: *Macbeth, Romeo and Juliet, The Tempest.* Lon had seen to that.

As a result, we knew what plays were like: plays were people on a platform pretending to be other people and talking to each other. They stopped talking sometimes to kiss, fight duels, put poison in a goblet, die, dance jigs. The chief thing that must never happen in a play was silence. However, a play that was all talk and no action was dull, too. Unceasing talk was not lifelike. Even in a book made up of words, many of the words describe action. "He pressed her to his breast." "She closed the door with a bang." "He gave him a ringing clout above the left ear."

The subject for our play was perfect for us: the Children's Crusade. I wrote most of it. A better teacher would have had the pupils write all of it; they could have done it. They did write some of it.

"The Children's Crusade" suited a one-room school because the small children could play the would-be crusaders and the big seventh and eighth graders could be their parents.

The scene took place in the Norman castle of Nettie Mozier (naturally) and Lord John Buckmaster, her husband. Their three

93

children, including stuttering Bernard, were determined to join the band of children all yearning for travel and warfare. Some of the parents were willing that their children make the journey and die, if necessary, to free the hallowed ground from the clutch of the heathen.

Nettie, if she had been alive at the time, might have prevented, single-handed, the folly of the Children's Crusade. As it was, the good sense she ad-libbed almost wrecked the play.

"Sir Giles," said she, "do you worship Christ Jesus?"

"Yes," said Sir Giles, the play father of a second grader.

"Is He present in the world as a spirit or as a piece of land?"

"As a spirit," said Sir Giles.

"Would Jesus want children to die in order that dirt be kept for Christians only?"

"I don't know," said Sir Giles miserably.

"Command your children to stay home, then."

George Washington Harriman, a putative crusader, piped, "I will save the Holy Land. Mama raised me to be pure."

This, which was nothing I had written, made me laugh. I doubted George Washington could hold his water all the way to Jerusalem, but at least there would be no privies along the road where big boys could mislead him.

The play stopped when I laughed, and I had time to notice, outside the windows, which only I could see through, and I only when I was standing, the number of rigs that had pulled into the schoolyard. It was a stormy afternoon, and parents, if the weather was bad, sometimes did come to pick up their children. Two or three rigs were the most I had ever seen at one time. Now there were six or seven.

I had the children continue with their play. I thought that the parents would be impressed with a school so disciplined that a few visitors didn't prevent it from continuing its program.

I was wrong. They hadn't known we put on plays. Plays were wrong. Actresses were in plays, and matinee idols made love to them. Outside the theater, stage-door Johnnies awaited them. Playacting wasn't what the parents had come for; however, since they had arrived in the midst of a play, they had their say about that, too.

Mrs. Mozier saw her daughter sitting on the make-believe dais with her husband, Lord Buckmaster, and heard her talking about Jesus Christ.

"Nettie," she asked, "what in the world are you doing up there?"

"I am acting in a play, Mama."

"Well, you get right down from there and stop acting. Acting is wrong. It makes believe that what never happened, happened. You go to school to learn, not playact."

"This is not 'make-believe,'" said smart Nettie. "This is the Children's Crusade. It happened. Children went to the Holy Land to save it from the pagans."

"They were fools," said Mrs. Mozier, no fool herself. "The best thing for us to do about the wrong happenings of the past is to forget them."

"No," said Nettie. "If we forget them, we'll do them again."

Mrs. Mozier was not the real leader of the group of visiting parents. She was only the most talkative. The real leader was Alpha Bissell's mother.

Half of the Fairmont parents and influential citizens had come. The fat sawmill man. Mrs. Matthews, of course. Mr. Mozier and Mr. Bissell. Mr. and Mrs. Adolph Hare. Etta Burney. Jake Hesse. The Fitzgeralds. Mrs. Harriman and her husband, who looked like Santa Claus.

Alpha's mother took charge.

"Mrs. Dudley, our plan was to send the children outside while we had our little talk with you. But in this kind of weather we can't do that. Since every one of them knows what there is to talk about, it don't make the best sense in the world to expose them to lung fever or worse to keep them from hearing what they already know.

"Playacting isn't what we're here about. Though don't think we aren't taken aback by that, too. What we're here about strikes a lot deeper. Do we want our children sitting day in and day out in the presence of the wife of a murderer and self-killer?"

"She didn't do anything," yelled Nettie.

"Be quiet," said Mrs. Bissell. "You children have to be seen. You don't have to be heard."

Mrs. Matthews said, "If she had been the right kind of a wife, my husband would still be alive."

Pat Fitzgerald, a reasonable man, said, "We're out of line if we start blaming Teacher for what Alonzo Dudley did. But that don't change the fact that it don't do our children any good setting day after day in the presence of a woman who was the companion and bedmate of a murderer."

Mr. Hesse said, "The word for that, Mr. Fitzgerald, is 'wife.' That's what you call Mrs. Fitzgerald, I think."

"She never watched me murder anyone."

Brian Fitzgerald, who never opened his mouth in class except when asked a direct question, stood and faced his father.

"Everything I ever learned, Teacher taught me, not you."

I hadn't taught him much, except how to throw a sinker.

Mrs. Mozier tried to get the meeting back on the track. "What we are here for, Mrs. Dudley, is to ask for your resignation."

"To fire you," said Mrs. Fetters.

"It needn't come to that," said Mrs. Mozier. "Orpha Chase Dudley comes from an old family, is a church member in good standing. I think that she can see that what we are asking is reasonable."

"I was hired by the Board of Education," said I. "They are the only ones who can fire me."

"The Board of Education, when it sees that half and more of the parents won't have their children taught by the wife of a murderer, will come around pretty fast to our way of thinking."

"She don't teach murder," yelled Nettie.

Jake Hesse, who was held in considerable respect by the neighborhood because he owned shoe stores in Piqua, Cincinnati, and Amesville, in addition to his Amesville farm, came to my defense. It was certainly his business success, not his looks, that held their attention. He was a high-waisted, big-bottomed man of medium height. He had a broad face and not enough features to fill it up. Negligible eyebrows, mouth like a buttonhole, eyes you had to look for, and a head flat as a board in back.

What he had to say was not only sensible, it was in praise of me. As I listened to him I thought, Who knows how Jesus Christ really looked? The pictures we have of him were painted by men who had nothing to go on but their idea of how a man who spoke such words would look. Shut your eyes, I told myself, and listen to Mr. Jake Hesse speak. Don't watch the jerky, angular gestures that are supposed to illustrate and explain, but that make him look like a man slapping gnats on a sultry day.

The gist of what I heard was that I was a fine teacher, had suffered a great deal already, and that Fairmont parents would be cutting off their noses to spite their faces if they took out on me their natural anger because of Lon's terrible act.

"I don't hold with plays myself," said Mr. Hesse. "But what you've just seen's not a play. It's just an illustrated history lesson. Set the kids around a table and let them pretend to be signing the Declaration of Independence. That's not a play, not the way we rate plays in Cincinnati, anyway.

"You don't hire teachers on the basis of what they've seen or haven't seen in their past lives. There'd be no way of determining that for sure, anyway. You hire them to teach reading and writing and arithmetic. Mrs. Dudley's done that. You hire teachers to set your children good examples by their upright lives. Mrs. Dudley has done that. She's been a strict, upright, churchgoing young woman."

He hadn't finished, but before he could get the next sentence out, Mrs. Fetters, still remembering Lon and the carbolic acid, shouted, "She drove him to it. If Lon'd had a good stay-at-home woman, Crit Matthews would still be alive; and Lon would be alive. Fire her. Throw her out. Get somebody not mixed up with murder. I won't have my children learning their lessons from someone with blood on her hands."

Mrs. Fetters didn't have chick or child to her name, not a niece or a second cousin.

The minute she yelled "Throw her out," Nettie screamed, drowning out Mrs. Fetters's further remarks, if she had any. "Don't you say anything, you dog-poisoner, you."

Well, she wasn't. Her husband did that; but that was enough to start the kids off. "Dog-poisoner! Dog-poisoner!" they yelled. Then they all surged away from the back of the room, where they had been herded by their parents, to where I stood facing my accusers. The little ones, Bernard and Naomi and Nancy, clasped me around my knees. The big ones, John Buckmaster and Nettie and Alpha and Brian, reached across them and put their arms around my shoulders. They didn't say anything; the grownups were also silent. The gusting wind rattled the windows in their frames. Something between sleet and hail grated against the glass like sand off a desert. I wanted to lean down and kiss every kid, but kissing, I knew, was the last thing they wanted.

"I will stop teaching, if that's what you want," I said.

Nettie Mozier said, "If Mrs. Dudley stops teaching, none of us will ever come to this school again. Will we?" she asked the cluster around her and me.

"No!" they shouted.

Then Jake Hesse left his place and came to the front of the room. Since he was a shoe merchant he wore fancy laced shoes, with green-gray felt tops. He toed way out when he walked; the stocky trunk of his body rested on the top of the pyramid of his spindly legs. Perhaps I was the only one who really looked at him, for when he spoke the arguing parents and the shouting children shut up and listened.

"Nobody," said he, "under the law can be punished for witnessing a crime. And apart from the law, it don't make sense to punish your children because their teacher witnessed a crime. The best judges of a teacher, if the children have been well brought up, are the children themselves. Children judge by what goes on in the schoolroom. What teacher's seen or hasn't seen on the outside don't change the sum of six plus nine or the capital of California or too free a hand with a switch. You've got a good teacher. You'll make a mistake if you fire her."

Mrs. Harriman lumbered up to join Mr. Hesse.

"Mrs. Dudley is as pure-minded as a four-year-old. If she's got a fault, it's not being a murderer's wife. It's knowing too little about what the kids are up to. But she's willing to learn. I've talked to her. I'm against firing her."

"*We* can't fire her," Mrs. Mozier said. "The Board does that. But we can advise the Board."

Mr. Hesse said, "I invite everyone to my house Saturday night. We can talk this over without teacher or children present. That would be more sensible than the powwow we're now having."

That was what they all agreed to do.

As they left, the kids were still hugging me and saying, "We'll see you Monday, Mrs. Dudley."

Mr. Hesse, who wasn't much taller than some of the kids, spoke over their heads to me. "Don't let this upset you. They've blown off steam. That's all they needed to do."

He started to leave, but came back for a final word. "I'd leave off the playacting if I was you, though. Murder or no murder, that don't set well with parents. They don't send their kids to school to learn to be John Barrymores."

"I'll stop it," I said. I wasn't unreasonable. I could meet people halfway.

Nettie Mozier, who could have ridden home with her mother,

decided, snow or no snow, to walk. She was mad at all parents. "Idiots," she said as she helped me hitch Mouse.

"Mr. Hesse was sensible."

"He's funny-looking."

"Handsome is as handsome does, Nettie."

"He'd better lead a good life."

Nettie was a gypsy-looking girl. Black hair, black eyes, a smile both acid and sweet.

"Well, the Children's Crusade won," she said.

"Don't you go home making any such claim."

"I know when to keep my mouth shut."

"I hope so. We haven't won yet."

"We will."

"I'm not any holy land and you kids aren't crazy crusaders willing to die for me."

Nettie gave Mouse a whack on the rump. "We won't have to. The pagans will give up. See you Monday, Mrs. Dudley."

We parted the veil of snow waving at each other.

She was right and Jake Hesse was right. I wasn't fired and I did see Nettie on Monday.

At school and in the neighborhood, what had happened may not have been forgotten, but in front of me, at least, there was no more talk of it. Leota got bigger and bigger, so she must have been further along than she had admitted. That was a reminder of the past to everyone; especially to me, and words weren't needed to remind me of it.

5

Coming home with Ebon there was about like coming home to another school. To Ebon, I'm sure, I was just a substitute teacher, a stand-in for Lon. Lon had been right; Ebon was a boy who wanted to learn, who deserved teaching—and deserved someone more learned than I to do the job. Actually, I wasn't Ebon's *teacher* at all; only another student willing to study with him.

Ebon took for granted that I would want to continue with him the evenings at the study table as I had with Lon. In the long run, it was best, but I resented his assumption at first. Ebon was my hired man, not I his teacher. Lon was never more absent than when we pulled our chairs up to that table where Lon had presided. But I wasn't able to say to Ebon, "I don't like it. I won't do it." Say no to the boy who always had something cooking on the kitchen stove when I got home from school? He did leave the finishing touches to me; he knew you couldn't stew an old hen or bake a Hubbard squash in thirty minutes. Say no to the boy who was too kindhearted to leave the barn cat, and her kittens, who had belonged to his father, alone at the Matthews' to shift for herself?

We followed Lon's course of study. Bible study meant less to both of us than it had to Lon. I was already saved and Ebon wasn't looking for salvation.

Singing hymns was what Ebon really enjoyed in the church line. Probably because he had such a good voice. If he'd had a chance to hear any songs except hymns, he'd have preferred them, I'm sure, to "Rock of Ages" or "Blessed Assurance." Those were the songs we knew, and we sing what we know. I couldn't sing at all except behind a strong leader. I loved singing, in spite of this, loved the exuberant gush of sound from my chest, loved to repeat the words I had heard since childhood. "Heir of Salvation." "I Am a Stranger Here."

I don't know what people who heard us thought, the widow and the hired man singing hymns together. Yes, I do know, but that comes later.

After our opening exercise, which was two hymns, one Ebon's choice, one mine, study began. Study was fifty percent history. Ebon was a hero worshiper. He wanted to know what men had done in the past and what they were doing right now in New York, Philadelphia, and Washington, D.C. Our textbook for the past was *World History*. Our textbook for the present was the Louisville *Courier*.

Out of *World History*, heroes emerged for Ebon; not wars, treaties, dates, inventions, explorations. The gladiators who, before they fought, said "We who are about to die salute you, Ceasar" made Ebon tingle clear to his fingertips. He said so. He held up his hands to show me, though there was nothing visible. What Leonidas said at Thermopylae made his heart beat faster. In his imagination he lived with men who shouted "Don't shoot 'til you see the whites of their eyes" and "I'll come back with my shield or on it." Even wicked men like John Wilkes Booth, with his "Sic semper tyrannis" and his broken leg, aroused Ebon's admiration.

100

These men of the past were less interesting to him, however, than the country's living leaders, whose acts and words were reported to us each day by the Louisville *Courier*. Such men were still making history. Distance alone separated us from them, not time.

Harding was certainly no Leonidas, and Coolidge no Israel Putnam, though Coolidge temperamentally was a man capable of waiting until he saw the whites of their eyes before firing. Harding and Coolidge were what we had. And nothing was yet known, in Amesville at least, of Teapot Dome or Harding's White House girls and poker games; or of Coolidge's sorry practice of using worms for bait when fishing for trout.

Harding was as handsome as a river-boat gambler, a man who, after schoolmaster Wilson, with his big thin nose and clip-on spectacles, *looked* like a statesman, whatever his practice.

I knew that thirty percent of study time spent in hymn-singing, thirty percent on great men of the past, twenty percent on the Louisville *Courier*, five percent on Bible-reading, with only fifteen percent left over for what other subjects I could force into the curriculum, did not constitute a sensible procedure.

I also knew that it was better than nothing. Those were queer evenings; perhaps no queerer than others in Bigger Township. Twenty-two and nineteen, sitting at an old grafting table following a pattern established by a dead man. I may have been Lon for Ebon. There was no way in which he could be Lon for me, though I often felt that Lon had just stepped out of the room.

To the life of study and industriousness, we had made additions of our own that would have been strange to Lon.

The cats, for instance: except for two of the kittens that Ebon was bringing up to be barn cats, all had moved into the house. Been moved by me, actually, when the weather turned bitter. The mother cat was the most domesticated animal I've ever seen. Round, gray, plump-jowled like a grandmother, she washed, ate, and saw to it that she and her offspring went outside for calls of nature as regularly as any privy-bound housewife. With a recipe written in cat language, she could have baked cookies or fried a chicken.

What would Lon have thought if he could have seen cats playing and heard "Jesus Saviour, Pilot Me" in his old home? Less amazed, I think, than to see Ebon going to church with me every Sunday morning and to prayer meeting every Wednesday evening.

Ebon, either as a disciple of Lon's or of his own accord, was a

101

nonbeliever. He didn't let that keep him away from church and the hymn-singing he loved. And the United Brethren took for granted that such vocal harmony must have its source far deeper than the cords in his throat. A man who could sing "Washed in the Blood of the Lamb" the way Ebon did surely knew a spiritual cleansing deeper and purer than water.

So Ebon sang in the choir and I worshiped in the congregation. Looking out the window, I saw the upcurve of the slope at the bottom of which the church was built and felt, in addition to the joy and peace of my own God-seeking, the support of those about me whose souls joined and supported me in silent worship.

6

Church, cats, singing, teaching, the winter lull of farmwork, all was orderly in the house of death and widowhood. Joey's sickness and departure for California gave me less time for grieving over the past than I otherwise would have had.

The Baltimore and Ohio ran through Amesville and there picked up western-bound passengers from the surrounding countryside. I listened to its long sad whistle in the night. It was a big iron needle stitching the country together. Whole families were heading west in the twenties. Their furniture, china, and sometimes even livestock (not chickens and pigs, of course, but a team that spanned particularly well), followed by freight. In Chicago, B. & O. passengers transferred to the Union Pacific or the Southern Pacific, depending upon whether they were heading for California or Oregon.

It was this wait of two or three hours in midwinter in a big, drafty, I supposed, depot that worried me most about Joey, California bound. I was obsessed by the superstition of three: calamities happen by threes. Two men had died: Lon and Crit. The death of a third was required, a man close to me. In the world as a whole, people were dying like flies. I knew that. The flu was beginning to be felt. But the symmetry of three demanded the death of someone I knew and would grieve for: Joey would be that one with a vengeance.

I spent the night before Joey left for California at my parents' home, so that I could ride into Amesville with them next day. My father had an automobile by this time, one that has long since disappeared from the market. I remember it well because it was the first I ever rode in. It was a Durant, big compared to a buggy, shiny and black. My father learned to drive by driving. Objects he must avoid—abutments of stone bridges, wandering cows, bottomless mud-holes—had an almost fatal attraction for him. He headed straight for them, then missed them by inches. I thought that the symmetry of three might be filled double before we reached Amesville: Joey's death would finish the trio started by Lon and Crit, while Mama, Papa, and I would need no additions to make our catastrophe fulfill all superstitious obligations.

Joey and I sat in the back seat with a lap robe round our knees. No heat in automobiles then, but Mama treated Joey as if he were going for a sleigh ride, with a hot brick wrapped in a piece of old carpeting at his feet.

I held Joey's hand, a big hand, but skin and bones now. When Papa headed for disaster, I unconsciously squeezed it.

"Take that wedding ring off," Joey said, "if you're going to keep up that squeezing. It's cutting my hand."

That ring I never intended to take off. I could stop squeezing.

"Don't Papa scare you?"

"He's a fast dodger," Joey said. "No, he don't scare me. Nothing's going to stop me getting to California and getting well."

"You're safe, maybe. How about the rest of us?"

"You're in the car with me. That's your safeguard."

I didn't know then that consumptives are the most hopeful in-valids in the world. People with cholera morbus or kidney stones expect death at any minute, while consumptives with only half a lung left are making plans for next year. Joe, I think, wasn't stimu-lated by the fever or the bacilli poison that was being pumped into his blood. It was his nature to be confident. The earth was made for the use of Joseph Chase. He did not intend to be ground down by it.

When I first began this piece of writing, I called it "The Girl Who Married a Brother." Joe has influenced my life more than any other man, and that's a marriage beyond any union of bodies.

I discarded that title because it would give the impression, I feared, that this account would be one of an incestuous relationship. And this would be emphasized since I would be making it clear that such unions were not unknown where I grew up.

If we had not been brother and sister, I doubt that Joey would ever have had an eye for me as a woman. He had a concern for me because I *was* his little sister; his "big-little sister," he called me.

Joey thought me a stick-in-the-mud, a person who, without his help, would stagnate. He was right. The grass never looked greener over the fence to me. I saw the fence, not the grass, and imagined breaking my leg, at least, and probably my neck in any effort to climb it.

I would never have gone to California seeking a cure for my lungs. I would have taken to my bed and never left it. I was afraid for Joey to go. Strange land of earthquakes and flash floods and invalids. I had heard California called "the one-lung state."

"Will Uncle Charlie meet you?"

"He will. He will meet me at San Bernardino and drive me to Tent City in Banning."

"Are you going to live in a tent in the middle of the winter?"

"It isn't winter there. Valencia are blooming and navels are ripe."

These were oranges, I knew. "You can't live on oranges."

"I don't intend to. Meals are served in your tent."

"That must cost money."

"It will. Uncle Charlie will help. You, too. Remember?"

"I will, I will," I said. "Every cent I can spare."

I had seen in my mind a picture of Joey dead under canvas on an army-cot kind of bed. Outside was a bleak cold desert, nothing growing but cactus and sagebrush. If Joey by the power of his mind could cure himself, I might by the power of the fear in mine prevent the cure.

I wiped my mind clean of that fear. Joey was still no one's picture of a man sick to death. Or even sick. Thin, yes. A flush, which to the unknowing, looked like the bloom of health. I made myself see him heavy again, brown again, never coughing.

I cried, because I was afraid it might not be so.

"Cut that out," Joey said. "I don't want to get on the train surrounded by sobbers. I'm going to get well. And sooner or later you'll come to California, too."

"Do you think I've caught it?"

"Nope. You haven't enough get-up-and-go to catch it. You're coming because I'm going to get well and ask you and you won't have anything better to do."

We heard the B. & O. whistle off in the southeast as we drove into town. But there was no rush—there was a twenty-minute layover in Amesville.

104

Mama had a basket of fried chicken, a jelly roll, buttered slices of home-baked bread. I had a box of cookies and apples. Joey boarded his car, jaunty as a man off for a pleasure trip to New Orleans. I cried again. Papa had tears in his eyes. Mama was the one Joey got his steel from.

She said, "Joe, we'll meet you here in one year."

Joey, standing in the vestibule as the train pulled out, yelled, "No need. I'll hike home."

We stood beside the tracks until Joe and the B. & O. were out of sight.

Then Mama said, "Pray for him every night, Orpha."

"I will," I said. I did. But I wasn't sure Joey would want me to. It seemed to show lack of faith in his own ability.

VI
WANDA

1

It was a hard winter, very cold but short. The contents of the chamber pot and the washbowl were frozen over by morning. Ebon kept a fire banked in the grate all night. Even so, I got chilblains that winter: feet too cold before I got to school, then, once I had a fire roaring in the schoolhouse baseburner, too warm too soon.

There were no more visitations of parents. I put on no more plays. We won the spelldown against Rush Branch District School.

Ebon did his work, I did mine. In the evenings Lon's old-time night school flourished. I was nearer Ebon's age than Victoria Cinderella had been to Ormand's. But Ormand had had for both of us a look in his eye that Ebon never gave me. I might have been a bird or a cloud, for any warmth I could see in Ebon's eye.

The men you fall in love with, though they later repudiate you, have, I think, been asking for it. Love me, their eyes say. It's an exercise in power. Come to me, their eyes say. (The other message—so that later I may have the satisfaction of throwing you over—is hidden.) Ebon's eyes said nothing like that. All he asked of me was to be Lon. Let the teaching continue. I tried, but nothing was the same without Lon. There were too many kittens. There was too much singing. You can sing your way to glory but not to knowledge.

April came, bringing the weather doctors hate to see: too much warmth too soon after too much cold. Long underwear is discarded. Winter coats are stowed away at the back of closets. Bodies, white, thin-blooded, go out into the bright but still-sharp air with nothing but goose pimples as armor against its unexpected bite.

There was much sickness. Papa was down for two weeks with the grippe. Lord John Buckmaster's mother died. Neither Ebon nor I so much as sneezed.

This false summer is just as routine as the Indian summer of fall, though nameless—unless the blackberry winter that often follows gives it its true name: "Blackberry winter: Warning."

The false summer held until mid-April. Redbud and dogwood bloomed. The letters from Joe were as sweet as the weather. Something wonderful was happening to him. He, who usually was so full of brag about his health, was saying little except, "I have been too blessed to brag." What did that mean? Had galloping consumption caught up with him? No, for he said, "I don't think you'll ever have cause to worry about my health again."

School let out for summer vacation early in those days. The children were needed to help with spring planting. I liked teaching, but it's a treadmill job just the same. I drove home one evening, the redbud beginning to fade, the dogwood soft as candlelight against the new green, saying to myself, "Three more weeks, three more weeks."

Ebon, who usually was still at work when I came home, was waiting in the barnyard for me.

"I'll help you unhitch," said he.

"You can do the whole job," I told him, "since you've already stopped work." I had a summer-vacation feel already: good-bye to school hours and everything done by the clock. I would go in the house and make something far beyond Ebon's cooking ability: floating island pudding or oatmeal rocks with raisins and black walnuts.

"Don't go in the house," Ebon said.

"Why not?"

"Wait for me."

"Is something wrong?"

"Yes," said he.

My heart stopped beating. So much wrong had already happened there, anything more would be terrible.

"A letter from California?" A letter saying Joe was dead, though I wouldn't let that thought do more than flit through my mind.

"There's nothing wrong with Joe."

"Is it something bad for you or me?"

"Both of us."

Ebon slapped Mouse into her stall, didn't wait to feed her or hang up her harness. I was the one who ran toward the house, but Ebon kept up with me. What I saw was the opposite of death and blood.

In a box fitted out with rockers was a baby. The box was on the floor near the cookstove, which had a good fire going in it.

"Where did this come from?"

"Read the note," said Ebon.

The note, on ruled tablet paper, was on the table.

"This baby," it said, "is named Wanda. She is two months old. She is your husband's baby and she belongs to you more than anyone else. I am going off to get married. My husband-to-be don't hold with taking care of another man's baby and I don't blame him. If you don't want her there are orphan asylums that will take her. My mother won't have her on the place and I don't blame her either. You may thank me someday. Leota."

I kept a rocking chair in the kitchen where I could sit by the fire when I peeled apples for pies or potatoes for frying. I sat down now and looked at the baby. I was rocking without knowing it, but I stopped suddenly, remembering poor crazy Ina. Was rocking the beginning of losing your mind? At least I had all my clothes on.

"She doesn't look like Lon."

Not many babies do look like their fathers, I suppose. It would be hard for any baby to look like big-boned, hard-muscled Lon. But Wanda, round-faced, with a mop of black curly hair, looked more like an Eskimo or a Kickapoo than fair-haired Lon. Not even Lon's color, let alone his features.

"Lon isn't her father," said Ebon.

Those were the words I heard, but I couldn't believe them.

Ebon repeated them. "She don't look like Lon because she's no relation to Lon."

"Your father came over to tell Lon—and me—about Leota. That's why Lon shot him. I was there. I saw it happen. You know that."

"Did you hear him mention Leota?"

"Lon shot Crit before he could say what he'd come over for. Lon shot him to keep him quiet."

"Pa didn't come over to tell him anything about Leota."

"He had some terrible news to tell. He said so."

"It wasn't about Lon and Leota."

"Lon dead, your father dead, for nothing?"

"Not for nothing. It was about Lon and me."

There was no way, at that time and at my age, I could take that in.

Almost everything that happens to us, except when we're babies, is something we have read or heard about. We've read or heard about death and cannibalism and snowfall, and the tides and the birth of animals and earthquakes and ice cream and eclipses of the sun, be-

111

fore we experience them. In our minds we have experienced the act of eating human flesh, of bodies going rigid and ceasing to speak, of cats producing kittens; before we even perform or see any of these acts, the words have prepared us for them.

When I was young, I had never heard the word "sex" at home. I hardly knew what it meant, except that it stood for something dirty. A girl or two, knowing my ignorance, wanted before my marriage to warn me, prepare me. "You'll be surprised," they said. "It might scare you, make you sick to your stomach. Maybe."

I wouldn't listen. Who wanted the marriage bed to be an old story? It would be like opening your Christmas packages before Christmas morning. A sneaky little midnight preview instead of a snowy morning miracle.

For me and Lon, I had done the right thing. Love has a wordless language by which the untutored body is taught. What happened was nothing I had ever imagined; stranger than earthquakes or eclipses. But my body was as eager for it as for breathing or eating. Such acts, before they are experienced, are never imagined either.

So I, a married woman, had learned about men and women; and, in that neighborhood (as in the world), knew that "I, John, take thee, Mary" doesn't mean that I, John, won't often want to take Bertha, Kate, Simone, Henrietta, *and* Leota, also.

But what Ebon meant, I did not know.

"Didn't your father want Lon to teach you?"

"He didn't want him to teach me what he did."

"To be an atheist?"

"Lon never tried to teach me that. He never tried to make you an atheist, did he?"

"No. Lon loved me the way I was."

"Me, too."

Ebon was no Mrs. Harriman. He wasn't older than I and he wasn't trying to teach me facts I needed to know in order to protect children of his.

"Lon loved you more than he did me," he said. "He married you. He wanted to live with you. He never wanted to live with me."

"Of course not. Live with you? Men don't live with each other. Except old bachelor brothers sometimes. Or some men with broken-down fathers. Lon would never have lived with you."

"He never did. Except on a couple of speechmaking trips."

112

"Lon never told me you even went with him."

"Pa knew."

"How do you know this isn't Lon's baby?"

"Lon didn't like girls."

"He liked me."

"You're different. Besides, Lon was trying to change. He didn't like to like boys."

"Most boys wouldn't like it, either."

"I'm different."

"Why did Leota tell your father it was Lon's baby?"

"She didn't. It was about Lon and me Pa wanted to talk to you and Lon—and Lon knew it."

"What good did shooting your father do?"

"No good. But Lon couldn't stand for you to hear the words. And he thought with Pa dead, you might never know."

"You don't know this. Not for a certainty."

"It's what I've figured out that Lon thought."

"Lon should've shot you, too, if he didn't want me to know," I said.

"You're better off knowing."

"I don't feel better."

The baby stirred in her cradle, then quieted. Ebon put a couple more sticks of wood in the stove.

"Whose baby is it? If it isn't Lon's."

"A married man's. That's why Leota accused Lon. He was dead and past being harmed."

"Don't she want her own baby?"

"Maybe. But it was choose between the baby and a husband. The husband didn't want another man's kid to look after."

"Didn't she know you would tell me?"

"No."

"You're not a very dependable boy, are you, Ebon?"

"I'm truthful."

"Maybe she thought *you* would want it. You're its uncle. That's the truth, isn't it?"

"That's the truth."

"It don't look like you, either."

"It looks like the man she's marrying."

"How could it? He's no relation, is he?"

113

"He's a stepbrother."

Without knowing it, I had begun rocking again. When you hurt, rocking helps. That's why babies have cradles. They can't talk, but when they cry, they're hurting and someone rocks them. When you've grown up, you have to rock yourself.

I rocked and I stared at Ebon.

I still didn't know what I was talking about: something so bad that Lon would shoot the man who would tell, then shoot himself.

Ebon was no longer the hired man. If an angel fell, maybe he would look like Ebon: pointed chin, curly hair, slanted eyes, a mouth like a big ripe apricot. And he was kind. I couldn't deny that. Fallen, maybe, but kind. A hard worker, too, a kitten lover, a singer, a bean cooker.

For quite a long time I did nothing but stare at the boy. I did not understand him.

"Did Lon ever kiss you?"

"Yes."

That was as far as I could go. I didn't want to imagine any more, and, as a matter of fact, I didn't know how to imagine more. But they had touched, mouth to mouth.

For a minute or two I thought, The one you should have shot, Lon, was me.

We were there most of the night. The baby began to cry. Leota had left a baby's bottle of milk, and I picked up the baby and fed it. If that baby had been Lon's, I don't think I could have done it. Maybe I could. I'm not a good hater.

There are women who claim to love all babies and children. They can't see a baby without wanting to scoop it up in their arms. I am not that kind of a baby lover, or a children lover or even a people lover. I can love individuals.

Ebon put more wood on the fire, moved the beans to the back of the stove. I had intended stirring up dumplings to cook on top of the beans, but I had lost all interest in cooking.

It's true, as I've said, hating doesn't come easy to me. I'm not proud of this. The hateful should be hated. I sat with Wanda in my arms wondering why I didn't hate Ebon. Except for Ebon, Lon would be alive. No, that wasn't true. Lon was the victim of his own nature. And I wasn't jealous of Ebon, as I would have been

114

of Leota. If Wanda had been Lon's child, Leota would have been his paramour, his mistress. Ebon seemed to me more like Lon's pet hawk or his housebroken otter. The attachment was unfathomable, but it had nothing to do with marriage.

If Ebon was more than hawk or otter, perhaps he was what a junior wife is in a Mormon household: senior wife's helper as much as concubine. That was the way it was working out with Ebon and me. But I couldn't accept that, either. I didn't want a junior wife. Truth to tell, it was all beyond my comprehension.

"What are we going to do, Ebon? What'll we do with the baby?"

"The orphanage will take it."

"Don't call her 'it.' Her name's Wanda."

"The orphanage will take her."

"She's your own flesh and blood."

"Not by anything I did."

"I can take her to school with me."

"They'll think that's worse than playacting."

"No, they won't. There've been babies there before."

"Not Teacher's."

"This isn't mine."

The room was so warm and I was so tired I went to sleep. I can't remember another time in my life when I went to sleep without intending to. My problem is the opposite: I intend to and can't.

When I woke up, the baby was in her cradle, the beans were in the oven. The fire was low. Ebon was where he had been all evening, in the ladder-back chair, wide awake.

"What time is it?"

"Three. I changed the baby and fed her."

"How do you know how to do that?"

"At our house somebody has to."

"I never did."

"You're the youngest. There weren't any babies."

"I've made up my mind. I'm going to keep her. I'll take her to school with me."

"You'll be sorry."

"It's the right thing to do," I said. Though I wasn't doing it because it was right. I was doing it because I had fallen in love with that baby. Some people don't fall in love at all. One baby, kitten,

115

man, tree, looks pretty much the same as another to them. They may be fond of them all, babies, kittens, men, trees; but no single specimen makes them lovesick.

Not so with me. My love is singular. *One* of Ebon's kittens was my kitten, not the whole litter. I'm not fond of forests, but that sycamore above Lon's grave was as companionable as a person. No baby except Wanda has ever made me feel that we belonged together.

If Wanda had come to me at any other time, my feeling for her might have been less intense. As it was, she came when there was no one else. My husband was dead. I had outgrown the home of my parents. Joe was far away.

True, there was Ebon. Most wives would have hated him. Instead of hating him, Ebon's love for Lon was a bond that united us. We kept Lon alive with our talk. And, in a way, he may have brought me Wanda. Leota might never, I think, have given me Wanda except that her brother was in the house. With Ebon there, she was, strange though it was, keeping Wanda in the family.

2

Wanda was no problem at school. In the first place, she was a quiet baby. In the second, there were seventh- and eighth-grade girls at Fairmont who knew far more about taking care of babies than I did.

Alpha, the rhymer, fed and changed Wanda; they cooed together like doves in a dovecote.

Ella Teeters, who had had a baby of her own at thirteen and had been forced to give it up, would have kept Wanda in her arms the day long, if I had permitted. Wanda had to be rationed for her own sake: a child spoiled from the cradle is destined to be miserable. She had to be rationed for the school's sake, too; my first job at Fairmont was to teach, not to raise a baby. I had been Lon's pupil for long enough to know how to run a good school.

No one could say, and no one did say, that there was a jot less teaching done during the time Wanda was at Fairmont than there had been done before. I forestalled any accusation of that kind by assigning longer lists of words to spell, more difficult arithmetic problems, more pages of reading.

What was said about me had nothing to do with my teaching; or with Christian charity either.

The first to bring me the news was Mrs. Harriman. She drove over to Fairmont to pick up her boys after school one day. A real blackberry winter had followed the untimely spring-summer. There were icy rains, sleet, flurries of snow, high winds.

The sycamore on the slope above Lon's grave was toppled. I heard it go down in the night—a strange sound, since there was no crackling (the tree was uprooted, not splintered), only a great sorrowful sigh or groan, as what had been upright for fifty years stretched itself along the ground.

Mrs. Harriman sent her two boys up to the front of the room to practice their writing on the board. It was the time of the Palmer method of writing. One was supposed to write with the whole arm, not the fingers. The atrophy of the fingers was encouraged by the making of loops and circles which could be done without the use of the fingers at all. The method supposedly prevented finger fatigue and produced legibility.

While the boys looped and circled, Mrs. Harriman sat down near the stove beside Wanda, who was in her box cradle, and me.

"People are talking again," she said.

"About what Lon did?"

"No, no. About you and Ebon."

When there's "talk" about a man and a woman, it means sex. I knew that, though "sex" was not a word I used at that time.

"He's my hired man. I pay him wages."

"You were spied on the other night."

"They can watch every night, for all I care. There's nothing to see."

"I won't tell you who did it. Their kids are here in school. It might make it hard for you to be fair to them."

But she told me.

"What he saw was Ebon rocking the baby and feeding it while you were putting pies in the oven."

"Ebon can't make pies."

"The pie don't cut any ice. It was a fatherly act."

Ebon the father! That was a wild idea. But what if he was?

"He isn't. But what if he was? What's wrong with your hired man's having a baby?"

117

"Nothing. It's who the mother is that counts."

"You think it's his baby by his sister?"

"I'm not talking about what I think. I'm telling you what's being said. It's being said that you're the mother."

"How could I be that? Teach school all winter carrying a baby. And nobody see?"

"It don't show on some women."

"How could I have it without anyone knowing?"

"I had two without any doctor."

The heat of the stove, the suggestion that I might be Wanda's mother, the endless circles and spirals that George W. and Thomas J. were putting on the board made me feel dizzy. It had not happened. But a year ago my becoming a mother would have seemed more reasonable than Lon's committing a murder and suicide; or of Ebon's becoming whatever it was he had become to Lon. Maybe this *was* the truth and everything else was a dream.

"What about Leota?"

"Leota's gone. You're here, the baby's here, Ebon's here. That's all they see—or need to see."

"They are crazy," I said. I did not tell her how crazy. "You don't think Wanda's my baby, do you?"

"No, I don't. But what I think don't matter. It don't even matter what they think—or what they don't think. They're going to get rid of you. If what Lon did wasn't enough, this will be."

I drove home at a snail's pace. The snow was gritty as gravel. Wanda was tight-wrapped, first in her shawl, then in a blanket. I had left Mouse's horse blanket on. She held her ears close to her head, afraid they'd freeze and shatter if held upright.

What else could happen? I began to laugh, and that scared me. If I read in a story "The widow, accused of having a baby by her teen-aged hired man, went home laughing," I would say to myself, "The poor woman is losing her mind." It was no laughing matter. But the difference between what people invent for their own mad purposes and what really happens is enough for an outcry of some kind—laughter or sobs.

Laughing or crying, who could I talk to? If I went home and told Mama, she'd say, "I told you so." Then she'd say, "Get rid of Ebon. Send Wanda to the orphanage. The sooner you shake yourself loose from the Matthews tribe, the better. They've brought you nothing but trouble."

It was true. But Wanda and Ebon weren't trouble. They were my family.

As I drove slowly home, the mistake of my life up to this point came to me: I had not been a thinker. I had not done what was reasonable. I had done what I felt like doing. I had never asked myself, "What will be the consequence tomorrow of what you do today?" I had fallen in love with Lon and had never asked myself the meaning of his long postponement of marriage or of his peculiar wooing. Peculiar? Well, how could I know? I had never been wooed before and, eager as I was for Lon's love, I would have accepted him if he had nuzzled me like a stallion or rolled me around with bites and scratches like a tomcat.

But that was the past. From now on I was going to think. I would be reasonable. I would ask myself: "Does this make sense?"

I would do all this after arranging to keep Wanda and providing for Ebon. My life of reason would include them. They had become a part of my life.

My first act as a thinker was not to tell Ebon all that Mrs. Harriman had said, but only about my being fired. The idea of his being the father and I the mother of Wanda would trouble him. He would move to the barn. He would not be able to help with Wanda or start a fire or boil a pot of beans, if that would be labeled "fatherly."

"I'm going to lose my job," I told him.

"The same reason as before?"

"Yes," I said. Lies come from the head, not the heart.

"You couldn't bring up Wanda in a schoolhouse, anyway."

"I could have, but I'm not going to get the chance."

"Lon's father made enough off this farm to bring up the family."

"I'm no farmer."

"I am."

"You won't farm for nothing."

"I'll farm on shares. Your father'll help you."

"I want to send money to Joe."

"You could get a teaching job someplace else."

I didn't care about eating that night. I fed Wanda. Ebon rustled up enough leftovers to see him through until morning.

He was still eating, sitting like a proper hired man alone at the

119

kitchen table, when there was a knock at the door. After-supper callers on stormy nights were unusual. The knock meant that who-ever was there was at least willing to be known—the visitor was not a Peeping Tom.

The sight of Jake Hesse didn't surprise me. He was the next one after Mrs. Harriman who *would* come to talk to me about my job.

Ebon put his dishes in the sink and went to his room before Mr. Hesse had his coat and muffler off.

"You've got a nice accommodating boy there," Mr. Hesse said, nodding toward the disappearing Ebon.

"I couldn't have managed the farm without him, Mr. Hesse."

"Don't call me Mr. Hesse. Call me Jake, the way everyone else does. As far as I'm concerned, you're Orpha, not Mrs. Dudley. I've stood up for you in more than one Board meeting, and what I did was for a girl named Orpha, not Mrs. Dudley."

I would just as soon have called my father Wesley as call Mr. Hesse Jake. But if that was what he wanted, I could do it. It wouldn't burn my tongue to say Jake. And he was certainly far nearer my age than my father. Not more than ten or twelve years' difference at most.

"Orpha or Mrs. Dudley," I said, "I hope you took my part because you thought I was a good teacher, Mr. Hesse."

"Jake."

"Jake."

"That's better. I did. I still do. But this time it won't do any good. I had my say, but they won't renew your contract. I wanted to get the news to you before it came to you from the Board. I don't know any way to soften it, but I thought it would go down easier coming from a friend."

I had never thought of Jake Hesse as a friend—though it was friendly of him to make this trip on a stormy night; and to stand up for me in Board meetings. I ought to do something friendly in return.

"Would you like a cup of tea? And some cinnamon toast?"

"That would be very acceptable."

The kettle was already on and, with a little stirring up, the stove was soon hot enough to make toast in the oven. The wind made the old Dudley house creak. The kettle sang. Wanda slept quietly. Only the mother cat moved around Mr. Hesse's ankles caressing itself.

"A cat should never be in a room where people eat."

120

"I'll put it in the sitting room."

"It was not born in a house. It's no kindness to it to keep it locked up."

"It's such a cold night."

"Look at that fur! It can't take off its fur coat the way people can when a room heats up."

I put Pussy, she had no other name, outside. I whispered in her ear as I set her down on the porch, "The minute he leaves I'll let you back in. Don't run away."

"That's better," said Mr. Hesse. "Have a cup of tea with me?"

"I've eaten," I lied again.

"I've eaten alone for so long it's a treat to have someone sit at a table with me."

I had manners enough to sit at the table with him. Not enough, though, to keep me from staring as he lifted his nose until it wrinkled in accordion pleats at the bridge when he took a sip of hot tea. It was the time of the pompadour, and Mr. Hesse had the right hair for it: bright chestnut with just enough curl so that the pompadour occupied as much space above his eyebrows as his face did below. Mr. Hesse's face, now that I was close and had nothing to do but look, was, I saw, not only young but also ladylike. Comb that pompadour down so that the curls, instead of standing straight up, clustered around the ears, put a hat with flowers and ribbons on him, and he would have a feminine face.

"Once a man has had a table companion, he misses her," Mr. Hesse said.

"A table companion" was what Mr. Hesse called a wife, I supposed. He wasn't the kind of man to talk of a wife as a "bed companion." Everyone knew that Mr. Hesse had been married before he came to Amesville, and that he had left Cincinnati "to forget." What he had to forget, I didn't know until that evening.

"Oh, Rosa!" exclaimed Mr. Hesse. "Orpha, you remind me of her. Young and innocent."

This was sweet talk to my ears. After being called a murderer's wife (which I was) and the mother of a woods colt (which I wasn't), I could have said, "You don't know the half of it, Jake." But approval was what I craved, not a father confessor.

"I am thirty-three years old," said Mr. Hesse.

Ten years' difference equals twenty when someone is older than you.

"When I was twenty-three, Rosa Wetzel, who was eighteen, came from Germany to live with her aunt and uncle in Cincinnati. We were married when I was twenty-four. After we had been married five years, she got so homesick for Germany she packed her bags and ran away without a word of warning to me. I came home from the shoe store one night—and she was gone, cleared out. The table was set and there was a note on my place saying, 'I can't stand it here any longer.' "

"Didn't she write you?"

"Not a word. I wrote to her, and my letters were returned unopened. And that woman was my wife. You could never do that, could you?"

I said no because it was the polite thing to say. But it was the truth, too: truer than I then knew. I can be left. I have been. But I cannot leave. Out of pity or cowardice, I'm not sure which. A combination maybe.

"She was a beautiful girl. A good housekeeper. But homesick."

"She should have told you."

"You would, wouldn't you? You're the straightforward kind. I couldn't live in our house after Rosa left. I don't rent it. When I go back for business, I stay there, but I dread those visits. Look, I didn't come here to tell you my troubles. But you and I have both suffered."

Mr. Hesse reached across the table and took my hand. I had never seen, let alone touched, a man's hand like his. All the men I had known were outdoor workers. They had muscles in their hands and callouses on them. Mr. Hesse's hand was strong, all right; it wasn't flabby or weak, but it was small and plump and white. It was a hand that had touched leather, which is smooth, and flesh, which is soft. He didn't work with axes or plows. What he did was to help ladies try on shoes.

His hand was warm as well as firm.

"I knew I could talk to you, because you have suffered. And now you have to suffer some more. The Board's made up its mind. They're making a mistake, and I told them so—but they're stubborn."

"It's all right," I said. "Mrs. Harriman's already told me."

"Alone now, like me."

"No. I've got the baby. And Ebon will run the farm. And maybe I can find another school."

"Alone," said Mr. Hesse.

He got up from the table, put on his coat and muffler. I went to the door with him. He stretched out his hand—intending, I thought, to give my shoulder a farewell pat. Maybe that was what he planned; but his hand slipped lower, until it was full on my breast. And once there, it did more than pat—it grasped, and fondled.

My mouth had been ready for Lon's first kiss, had been asking for it. But my breast had not asked for or even expected a touch from Jake Hesse. I backed away from him faster than I would have from a slap or a pinch—backed so fast and so hard, Ebon's ladder-back chair fell over with a clatter, and Wanda, awakened, began to cry.

If Mr. Hesse knew what caused the collision, he didn't show it.

"I'm awkward as a bay steer," I said, which was an awkward thing to say, but Mr. Hesse didn't seem to notice that, either.

He took my hand between his warm plump palms and said, "Thank you for the tea, Orpha. I hope it's not the last cup we share."

I hadn't shared tea with Mr. Hesse, but I didn't add rudeness to awkwardness by reminding him.

The minute the door closed behind him, the door to Ebon's room opened. Ebon had on the long underwear all men slept in in wintertime. In summer they slept in their work shirts—or nothing.

"What happened?" he asked.

"Nothing. I backed into your chair. And knocked it over."

I picked up Wanda, who didn't need anything but some fondling to put her to sleep again.

"Get Pussy, will you?"

"Where is she?"

"On the porch, I hope."

"What's she doing out there in this weather?"

"Mr. Hesse didn't want her inside."

Pussy was at the door.

Ebon said, "Do you want me to bring the cradle upstairs for you?"

So I with Wanda, Ebon with the cradle, and the cat behind us climbed the stairs. If anyone had seen us that night, Ebon in his underwear carrying the cradle, I with the baby, going upstairs, I would have been fired all over again. Even the cat made us seem domestic in some secretive forbidden way.

Ebon, hustling back downstairs to stoke the fire in the cookstove before it went out, *was* fatherly, I suppose; but not in any secretive or forbidden way.

What was secret, what was forbidden, was the state of my troubled breast, all atingle, as if it had a life of its own apart from the rest of my body.

3

At that time and in that place it was humiliating to be fired. In hard times people lose their jobs and no one blames them. But times weren't hard in 1923. If you lost your job then, it was your own fault. It was a sign to all that you were lazy, incompetent, irresponsible. And as a result you felt hangdog and shamefaced.

I was fired, and I didn't feel that way at all. I felt downright scornful and amused. It has always been this way with me. If there is enough irony in a situation, even though I have to take the blame for something, I am amused. The irony lies in the fact that things are not what they seem. I don't suppose that I'd be amused by even the one-hundred-percent irony in a verdict that sentenced me to hang not only for an act I didn't commit, but also for one that didn't take place at all. But I might think, as the rope was tightening, The stupid dolts. If only they knew what I know.

Pleasure in irony, either in your own life or in what you read, is an ego trip. "I know what others do not."

When an author writes ironically, he gives this pleasure to his readers. They know facts of which the characters in the story are ignorant: "He believes she is doing this because she loves him. Little does he know." Irony in writing is a technique for increasing reader self-approval.

Irony sustained me in my being fired. "Fired because they think Ebon and I are in love! Little do they know." But there was no one to whom I could tell the joke.

4

While I was teaching, Friday was a special day for me. It was the day school got out, the day before the two-day vacation. I awakened on Friday mornings with the special-day feeling I also had on Sundays. It was not the same feeling. Sunday meant worship and singing; it meant better clothes and different food. Sunday had a sheen workdays didn't have. The Friday-morning feeling was a foretaste of what was to come: Saturday at home and Sunday at church.

Now both feelings had gone. Friday morning didn't promise release from the treadmill (yes, I loved the treadmill), or Sunday any haloing of ordinary living. I opened my eyes on both days and both had as well be Tuesday.

But the Friday of my last day of teaching, after I was fired, was special in an unusual way. I was free not just for two days but for a lifetime, if that was what I chose. If I hadn't been fired, if teaching hadn't been taken away from me, I doubt I would ever have had the courage to leave it: something I liked, something I was good at, with kids I loved. What, over the fence, could be any greener? I could at this minute be living in a home for retired teachers, if I hadn't been fired. And except for Ebon, I wouldn't have been fired. And except for Lon, there wouldn't have been Ebon.

You make what seems a simple choice: choose a man or a job or a neighborhood—and what you have chosen is not a man or a job or a neighborhood, but a life.

I must have had some of that feeling the afternoon I drove home from Fairmont for the last time. I felt that I was driving into a new life.

Spring postponed by the blackberry winter was making up for the time it had lost. Or perhaps because of the recent cold, the weather seemed warmer than it really was. But it was truly warm. I was bare-armed and comfortable. Under her harness, Mouse was sweating. The cold snap had held the dogwood and redbud back. The white dogwood was blooming now amid the newly leafed trees like froth at the top of a cresting green wave. Corn was being planted; late, but in farming you do what the weather permits.

Birds I hadn't noticed until then were sitting on fence rails preening and singing. Redbirds in moderate numbers. A few robins. Plenty of jays and woodpeckers. I saw a brown thrush or two.

Oh, I got fired in the dead of a false winter, but I drove away from teaching amid blooming and nesting, my baby at my side.

When I got home I found that Ebon had chopped off an old hen's head and put her in the oven to bake. He supposed I would be downcast and thought some hearty food might not come amiss. For some reason I wasn't downcast. The irony of my firing, the unexpected opening out of my life, the tardy summer finally arrived, made me feel more like celebrating than grieving.

Ebon was prepared for celebrating, too. The easygoing Matthews' always let some of their cider ferment, and Ebon had brought over a small jug. I felt like trying new things that evening. After a sip or two I decided that hard cider would not be a part of my new life. But a sip or two was right for that early-summer supper when the schoolhouse door closed behind me; and learning, not teaching, became my lifework. And I've needed a lifetime for it, because I'm a slow learner.

Fifty years ago, Sunday afternoon was the time for visiting. People were home from church. Sunday dinner was over. Serious work, even anything as slight as darning socks or killing potato bugs, was out of the question. Autos were becoming more numerous, but the Sunday-afternoon drive, except for courting couples, was not yet the order of the day.

Radios were fairly common, but what you could hear on Sunday afternoon wasn't as stimulating as the news visiting neighbors often brought. Anyway, we were still talkers as well as listeners then.

On one Sunday, Ebon and I went to church, and after dinner was over, Ebon hitched up and went off on his own business. Not much later, Mama and Papa arrived.

The first thing Mama said was, "I'm glad to see that boy's gone."

"He's just gone somewhere for a visit."

"He ought to be gone for good."

It was warm enough to sit on the front porch. Because of what had happened there, the porch was a place I usually avoided.

Once we were settled, Mama said, "You can't say I didn't warn you."

"No, I can't."

"I've got to admit that nothing as outlandish as the story that's going round ever crossed my mind."

"So you've heard that, too."

"Everyone's heard it."

"How can they take stock in anything so unbelievable?"

Papa said, "That's its great attraction. 'Who'd have thought it!' That's what they say. 'Girl's husband kills wrong man.' "

"Wesley, nothing's to be gained by going over that gossip."

"Wrong man?" I asked.

"They think Lon thought Crit was the father."

"And me the mother?"

126

"Yes."

"If Lon was alive, he'd shoot a lot more people and I wouldn't blame him. Wanda is Leota Matthews' baby, and Ebon is her uncle."

"What was all the shooting about?" Mama asked.

"Mama, you said let's not talk about it. So let's not. It was a quirk in Lon's mind. Like pouring carbolic acid down Mr. Fetters's throat. We can't figure it out and no use trying. What I've got to figure out is what to do now that I've lost my job."

"That's really why we're here," Mama said. "We've got a plan. The first thing to do is to send Ebon Matthews packing."

"I can't farm."

"I can," Papa said, "and I won't cost you anything like what you'll have to pay Ebon."

"As for the baby, the best thing to do is to send it to an orphanage, where it belongs."

"I can't do that."

"You mean you won't?" Mama asked.

"Yes. I mean I won't."

"In that case I'm willing to take care of the baby myself."

"What am I to do?"

"Get a school someplace where this talk hasn't been heard. You can come home holidays."

"I'll lose my baby that way."

"You said it wasn't yours."

"I didn't give birth to her. But she's mine because I love her. I'm the only mother she knows."

"Both of you come home to stay if that's the way you feel," Papa said. "With Joe gone there's more than enough room."

"No. I'd just be underfoot. The baby cries. I'm used to running my own house now."

Where that argument would have gone or how it would've ended, I don't know, for at that minute Jake Hesse drove in the driveway. He had a new car he was showing off—to me, he had thought; but he was glad to find Papa there. Papa, with his new Durant, could talk cars a lot better than I.

Jake had a Paige, bigger and fancier than Papa's car.

Papa and Mama were happy to see Jake. He was well-thought-of and well-to-do. It pleased them that a man of his standing wasn't giving their daughter the go-by.

Before we went to look at the new car, Jake said, "I want you

127

folks to know that I did what I could to persuade the Board of Education to give your daughter a new contract. She's the best they've had around here for some time. Or will have."

"She's done some things to cause talk," Mama said.

"If you want to talk about giving a homeless baby a home, or a fatherless boy a job, the talk ought to be full of appreciation, in my opinion. And I told the Board so. A board's chief concern should be 'Can the teacher teach?' And I told them that, too.

"Well, what do you think of this buggy, Mr. Chase? It's no Packard, but show me a prettier car and I'll eat my hat."

It *was* a pretty car—and a strange one by 1923 standards. It was a touring car on its way to becoming a sedan. There was a glass windshield between the back seat and the front, with wind wings attached to that so back-seat passengers were as well protected as they would be riding in a sedan. The car was pale green and the leather upholstery bottle green. I thought of something funny to say, but didn't have anyone to say it to: Riding down the street in that car, I'd feel like a worm in a head of cabbage.

It wasn't a fact; the car was far from cabbage-shaped. And the idea wasn't very funny, either, except maybe to someone who liked to laugh with you.

The car was impressive, though, and Jake Hesse's invitation was, too.

"I came over to ask Orpha to take a spin with me. I thought she might need a little cheering up."

Before I had a chance to say I didn't need cheering up, Mama said, "That's kind of you, Mr. Hesse. Orpha, I'll look after the baby while you're gone."

"No, no," Jake said. "We'll take the baby. This is a family-sized car, and it'll look better and I'll feel better with a family in it."

Mama wasn't going to argue with Jake Hesse. If he wanted to take the baby along for an airing, that was up to him.

"I'll help you get ready, Orpha."

I *was* ready, as far as I knew. And I hadn't even said I was going. But I was. I knew that. I might look like a worm in a head of cabbage in that car, but at least I'd be a traveling worm.

While I changed Wanda, Mama picked out a Sunday outfit for me. I had put on a housedress when I came home from church.

"You can wear my gloves," Mama said.

Mama would no more think of going "out" without gloves than she would of going outside without shoes. Lack of shoes meant you were poor, which was nothing to be ashamed of. Lack of gloves meant you didn't know right from wrong when it came to dressing.

I looked all right, in Mama's eyes anyway, when I came down the front steps with Wanda in her crocheted shawl and I in my summer hat, pongee suit, and wearing Mama's white gloves. The suit was too warm, but it looked like motoring, which was what I was about to do.

Mama thought Mr. Hesse was out of his mind to want to take Wanda with us. Perhaps she thought he was out of his mind wanting to take me. But she was glad for *me*. I could see that. She stood in the driveway waving for as long as we were in sight.

"I thought we'd drive along the Rattatack," Jake said, "to see the dogwood, then end up in Amesville at an ice-cream parlor. It's warmed up enough for ice cream, don't you think?"

It was certainly warm enough.

I didn't ask Jake in when we got home. It was past sundown and past Wanda's feeding time. Maybe Jake didn't expect such an invitation or want it. I didn't even let him see me to the door. Not know the way to my own door? What nonsense! I was a real backwoods girl then, full of common sense about small matters.

Ebon was home before me, with a package and letter Mama had forgotten, in the excitement of Jake's arrival, to give to me. Both were from Joe.

After Wanda had been put to sleep, I sat down to read Joe's letter. Ebon, while I read, looked through the book Joe had sent.

I still have Joe's letter. He wrote like a man chiseling information for the ages on stone: black ink, bold strokes, durable paper. The lines of his writing don't wander. The slant of his writing doesn't vary.

Joe, handwriting apart, was the best kind of letter writer. His pen was just an extension of his tongue. His letters talked to you.

"Hi, Sis," he wrote. "O.K. I know that at the first of the year I told you you would never have to listen to me talk about my health again. I was wrong. You'll have to listen to it a little longer. What I should have said is, 'You'll never have to listen to me talk about my *bad* health again.'

129

"When I came here the doctor told me I had three months at the most to live. I told him that wasn't my plan. He said, 'Was tuberculosis your plan?' I said, 'No, of course not.' He said, 'Well, I'm sorry to tell you that the bugs who planned your T.B. plan to finish you off.'

"O.K. Now we come to Tony Musgrove. He's a preacher. Don't get me wrong. He's no Holy Roller or Primitive Baptist talking in tongues and kissing snakes in the pulpit. First of all, Tony was in the war. That's where he got his T.B. Next he came here. Here he was healed. When he was healed, he became a preacher, straight-line, regular church minister.

"Now brace yourself. He was healed by Jesus Christ. Oh, sure, I know. That kind of embarrasses you, doesn't it? It didn't embarrass you to have Lon say that he was never able to believe in Jesus Christ, did it? Let alone that He healed people or raised them up from the dead.

"Why is that? Doubt makes us feel smarter than those we doubt? Belief makes us feel we've been sold a bill of goods?

"Oh, sure, I know you're a churchgoing, Bible-reading, hymn-singing Christian. More than most. But the faith Musgrove has, willing to put Jesus to the test? Take Him at His word? 'Ask and ye shall receive,' He said. You willing to do that publicly, Sis? Then give Him public credit for what you received?

"That's what Musgrove did. He asked, he received, and he gave the Lord the credit.

"Tony comes here once a week to visit patients. He's a preacher over at San Jacinto, twenty, twenty-five miles from here. It's better than medicine to see a man like Tony, who came here a far-advanced case, walking around now looking more like a lumberjack than a lunger. Or a preacher, for that matter. Tony told me all about himself, the war, his breakdown, and the healing.

"It don't shove me one notch up any ladder to doubt other people. To say to someone like Tony, 'You aren't pulling the wool over my eyes, Mr. Houdini.' I took his word for what happened to him. But Joe Chase is no Tony Musgrove. I didn't doubt that his cure happened just as he said it did, but I told him, 'I don't have enough faith for that kind of a cure myself.'

"Tony said, 'You don't have to have faith. I've got the faith. I can ask and I will receive.'

" 'Receive what?' I asked.

" 'Your healing. You got any objections?'

"I wouldn't have had objections to being cured by a witch doctor. I'd of kissed a snake to get out of this place.

"O.K. I know I said no more talk about sickness, and there won't be much more.

"To Musgrove I said, 'Reverend, pray your head off. And you better know before you start that Doc says I've only got three months more, so tell Him.'

"But I couldn't go on with that: 'Say, tell Him it's now or never.' I may be flip, but I'm not downright scornful about someone else's religion.

" 'So Doc's given you up?'

" 'Three months, he said.'

" 'Jesus Christ hasn't given you up.'

"The strange thing is that I didn't doubt him. I'd of doubted you, or Reverend Vawter, or Papa and Mama both on their knees and crying quarts.

"He said, 'I'm not going to ask that you pick up your bed and walk. I'm going to pray for your healing. You'll be healed.'

"Well, I can't pick up any bed, but I can walk. Night sweats, coughing, spitting blood—all gone.

"Well, I said no more talk about sickness, and at present there isn't any sickness to talk about. There's a good deal more to tell you. That'll be the next installment. Don't want to give you too many shocks at one time. You probably figured I'd get well, since only the good die young. Now something's happened I bet you never figured on. Me, either, for that matter.

"I didn't tell the folks any of this except that I was better.

"S.W.A.K., little sister. Thanks for the money. Write and I promise you the first thing I'll do won't be to shake the letter looking for a check. xxx Love and kisses, Joe x x x."

VII
JAKE

1

The summer of 1925 was glorious. They said the summer of 1914, the summer before the Great World War (no one then thought world wars would have to be numbered), was memorably beautiful. Perhaps memory, sickened by the blood and suffering that followed, gilded the summer days that came before killing started.

Perhaps the summer of 1925 was the same for me—nothing unusual really. Phlox and lilacs not bigger or sweeter than common. The swimming holes along the Rattatack not a whit deeper or clearer than in 1924 or 1926. The cream on the milk crocks not exceptionally yellow or thick.

It is a matter of statistics that lightning hit fewer barns that summer and that fewer children died of milk fever. There were no tornadoes. There was an outbreak of hog cholera south of us, but it never got as far north as Bigger Township.

I had my twenty-third birthday, Ebon his twentieth. Wanda's imagery was often sheer delight. When I held a white phlox blossom to her face, she said, "Snow." White and cool: that meant snow to Wanda. She was two years old.

The clouds were unusually large that summer, dumpling-shaped but fleecy white. The stars, stars of a summer night, were not hard and crisp like winter stars, but had a nimbus of light at the edges as if melting a little in the heat.

I don't remember the clouds and stars of any other summer so clearly. Did I look up a lot? Did I lift my head and sing "Praise God from Whom All Blessings Flow"? I felt blessed.

First of all, Lon no longer fired his gun and died before my eyes each day. He was gone. "Departed" is easier to bear than parting.

I had the promise of another job. The teacher at Turkey Creek had been fired. I drove over to apply. The President of the Board, Mr. Cyrus Shannon, was on the back porch of his home at the wash bench, cleaning up before supper. He was so lathered I couldn't see him very well; and so full of snorts from the depths of the wash-basin, I couldn't hear him very well, either.

What he said was, I thought, "Go in and talk to my wife."

I did. She was Emma Shannon; table set, supper keeping warm on the back of the stove while she waited for Cyrus. She was the one who hired me, really. Cyrus came in bright and shiny as a crab apple and about the same size. Emma was a big Grimes Golden or Maiden Blush.

"This is Orpha Dudley," she told Cyrus. "She's applying for the job."

"You the one whose husband shot Crit Matthews?" he asked.

"And himself," I reminded him.

"We ain't hiring her husband," Emma said.

"Can't very well, him where he is."

"Did you ever take a stick to a child?" Emma asked.

"Never. I never laid a hand on one of my pupils."

I didn't tell her I would have if their actions had merited it. But a teacher who would whack one of my Fairmont children would have punished a rose or slapped an owl. They were that sweet and wise.

"The man we're firing, Brad Beamish, kept order with a razor strop."

"My grandson came home with welts on him. Near to blisters, some were," Emma said.

"I couldn't do such a thing, except to save my own life—or some-one else's."

"We can make inquiries over in the Fairmont district."

"You should."

They did and I was hired—the result, I think, of Mrs. Shannon's saying, "We ain't hiring her husband," and of the blisters on her grandson's bottom.

2

This was the happiest summer of my girlhood—if a twenty-three-year-old widow can be called a girl.

As a child I had been happy. I lived in a world made just for me. At twelve I became a girl and began to live in the world of grownups, to work for them, to accept their standards, and to be at their beck and call.

I had two summers as Lon's wife. Wasn't I happy then? No, not in the sense of contentment, ease of mind. Passionate love doesn't leave room for untroubled happiness. Happiness is a saucer of water compared to that sea of tossing emotions. I certainly wasn't sad, if that is the opposite of happiness. But one cold look, or one look I thought cold, could fill me with despair. "He doesn't love me any more." And probably Lon never loved me as I loved him. The myth that every woman is a rake at heart is man-made. She isn't physically equipped for that kind of life. The man can take any woman he likes; the woman can only hope that the man she likes will take her. She doesn't have penis envy. That's a fool notion. *She* doesn't want a penis for herself, except as it comes attached to a passionately loving man. Then she isn't happy; then she is exultant.

So I had the happiest summer of my girlhood. I wasn't in love and, so far as I knew, no one was in love with me.

I was a widow, with a toddler able to walk, straining to run; a farm that needed more than the work of one hired hand; a sick brother in need of money; a job awaiting at a school accustomed to being run with a razor strop. How does that girl manage a happy summer, even if the weather is perfect?

I'll tell you how. Everyone delights (I then thought) in kittens. But what if the kittens could talk? Everyone delights in reports from foreign lands. But what if the lands reported on were as strange as the realm the baby is leaving? Every growing child provides these pleasures. Wanda, being Wanda, brought them more vividly than most. I can say this without vanity, Wanda not being flesh of my flesh.

Wanda was growing up that summer while I was growing down— down into the girlhood I had missed.

Ebon and I were two human beings together. That's an unusual coupling to find among persons programed, as we are, to reproduce, not to be. Homosexuals aren't two human beings together. They're just lovers using sex in an unusual way.

Reproduction certainly wasn't on Ebon's mind or mine that summer. Leota had taken care of that for us. We had in Wanda all the benefits of reproduction without the turmoil.

If Ebon's and my ages had been reversed? If he hadn't been a boy who had loved a man? That wasn't the case, so I had a summer that was lost to me when I was twelve. I had a summer of play. Oh, I worked. The farm was too much for one, and I could do everything Ebon did except plow. There's not much plowing done in the summer, anyway: harrow, disc, harness, milk, feed, slop. I could do all of that. I did, and what I remember is the play.

Most playing takes a partner. "Playing with yourself" is a phrase for something improper. Talking to Wanda was a partnership activity, proper as could be and as much fun as any game.

People were crazy about bridge in the summer of twenty-five. The newspapers reported contests between famous players. Euchre and seven-up and pedro and poker were still the most popular games in Amesville. But in my home, and the Matthews', too, for that matter, playing cards had not been permitted. Playing cards were the devil's calling cards, an invitation by Old Nick himself to gamble, cheat, waste time, consort with loose livers, and, quite possibly, resort to violence. Such a reputation naturally made those pieces of cardboard devilishly appealing to the young.

I hadn't the temerity to buy a pack of real cards in Amesville, but I did buy a game of five hundred, which is nothing more or less than bridge disguised. You bid, have suits, have trumps, just as in bridge. A bid is really a bet, just as it is in bridge. Five hundred is designed, as bridge is, for four players, but there's a version called "honeymoon five hundred," just as in bridge, that two can play.

Ebon and I went crazy that summer playing honeymoon five hundred. I don't think our fascination with the game was any more a sign of depraved living than is the popularity of the slot machines and roulette wheels at Las Vegas. Less so. We didn't travel miles, pay stupendous prices, or lose hundreds in our fever to win.

We gambled, yes. Pennies. And the winnings went to Joe. This wasn't a very fair arrangement for Ebon. I wouldn't have sent a penny to Leota. But Ebon didn't lose often, so his contributions to Joe weren't great.

Without Las Vegas as an example of the intoxication, of chance-taking, I would have to think Ebon and I were crazy during that summer of five hundred madness. We could hardly wait until our time at the study table was over to get to the little center table in the sitting room, draw up the chairs, and start the worldly music of the flip-flap of playing cards.

The game had such a hold on us we had to make strict rules about times for starting and stopping. Study until 9:00, cards until 11:00.

138

For farmers getting up at 5:30 (as we did), bed at 10:00 would have been a better rule.

The study time Lon had started still continued, but with changes in subject matter. There was much less Bible study than when Lon was with us. We gave up mathematics, too. With a teacher, we could have plodded ahead; alone, we were lost.

The daily news, what the schools had begun to call "current events" (I don't know why; they didn't call history "past events," which it is), we read, though we didn't completely understand what was going on.

Ebon was still a hero worshiper; and the President of the United States was a great man for him just by virtue of holding the job. Coolidge was not really cut out for hero worship, but Ebon worshiped this President who acted like one of the people. "Humility" hadn't yet become a popular word. All Ebon could say admiringly about Coolidge was, "He didn't get the big head."

The answer to that was, "What's he got to have the big head about?"

"He's President."

"Only because Harding's died."

"He's better than Harding."

"Using that as a yardstick, the country's full of heroes."

The year before, a tornado had killed hundreds of people in Indiana, Kentucky, and Tennessee. Everybody still had the tornado jitters. It was said that a shift in the tilt of the earth's axis was the cause of the twisters and that the midsection of the United States was entering what was being called "the Tornado Age." People who had never before had cyclone cellars dug them. Every dark cloud on the horizon, every rattle of a shutter or creak of a barn door at night, made people run to their porches to sniff the wind for the sulphur smell it was said ran on ahead of a tornado.

We didn't have a cyclone cellar, not even a fruit cellar. We talked about what to do in case we had any warning and didn't, as happened to many people, simply find ourselves flying through the air still in our beds and bound for destruction.

"Get down to the branch, flatten out at the bottom, and hook your fingers under the biggest boulder you can find."

The branch had only about six inches of water in it, so there was little danger of drowning.

139

"What can we do about the animals?"

"Forget them," said Ebon. "Hope one won't land on top of you in the blow. How could you keep a cow from blowing away in a twister? Whole barns get picked up. A cow in a cyclone would fly along as smooth as a buzzard in a breeze. You take Wanda. I got a sack I'll stuff the cats in."

The tornado never came.

Henry Ford changed the color of his cars from solid black to red or green, if you wanted either of those colors. It was as upsetting as taking nuns out of their habits.

"It'll never work," said Ebon. "Black *means* Ford."

"It'll be the same car."

"It won't look the same. People judge by looks. If the looks change, what reason they got to think the engine's not changed, too? And the brakes and the springs and the carburetor?"

Ebon knew a lot about cars. With the first money he saved, he intended to buy one. His favorite was the Hupmobile.

In Tennessee the monkey debate was raging. Scopes was being tried for saying (that's what the people *said* he said) that we were descended from monkeys, not made in God's image.

Ebon said, "Who knows what God looks like?"

"If we were made in His image, He looks like us."

"Maybe He looks a lot worse than us. Maybe He is a big-hearted God and when it came to making people, He said, 'I'm going to give them a break and make them good-looking.' Maybe *He* looks like a monkey and made people as an improvement."

"That's not what Scopes is talking about," I said. "He's saying our looks have changed. He's saying a billion years ago we lived more like monkeys and looked more like them than we do now. Not that we descended from them."

"Did you ever see a monkey?"

"In the Cincinnati Zoo. It looked like my grandfather."

"They didn't wear clothes in Eden. That's more like monkeys than people."

"Do you think they should put Scopes in jail?"

"No. He didn't say the kids had to believe what he believed, did he?"

"He said he believed it. Kids believe what the teacher believes. I know that from experience."

"Maybe he's right. Everything isn't in the Bible. Automobiles aren't there, or guns. Or railroads. The people who own automobiles aren't going to jail just because God doesn't have one."

"Maybe He has. How do you know?"

"I don't. But if He has one, it's a Hup."

"Just because you like Hups is no sign God does."

"He don't like them because I do. God knows what's best, don't He?"

"Of course."

"Then He's got a Hup."

That was crazy talk. Lon would have been disgusted. He hated silliness. Ebon and I in our summer of childishness laughed a lot.

Most of our talk that summer wasn't about the news in the paper: Ford or Scopes or tornadoes or Coolidge. Most of our study time and talk went to the book Joe sent me, the book that had been given him by his friend the preacher. It still had his name in it. "Tony Musgrove."

"Read this," Joe's note said, "and see how people could live if they were truly Christian."

The book was John Spargo's *Socialism*.

If we had been doing the studying Lon outlined, Spargo wouldn't have taken such a hold on us. After so much gambling on five hundred, playing with Wanda and the kittens, it probably eased our consciences to tackle something serious. That wasn't the entire explanation, though. Sometimes the ideas you are ready for come just at the time you need them. I'm not sure about Ebon, but I was ready to be a socialist.

Spargo gives the history of socialism, shows its roots in religion, names the great heroes and put, for uneducated readers like me and Ebon, the whole matter in a nutshell.

The earth contains just so much of material goods: animals, vegetables, minerals. Put them all in a heap and say: The man who can, grab the most. It doesn't matter how he grabs, tramps on others, knocks down women and children. Or what he does with what he gets; hoards it while others starve. This efficient grabber is entitled to all he gets; and is even in our Christian country admired as a go-getter and, if he gets enough, a tycoon.

"O.K. What should be done?" Ebon asked. "Share and share alike?"

141

"No. It should be divided according to need. A sick person needs better food than a well person."

"Who'll decide who needs what?"

I didn't know. "The government, I suppose."

"It won't work," said Ebon.

"Why?"

"You willing to let some lazy no-good come here and without turning over a hand take a share of our crops?"

"There'd be rules."

"If there's rules, they won't let us play five hundred any more."

"What's five hundred got to do with socialism?"

"It's a bad example. There wouldn't be any game if every player got just the same cards. What fun would there be in that? There's got to be some chance. The bright players have to have a chance to outsmart the others. That's the way I beat you."

Once in a while my old jealousy of Ebon flared up. I remembered Lon's saying he was a boy who deserved teaching. I remembered that except for him Lon would be alive. And here he was boasting of beating me. And here he was sharing in the profits of Lon's farm but unwilling to share with others.

I looked at Ebon and had these thoughts but didn't voice them. Later on, though not with Ebon, I took to putting down on paper thoughts that were black, contemptuous—and true. It was almost as good as saying them—better in some ways. The bitterness, the contempt was out of my system. They were buried in ink on paper as safely as a body in the ground. I was purged and no one was hurt— except, in the long run, me.

There was in addition to the peace a kind of awful pleasure in this practice: the pleasure of deceit, of being two persons at once; the pleasure of charlatanism, of putting something over on unsuspecting persons. A Judas without even having to give a kiss. It was not a question of lying. It was a question of listening without an expression of disbelief, astonishment, disgust. It was power. It was godlike. It was being a two-faced Janus. "You do not know to whom you speak." Who could hurt you when you were invisible?

This practice did not work with Ebon. He knew without my saying a word what my unsaid words would be. When confronted with such a silence, he would say, "I think I forgot to feed Jumbo." Or, "We better finish this game tomorrow night."

So there was no need with Ebon to purge myself of unspoken thoughts by putting them down on paper. My thoughts with Ebon might be unspoken; they weren't unknown.

This has been a flash-forward. I hadn't yet come to the time of thinking much that I didn't say. So there was no need of cleansing my mind of corrosive opinions by the use of paper and pen.

No, it was my lost girlhood's happy summer: happy and strange and unexpected. Summer of socialism and five hundred; of Wanda's first words, and promised work at Turkey Creek; summer of winds that didn't blow, of Fords no longer black, and of Coolidge always cool.

3

These, though part of my happy summer, were not the chief causes for my happiness. There were two, each, as time proved, of equal importance, though not of equal value.

First, because it came first in time, was Joe and what was happening to him. The most important thing that happened to Joe was not dying. Most important to me, too. If Joe had died, half my life would have been unlived; this (important to me) would never have been written.

Joe lived; and after his living, not his dying, came life and transfiguration. Joe's letters, in spite of his resolve never to mention sickness again, did on occasion mention his health. He was afraid that I might think that a truly loving, promise-keeping God ("Ask and ye shall receive") would have cured him instantaneously. A show-off God might have done that. Such a cure might have pleased a vain insecure God. It would not have been helpful to Joe.

"I needed to lie here on my back, sweating, coughing, occasionally bleeding—and thinking. Cured overnight, I would have been the same old Joe, taking all the credit for my recovery to myself. You saw how I was at Christmas. 'Joey Chase doesn't need any help from anybody.'"

That Joey had disappeared. Many letters said so. The very first said so perhaps more clearly than any of the others. This is so much like a prayer, or a confession made for a priest's ears only, that I have thought twice about including it.

"Dear Sister," he wrote, "I have told you a lot about my sickness.

143

Now I'll tell you about my health. I was born, as you know, on August 2, 1897, the son of Wesley and Myra Chase. I was born again on February 11, 1925, a son of God. My rebirth was not the result of my prayers or churchgoing; of any Bible-reading or good deeds. It was a gift of grace, God's will, an answer to the prayers of a man of God and minister of the gospel.

"I don't know how to make what has happened to me clear to you. It would be easier perhaps to explain it to a heathen—or an unbeliever like Lon. You've got religion and a church that shields you from miracles.

"It was and is for the most part a feeling, and I don't know the words for a feeling I've never had before and I don't think you've had, ever.

"Alone, far from home, given up as incurable by doctors, a past life of—well, no need to tell you. Then, prayed for, unbelieving (hope is salt in your wounds), one night there came to me, into me, a chestful of glory. 'Love' is the right word. I was loved by God. His Son and I were brothers. Brother to Jesus? Son of God? It's what Jesus said over and over.

"The only way I know to make this even halfway clear is by asking you to remember how you felt when you knew that Lon loved you. You had wings, didn't you? That's the way you sounded when you talked about him to me. And Lon the man he was. You've faced that by now: a murderer. If love for him made you so happy, think how I feel, come home to God's love. You wanted to please Lon in those days, didn't you? I want to please God. Will I be able to? I don't know. I know I'm going to try.

"You'll hear from me often. I also want to talk about Him.

"God bless you and keep you. Joe."

He did write to me often. His letters were a part of my summer's happiness and strangeness.

We were a churchgoing family. Remembered the Sabbath day to keep it holy. Honored our fathers and mothers. Had no graven images before us. Talk about being a son of God and a brother of Jesus was not, however, common. Let alone comparing your religious feelings with the feeling you had for an earthly lover. The feelings your body had in bed, even with a man joined to you in holy wedlock, were not wrong, surely; but you didn't talk about

144

them. And you certainly did not say, "Union with God gives me comparable joy."

Joe's letters made me happy for Joe, though they embarrassed me. I wouldn't have shown them to Mama and Papa for anything. They would have thought the tubercle bacilli had traveled from Joe's lungs to his brain. I never showed them to Ebon. There were subjects I stayed away from with Ebon. Not religion: he enjoyed church because of the singing. But Joe's religion, where he said he loved God the way I loved Lon? No, no. That was sex, or skirting on its edges; and if Joe's talk of religion embarrassed me, any talk by Ebon of sex might have infuriated me. Or disgusted me. Anyway, I didn't risk it.

Joe's letters were my private treasure. Amazing grace. I read them over and over. If Joe had told me about a love affair with a girl, I wouldn't have been surprised. Amazed, perhaps, at his frankness. But a love affair with God?

4

The greatest happening that summer, however, was not Joe's redemption, or Wanda's sudden bursts of talking, or five hundred fever, or the discovery of socialism. It was being wooed.

Is this a female weakness in general? Or mine in particular?

There has been a change in fifty years, and for the better. In my time and neighborhood (and in my soul) there was only one standard by which a woman measured success: did some man want her? Was she wooed, courted, sparked, stepped-out?

When Jake Hesse began to ask me to go with him, first once a week, then twice a week, on drives, to the movies, to basketball games, to Amesville's Oyster Bar, I knew I was being courted. This made me happier than all the other summer's bounties heaped together. All right, he wasn't handsome. Where had handsomeness gotten me? Lon was a beauty and so was Ormand. All right, I wasn't in love with him. Where had love gotten me? I loved Lon and might even have loved Ormand if Victoria Cinderella hadn't claimed him before I ever laid eyes on him.

I respected Jake. When they had wanted to fire me at Fairmont, he had stood up for me, and with sensible reasons, too. When Lon died, Jake knew what to do. I couldn't, brought up where I was, fail to admire success. Business success, I mean. My socialism hadn't yet robbed me of that.

Everyone knew by his car, his house, and his farm that Jake was successful. The three shoe stores he owned—the big one in Cincinnati, the two smaller ones in Amesville and in Piqua—made him a kind of merchant prince in that backwoods country.

Jake naturally talked to me about shoes when we first started going together. All I knew about shoes was wearing them and buying them. The only person I knew who had any connection with shoes, except wearing them, was the shoe salesman, the man who had to sit on a stool at a customer's feet and shove shoes on and off a maybe not very fresh-smelling pair of socks. Or maybe the salesman enjoyed his job in spite of that because he got a peek once in awhile up a lady customer's skirts. Two jobs that I never hankered for were dentistry and shoe salesmanship.

Jake changed my mind about shoes. We never talked about dentistry.

On one of our first dates, just a summer drive, not going anyplace and Wanda home with Ebon (the word "baby-sitting" hadn't been invented yet), Jake reached down and clasped my ankle. Jake could drive with one hand without any trouble.

"Where'd you get those pumps?"

I was reluctant to tell him Stern and Goodman, not Hesse's Bootery. But I told him the truth.

"I can't afford Hesse's prices," I told him.

"How much did these cost?"

"One ninety-eight."

"What do you think you've got here?"

"Cordovan leather, Cuban stacked heels, they said."

Jake snorted.

"The heels are Cuban-shaped, all right, but they're not stacked. They're wood. Do you know what Cordovan leather is?"

"The best, I thought."

"When it's Spanish, which is what Cordovan is, it's good. This was never east of Chicago, let alone across the Atlantic."

"How do you know so much about shoes?"

"It's my business."

"How did it come to be your business?"

"My father was a cobbler. He left me some money. I couldn't

146

cobble, but, from the trade he had, I saw the shoe business was a moneymaker. Everybody don't have to have hats or even handkerchiefs. There's practically nobody who don't wear shoes. Some for one reason, some another. A farmer don't care about style. You do. I planned to carry a stock that would have something for everyone. The big store in Cincinnati isn't where I started. I started little in Piqua. Before I finish, I plan on owning a dozen stores at least. Chain selling and buying is the coming thing. It gives you some leverage."

All men tend to talk their business. When they talk it to those who are not in the same business, their talk becomes a monologue. So I certainly heard a good deal about shoes, from the kinds of leather that went into them to the most effective ways of selling. I listened, I heard, but I don't remember. Oh, I remember a thing or two. I remember the advance that was made in shoe construction when someone figured out a way to sew in the tongues so that they didn't crumple down into the toe of the shoe when the shoe was put on.

I remember that in selling a lady a pair of shoes, a salesman should always bring her first a pair that is too small. He should say when this is discovered, "I would have sworn you wore a four at the largest. Your foot is long, but it's so delicately boned, it looks small."

Small feet, in the decades before big bosoms, were the trademark of a truly feminine woman. I know this is true because my feet, in addition to being peculiarly shaped, were big. I could wear Jake's shoes. I never let him know it; shoeman that he was, he probably noticed.

He was proud of his small feet and slender ankles. "My doctor told me," he said, "that any girl would be proud of ankles like mine."

Any girl maybe, but any man? I thought this, and had the good sense not to say it. Or write it down, either. I hadn't yet come to the two-faced practice of living a double life: one life on paper, another spoken; a life of words, a life of acts.

If all the words ever uttered by me and Jake Hesse had been recorded, fifty percent of them would have to do with shoes. But ninety percent of those words have faded from my memory. Memory is a magnet. It will pull to it and hold only material nature has designed it to attract. My magnet didn't attract shoes.

It has held onto statements of little consequence. Once, Jake said,

"I was riding my bicycle one evening back at Piqua when it came on to rain. It was a warm spring rain and I thought, Riding a bicycle in the rain is one of the nicest things that will ever happen to me."

My magnet grabbed that. Not the bicycle or the rain. I can't ride a bicycle; and I prefer sun and wind to rain and clouds. What the magnet reached out for was the sadness. Riding a bicycle in the rain one of the best things of your life? How pitiful. I thought that, but didn't write that down, either. Though I do so now.

When you read of the twenties now, they're "the Roaring Twenties"—bootleggers, "How you gonna keep them down on the farm after they've seen Paree," the Charleston, Rudolph Valentino, Lindbergh. In Bigger Township the Roaring Twenties never roared.

Jake and I did go to the movies, and we went there in an auto instead of a buggy; otherwise there wasn't much difference between my courtship and my mother's.

I was capable of one Roaring Twenties act. Late, it is true. Women were bobbing their hair in 1915. I didn't bob mine until 1925. I'm not sure why. I liked my long hair. It was thick and heavy, tow turning to brown. I wore it in the prevailing fashion: back-combed on top to form an airy mound; back-combed on each side to make what was then called "cootie garages." What hair was left over, after all this back-combing, was made into a bun which filled up the space at the nape of my neck where the two cootie garages ended.

Women wore their hair "up" in public then as certainly as they wore clothes. Mad Ophelia wore her hair uncombed and hanging. Lady Macbeth wasn't coiffed when she went killing. If we had seen in 1925 a street full of today's girls, long hair switching about without benefit of side combs, barrettes, or back-combing, we would have thought some catastrophe had sent them out into the street: Ophelias fleeing from some burning building, asylum inmates in a breakout.

Hair was sexy in 1925. Letting it down in front of a man in broad daylight was token nakedness. It was female exhibitionism. "Look what I've got," it said.

Once with Lon I had done that. One evening when I had stayed after school to help him, I was so filled with the desire for him to make some declaration of love, and so unable to do so myself in any direct way, that I, without understanding what I was doing, took out my hairpins and let my hair hang free to my waist.

It was a sexy act. I knew that. You took down your hair to go to bed. It was not quite the same as coming out to a man with your

148

nightgown on. But the nightgown would be the next step—and the hanging hair said, "Look, I'm preparing for bed."

Perhaps my loosened hair did say to him what I had unconsciously intended it to say—and unready for such a declaration, he told me my work for the day was finished. I put my hair up into a washerwoman knot, not taking time for any back-combing, and left sad and shamefaced.

I was at least five years behind other women in bobbing my hair. I shouldn't have been so tardy. I wasn't skilled at hairdressing; back-combing took hours; my cootie garages were never of equal sizes; my hair was fine and soft; strands of it were always escaping from the back-combing to hang in wisps over my forehead and ears.

Bobbing not only solved all this, it also made me look fashionable and younger. At twenty-three I wasn't really old, but what had happened to me made me feel old.

I had a Buster Brown bob, and when I looked at myself in the mirror I felt less like a widow and more like a ball pitcher again. There isn't anything very sexy you can do with bobbed hair; at least, not with a Buster Brown cut. For Lon I had let my hair down and said "Bed." For Jake I cut it off and said, "I'm keeping up with the times." At least that's what I thought I was saying.

When Jake saw me, he said, "What's happened to your hair?"

"I had it cut."

"Why?"

"It's the style."

"In China, women have their feet bound. It's the style. Do you think it makes them look prettier?"

"Binding cripples them. Cutting my hair frees me."

"Frees you from what?"

"Hours of combing and washing. I thought you'd like it. I thought you'd like me to keep up with the times."

"You could have asked me if I'd like it."

"It was to be a surprise."

"I'll say it is. Last time I saw you, you were a woman. 'A woman's glory is her hair.' Haven't you ever heard that? Now you've said, 'I don't want to be a woman.' How do you think that makes me feel?"

"I don't know."

Jake told me.

"Makes me feel that you want me to forget that you're a woman.

Says to everyone who sees you, 'Here's a woman who don't care what her husband thinks of her.' "

"I don't have any husband."

"You never will have as long as you'd rather be a boy than a wife."

"Bobbed hair doesn't have anything to do with being a boy. It's a fashion."

"It's a fashion I don't like."

"It'll grow out."

"Meanwhile?"

I didn't know about meanwhile. Jake did.

"I'll get you a switch. You can fasten it with combs to the back of your hair. No one will know you've cut your hair."

Switches weren't unusual then. Mama had worn one for years. All of her hair went into a tall back-combed pompadour leaving almost nothing for a knot. Her knot was a switch, long strands of hair she coiled into a bun and fastened solidly with big bone hairpins.

One Fourth of July, swimming in the Rattatack, Mama put her switch on the bank under her shoes and dress. (Her swimming suit was a makeshift combination of bloomers and corset cover.) While she was in the water Old Pedro grabbed up her switch and ran along the bank of the river, half the switch streaming behind him from one side of his mouth, half from the other. He looked like some prehistoric animal come back to life. Joey chased him down and recovered the switch. Mama, usually thrifty, would never, though the switch was unharmed, wear it again. People had seen Old Pedro's performance.

"Wear a dog's whiskers on my head? Certainly not."

She bought a new switch, though she didn't throw the old one away. It hung at the back of her closet till she died. Mama had a pessimistic streak. If the worst came to the worst, and she expected it would, dog whiskers would be better than nothing.

Jake bought me a switch. It was believed in those days that men should not buy girls personal things: not stockings or jewelry, and certainly not underwear. Hair is about as personal as you can get, but since it was something I didn't want and took as a favor to Jake, the act was purer than it would have been otherwise.

Sexually pure, that is. Not pure as an honest human act. It was an effort to please. It was an attempt to fabricate an imaginary self who would please Jake. And fool him. Be for him a girl who kow-towed to men; made a silly mistake and rectified it. Carried away by a passing fad, but able to admit its unsuitability.

Why did I do it? Personal weakness. I've done more harm by the falseness of trying to please than the honesty of trying to hurt.

Jake bought the switch and I wore it. I put a heavy rubber band around the stubby hair ends at the nape of my neck. With another rubber band I anchored the switch there; then I coiled it into a Psyche knot. It deceived everyone. Even Jake forgot that my long hair was store-bought. And that's the only kind of long hair I've ever had since the cutting. Beneath the long false hair I stayed bobbed. Bobbed, bobbed! Short hair under the drape of falseness. Some people noticed and wondered. Not Jake. What I said I would do, and what looked as if I had done, was enough for him.

To augment your hair is no more a criminal act than to add to your breasts with falsies. Breaking promises, lying, wearing disguises may be the beginning of criminality. I don't know for sure; I never went the full route. I did experience some of the deceiver's thrill when I was complimented on my devotion to old-time values, while I said to myself, "Little do you know."

What I felt, short-haired and disguised as a long-hair, was what any boy, smoking corn silk behind the barn, feels: "I am doing what is forbidden and getting away with it." The corn-silk smoker doesn't hate his parents. He loves them and knows he can fool them. I didn't love Jake; I recognized his good sense and enjoyed fooling him.

5

Mama asked us to have supper with them. She rejoiced in the attention Jake was showing me and in my response to it. Fired from my job, a woods colt for a daughter, a gossip-provoking choice for a hired man; and the less said about Lon the better. Jake was the best sign she'd yet had that, in spite of these misfortunes, I was going to turn out normal.

Even Mama's daughter had been her enemy when the man her daughter talked to was Mama's husband. When the daughter was safely committed elsewhere emotionally, then the daughter was no longer her enemy. After I left home, my mother always fought on my side.

Having me and Jake to dinner was her way of saying to Jake, "You've heard the old saying 'Like mother, like daughter,' haven't you? Come and see."

And he did hear *and* see, for on the way home Jake said, "I've always heard that if you want to know how the daughter will turn out, visit the mother. What a woman!"

The visit was on one of those August days, tired of July's blaze and already looking forward to September. The leaves looked ready to drop. They hadn't changed color yet, but they were already earth-bound. The clouds, no longer summer's domes, were streaked with autumn's mackerel strands. Goldenrod was blazing and fare-well-summer was saying good-bye.

The Paige wasn't a sedan, so we weren't shut away from the air and the sky, from the tired leaves and the flowers of fall. It was Sunday, and we all had on Sunday clothes. They also gave the day a special feel.

Wanda wore a dress Jake had bought for her in Cincinnati. Clothes as a gift for a woman were a sign of intimacy; of too much intimacy, that is. For a child they were a kindness. Wanda, as big as most three-year-olds, and toilet-trained to a fare-ye-well, wore a dotted Swiss with a cherry-colored sash. She had cherry-colored shoes to match. Having spent her first months in a schoolhouse and her life since then with grownups, she had no practice in baby talk; she was more talkative than Coolidge himself.

Jake didn't play golf, but he wore a golf suit—knickers with long woolen socks and a fancy pair of Hesse brogans with fringed tongues. Jake was built for trousers that hid, not knickers that revealed. I wasn't built for the fashions then myself: dresses with waistlines at the hipbones and no indication that between shoulders and hips the body tapered. So we were fashionably if not attractively dressed. And if Jake's approval of me hinged upon the impression Mama made upon him, we were already engaged.

Mama had said more than once in my hearing, "I marry my children off, not on." She wasn't unloving. She knew that a marriage that made a girl long for home and mother was not an ideal marriage for mother or daughter. Jake wasn't a man, judging by the one she had married. He was, though, as she sometimes said of

152

ingredients for gravy, "good husband timber." Particularly for a daughter who would not, by those who knew her past history, be judged "good wife timber" herself.

In Papa, Jake had someone he could talk shoes to. Jake sold shoes and my father sold nursery stock. They were both businessmen. Papa, with the help of nature, produced trees, grape and berry vines, currant bushes, rhubarb and strawberry plants. Jake, with the help of cows, steers, and bulls, provided shoes. There was no point in either if it couldn't be sold. Papa and Jake talked of sales.

"You got it all over me, Jake," Papa said. "People come to you for shoes. I've got to go out and peddle my wares. I'm just a step ahead of a pack peddler."

"I'm the pack peddler," Jake said, "settled down. Pack peddlers didn't manufacture what they sold. Neither do I."

"You're right about one thing," Papa admitted. "I like growing more than selling. I don't know's I'd make out very well as a salesman on the road for someone else's stuff."

"If people had to depend on me for making shoes, they'd go barefoot. Selling is all I know how to do, and nowadays I hire others to do even that for me."

Mama and I were clear out of this conversation; we didn't know anything about selling and didn't want to learn.

Wanda, such an early talker, clear beyond words and into sentences already, charmed Mama.

"It's the same with some wild flowers," Mama told me. "They beat anything the seed companies offer. All the seed companies can do is try to make the wild flower bigger and brighter. And Lord knows, if Wanda was any bigger or brighter, they'd put her in a side show."

Wanda certainly understood none of these words except possibly "big" and "bright," and these as "big" dog and "bright" fire. Nevertheless she toddled over into Mama's lap and said, "Grandma bright."

Mama squeezed her. "It runs in the family, Wanda." To me she said, "Let Wanda stay with me, Orpha, while you and Jake take a drive."

"Jake doesn't mind having her along. He says he'd always hoped to have a little daughter."

"That's a good sign in a man. Most men want boys. That means

153

they think the world would be better off with a lot of little duplicates of themselves running around. A man who wants girls appreciates his wife."

I didn't repeat Jake's name (he was two chairs away from me) for fear of attracting his attention. " 'Wife's' a word he never uses. Except about the one he had who got homesick and ran away."

"He's going to use it. I can tell. And I hope you've got the good sense to say yes when he does."

"Maybe he won't ever say it. He's had one bad disappointment."

"You, too. You're both burned children. Don't you let it keep you out in the cold for the rest of your life. You'd make a perfect couple. Jake'll never murder anybody and you'll never run away."

We weren't a perfect couple, but the last part was true, anyway. Jake never murdered anyone and I never ran away. The first is certainly a virtue. The last isn't. It depends upon what you've got to run away from. In some cases, running may show good sense and even courage.

6

Mama was right about Jake's intentions. She kept Wanda, while Jake and I drove north past the tall corn, past tobacco so green it was hard to guess how anyone, looking at those leaves, ever had the idea of making them into smoking material.

I was young enough to like the foretaste of autumn in the air. Now I like spring, with its promise of renewal. Then I welcomed the threat of autumn, with its gales and flurries of snow and chain lightning.

Jake may have felt otherwise. We didn't talk about the weather or the seasons. Or even shoes. We talked, to begin with, about Rosa.

"I expect you've heard about my first wife, Rosa."

"I knew you were married." And I'd heard more. But I didn't think Jake wanted to talk about Rosa any more than I wanted to talk about Lon.

"I was, but it didn't last long. I don't know anyone who looked more like she would make a good wife than Rosa. She was born in Germany and came here to live with her uncle. She could bake, churn, make smearcase. She knew just how much starch to put in a shirt front. She hung all the bedclothes out once a week to air."

"How did you find out all this before you married her?"

"I didn't."

"Why did you marry her then?"

"I married her because she was pretty."

Two beauties. Rosa and Lon.

"Why did she marry you?" I was sorry the minute I said it. It sounded as if I meant, "That wasn't the reason she married *you*."

If Jake thought that was what I meant, he ignored it. "She married me to get away from her uncle."

"Didn't she think she loved you?"

"I don't know what *she* thought. I thought she loved me. You wouldn't do that, would you? Marry someone you didn't love?"

I said, "I got married because I was madly in love. That marriage didn't pan out very well."

"So you don't plan to be madly in love again?"

"How can you make plans about anything like that?"

"Do you plan to marry again?"

"If the right person asks me. Girls don't do the proposing."

"To your mind, who would be a right person?"

I knew what he wanted me to say: "Someone like you." I tried to be honest. It didn't have to be Jake. Or even someone like Jake. I described a good man. Jake recognized himself.

Before you get to the Rush Branch bridge there is, or was, a turn-off for swimmers, fishers, or just plain parkers. Jake stopped the car there. Sunday afternoon at the Rush Branch turnoff is no place for neckers, and I don't think necking was really what Jake had in mind. What he really wanted to do was talk, but talking did lead to touching, which, with his hands off the wheel, he was free to do.

Being touched by Jake Hesse was nothing I'd ever had in mind or looked forward to, and he was a peculiar toucher; little nips and strokes and pressures. His touching was like that of a machine that has had a specific button pushed. Push the mouth button and mouth hunts mouth, takes hold of one corner in a kind of nervous little nip. Push the hand button and a hand pats a knee, then slides a little way up a stocking. (I had bobbed my hair but I didn't roll my stockings.) The hand kept moving until it touched bare flesh at the top of my stocking. The hand jerked away then. The hand button had been pushed for stocking stroking only, not for an exploration of teddies or bloomers.

My mind made these calm observations. But my body was not

155

calm. I had not been touched by any human hands other than Wanda's or by any creature more loving than my cat for almost three years.

Body did not analyze or label; it burned and tingled. Body wanted mouth to be really kissed: the whole mouth, right side, left side, inside and outside. It wanted to be taken charge of. It was hungry, and while a crumb was better than nothing, a crumb didn't satisfy. Body didn't have teddy boundaries. It continued long after teddy stopped. Body had its eyes closed and couldn't see from where the touching was coming. It didn't care.

I had done a lot of hugging of Wanda and much stroking of Puss with little response from either. Puss did purr. Wanda sometimes took hold of my finger. But touch was a one-way street with them: I gave, they received. Is there a scarcity of human fondling in the world, considering the appetite for it shown by cat-caressers and baby-huggers?

A slowing car made us sit up straight.

When the car was gone, Jake said, "I got carried away. I should have saved that till we were engaged."

I held back a number of replies.

"Will you marry me, Orpha?" Jake asked. "I'm considerably older than you and I'm never going to set the world on fire. I've been noticing you ever since the day you rode in to Matthews'. Well, let's not talk about that. In fact, ever since you began teaching at Fairmont. I did more than tell the Board you'd make a good teacher. I told myself you'd make a good wife. I still think so. Will you marry me, Orpha?"

I certainly intended to say yes.

Marriage then was a woman's vocation. She had only two choices: be an old maid or be a married woman. For a woman, spinsterhood was failure. Old bachelors weren't failures; all they had to do was ask and they'd lose their bachelorhood in a minute. A woman couldn't ask. An old maid was a failure in the same way that hobos and bums were failures: she was unemployed. Housekeeping, having babies, taking care of a man—all this was her profession: a profession she couldn't practice without a partner. And if no one wanted her for a partner, she was jobless.

Most women had always taken for granted that the husband's work came first. I certainly did. I had no God-given talent except to

156

make a home comfortable and a husband happy. I had always intended to do that if anyone would give me a chance.

And I had learned with Lon that there are better reasons for marriage than a burning desire to throw oneself into somebody's arms. Love should play some part in the arrangement. The woman could love the idea of marriage, and children, and housekeeping. The man, without any of these, had better love the woman.

"There is one word you haven't said," I told Jake.

He knew what it was. He wasn't a bold man, and his experience with Rosa had made him cautious.

He took a chance. "Orpha," he said, "I love you. Will you marry me?"

"Yes," I said, "I will."

7

We were married on September 4, 1925, in the United Brethren Church. It wasn't my first marriage, but it was my first wedding. Lon didn't believe preachers had anything to do with a man's and woman's decision to live together; the law, either, for that matter. Our marriage was legal; a justice of the peace had made us man and wife, but there had been no wedding.

The church ritual was better, with its prayers and blessings and tears. I liked saying "in sickness and in health, for better or for worse, until death do us part." Marriage was my career, Jake was my partner, and God was our witness.

For the wedding, Mama had made me and Wanda duplicate dresses of pink organdy. I had never seen Mama happier. Wanda and I were as ruffly as hollyhocks in our our pink dresses.

"If only Joe were here to be best man," Mama said.

It was Jake's place, not Mama's, to choose the best man.

"Better to be without him than risk his health in a trip."

After the ceremony at the church, Mama had a reception. She had cleaned, baked, and decorated for days. The wedding cake was five tiers high. Jake and I, following the example of couples pictured in the Louisville *Courier*, cut it, each a hand on the butcher knife Mama had disguised with silver foil.

There was fruit punch with sliced bananas floating in it. The paper napkins were decorated with silver wedding bells. If the

United Brethren ceremony hadn't made Jake and me man and wife, Mama's reception would have. Grace was said before the cake was cut and "God Will Take Care of You" sung before anyone left.

It was the practice in those days to abduct the bride, if possible, before the newly married couple left on their honeymoon. Then the groom had to spend his wedding night scouring the countryside searching for his wife. The groom's car might have the air let out of its tires. The bridal room in the honeymoon hotel might be decorated with vulgar signs or the bedsheets be pinned together.

We weren't going to a hotel, though I had longed to do so. "It will be more homey just to go to my place," Jake said.

Papa's Durant, not Jake's Paige, would be our getaway car; thus any tampering would be done to the wrong car.

I wouldn't be abducted, because no one would be able to find me. After I went upstairs to change into my "traveling dress," I would come down the back stairs with Ebon carrying my suitcase. We would run to the toolshed and stay there until Jake, driving the Durant, stopped in front of it for a second. I would then jump in, and the honeymoon would start.

Ebon and I made the toolshed without being caught. We left the door slightly open so that we could see Jake approaching. As he came in sight, Ebon gave me a great hug, his long arms crossed tightly over my back, and his kiss covered the whole of my mouth. I was too astonished to move. If Ebon hadn't pushed me out the door, I might have spent the night of my honeymoon in the toolshed.

"Good luck, Orphy," Ebon said. "I'll take care of everything."

He threw my suitcase into the back seat, and I climbed into the front with Jake. After the excitement of running and hiding and the unexpected kissing, the ride to Jake's place was quiet. The calm of marriage had set in.

8

Perhaps there was something to Jake's belief that his home would be better for a honeymoon than a hotel. Ebon had taken all of my belongings to Jake's. When we opened the door to the kitchen, there was my cat, purring and rubbing herself about my ankles. It was as if I had never left home.

158

I lifted her up and held her close.

"Pussy, Pussy, Pussy."

"Where did that cat come from?" Jake asked.

"She's mine. Don't you remember? I've had her for a long time, Ebon brought her over with the rest of my stuff."

"She'll have to go to the woodshed."

"She's housebroken. Leave a window open and she jumps in and out when she needs to."

"Cats smell. I'll take her out."

"She's lived in a house with people all of her life. Poor Pussy."

"That's not a nice name for a girl to use."

"Why not? It's just another name for a cat. Like Tabby."

"It's a name for something else, too. Not a very nice name, either. We'll rename her. Ma had a cat named Mouser. How about Mouser?"

"She doesn't catch mice."

"Out in the woodshed she will. Here, I'll take her."

"Let me. You're a stranger."

On the way to the woodshed I picked up the rag rug that lay in front of the wash bench on the back porch. With it I made a nest in a dip in a rick of wood.

"Good-bye, Pussy. This is different, but you'll be all right. I'll never leave you."

Inside I said to Jake, "How about Tiger for a name? She's got tiger stripes."

"That's more like it. The name you had for your cat shows what a sweet girl you are. But it wouldn't do for people to hear my bride saying, 'Have you seen my pussy?' "

I didn't know why not, but I had already discovered that Jake had a squeamish streak about words. I was just as ladylike as could be about words myself. I never said belly for stomach, butt for bottom, or puke for throw up. True, there were quite a few words I didn't know were bad, and these, like pussy, I used freely.

I often said of something I didn't like, "That makes me sick." This, as Jake had already told me, was not nice, either, though he didn't tell me why. A woman's "sick time" is when she "comes round," which means that she is having her menses. So, for a woman to say "That makes me sick" was the same as to say "That makes me menstruate"; a perfectly normal happening but no more to be mentioned in public than urination. Less to be mentioned, since it, like

159

pussy, has to do with sex. Jake asked me to stop saying it, and I, anxious to please, stopped without knowing the real reason.

A woman of good sense or spunk would have said to Jake, "What's wrong with pussy? What's wrong with feeling sick?"

A woman with a little knowledge would have known. *She* would have said to Jake, "Don't be nasty-nice, Jacob, my boy. You didn't marry your mother."

I was neither knowledgeable nor spunky. So thus I began with Jake my life of double-dealing. Didn't know, didn't find out, went my own but hidden way.

Pussy never became Tiger, let alone Mouser, except when Jake was around. She never even learned that Tiger was her name. But let me say, "Pussy, Pussy," and she came at once.

Instead of "That makes me sick," I learned to say, "I don't care for that." What I still felt was sick.

So our honeymoon started. Except for Pussy in the woodshed, where, I was afraid, she'd feel lonesome, and maybe run away, I wasn't troubled. My plan was to please my husband. If there were words he didn't like, I would find others. There are thousands of words in the dictionary. My first husband had at least taught me that.

Jake carried my suitcase up the stairs. "By rights," he said, "I should carry the bride."

That was a sweet thing for him to say. We both knew he couldn't do it and we both laughed.

"I can walk," I said, "and the suitcase can't."

Mama had made my bridal nightgown out of the finest nainsook. When Papa saw it he said, "You'll be covered, but not hidden."

When Jake saw it he said, "Before you put that on, I'd like to see you without it."

When Lon had stripped off his clothes, I had thought, Most men would want to see the girl without *her* clothes. Now here was a man who did, my newly married husband, and I thought he was strange, too. Perhaps I was the strange one. If the nakedness had come after loving and kissing, with clothes that got in the way thrown off in a hurry, nakedness would have seemed natural, actually necessary.

I had recovered from my early training in modesty. Stripping for inspection was, even so, a new experience. I was no longer bashful. Jake was my lawful husband. I wasn't ashamed of my body. In spite of this, I felt as I imagined a slave on the auction block felt when

160

being inspected by her new owner. Jake hadn't even untied his tie yet. He did have his hat off. He sat on the edge of the bed and watched and waited.

I paused when I reached the teddy stage. There wasn't much left to uncover. What there was, Jake wanted to see.

I was willing to show him, though I didn't think that this was the best way to arrive at nakedness on your wedding night. I wouldn't have said to Jake, "Take off your clothes before you go to bed so that I can see you." Everyone, I was beginning to understand, didn't have to be like me. Jake was my husband and he wanted to see me and I had a good body.

I took off everything. I stood in front of wallpaper covered with yellow roses that grew over a trellis. I was naked in a garden; nakedness had started in the Garden of Eden and was thus Biblical.

Jake looked his fill. Then he said, "You have a body like a dancer's."

That was the first thing I ever wrote in my "Book of Unspoken Thoughts."

Instead of saying to Jake, "What do you know about the bodies of naked dancers?," I thought it to myself. It did not seem a suitable remark for a wedding night. I got it out of my mind by writing it in my book, which had been intended as a class record book.

What I wrote was: *The man said to the naked girl, "You have a body like a dancer's." A touch would have pleased her more than this fabrication.*

Perhaps it wasn't a fabrication. There was a good deal more to Jake's life than I had any idea of at that time. And the truth of the matter was, whether he came by the knowledge through experience or intuition, I *was* built like a dancer: long muscled legs, capable of bounding and leaping, unburdened with a heavy torso; the stomach concave; the ribs barely covered; the breasts not weighted with flesh. I knew more about baseball than ballet then. I was probably shaped as much like a first baseman as a dancer. This was intuition on my part, too, not knowledge. I had never seen a naked first baseman, any more than Jake (I believed) had seen a naked dancer.

I went to bed in the nightgown that covered but did not hide. With marriage, Jake had lost courtship's need to kiss and fondle. Marriage had licensed him for more intimate practices.

Women born at the turn of the century have been conditioned not to speak openly of their wedding nights. Of other nights in bed

161

with other men they speak not at all. Today a woman having bedded with a great general feels free to tell us that in bed the general could not present arms. Women of my generation would have spared the great general the revelation of this failure; a failure considered by most men as humiliating. I would have, though Jake needs no such protection.

9

September without teaching was like an autumn when the leaves don't turn: something wrong somewhere.

Before we were married, Jake had asked me to give up my teaching job at Turkey Creek.

"It is a slur on a husband's manhood when his wife is forced to go out and become a breadwinner."

"I like to teach."

"It would be hard for anyone to believe that a woman would tie herself down to twenty kids five days a week unless she had to."

"I promised to send money to Joe. He needs it to go to college. He wants to be a preacher."

"Preachers with a call from God don't need college in order to preach. Prayer and the Bible are all that is needed."

"Joe wants to go to college whether or not he preaches. I promised to help him."

"There'll be plenty of money without your going out to earn it. You take care of the house and me and Wanda, and I'll see that Joe gets as much as he would from your teaching."

The house didn't take much care. Jake had left in his house in Cincinnati all of the furnishings and most of the keepsakes of his days, first, with his mother, then with Rosa. Cincinnati was the center of his business, and he went there five days out of every week. When he was there, he stayed in the old home. It served him as an office as well as a place to sleep. He was building a new shoe store in Louisville, and the man who would manage it, together with the Piqua and Cincinnati managers, met there to discuss business and lay plans.

I had looked forward to going to Cincinnati, a great city, the "River Queen." Although I had visited it once, as a child, and re-

162

membered the zoo, I had only heard of its shops, its libraries and lyceums, of its ships on the river. Jake said no. His days in town were filled with business. Travel would be a hardship for Wanda. He wanted me to establish us firmly in Amesville: join clubs, go to and give parties, attend church.

Bridge clubs were fashionable in Amesville. For married couples, these met at night after the men were home from work; women played bridge in the afternoon. Before the game they sat down to an elaborate luncheon served on card tables covered with a cloth heavy with Madeira embroidery.

As the new Mrs. Hesse, wife of the shoe merchant well known in two states and about to branch out into a third, I was asked at once to join the Thursday Afternoon Bridge Club. I no longer believed that card-playing was wicked; and after a summer of five hundred, bridge was just more of the same. The second time I played, I won first prize, a framed reproduction of Maxfield Parrish's "September Morn."

The problem for me was not the game itself, but what preceded it—the luncheon. I could cook for harvesters, church suppers, growing boys (Ebon), toddlers (Wanda). Whether I would ever be able to cook a bridge luncheon, I didn't know. The first one I ever ate awed me.

This was the menu:

1. An unknown mixture in a shell too small for an abalone, too large for a clam.

2. Two hollow globes called "puffles." These globes were colored blue and yellow and were the texture of coarse potato chips. They did not taste like potato chips, but like pasteboard lightly seasoned.

3. A large green dill pickle.

4. At each plate, a slice of blue-and-yellow bread.

5. Lemon-yellow ice cream, topped with whipped cream colored blue.

6. Small cakes shaped like hearts, diamonds, clubs, and spades. Hearts and diamonds were yellow; clubs and spades were blue. (Blue and yellow were the colors of Amesville High School, and the football season was just beginning.)

Jake was proud of me for winning first prize. When I said I would never be able to produce a prize-winning luncheon, he told me not to worry. "Anything a club lady in Amesville can make, I can buy at a delicatessen in Cincinnati. I never heard of a puffle and from what you say I never want to eat one. But if puffles are what the ladies of Amesville want, Cincinnati can produce them."

10

In my Book of Unspoken Thoughts, I listed Jake's virtues. Why weren't they spoken? Because they were arguments I needed to remind myself that I had married wisely. Spoken, I was afraid Jake might understand their purpose and my need for remembering them.

1. Jake is generous.

He was. He would bring home anything I needed from Cincinnati for my bridge parties. He sent twenty-five dollars a month without fail to Joe. He doted on Wanda. (Mother kept her for the first two weeks we were married.) He spoiled her. It was Christmas for her almost every time Jake came home from the city; she cried if he came home without a gift—a doll or a teddy bear or a ball with little bells inside it that tinkled when she rolled it. Other women had their household accounts checked, were without pocket money except from the sale of their own butter and eggs. Not so for me. True, Jake had money, but rich men can be closefisted, too, with wives.

2. Jake is not jealous.

When Jake saw that I missed my teaching and missed the nights of study to which I had been accustomed with Lon, he suggested that Ebon come over once a week for what Jake called "classwork." With no known reason for jealousy, I had burned with anger when Lon let Ebon become a part of our evenings of study. Are you jealous because you believe others capable of your own infidelities? Does a lack of jealousy mean a lack of imagination? A lack of love? Do love and jealousy go together? I didn't know.

3. Jake is hard-working and successful.
4. Jake is clean and tidy.
5. Jake does not drink or gamble.
6. Jake is a faithful husband.

All these, written in my book, *were* thoughts never spoken. They weren't spoken because each was only one-half of a sentence. The whole sentences would have been: "Even though Jake put Pussy's

164

kittens in a gunnysack and killed them by shooting into the sack with a shotgun, he is generous, faithful, clean, hard-working, etc.

"Even though Jake took my book on socialism and burned it in the cookstove because it preached revolution, he is generous, clean, faithful, hard-working, etc.

"Even though Jake will not let me say that anything 'makes me feel sick,' when I really am sick he does then exactly what he does when I'm well; yet he is nevertheless generous, sober, hard-working, etc.

"Even though Jake hoots at Joe's letters and says Joe is either out of his mind or fishing for money, he is generous, hard-working, sober, etc."

The killing of the kittens was in some ways the worst. Pussy would have gone, too, if I hadn't rescued her. I was accustomed to the drowning of kittens, usually before their eyes were open. Pussy's five were four months old and at their most playful and cuddlesome. Jake said that in the mix-up of grabbing kittens and stuffing them into the sack, he had mistakenly grabbed Pussy, too. Perhaps. Suspicious, Pussy leaped out; I held her and saved her. There was a lot of bloodshed and a lot of cat-screaming. When the sack no longer moved, Jake opened it: four dead kittens and one unwounded, but dazed. Since this kitten was a male, Jake said, "It's the law. Even a criminal don't have to suffer double jeopardy." So Pussy had one kitten left to console her. The kitten couldn't be consoled. The shooting had permanently frightened him. We called him Crazy Cat, and he lived for a long time, always fearful, jumping out of his skin when a door banged.

The book-burning was in its way like the cat-killing, with this exception: a duplicate of a book can be obtained. A dead kitten is dead forever. I valued the burned book especially because it had come from Joe. Joe would have laughed at that. A book's value lies in its words, not in the hands that may have touched it.

I was able to get another copy of Spargo's *Socialism* through Tom O'Hara, then the manager of Jake's store in Cincinnati. When the new store in Louisville opened, O'Hara was to manage it. He came down to Amesville so that he and Jake could ride to Louisville together; when he did this, he stayed overnight at our house.

165

O'Hara was a big black Irishman. He looked more like a man to put shoes on horses than on ladies. The ladies, however, according to Jake, doted on being shod by Tom. They would buy more pairs of shoes than they needed simply for the pleasure of having Tom at their feet tickling their toes now and then as well as praising their high insteps and slender ankles. Tom was a free-talking, hearty, laughing man of the kind you'd think Jake would disapprove. Perhape Jake was with Tom as Grandfather had been with Toss; as if each man found in the other a hidden opposite he admired but had never been able to expose in himself.

I asked Tom if he would buy me Spargo's book in a Cincinnati bookstore and bring it to me in a plain wrapper.

Tom, who didn't know any more about socialism than Wanda, said, "Reading dirty books, eh, and trying to keep it secret?"

"Socialism isn't dirty. It's politics."

"What's the difference?"

"Socialism is against dirty politics."

"It's against Republicans then?" Tom was a Catholic and a Democrat.

"Republicans *and* Democrats."

"Jake's not going to like it."

"That's why I'm asking you to buy it. That's why the plain wrapper."

"Well, you're free, white, and twenty-one."

Tom brought me the book, and I kept it, along with Unspoken Thoughts, well hidden. Up to that time, I had been two-faced only in thoughts. Now I became two-faced in deeds as well.

Jake paid no attention to our "class meetings"; he read the paper for half an hour after supper, then went to bed. Tom, if he happened to be at our house when Ebon was there, attended the class meeting for a while, laughed his head off when he saw that Ebon and I were studying the forbidden book. He usually ended up playing with Wanda instead of listening to us.

Wanda, who could talk at one, could converse at three. "She makes more sense than you two," Tom told us. "Don't you, Wanda?"

"What's sense?" asked Wanda. "I can make cookies."

"You're my cookie," Tom said.

Tom, at thirty-four, had four children of his own and knew how to toss them in the air, swing them between his knees, and let them climb from his ankles to his shoulders like a cat going up a telephone pole. He never brought Wanda a present, not even a sucker; and Wanda, who always met Jake at the door crying, "Where's my present, Papa?," met Tom crying, "Let me climb."

Tom told jokes and used words Jake wouldn't have tolerated in anyone else. To me once, after Jake was in bed, he told of a strange man he had met in Louisville. This man went about the streets of Louisville, where there were still a good many horses at the hitching racks, trying to find a horse who would lick the palm of his hand.

"Did he put something on his palm the horse would like?"

"No. He didn't think that would be fair. He had to find a horse who would lick his hand of its own free will."

"Why did he want his hand licked? Free will or no free will."

"It was the only way he could have an orgasm."

I didn't know what that was, and I didn't try to find out from Tom. Either it was something I would appear stupid not to know, or it was something so far over my head I wouldn't understand if it was explained to me.

I did look up the word in my little dictionary, but it wasn't there. I wrote it lightly in pencil on the flyleaf. Lon had taught me to look up every word I didn't know. I wanted to remember to look up this one when I had the use of a bigger dictionary. If I had known what it meant, I would never have written *that* word any place where Jake would see it.

Jake opened my dictionary and saw that word in my handwriting. In my opinion he looked up the word himself in some big dictionary before he spoke to me about it. Where on a backwoods farm or even in a big-city shoe store would you run into a word like that? O'Hara would, yes. He was an Irishman, and the Irish pick up words the way a dog picks up burrs. He even knew Indian words, and there hadn't been an Indian in Bigger Township for a hundred years.

Jake brought me my dictionary one evening after I had finished the supper dishes and he had finished the *Courier*.

He opened the dictionary; then, like a prosecuting attorney, asked me, "Orpha, is this your handwriting?"

"Of course it is."

"Why were you writing a word like that?"

"I was writing it so I wouldn't forget to look it up. I didn't know what it meant."

"Where did you read that word?"

"I didn't read it. I heard it."

167

"Who said it?"

"Mr. O'Hara."

"How did he happen to be using a word like that to you?"

"It was in a story he told."

"What was the story?"

I told him. Jake said, "O'Hara is a loose talker. He's a hard worker and knows shoes, inner sole, outer sole, heel and tongue. But he was brought up in shantytown and never learned that there are some words you don't use to ladies."

"What does it mean?"

"Nothing a well-brought-up young woman needs to know."

"Is it dirty?"

"It's not a word you'll ever need to use."

Jake tore the page out of the dictionary, crumpled it, and handed it to me. The word by that time was so fixed in my mind that there was no need to have it written anyplace in order for me to remember it. I lifted the stove lid and dropped the page onto the still-live coals.

"Good girl," Jake said. "That's where it belongs."

Orgasm went to join socialism, Pussy, and "feel sick."

Bad words, bad books, doomed kittens. Strange bridge parties, Unspoken Thoughts, bobbed hair disguised with false! Wifehood was my profession, and I had never expected it to be a bed of roses any more than teaching or farming or carpentry.

Dead cats, crazy cats, puffles, bad word, Unspoken Thoughts, "sick times" ignored. So what? Look what I have, I told myself. Wanda, a human talking doll. Pussy, a piece of purring fur. Class meetings, with Nettie present now. Teaching a Sunday-school class instead of schoolteaching; miracles instead of fractions and current events. Letters from Joe, each one a psalm. My parents, proud.

Rob me of all of these and I was still twenty-five and living in a bower. Jake, because his farm was rolling, grew apples, not corn, tobacco, or timothy. Apple blossoms beat roses and lilies. You look up to apple blossoms and what is overhead beats any beauty underfoot.

My memory magnet, which didn't attract shoes, attracted and held onto the names of apples: Grimes Golden, Maiden Blush, Summer Sweeting, Golden Delicious, Rome Beauty, Early Harvest, Northern Spy.

Most of the apples went to market in bushel baskets. Not all. Wanda and I picked up the windfalls. We made apple butter in a copper kettle in the back yard, jelly and sauce in the kitchen.

I say "we" because Wanda, in addition to learning to use her tongue early, had early control of her hands. At a time when most children are still fumbling with their spoons and upsetting their mush and milk, Wanda could peel and core an apple.

Once, when I was upstairs trying to sleep off a headache, Wanda started supper. She cooked dried apples that had been set aside for the pigs because they were wormy. Jake doted on Wanda so much that he had a spoonful or two of her applesauce, afloat though it was with worm grease. I wouldn't do that. How would a child ever learn to inspect dried apples before cooking if people ate what was cooked, worms and all?

"A worm is meat," said Jake, "like a pig. Just a different shape."

A woman who keeps house is thought to be on the same sad level as a man who digs ditches.

A woman who paints the picture of a room is an artist and is admired. I with my broom, Wanda with her dustcloth, working on a level with the rungs of chairs, made the picture of a room more real than anything on canvas.

A woman who dances is admired. Wanda and I moved like dancers, brought in the wood, took out the slop, ran down the stairs with the dirty bedding, ran up the stairs with the clean.

Dancing and picture-making went on there every day. The phonograph played "The Stars and Stripes Forever." That was good music for broom strokes and dancing trips upstairs and down.

Nettie Mozier, eighteen now, looking like Wanda's big sister, Kickapoos both, continued coming to the class meetings. Ebon liked her, Jake didn't.

"She's headed for trouble," Jake said. "Why do you attract all these peculiar women?"

There was nothing peculiar about Nettie, except that she looked a little like an Indian, enjoyed study, and wasn't afraid to talk back to Jake.

"What's peculiar about Nettie?"

"Somebody'll take advantage of her."

"That won't be our responsibility."

169

"It will if she's here."

"I trust you and Ebon."

Jake didn't think that was funny.

Mrs. Harriman came over late one afternoon before a class meeting started. I hadn't seen her since Fairmont days. She was still, for me, the mother of George and Thomas and the woman who had defended me as a teacher. I supposed that she wanted to talk teaching. She didn't. What she wanted to tell me was about her health. Jake and Tom O'Hara were both there. I talked to Mrs. Harriman in the kitchen; they were in the sitting room. The door between the two rooms was left open. This didn't bother Mrs. Harriman. She was too concerned with her own trouble.

She unbuttoned her dress and showed me a large, veined breast with a nipple that fell inward to form a crater. At the breast's outer edge was a raw spot, something like a boil that has been lanced or an abcess building toward draining.

"Ain't that an awful sight? If it ain't cancer, I'm a rich woman. If it starts to run, I'll live in the barn. I won't have George or Tom catching it. I'm so careful. I don't let them eat from anything I've touched. I don't get near them. I don't let them catch my breath."

At that moment Jake shut the door between the two rooms with a bang. Mrs. Harriman didn't even notice its closing.

It was Mrs. Harriman's outburst that made Jake touchy about the class meeting that night. Nettie, whose father had driven her over, hoped to be taken home by Ebon. Ebon couldn't take her because he had come over on horseback. They could have ridden double, would have, except that Tom O'Hara proposed giving Nettie a ride home in his Ford.

"Hard on the horse," he told Nettie, "and a long bone breaker for you."

"Are you sure it won't be a bother for you?" Nettie asked.

"Be a pleasure," Tom said.

Jake was sure this would be true—and double. He took me to one side. Before he told me what he had in mind, he scolded me for leaving the door open while Mrs. Harriman talked.

"There she was, naked from the waist up and talking about a pretty nasty disease. And neither of you cared that the door was open so two men could see and hear all that went on."

"She didn't even know you were there."

"You did."

"I couldn't leave her while she was telling me something so sad."

"O.K. You did what you had to do. Now we've got someone else on our hands who needs looking after—Nettie."

"What does Nettie need?"

"She shouldn't go off alone with O'Hara."

"What can we do? Ask her to stay the night?"

"No, no. You just go along as chaperone. Tom'll behave himself with you along."

"Maybe he won't want me along."

"Don't ask him what he wants. Just go."

So I just went.

Nettie didn't mind. Ebon was the one she had her eye on, and with the slightest encouragement from him she would have straddled old Mouse behind him. If Tom minded my presence, he didn't show it. Until we got rid of Nettie, it seemed that Jake was completely wrong in his opinion of Tom: not a misbehaving word or gesture. After that, it was misbehavior all the way.

If I had been in love with Tom O'Hara or longing for his touch, I didn't know it. I was married. If marriage was a cage, I had entered it with my eyes open. It was where I wanted to be and I intended to stay there. If someone like Tom hadn't come along, and someone like Jake hadn't opened the door and given me a shove, I would never have ventured outside.

11

My Unspoken Thoughts had been my mind's work, I believed; I didn't recognize them as my body speaking.

Jake's name, though many thoughts were in one way or another about him, rarely appeared. I had that much delicacy—or slyness. No one reading them, not even Jake, would suspect that he was their subject.

So I thought.

It is a waste of life, I wrote, *trying to teach a turnip to bleed.*

The life you live contradicts the one you desire but don't approve.

To live with someone you don't love, quietly, unflinchingly, is to live a slave's life. Out of that endurance comes a slave's strength.

Beneath the assumption that marriage is for all time, the uncon-scious dream life flourishes.

Why do men who eat cows condemn cats who eat birds?

She awakened thinking, I wish I could smile at someone.

Nature protects you. What you can't get, you cease to be capable of enjoying.

Womanliness makes a good man better but a bad man worse.

Her spirit was so disassociated from her body that her body's use or misuse meant little. Once, the two had been identified. Then spirit had kept up a constant clamor, an endless plaintive "no." Body was silent; made no unseemly sounds: mouth closed, jaws set, eyes shut. From beneath the closed eyelids tears flowed.

Body and spirit in time took up their abode in different lands. Or if the same land, it was a realm of an indifference so great it could not be told from death.

The harvest of hazarding less than all is nothing.

To be left is fate and bearable; to leave is decision and unbearable.

Hope is a killer.

I did not know that in my Book of Unspoken Thoughts I was doing more than recording opinions; that I was prophesying acts. I did not complain, or cry out. My pen did the speaking in words the ear could not hear.

12

After we turned homeward, Nettie safely delivered, Tom said to me, "Well, take it off, kid."

When I heard that I thought, Jake knew what he was talking about.

"Take off what?"

"Your shoes, of course. Just because I'm a shoe salesman doesn't mean you can't be comfortable."

"I'm used to wearing shoes."

"You poor kid. Don't anybody ever pull your leg?"

"I don't know what you're talking about."

"Your hair, your hair. Take off that mess of false hair. What're you hiding, anyway?"

"I'm hiding my bobbed hair."

"What for? It's the style now."

"Jake doesn't like it."

"Why?"

"He thinks it looks cheap."

"Nuns have short hair. What's cheap about a nun?"

"They hide it, though."

"Well, Jake don't want you to act like a nun, does he?"

That wasn't a question I thought I should answer.

"How do you make it stick on?" Tom asked.

"Rubber bands."

Tom reached over, ran his fingers under my Psyche knot, gave a firm tug, and had my false hair in his hand.

"That's a hundred percent better. What the hell makes you want to tie that wad at the back of your neck?"

"I told you. Jake doesn't like short hair."

"Didn't he ever see you like this?"

Tom ran his hand through my short hair.

"Of course. That's why he bought me the switch."

"What do you do at night?"

"I sleep with it on."

"My God! Don't it ever come loose?"

"No."

"Don't you like short hair?"

"Of course I do. That's why I bobbed it."

"Why do you try to hide it then?"

"I told you that already, twice. To please Jake."

"Did you ever think of letting him try to please you?"

"What makes you think he doesn't?"

"I've known Jake a lot longer than you have."

"You've never been married to him."

"Thank God, no. I work for him, though. Same as you do."

"Don't run down my husband."

"Here's your switch. Pin it back on. Be Jake's old lady again."

"I don't have to when Jake's not around."

"What are you when Jake's not around?"

"A flapper, I guess."

"Hey, hey. You had me fooled. I thought you were old Mrs. Prim, the ex-schoolteacher."

Tom ran his hand through my short hair again, softly, the way I smoothed Wanda's black mane when she put her sleepy head in my lap at suppertime. He cupped the palm of his hand across the

173

curve of my skull the way I cupped Pussy's head. His hand was big enough to make me feel that I was a pet he was caressing, little, furry, and lovable.

"You've got a nice-shaped head."

"Same as everybody else's."

"You a head feeler?"

"No."

"They ain't all the same. Some people got heads like marbles. Some people got heads the shape of ironing boards."

"What's mine like?"

"A greengage plum. Swell out, curve in."

"Wonder what Jake would think if I shaved my head?"

"He wouldn't like it. What'd you pin your switch to? Say, I can't talk and drive. I got a one-track mind."

He pulled off into the lane of the Grigsbys' old abandoned log house.

"I've got to get home to Wanda."

"Jake's home with her, ain't he?"

"He's home, but he's asleep by now."

"You spoil that child. You ought to have another, for her sake."

"I'd like to."

"What's to hinder?"

"I don't know. I went to a doctor to find out."

"What'd he say?"

" 'Send in your husband.' "

"What'd he tell Jake?"

"Jake won't go."

"What's wrong with Jake?"

"Nothing that I know of. He thinks examinations like that are kind of indecent."

"What'd he think about you going?"

"He says it's different for women. They have children and female diseases and are used to having doctors examine them. They don't get embarrassed as easy as a man."

"Is that a fact?"

"It embarrassed me."

"Say, let's cut this out. I talk to Jake three times a week. No use wasting a whole evening talking *about* him."

"You asked the questions."

"It was a mistake. You should've told me to shut up. Look, you're

174

no kid. You're a grown-up twice-married woman. Papa won't spank if you bob your hair. Or tell some nosy guy it's none of his business if he asks you a question you don't want to answer."

"What do you think's wrong with me?"

"Only one thing, as far as I know. And that's on a subject I decided not to talk about any more. Decided not to talk at all, as a matter of fact."

And he didn't. I'm not sure whether or not he was absolutely silent. There was certainly no conversation. The sound I heard was perhaps only the blood pounding in my ears; it was like a stream flowing, or leaves blowing. Tom wasn't a man who started out with an ear, in a hunt for other openings. Or a man operating like a dowser rod searching for the area that provided the greatest response. He was like a man loving, and his loving was a getting-acquainted. It was his arms and mouth saying, "Hello. How are you?"

I was fine. I was learning. Every thought whispered, "Wrong. Forbidden. Unfaithful. Wicked. Cheap. Disgraceful." Every vein, nerve, muscle shouted, "Hallelujah. Glory be to God in the highest." My eyes were shut, but here were no tears. My mouth was not closed, but smiling.

We don't live by heart thumps, nerve thrips, or muscle contractions. That's the life of animals, and we left that behind when we began to speak. We live by words and sentences now. They're what we developed as we hunted for labels to put on the thrips and the thumps and the spasms. Tried to discriminate, actually. So where was I going? Back to the animals? It seemed more like back to Wanda. Back to the innocent pleasure of fondling. Innocent? Well, there was no adultery, the Biblical word for the spasms that is theft as well as retreat from the word to the wordless. What happened to me could have happened to Wanda and no one would have been arrested for child abuse. What's the opposite of abuse? Delectation? Is woman-delectation a crime? If you listen to the words, yes. Outside of marriage at that time and in that neighborhood, it was. And I knew it. If you listen to your body, "Grace abounding" was what *it* said.

We were home by eleven. Tom, who was spending the night at our place, paused before going into the house.

"You know this is just the beginning," he said.

I did, but I didn't answer.

Tom handed me my switch. "Why don't you leave this off?"

I didn't answer that, either.

I went to the woodshed first, where Pussy continued to sleep. She had poor old Crazy Cat by her side. I looked in there almost every night to see if she was safe. I went that night to stroke her, to say, when she purred, "Are you happy?"

I went to Wanda's room, more than once most nights: not that she ever needed anything; she slept as unmoving as a wooden Indian. I went just for the delight of her black hair against the white pillow and the neat little mound of her four-year-old body lifting the covers. I turned a cover down or pulled it up and had a mothering do-gooder's satisfaction. That night, selfish with my own happiness, I couldn't resist patting as well as rearranging.

Wanda opened her eyes. "You've got your short hair on, Mama."

"Sometimes I like to wear it. Go back to sleep."

She didn't need to be told. She slept.

When I went into Jake's and my room, I had thought that I would do what Tom had suggested—become what I truly was, a short-haired woman, no longer pretending. I put my switch on the dresser, put my nightgown on my body. I took two steps toward the bed. Then I went back and once again anchored the false hair to my own stubby ponytail. Thus disguised, I was ready for bed.

VIII
TOM

1

Hemingway had not yet said, "If it feels good, it *is* good." Or if he had, I didn't know it. When Sir Thomas More had his head cut off, that surely didn't feel good. Sir Thomas chose an agony rather than endure the lifelong heartache of knowing that he had preferred what felt good rather than what *was* good. Or what he believed to be good; which is all we can know about the good anyway.

It was with Wanda, not Jake, that I felt the burden of my guilt most strongly. With Wanda I dealt in words.

"Wanda, you must not tell stories."

"Wanda, if you make a promise, you must keep that promise."

"Wanda, the Ten Commandments are the rules God has given us to follow."

What kind of a mother was I, liar, promise-breaker, Ten Commandment–defier, talking thus to a child of four? I was a whited sepulchre. A Judas-kisser. Surely Wanda, who was not easily fooled, would detect my falseness and be harmed by it.

With Jake, there were no false words. There did not have to be. If I had said, "Jake, I lie, break promises, do not keep the Commandments," he would not have believed me. Not because Jake thought me to be a saint but because I was his wife. And because nothing had changed in our relationship. False hair firmly anchored, I went to bed with him as usual. What happened there had not changed because of Tom. I was not capable of what young people today apparently find possible: simultaneous sexual relationships of feeling with more than one person. Are they wrong today, and was I right? I doubt it. Both quite likely wrong; and I more so, being false as well as unfaithful.

Jake detected some change in me. I was merrier, less resentful of the bridge luncheons, more and more knowledgeable about shoes, less despondent about not teaching, less dependent on class meetings.

"Nothing is more satisfying to a man," Jake told me, "than to hear his wife laughing and humming around the house."

179

I *was* laughing and humming. That was true. Tom was the cause of the laughing and Ebon's singing had taught me tunes to hum. Jake considered himself the source of all these happy sounds. Jake, though I didn't know it then, was in great need of such a belief. I tried to let him keep it.

So Jake was happy. I was happy. Tom was happy.

I wasn't first with Tom, never would be. Because of him, I did laugh and sing. Laughing and singing aren't marriage, however, and Jake had married me. Marriage is sometimes glum but it is a habitation. You live there. Laughing and singing are sounds in the void, not even a window to issue from and be shaped by.

2

"Well, kiddo, we are going to Cincinnati today," Tom said.

I loved that "kiddo." I was twenty-five years old. (I loved the first time I was called "baby," when I was forty. Is there a baby in all of us, or just in women, that never grows up? Or at least never wants to.)

"I can't go. Jake doesn't like women who go skylarking off to shop and see movies."

"I promise you—no shopping, no movies."

"I promised Jake."

"I didn't know that cut much ice with you."

"Oh, Tom. It's because I break the big promises, I have to keep the little ones."

"I know that, kiddo. This won't hurt Jake. He's in Louisville for two days. I expected to go with him, but he changed his mind. He wants me back in the store."

"Who'll feed?"

"We'll be back in time. Late, but in time."

"What'll we do with Wanda?"

"Take her."

"Jake says the city is hard on children."

"Horsefeathers! Wanda could go to the North Pole, and you know it, and never turn a hair."

"What if Jake comes home and I'm gone?"

"Jake'll find excuses for anything you do."

"You think he loves me that much?"

180

"Hell, no. Jake loves Jake. He'll hit upon some explanation that doesn't hurt him."

"What about your wife?"

"What about Nora?"

"What if she sees you wandering about town with some strange woman?"

"We aren't going to be wandering."

3

So we went. It was May, The rolling hills were like green cushions. They were embroidered with the remnants of Maybuds and dogwood. Wanda sang "Over the river and through the woods, to Grandfather's house we go." Ebon had taught her that. Tom sang "Galway Bay." His mother had taught him. Everyone could sing but me. I could hug, I was in the middle; Tom, as big as a barrel, Wanda, as slender as if she had taken her name from a wand. And I could laugh.

I never understood it. The idea of disobeying Jake, of deceiving him, made me unhappy. The fact made me happy. On that ride to Cincinnati, Jake never entered my mind. I was a woman (at twenty-five, youth, I supposed, had ended) with a man and a child I loved to be with. I had given up trying to define love. "Love to be with" didn't need definition. It was demonstrable.

"I have to go to the store for a while," Tom said. "I'll leave you and Wanda off at a friend's and pick you up later."

I didn't want to be left off at a friend's. I wanted still less to go to the store. In Cincinnati, fifty years ago, as almost everywhere else, the mansions were on high ground, the houses with geraniums and porch swings were on the flats. Tom stopped in front of a house with geraniums and a porch swing, neat, white, but squeezed in between two houses that were duplicates.

"They're expecting you," he said.

I wanted to be introduced, explained, apologized for. A lady came onto the porch. Tom called to her, "Here they are, Nora."

To me he said, "Hop out, kiddo. Everything will be all right. I'll pick you up in a couple of hours."

I didn't hop. Wanda did. I climbed out slowly and watched Tom speed away. Then I turned to look at Nora. She had come off the

181

porch to the sidewalk where I stood. She was Irish; I knew that. If I hadn't, I would have guessed she was Swedish, a milk-blond with pale freckles and a great mound of hair, more carrot than red. I was wearing my natural short hair. Nora made me see why Jake liked long hair. It was, for a woman, the difference between being crowned and uncrowned.

"Hello, Wanda," she said.

For Wanda, Nora was a woman with a porch swing.

"Can I sit in your swing?"

"Sit and swing. That's what it's for. Come on in," she said to me.

I was trying to make up my mind whether to stay or run. I was brought up with jealousy. I had experienced jealousy. I was reacting as I would if Lon, or even Jake, had dumped on me a woman I knew as much about as Nora evidently knew about me. I might not do it, but what I would like to do would be: hit her.

"Come on in," Nora said again. "Lunch is ready. You must be hungry."

I still had not been able to move, or say a word. Nora was a woman I had wronged. I was more at ease with those I thought had wronged me. I knew how to be a victim. Maybe I wanted to be a victim.

Can we, by our thoughts and emotions, shape our own faces? What would a face whose owner had never felt vindictive, cruel, greedy, hateful, jealous, be? Even in a town as small as Amesville, the faces I saw on the street when I was a child sometimes frightened me. Once—in the courthouse when Lon and I were getting our marriage license—I did see an elderly man and woman whose faces were transfigured with purity.

Nora's face, because she was younger, was even more startlingly pure. Age, with its ivory skin, white hair, and frail bones, appears to have shed all baseness. Nora's skin was not white; she was not frail. She was young, full-bodied, and vividly colored: coral lips, carrot hair, and eyes so blue and open to inspection you could take a baptism of trust there more easily than the United Brethren provided in branch water. Her face had never been twisted by hatred or jealousy or cruelty. I was more afraid of going into the house with her than I would have been with a woman who had an inclination to strike. With such a woman I could have held my own.

182

Wanda was already swinging.

"Come on in," Nora urged.

Inside the house were four children and two dozen objects I could less accurately name. They had to do, I knew, with the rituals and beliefs of the Roman Catholic church: crucifixes, votive lights, crosses, candles, pictures of Jesus and His mother. These were not strewn around helter-skelter, but neatly placed. The effect was ecclesiastical and tidy.

Nora introduced me to, or, rather, told me the names of, her children. The oldest, Mary Frances, was six. Following her were James, five, Theresa, three, and Peter was two. Mary Frances was carrying Peter. Peter had the most completely crossed eyes of any human being I had ever seen. It made my eyes hurt to look at him.

"The children have been fed," Nora said. "I'll give Wanda a sandwich and they can all go outside and play. You'd like that, wouldn't you, Wanda?"

"Yes," said Wanda, who had come indoors after us. "What's wrong with your baby's eyes?"

"They're crossed."

"Can he see?"

"He can see. Now all of you run outside. We want to talk."

They wanted to run outside, and did. I, still wordless, was left to talk. All that I could think to say was, "I am sorry. I have wronged you. I have broken the Commandments. I will never see Tom again."

I never said any of this. She put me at a table with what was almost a bridge-luncheon meal. Waldorf salad decorated with halves of English walnuts, home-baked bread cut into triangles but, thank goodness, uncolored. Also tea, which was then considered festive and which for politeness's sake I drank.

"You noticed Peter's eyes, didn't you?"

"Yes, I did."

"They're terrible, aren't they?"

"It's too bad; he's such a nice-looking little boy."

"I caused it."

"How could you do that?"

"I tried not to have him."

"Abortion" was not a word I knew then. But I did know that women who found themselves pregnant and didn't want a child

183

took castor oil and pushed sharp implements into their wombs in an effort to dislodge the unwanted child. No one with a face like Nora's could possibly have done such a thing.

She hadn't. "I think it is wrong to do what causes children, then try not to have what God made the act for."

"Some people don't think it's wrong."

"I do. I had my first three children so close together. Then I listened to someone I shouldn't have. She said a douche of half ice-cold water and half vinegar would kill the sperm before it got to the egg. So that's what I did."

"That must have been painful."

"I wish it had hurt more. Then I would have stopped. It kept on. And you saw the result. The sperm wasn't killed but it was damaged. And the baby that came from it was damaged. Don't those eyes look as if poor little Pete had just had a slosh of ice-cold vinegar-water in his face. That would make your eyes cross, wouldn't it?"

"It would just make me shut them, I think."

"In the womb it would be different. Now I am never again going to use anything to stop a baby from coming. It's wrong. It's terribly wrong. Do what makes a baby, then say to the baby, 'You can't live.' That's murder."

"So you aren't going to have a lot more babies?"

"No. I will never do anything to have a baby again. I like babies. I never liked what you had to do to get one. I have stopped doing it."

"What is Tom going to do about that?"

"You know what he is doing."

"Don't you think he is wrong?"

"It isn't murder."

"What if I had a baby?"

"You won't. You've had two husbands and no baby. You won't change."

"The doctor said there was nothing wrong with me."

"Doctors tell women what they want to hear."

"I'll promise never to see Tom again if you ask me to."

"What good would that do? Tom's a man. He'd just pick up with some woman who'd have a baby or whose husband would shoot him. Tom's a good husband. He loves the children, he's a good provider. That one ugly little act. I don't like it and men have to have it. It's wrong, but, with you, no child's being murdered. And Jake don't object."

"Jake doesn't know anything about it or he would object."

"He wouldn't have any right to."

"I don't know what you mean."

"Of course you do. You know Tom and you know Jake."

"You don't know Jake."

"Tom does."

"Just because Tom's not a true husband doesn't mean that Jake's like him."

"That's not what I meant. That's not what Tom said. Look, I asked you here to make you feel better, not worse. I don't think what Tom's doing is right. He don't, either. He goes to confession. He don't have a priest's control. But what he's doing isn't against anyone's will. Some women are almost like men that way. I'm not. God made us all different. No baby is deformed or dying by any act of Tom's. He makes you happy. If I was Jake's wife and a different stripe, I might think Tom was a treat, too."

"Look," I said, "you talk about your husband and I'll talk about mine."

"Tom said you grieved because of me and the children. I didn't want you to grieve for that reason."

I couldn't say, "Thank you for your thoughtfulness." I would prefer grieving to thinking that I should be thanked for an "ugly little act" that Tom had to have; and which, while wrong, was at least better for him to do with me than with almost anyone else. I could stand the idea of sin and of unfaithfulness and deception better than I could of being some kind of good-hearted nursemaid to nastiness.

Nora saw that she hadn't made me any happier.

"You haven't taken him away from us, you know."

"I know that."

"After your first husband, who was a murderer, then next Jake, who—"

"Let's not talk about Jake."

"I could tell you—"

"I don't want to hear."

"Let's play with the children, then. All I wanted to do was to make you feel better."

I think that was true. That pure face belonged to someone untroubled by seeing more than one side of any situation. She thought Tom and I were wicked—I thought so myself—but I was not to worry about *her*. Worry about God. God would be displeased. She wasn't. Tom's and my sin, that "ugly little act," prevented a greater sin; and it also excused her from something she detested.

She was even grateful to me. That wasn't her intention, but, as the result of her talk, I doubted that Tom would ever look the same to me again.

"You haven't eaten more than one bite," Nora said.

"I haven't much appetite."

"Let's call in the kids. They'll clear up the leftovers in a hurry. And cheer us up, too."

They did both. There wasn't a scrap left on the table when a car stopped in front of the house and Tom himself banged open the screen door.

"Oh, God," he said, "he did it, he did it."

There were tears on his face. He grabbed up two of the children, cross-eyed Pete and Wanda, and danced around the room, saying over and over, "By God, he did it."

"Don't curse, Tom," Nora said.

"I'm not cursing, Nora. I'm praising God."

"What did God do?" Wanda asked.

"A man named Lindbergh flew all the way across the ocean alone."

"With wings? Like a bird?" asked Wanda.

"Like a bird, but in a flying machine."

"What's a flying machine?"

"It's a machine. With an engine like an automobile, but it travels through the air, not on a road."

Tom put the children down and faced us, still seated at the table. "How can you sit there? Don't you know what this means?"

"It's just fast travel, isn't it?" Nora asked.

"Oh, God," said Tom again. "Thank God you're not in Paris greeting Lindbergh. Yeh, it was fast travel, all right. But look who did it! A kid all alone. If his engine went bad, he'd be down in the water without a thing to mark the spot."

"Would he drown?" asked Wanda.

"Like a man in the Ohio. Nora, light your candles. For God's sake, let's have a little rejoicing around here."

Nora lit the candles and knelt with her children. Tom tried to hold back tears. I looked on. Wanda knelt with the other children and clasped her hands.

"Thank thee, God, for taking care of Lindy."

186

Where she got the Lindy, I don't know. The crossing herself and kneeling when candles were lit she picked up then and there. She could be a hundred-percent Kickapoo, I thought, in touch with something we had lost.

The ride back to Amesville was quiet. I sat as far to my side of the seat as I could. Wanda was in the middle. Tom gave his whole attention to driving.

I was disgusted with both Tom and me. We had been romantic lovers, sinning, yes. Nora had taken away both the romance and the sin. Nora had hinted that, if there had been any desire on my part to punish Jake, I was mixed up even about that. I was not even feminine. "Some women are that way, too." Back to army mule again.

Tom was mad at me because I had been unresponsive to what had moved him so much. I hadn't been unresponsive to Tom or his tears. A man who can't cry is only half human. If we had been alone, I would have spoken. How speak in the midst of children, lighted candles? Or stunned as I was by Nora's offer of friendship; and her reasons for the offer.

Tom went forty miles an hour most of the time, as if his one wish was to get rid of me as soon as possible. The door handle I was shoved against put a dent in me that showed a bruise next day.

Wanda was the only one not depressed.

"Will Lindy fly home again?" she asked.

"No," Tom said.

"Why not?"

"It's too dangerous."

"Is it more dangerous coming home than leaving home?"

"No."

"Then why won't he do it?"

"He just did it to prove that he could."

"What will he do now?"

"I don't know."

"Your baby has funny eyes."

"I've noticed."

"What crossed them?"

"No one knows that for sure."

"Your wife said—"

"Young lady, you talk too much."

187

Wanda went to sleep. Nothing more was said by anyone until we reached home.

"I'll carry her in," Tom told me.

He did. Upstairs to the room that opened out of Jake's and mine. Without so much as a good night, he went down to the parlor bedroom, which he occupied when he stayed overnight. I undressed Wanda, then went to bed myself. It was scarcely dark. Everyone except chickens and the sick was up and about, getting supper in Amesville; Lindy was rejoicing in Paris; Jake was talking shoes in Louisville.

4

Under one roof two remained apart, separated not so much by walls as by three words. They were not true, these words. Why would I let someone who had no idea what I felt define for me an act of mine? Didn't I know better than she?

If you were born hating the act of chewing and the flow of saliva carrying food downward, it would be admirable to say no to eating. Never pull up your chair, unfold a napkin, separate flesh from bone just to please someone whose pleasure it was to serve it forth. Nora could say no. Her face showed the absence of conflict. Didn't she ever worry about Tom, who loved to serve it forth? If she had, now she had solved that problem, too. I was the solution. I was everyone's solution. Oh, doormat of the Zodiac!

That wasn't true. Jake was a solution for me; and Tom also. I just hadn't the luck of finding all my solutions in one person.

Were there still tears on Tom's face? I liked a man with so much muscle and backbone he wasn't afraid to cry. No one was going to call him a sissy, not more than once, anyway. It took two things to enable a man to cry—a tender heart and a strong arm. Bruisers with stony hearts never cried. The same was true of weaklings who couldn't swat a fly.

Tom loved God enough to take His name in vain. What other word belonged in the mouth on great occasions?

It shouldn't be a debate. "By this act I refute you, Nora O'Hara." It would be a refutation just the same if I went to Tom.

I stopped in Wanda's room before I went downstairs. She was sleeping as always, not curled up as if to protect herself, or still in the womb. Flat on her back, straight as a ramrod, silent as a log. Forgive me, Wanda, I thought.

Tom hadn't gone to bed. He was sitting, fully dressed, in the rocking chair by the west window, watching, or at least looking out toward, where the new moon was setting.

He didn't hear me come in. When I put my arm around his neck, he said, "I thought you were mad at me."

"The kettle is calling the pot black."

"I *was* mad at you. Fly across the ocean all alone and it don't mean as much as your darned cat climbing a fence."

"I love my darned cat."

"You ought to love Lindy."

"I love Lindy. Come on to bed, Tom."

I untied his tie, unbuttoned his shirt, pushed down his suspenders.

"You going to undress me?"

"If I have to."

"You don't have to, kid."

Tom was a big man, thick as well as wide and long. I lay by his side as if in the shade of a sheltering cliff.

"It wasn't Lindy," I said.

"Nora?"

"Yes."

"I thought you'd feel better to know. 'Your poor wife and children.' Those were your words. I thought you'd feel better if you really knew how it was."

"I do feel better about them. It's me I don't feel so good about."

"A vulgar dirty little act?"

"Nasty!"

"It is if you feel that way. Eskimos think kissing is nasty. Get your mouth all mixed up with somebody else's spit and teeth."

"Did you make that up?"

"No, it's true. That's the way they feel about it."

"Murder is wrong, no matter how you feel about it, isn't it?"

"Sure. Worse if you like it."

"God wouldn't have made a nasty little act the only way to have children, would He?"

"No God I know anything about."

"He made some rules, though?"

"That's what I'm told."

"And we're breaking them."

"Not recently."

Tom made me laugh. I kissed him.

"Teeth and spit," he said. "The Eskimos don't know what they're missing."

"I love you, Tom."

"I wondered if you'd ever say that."

"You never asked me if I did."

"What you have to ask for's no good."

"Beggars don't think so."

"Kid, I'm no beggar."

"Thieves don't even ask."

"If it ain't a gift, I don't want it."

"It's a gift."

We woke just at sunup. Tom had to be in Louisville early. I had to look after Wanda.

"Nora is wrong," I told Tom. "Worse than an Eskimo."

"Poor girl," said Tom.

I dressed before I went into Wanda's room.

"Put your hair on, Mama, before Papa comes home."

"He won't be here until night."

"He might surprise us someday." But, out of habit, I put on the switch.

We had the first strawberries of the season for breakfast.

"If Lindy was here, it would be perfect," Wanda said.

"Not for me or Lindy," said Tom. "How about you, Orpha?"

"I'm happy just as we are."

5

After Tom left, I took my switch off again. I was floating, floating, and it seemed to weigh me down.

Wanda, who noticed everything, noticed.

"If I hear Papa turn in the drive, I'll let you know."

I was teaching the child deception.

There were a thousand things I wanted to do that day. Among them was to put some words into my Book of Unspoken Thoughts. If Tom had been there, they would have been spoken. In a way, I

190

was still talking to him, putting into whole sentences what had been exclamations and questions and wonderings the night before.

Unless you are crazy, nasty acts make you feel nasty afterward. Only lunatics enjoy killing flies or slapping babies or eating so much they puke. Unless you are crazy, an act that makes you love the whole world cannot be nasty.

Where there is no feeling at all, the act is not nasty. The unresponding body takes no message to the brain. "Nasty" is the brain's word.

The bumblebee is also small and quick, but one knows that it has been there.

To receive and give simultaneously: if a flower could love us when we inhale its scent; if a sunset could respond to its admirers with a deeper crimson.

Wanda and I painted a beautiful picture of a farmhouse that day. Dusted the rungs of chairs. Beat braided rugs gently. Bade every picture hang even. Scoured the stains out of teacups. And the same-colored stains out of chamber pots. Bon Ami-ed the front windows. Made strawberry shortcake for supper. Also creamed peas (not until I got to California did I eat a boiled pea unaccompanied by any sauce), fried chicken, made gravy.

If Jake thought the splendor was all for him, that was not intentional deceit on my part. The house-shine and food-savor were the result of a happiness that didn't permit standing still. There was nothing wrong in letting Jake share that bounty, was there?

At six, without being warned by Wanda, I had my hair back on, the table set, biscuits and shortcake in the oven.

Jake didn't come at six, or seven or eight. In the first months, this had worried me. Had the car gone over a cliff? A runaway horse crashed into him? A bridge collapsed? Jake was always late, maybe an hour or two, maybe, as now, until next day. I didn't worry any more. I did fume. Why couldn't he let me know? We had a phone. He knew that I worried. I had walked with a lantern one night, pitch dark and pouring rain, to the south fork of the Rattatack, where, I was afraid, the bridge might have gone out. It hadn't, and Jake overtook me homeward-bound and soaking wet. Jake had two kinds of pride—one as a businessman, the other as a householder. The businessman's pride was never to be late; the householder's was never to be on time.

191

Neither Ebon nor Nettie had phones. Papa and Mama did not want to make the long drive at that hour of the evening. So Wanda and I ate the good food alone. Pussy ate a whole chicken wing on a sheet of the Louisville *Courier*.

After supper I reread some of Joe's letters. I sat in a rocking chair (home of the hurt). Wanda was on my lap, and on her lap was Pussy. Pussy purred, I rocked, Wanda stroked. I read Joe's letters aloud. They were all about Jesus. Was Jesus a storybook man to Wanda, a magician, a Santa Claus before Santa got old and bewhiskered? You asked Jesus for favors the way you asked Santa for presents. Only Jesus, of course, made promises. "Ask and ye shall receive." Santa said, "Be good."

Were my Unspoken Thoughts really talk with Jesus? In any case, He knew them. Could I have put them down if I had believed that no eye would see? No ear hear? Maybe. In the beehive of the brain, thoughts that never escape buzz around the cranium night and day. With pen and paper I cracked the cranium, freed the thoughts, and stopped the buzzing.

"Did I ever see Uncle Joe, Mama?"

"No, you never did."

"Does he look like you?"

"No. He's handsome."

"What's a seminary?"

"A school where men go to learn to be preachers."

"Can women go?"

"No."

"Why not? Don't God love women?"

"God didn't make seminaries. Men did."

"It's like a lodge? Like the Odd Fellows?"

"Kind of."

"Can Uncle Joe really see Jesus?"

"Yes."

"Can you?"

"No."

"You pray. He couldn't hear you if He wasn't there, could He?"

"No. He's there, all right. But only the pure in heart can see Him."

"If I prayed hard, could I see Him?"

"If you had enough faith."

"I don't," said Wanda. "I will never see Jesus. But I love Him and He loves me."

192

I rocked. Pussy purred. Wanda stroked.

Joe wrote, "I think my sickness was only the effort of my flesh to tell me something about my soul. My soul could rot and bleed and I would never have noticed it. Never even notice that I had a soul. God woke me up by making my body sick. I looked inward then. I was healed by faith. I will live by faith and preach the gospel of the Son of God. Which I am also."

The purring had stopped. The stroking had stopped. Two slept. I thought: Wanda, child of adultery; Orpha, adulteress. One owes her life to the forbidden act; one owes her happiness to it. The last, not absolutely true. I was happy when telephone wires sang in the wind, when roosters crowed, when summer's giant clouds cast their traveling shadows over sunny fields. Clouds and roosters and telephone wires (plus a little wind): was a life that asked no more than that for happiness damaged? And was happiness the answer? Did Jesus ever tell anyone to be happy? Or Moses? Or Paul? Was Jesus ever happy? Hanging on the cross, true to His Father's commandment, was He perhaps the happiest He had ever been? I needed to talk to Joe.

6

I intended to tell Jake next day of my visit with Nora. He objected to Cincinnati, not to Tom or Nora. I didn't get it done.

Wanda started school. Tom was transferred to Louisville as manager of the new store there. Nora and the children stayed in Cincinnati. I saw Tom as much as ever. Jake never noticed; or if he noticed, he didn't care. I resented this. I thought a husband should notice. I didn't ask Jake for what I would call "love"; I did think he owed me some jealousy. Some suspicion. Wasn't he even enough aware of me to wonder about my high spirits after he'd been gone?

When Nora asked me to visit her again, there was no reason not to go. Wanda in school, Jake in Piqua, Tom eager for a pleasant daytime ride through maple and hickory and sycamore at the height of this Indian summer war paint.

"What's she want to see me about this time?"

"Search me," Tom said. "Nora and me don't confide in each other. It'll be what she thinks is for your good."

"In the long run, I guess what she told me last time maybe did help."

"Maybe she wants you to see Pete's eyes."

"Did the operation cure them?"

"I wouldn't say cure. They're still a little off plumb. But it don't give you a downright headache any more to look at the poor kid. I'll pick you up in time to get you home by suppertime."

Tom never liked being with me when his kids were around. He felt the same guilt with them I felt with Wanda. He let me off at the gate and was gone before Nora came to the door, though she did wave at his disappearing car.

Nora was still just as sweet as her face. Tom was right. Her intention was to do me good. She had Pete in her arms, though now, at three, he was a lunk of a boy to be carrying around. The habit of coddling, developed early because of his eyes, still persisted, though the eyes no longer required it.

"I am going to take you to visit someone you ought to know," Nora said. "Someone who would make you feel better about Jake."

"I feel all right about Jake," I said. Which was a lie.

"Last time you were here, you didn't."

"I still don't," I confessed.

"I thought so. I feel better about Tom now that Pete's eyes are better."

"What did Tom have to do with Pete's eyes?"

"I told you. Except for him, there wouldn't have been any need of vinegar and water. That's plain, surely."

In a way, Nora's way, it was plain. We had gone over all that on my last visit. I changed the subject.

"Who are we going to see?"

"It's a surprise. We'll go by streetcar, with a little walk at both ends. You can walk all right?"

I don't know what made her think I couldn't.

"I can run," I said.

"Well, no need of that."

"Are we a surprise to the person we're visiting?"

"No. Rosa expects you."

"Rosa! That was the name of Jake's first wife."

"This is Jake's first wife."

"When did she get back?"

"Get back from where?"

"Germany. Where she went when she got homesick and ran away from Jake."

194

"She ran away, all right, but she was never homesick for Germany."

"But Jake told me—"

"You you can hear Rosa's story from Rosa. I reckon it won't be like Jake's any more than your story of marriage would be like his. I won't stay. You and Rosa need to talk private."

"I think I'll ride back with you."

"You can if you want to. I wouldn't if I was you."

"Nora, you and I are as different as night and day."

"Not that different. Tom liked me and he likes you."

"A man can like night *and* day, both."

"I can't make you go. It's up to you."

I went. We walked three blocks from the end of the trolley line to a larger house and a prettier garden than Nora's. Or mine. Rosa was now Mrs. Shaughnessey; Nora had told me that. Rosa was standing on the front porch waiting for me. I turned to Nora, expecting her to lead the way, and saw she was heading back to the trolley. When I reached the top of the steps, Rosa and I, without saying a word, sat down, I on a chair, she on the porch swing, and looked at each other.

I saw myself, ten years older. Rosa looked at herself, ten years younger. We were not twins, but sisters, one heavier with child-bearing and born ruddy instead of tow-colored. Rosa, I judged, by the set of her mouth before she had said a word, was outspoken and strong-minded; she didn't keep any book of Unspoken Thoughts. They were all spoken. Jake had told me she was beautiful. She never could have been, not even sixteen years ago. Never ugly, with regular features, high color, and sandstone eyes; but a chin as strong as Dempsey's. Jake was praising himself when he called Rosa beautiful; a man who attracted handsome women. He said it to impress me, and I was impressed.

Rosa, rocking herself in the shooting swing, said, "My God! So once wasn't enough!"

That was fine for Rosa. A man so attracted by her that when she ran away from him the only way he could solace himself was by finding someone as like her as possible. But where did that leave me? Not a real person. Not Orpha Chase Dudley. Just a look-alike. A replica. A Rosa who didn't rebel, who didn't speak out, but wrote in a book. Who gave him a ready-made child.

195

Rosa said "My God" again. Then, "Well, you can see what another ten years'll do for you. If that's any comfort. What else did the old bastard tell you?"

Rosa was a rough talker. Was it Germany? Or did being married to Jake, who was what Mama called "nasty-nice," bring out in her the defiance of roughness?

"He told me you got homesick for your folks in Germany. And went home to them."

"I didn't have any folks in Germany."

"He said you wanted to leave your uncle here in Cincinnati."

"And you believe everything he told you? Swallowed it hook, line, and sinker? I can see you did. You were born to be bamboozled. Well, the uncle part is true. At nineteen, I thought it would be better to be knocked up by a husband than by an uncle. I was probably right. Though Jake didn't give me the answer. Oh, he tried, all right. Knock, knock, knock, day and night. How do you put up with all that? Well, it's none of my business. No children, though, I'll wager. I've got three. They're all at school now. Shaughnessey is a fine man. I'm not his chamber pot, handy when he needs emptying."

"Do you hate Jake so much?"

"Not at all. No more than warts. Something that happens to you when you're a know-nothing kid. How long have you been married?"

"To Jake? Four years."

"How come you're just now finding out I'm not in Germany?"

"I don't come to Cincinnati."

"You're near. Why not?"

"Jake asked me not to."

"In God's name, girl, you're not six. He's not your pa. Where's your spunk?"

"Maybe I was born without any."

"You're still young. Grow some."

"I'm sly, not spunky. I do the little things Jake asks me to do. That way, he doesn't notice the big things."

"So that's the way it is."

I didn't have enough spunk to come right out and say yes, that's the way. I didn't need to.

"That's a rotten way to live. I don't know which one of you I feel sorriest for."

I knew which.

"Why did Nora bring you over here?"

"She thought seeing you would keep me from feeling so guilty about Jake."

"Guilty about Jake! How did *she* know you feel guilty about Jake?"

That was another question I didn't answer—and didn't need to.

"So that's the way it is," she said again. "Well, feel less guilty?"

"Not yet, anyway."

"What does she think about you and Tom?"

"She thinks we're sinners."

"Then why's she want you to feel good?"

"I'm not sure. Maybe she thinks if I don't, Tom may sin worse with someone else."

"How could he? You're a married woman."

"Someone who'd have to do away with a child."

"Oh, Jesus! Come in and have a cup of coffee. Or a glass of beer. You need something. Don't you have anyone you can talk to?"

"Tom. Wanda."

"Who's Wanda?"

"My adopted daughter. She's only six."

"She's not going to be much help. Don't you have a mother?"

"I'd be ashamed to tell her."

"Stop doing what you're ashamed of. I did."

"You had Mr. Shaughnessey."

"Not till I left Jake. Come on in."

There was a long mirror above the table in the front hall. Rosa took my arm and held me by her side in front of it.

"Take a look. You're going to look a lot worse than me in ten years' time. Nothing ruins a face so fast as double-dealing. Your face telling one story to the world. Your heart yanking your face to pieces, trying to let the truth be known. One eyelid'll hang down lower than the other, one side of your mouth'll stay stiff while the other smiles. I know a dozen cases like that."

"You think I should give up Tom?"

"Both of them. Jake first, then Tom."

Rosa had good black coffee, and pound cake so rich with butter and eggs it could be the mainstay of your diet. Jake had told the truth about one thing—Rosa was a good cook.

She was determined to talk to me about Jake, to let me know how awful he had been. She had some idea that since she had left

197

him and I hadn't, she needed to justify her decision to me. Was it an indication of the part words were to play in my life that Rosa's rough words seemed worse to me than my acts?

Rosa said all the words, unmistakable words. I had never before heard sex talked about; and certainly I had never talked about it myself. I didn't now. But I listened. Because Rosa and I looked so much alike, with the exception of the ten years' difference in age, I felt that I might be listening to an older, more experienced self warning a younger one. Ordinarily one learns from the past. Was the future speaking to me now?

Because of the prolonged talk, I didn't get back to Nora's at the time Tom expected to pick me up. He saved me the trouble of that trolley ride by coming to Rosa's.

On the front porch waiting for him, Rosa had two last things to tell me. The first was, "Tom O'Hara is never going to marry you. You know that."

"I know that," I agreed.

"Orpha, I didn't tell you the very worst thing about Jake. Never once in the four years I was married to him did he make me laugh. That is unforgivable."

For the first ten or fifteen minutes, I just leaned against Tom. Neither of us said anything. Then Tom said, "Maybe Jake was right telling you to stay away from Cincinnati."

"He certainly had his reasons. Did you know that Rosa looked like me?"

"Fifteen or twenty years ago, maybe."

"How do you think being her twin makes me feel?"

"She's a pretty good-looking woman."

"Makes me feel like a shadow. I'm nobody. I'm Rosa's shadow."

"Not to me, you ain't."

"I am to Jake."

"I didn't know you cared that much about Jake."

"I feel sorrier and sorrier for him. He's married to a shadow. How would you like to be married to a shadow?"

"You're the only wife I've got. You're no shadow."

"Don't joke about serious things."

"Joke? If you think that's a joke, you've got a peculiar sense of humor."

"Do you know what Rosa says is the very worst thing about Jake?"

"I can guess."

"No, you can't. The worst thing is that he never made her laugh."

"If that's what she wanted, she sure picked the wrong guy."

"You've been in Jake's house in Cincinnati, haven't you?"

"Sure."

"In his mother's room?"

"I didn't know there was such a room."

"There is. And what's in it are all the things a mother keeps of her little boy. A box with his curls. The first picture Jacob ever drew. And you can't guess what it is. A cat! That's before he found out that more than cats are called 'Pussy.' His first mush bowl and spoon are there."

"I though you said this was his mother's room."

"It is. Or was. It's filled with the things of his she'd kept. And *he's* kept them all just as she left them. Rosa knows. She lived in that house all the time she was married. He loved that room. He'd go in there, Rosa says, and be Mama's little boy again."

"What did Mama think of her little boy getting married?"

"While she lived, he didn't. He never would've, Rosa says, if Mama hadn't died."

"Poor Rosa."

"Poor me. Did you know his mother wore her hair in a bun on the back of her head, the way I do?"

"The way you do sometimes."

"Who am I, Tom? Jake's mother or his first wife?"

"Orpha, you're my sweetheart."

I sat tall enough in the seat to put my arm across Tom's shoulders. "I'm a stepmother to Wanda and a stepwife to you."

"You're all the mother Wanda has, and all the wife I have."

"Nora should've married Jake and you should've married Rosa."

"Where does that leave you?"

"With Shaughnessey, I guess."

7

Wanda was waiting at the end of the lane that led to our house. Tom stopped for her. She had my switch in a paper bag.

"Put it on, Mama. Papa's at home."

199

I could clamp that hair on and coil it at the stub at the nape of my neck in my sleep. I knew that Wanda had long since learned that I hid some things from Jake. I wasn't happy that Tom should know that Wanda was involved in my deceit.

"I told Papa that you had gone for a ride with Uncle Tom."

"Did you tell him where?"

"He doesn't care. He thinks it's nice for Uncle Tom to take you for a ride."

He did think it was nice. He tried to persuade Tom to stay for supper.

"Can't think of it, Jake. Nora's expecting me. I'll be late as it is. Thanks just the same."

After Tom left, Jake said, "Nora's got a real fine husband. A lot of men with a wife like that, her mind on just two things, church and the children, would develop a wandering eye."

The impulse to set Jake right was almost overwhelming. I wanted to yell, "Wake up, Jake, you idiot. Tom's got a wandering eye. And who it's wandering to is me. Just because there are some words you won't say and some acts you're ashamed of, don't mean those words and acts don't exist. You're living in a fig-leaf world, Jake, putting shoes on people's naked feet and hair on my bobbed head. If I loved you the way I ought, I'd yank off my false hair. I'd show you where I've hidden *Socialism*. I'd call 'Pussy, Pussy, Pussy' to my dear cat till you were willing to give a woman's center its right name without blushing. Oh, Jake, I pity you from the bottom of my heart."

It was the pity that kept me from saying a word. I cooked supper. Leaves, frost struck, drifted down. A basket of MacIntosh apples scented the kitchen. Wanda showed us animal shapes with shadows made by her fingers.

After supper, while Jake read the *Courier* in the sitting room, I sat at the kitchen table and wrote in my Book of Unspoken Thoughts.

What if a doctor pitied you so much that in order to spare you pain, he wouldn't operate?

Can you love the one you pity?

"Like as a Father pitieth his children." Yes, but does a grown man want to be treated as a child by a woman? Or does he in that way become once again Mama's little boy, his precious curls still in her keepsake box?

Somebody (Lon?) said, "Pity is next door to contempt."

Is pity the choice of those without the courage to be honest?

I wouldn't mind being pitied. I think I am pitiable. It would per-
haps depend upon who pitied me. R. probably pities me. Does W.?
I think so. T. doesn't.

When I heard Jake fold his paper, I slipped my Book of Unspoken Thoughts into its hiding place in the groove between the
table top and the support for its leaves. Jake didn't know about
Unspoken Thoughts. Except for letter-writing, he didn't like to
see me writing anything. Writing was a way of hiding what you
really thought, he believed. He was right.

Jake usually went to bed after finishing the *Courier*. Sometimes
he came to the kitchen to mix himself a glass of Celery-Vesc, a kind
of fizzing stomach-sweetener.

He came out this evening just to talk.

"I've got an idea for something I should have had long ago:
shoe-repair shops in connection with every shoe store. I got it into
my head that selling shoes was a step upward from repairing shoes.
That's nonsense. Garagemen likely make more money than car
salesmen. I got it into my head that by repairing shoes, I was cutting
my own throat as a shoe seller. The man who had his old shoes
mended wouldn't buy a new pair. Poppycock! Some'll do one thing,
some another, and the way to cash in on both is to cater to both.
Look at this."

Jake took off one shoe. Jake was the cleanest man in the world.
He could've stirred the soup with his toes without harming the
soup.

"Now, I don't suppose you can tell me what kind of a shoe this
is?"

"It's an oxford," I said.

Jake seemed pleased. "Just as I thought. Boot, oxford, moccasin.
That's about the sum total of your shoe knowledge. It's a McKay
shoe. Now, before you can start repairing a shoe, you've got to
know what kind of a shoe you're working on. There are two chief
kinds, Welt and McKay. I prefer the Welt, but I've been wearing
a McKay just to try it out. Better than either is a Turn shoe."

"Is a Turn shoe anything like a turncoat?" I asked.

"I thought maybe you'd like to know a little something about
your husband's business. After all, it's what puts the bread and
butter in our mouths."

"I was just joking."

"Kings, I believe, had court jesters. They don't fit into ordinary households very comfortably."

"I'm sorry. It was just a play on words."

"The shoe business is more than play and more than words. It's hides, workmanship, salesmanship, ending up with protection for the human foot. There's nothing funny about it."

"I'm sorry. What is a Turn shoe?"

"It's a shoe that is made wrong side out, then turned."

I kept enough of my mind on shoes to follow Jake's descriptions. But most of it was still hearing what Rosa had had to say about him. Except for the information about Jake's mother, nothing Rosa had said was news to me. It was all an old story, but a story I had never put in words. Hearing the words was the difference between blood in your veins and blood on the floor.

Realizing that Jake had finished his talk about repair shops, I told him that I thought it a fine idea. He said, "Bedtime, Orpha."

He stood behind my chair and cupped my breasts in his hands. This act, less intimate than the other, was longer and more felt. I remained still. I made myself immovable. Rosa told me what she had done. No husband deserved that more than once in a lifetime.

8

I always washed and put cucumber cream on my face and hands before going to bed. Since I hadn't done so that night, I got up as soon as Jake's breathing told me he was asleep. After washing and anointing, I went to Wanda's room.

"Mama," she said, "are you sick?"

"No, no. I just went to the bathroom."

"You smell sweet."

"That's my cucumber cream."

"What's cucumber cream for?"

"It bleaches freckles and softens."

"Get in bed with me, Mama. You used to all the time."

"That was before I had a husband to sleep with."

"You could come in for a little while. He would never know. Couldn't you?"

There was no answer for this. Wanda knew that I hid some things from Jake. This wasn't a nice lesson for a six-year-old to have learned. It had been a long and miserable day. My eyes ached for sleep.

Wanda, who knew things like this without being told, said, "If you fall asleep, Mama, I'll wake you up."

It would be freezing by morning. I had washed in cold water. When Wanda turned back her covers, warmth flowed up from her bed.

"Ten minutes only," I told her.

Under Wanda's covers, when I stretched full length, I touched something that startled me.

"What's in your bed?"

"It's only Mouser, Mama."

"Mouser?"

"I call her that to please Papa."

"It wouldn't please him if he knew you had a cat in bed with you."

"I bring her in after he's in bed. And I put her out before he gets up. You don't mind, do you, Mama?"

"I mind not being told."

"If you knew, Papa would blame you, too. Take off your hair, Mama."

I put it on the floor beside the bed. Wanda ran her hand through my hair. "You're cold, Mama."

I was, but the combination of the cat and the child radiated warmth. Wanda was short-coupled, as they say of horses, warm as a chunky little base burner.

"You were shaking, Mama."

I hadn't known it till I was told. Without being told, I knew the luxury of lying warm and still.

"Is Pussy in your way, Mama? She can sleep outside the covers."

"No, no, she's fine. She's a foot warmer."

"Are you cold?" "Is the cat in your way?" Somebody patting my head. Somebody worried about my comfort. I began to cry. It is strange: misery can be endured dry-eyed, but a little tenderness brings on a flood of tears.

Wanda was motherly. "Mama, let's say our prayers. When I was little, we always used to. Let's say our prayers and go to sleep."

"You say yours first, Wanda."

Wanda's bedtime prayer had always been "Gentle Jesus, meek and mild." She said the whole of it.

I always prayed for everyone in the family, most of all for Joey, far from home. My prayer ended as always, "Lead us and keep us, for Thy Name's sake."

Wanda said, "You didn't pray for Papa."

"You do it, Wanda."

Wanda did. Then she said, "Good night, Mama," and I slept until Wanda awakened me. "It's daylight, Mama. Time to get up."

Wanda was already outside the bed. "I put Pussy in the woodshed. Hurry or you'll freeze."

I was at the door when Wanda ran to me. "Your hair, Mama, your hair."

Jake was still asleep, on his back gently snoring. I put my hair on the dresser. With one knee on the bed, I had a change of heart. If a bun on the back of my head pleased Jake, why not wear it? When Jake awakened, there I was, as if never absent, disguise in place.

"Turn over, wifey," he said.

9

I never again saw Nora or Rosa. They asked to see me and I could have gone. Jake was so busy getting his new repair shops started, he was hardly aware of what I did.

He couldn't have chosen a better line of business or a better time to start it. By the early thirties, the Depression was already well under way. Sixty percent of the people in America were making two thousand dollars or less a year. "Brother, can you spare a dime?" had become a kind of national anthem. People who in better times would have bought a new pair of shoes now had the old pair half-soled. If they bought a new pair of shoelaces, they felt affluent.

Jake, in addition to having a shoe business that brought in cash, had a farm that made it unnecessary to pay out much for household supplies. True, we didn't grow tea or sugar cane; but there was plenty of corn, buckwheat, potatoes, apples, pieplant, berries, milk, cream, and eggs.

After talking to Nora and Rosa, I made a greater effort than ever before to be kind to Jake. The boy who had to endure curls; considering their length, he must have worn them until he was six or seven. The man who had heard those brutal words from Rosa; who had to lie to hide the real reason she left him. Didn't he deserve some kindness now? Was what I gave him really kindness? He thought so. That is why, I suppose, the final revelation hurt him so.

The elaborate parties for my bridge club pleased him. I could now make puffles as well as any woman in Amesville. Church suppers were better attended at our place than at the home of any other church member.

Even the class meetings, though Jake never joined us, seemed to give him pleasure. In addition to Ebon and Nettie, Wanda now attended these weekly study sessions. A child of eight obviously couldn't understand socialism. We didn't understand it very well ourselves. Socialism in that time of want and business failure was a more important subject than it had been when Joe first sent me Spargo's book. Would what was happening have been possible in a socialist state? The nearer Joe got to the ministry, the more of a socialist he became. He sent us additional pamphlets and circulars. In California, there was talk of giving everyone over sixty years old sixty dollars a month. The recipient would then be required to stop work and an unemployed young man would take the older man's job and receive his former salary. Ebon, already half a socialist, couldn't swallow this. "Giving money away for nothing," he said. "It will bankrupt the country."

We read *Main Street*. (This was a far cry from Lon's days with Shakespeare and the Bible.) Even Wanda enjoyed *Main Street*, and wished she had been named Carol instead of Wanda. Today, a child like Wanda would bring home from school a little booklet entitled *How to Live with Your Gifted Child*. In the thirties that terminology had not yet been invented. I.Q.'s were being determined in some parts of the country; not in the little town of Amesville. Wanda's classification with us was "quick," "bright," and sometimes "too smart for her own good." She remained Kickapoo in looks: dark, chunky, broad-faced. She didn't, insofar as anyone knew, have a drop of Indian blood in her veins, but in addition to her looks she had characteristics that were thought of as typical of Indians: she was calm, did not complain about small hurts; undertook and completed tasks most children would have whined about or run away from. She spoke up at our study sessions like a chief at a powwow; far from tongue-tied, but not garrulous, either.

I saw Tom more often than ever. Jake was like a man over whose wounds scar tissue, tougher and more protective than natural skin, had formed. I slept with Jake every night. I spoke no wounding words of the kind Rosa had used. He did not notice—or if he noticed, thought nothing of—my jaunts with Tom. Today, an analyst might speculate that if I really was, with my bun and my sensible schoolmarm lingo, Jake's mother to him, and with whom for decency's sake he was quickly incestuous, he was also too loyal to believe that his mother could care for any other boy as much as she did for her own dear little Jacob.

On my thirtieth birthday, Tom and I went to Clifty Falls, the Niagara of our part of the woods. What hidden sexual symbolism lies in a rush of falling water, I don't know.

At the falls, Tom said, "I am going for once in my life to spend an entire night in bed with you. Nothing makeshift. Our bed. A bed I've bought and paid for. I'm going to go to sleep with you and and I'm going to wake up with you."

"Jake may or may not be home tonight. You know that."

"It doesn't make any difference. Jake is gun-shy. No woman again is going to hurt him. I'll call Wanda and tell her the car's broken down, that we'll be home as soon as it's fixed."

"I don't like to lie to Wanda."

"Oh, Orpha, Wanda's whole life's been built on a lie. You going to start telling her you ain't her mother?"

"I don't like leaving her alone."

"Well, you've got to make your choice. Tonight, it's me or Wanda."

That night, it was Tom.

Tom was right. Jake did come home and received the message Tom gave Wanda. But when we pulled in next morning, his interest was in the mishap to the car, not in where we had spent the night.

After Tom left, he said to Wanda, "You go out and play for a while, Sis. I want to talk to your mother." As soon as Wanda was out of earshot, he said, "Sit down. Sit down. I have something to say to you."

We were in the kitchen. I sat. This was something I had long expected. The pain I felt was for Jake. The skin over his face was very tight. The openings for his eyes and mouth were so narrow, I wondered that he could see or speak. I almost blurted out, "I will never see Tom again." I meant it. I was thirty years old, no longer a girl. Jake had protected me as a teacher, treated Wanda like a daughter, and given me a home. Tom would find another woman, and I would settle down to be what I had planned to be when I married Jake: a woman guided by her good sense, not her feelings.

Before I said a word, Jake held out for my inspection two notebooks, two of my books of Unspoken Thoughts.

"So these are your unspoken thoughts, Orpha? You wrote in these books thoughts no good wife should ever have."

"Everybody has bad thoughts sometimes. I put these in writing and got them out of my mind. It was like burying them."

"Writing down your thoughts is not like burying them, Orpha. It is like preserving them. You know that as well as I do. You got them out of *your* head by putting them on paper. But by doing that, you put them where anyone who can read can get them in *his* head. They're in my head now. They cut me to the quick, Orpha. My little schoolmarm I worked to help. I thought I might read in your notebooks some appreciation of our early days. I was lonesome last night—"

"I am sorry I was away. I promise you—"

"Don't be upset about last night. Breakdowns will happen to the best of cars. Just be thankful you were with a friend of mine. All I ask of you now is that you do for me what you did for yourself. You buried those thoughts from yourself by writing them down. Bury them for me by burning these books. I've kept the fire going for just that purpose. When I see those pages burning, your words will go out of my mind, too."

Jake handed the books to me. He took the lid off the kitchen stove. There was a thick bed of coals with an occasional small burst of live flame.

I could not put my books in there. They were me. It was like asking me to throw my living brain into the fire, my beating heart, my hand that wrote the words. It was like asking me to die.

"You do it if you want to, Jake. If you don't like those words around, you burn them." I held the books toward him.

"No, no. That's not the same at all. They're your thoughts. I can't destroy them. You must do it. When you do, I'll know you have taken them from your mind. I'll forget them then, too."

How was I able to resist him? Knowing what he'd already been through, knowing what was in those books? I don't know how; but I could not burn those books any more than I could put my hand in the fire. Less easily. What I had thought was more a part of me than my flesh. They *were* me. Flesh was only what covered me.

Jake stood. I sat. The books remained in my lap. I was paralyzed. I could neither move nor speak. I watched the coals die out. I watched the life go out of Jake's taut face.

Jake said, "I am going upstairs and pack a suitcase. I will move into my house in Cincinnati. When you let me know that you have burned those books, I'll be back. But not until then."

I never burned those books and Jake never came back.

10

Joey, when I wrote him that Jake had left me, replied, "Come to California. I need a housekeeper. I've joined the Society of Friends and with God's help will soon be recorded as a minister of that Society. I'm sorry about you and Jake. That's his loss. I hope it's my gain. I need a housekeeper."

After Jake left, I no longer saw Tom as often as I had. Tom didn't understand my reason for doing so—and I didn't understand them very well myself. I hadn't written my Unspoken Thoughts in order to drive Jake away. If I began seeing Tom regularly, it would seem so. To whom? To me. So what? The "what" was that my Unspoken Thoughts would no longer be pure, my heart reflected in a mirror of paper. Impure, something devised as a club to drive Jake away.

Did I stop seeing Tom because I could no longer hurt Jake by doing so? I talked to Tom about it in the few times I saw him before I left for California.

"It beats me," Tom said, "why, when you had to sneak off like a chicken thief to be with me, you were willing to do so. Now, with Jake gone, no sneaking necessary, you treat me like a man selling Watkins products. Polite, but not having any."

"I don't understand it, either, Tom. With Jake here keeping his eye on us, it seemed fair. With Jake gone, I feel like I'm taking advantage of him."

"My God. What kind of reasoning is that? Sounds like what you loved wasn't me, but risk. Adventure. Putting something over on somebody."

"Could it be I loved both?"

"Well, God help you if that's true. How did Jake get hold of those books, anyway?"

"I hid them under the kitchen table in the place where the leaves go."

"I can think of about a thousand places more secure than that."

"Jake never pulled that table open before in his life."

"What was he doing it for when you were gone?"

"He was going to polish the whole thing, leaves and all, for a church supper."

"Could I see them?"

"If you want to. There's nothing in them to hurt you."

Tom read without saying anything, except "They don't sound like you."

"They sound like me writing."

"Hi," he said. "I hope this is me. *'His physical presence—not saying a word, silent as a star, more silent than the wind—gives me pleasure.'* That's not Jake, is it?"

"That's you."

" *'Loneliness is the suicide you commit each morning.'* What the hell does that mean?"

"I don't know."

" *'For years as a faithful wife, she had compared him to his great disadvantage with men of her imagination. This he had not resented. Then, when unfaithful, she compared him with real men to his advantage, he was sick with resentment.'* This me, Orpha?"

"You know it isn't."

"Someone else?"

"No one. That's just writing—when I didn't really have anything to say, but wanted to write."

209

"Orpha, you are crazy. I don't know how Jake stood it as long as he did."

"How about you?"

"Yeh, that's true. How about me. Is this me? *'It was the dream behind his face I loved.'*"

"No. Lon."

Tom threw boths books down. "Why wouldn't he burn them? I sure as hell would've."

"If he burned them, it didn't mean I was sorry."

"Are you?"

"I'm sorry Jake saw them. If I was sorry I wrote them, I'd have to wish I was someone else."

I went over to Tom and put my arms around his neck.

"Remember, I'm the Watkins man."

"Tom, you and Joey and Papa and Lon, when he was alive, are the only men I love."

"Why did you marry Jake?"

"I was trying to be sensible."

"I'd give that up in the future if I was you, Orpha. It ain't your style."

11

Being sensible was still my ambition, though. What was the sensible thing to do about going to California? Papa and Mama said, "Go." What would I use for money? To get there and after I'd arrived? Farms couldn't be sold—or even given away. Ebon could sell enough and barter enough off Lon's farm to support himself and keep me in pocket money. But raise enough money for a trip west? It couldn't be done. Papa and Mama, who wanted me to be with Joe, both for his and my own sake, were as hard hit in their nursery business as everyone else. Getting another teaching job might not be possible. The cry during the Depression was for women to stay home and let the men have the paying jobs.

Then Tom came with a letter from Jake.

When Tom handed it to me, I said, "Why didn't Jake mail it?"

"He wanted me to talk to you about what he has to say."

"You know what's in it?"

"Jake told me."

"Don't you feel uncomfortable talking to Jake about me? With him so ignorant?"

"I'd feel a damned sight more uncomfortable if he wasn't. Read your letter."

When I read it, I said, "What does this mean?"

"It could mean Jake loves you."

"You think he does?"

"No. Jake wants to love himself more than he does. You wrote that rotten stuff about him—"

"I didn't mention Jake."

"Well, it wasn't exactly a recommendation. Now, if he offers the woman that wrote that stuff five hundred dollars and a farm, he's turning the other cheek. He's saying, 'The woman was a bitch, but I forgive her.' "

"Jake doesn't use words like that."

"He's probably got some unspoken thoughts, too. Using whatever words he would use and telling himself, 'I'm not takin, it out on her. She was mean-spirited and I'm big-hearted.' And he pats himself on the back."

"You talk like you know Jake pretty well."

"I do. I know Shaughnessey, and Shaughnessey married Jake's first wife. This is nothing new with Jake. He puts out money and buys himself forgiveness in his own eyes."

"If you were me, would you take it?"

"Sure, I'd take it. Do Jake good and do you no harm."

"What can I do with another farm?"

"Right now, not much. Let Ebon get out of it what he can."

"What'll I do with the five hundred?"

"You already decided that."

"You don't care?"

"Sure, I care. But if you're not going to see me anyway, I'd rather you'd be in California than Amesville."

"If you were me, would you go?"

"I sure would. One husband a suicide. One husband run off. California or Australia, I'd put some distance between me and Amesville. You're bad news around here. I've got to wondering if I'm to be the next casualty myself."

"You don't really wonder that!"

211

"If I was smart, I would."

"You wouldn't ever marry me, would you?"

"No, I never would, Orpha."

12

Everyone wanted me to leave. Parents, brother, husband, lover, tenant farmer, and especially Wanda. California was the Land of Oz to her, the Emerald City. Papa Jake vanished from her life as if he had never been. Uncle Joey, the preacher-to-be, the handsome traveler, the French-harp player, waited. Oranges and lemons, roses in winter, waited. And the biggest ocean of all, crashing around the edges of that western land, waited.

Still I dawdled. Nothing to keep me, Joe waiting, parents urging, I lingered. I was not willing to try anything new. I lived in the big house like the occupant of a shell that has by some chance had all the irritating sand swept away. Wanda came home from school with *Five Little Peppers and How They Grew,* and I read it with her. I wrote more frequently in my Unspoken Thoughts, not to hide what I thought from Jake, but because I had no one to talk to. The study sessions had stopped. Ebon and Nettie had reached the point where Wanda and I were a hindrance to what they were learning. Once at dusk I thought I saw Jake's face at the kitchen window. I ran out, but there was no one there.

In my Unspoken Thoughts, I wrote, *In the empty bed, the memory of sharp limbs and a penetrating twig is stronger than absence.*

13

"It's the Watkins man again," Tom said.

"What're you selling today, Tom?"

"I'm giving, not selling, today."

Tom was born cheerful. His inside climate affected him more than what was outside. He had a wife who wouldn't sleep with him, a second woman who said she loved him but was going off to California, four stepladder children, a tedious job shoving feet into shoes, and still he was beaming.

212

"Hey," he said, "you still having unspoken thoughts?"

"None from you, Tom."

He picked up the latest notebook and read aloud.

" 'It was as natural as yawning and as hard to hold back. He was a rascal, it was plain to see, and took about the same pride in what he was doing as an Indian in scalping.' That me?"

"You're a rascal, aren't you?"

"Sure. And you're my boss's wife, ain't you? That makes us both rascals."

"And neither of us started out to be."

"Did we hurt anyone? Not Nora. Nor that shitepoke, your husband."

"Ourselves, maybe?"

"Nope. I don't buy that, either. Look at your present, why don't you?"

The present was in an envelope I hesitated to open.

"O.K. I'll do it for you. Two one-way tickets: Cincinnati to Los Angeles, leaving November 11, Pullman berth included. That's the only way you're ever going to get started. You'll mope around here until you've spent your five hundred: you'll get soft-hearted, burn your books, tell Jake to come home, and, for lack of any juice in your life, you and me'll be sneaking off together again."

"Where'd you get the money, Tom?"

"I didn't rob any bank."

"I'll pay you back out of the five hundred."

"That won't be necessary."

"The eleventh. That's only ten days away."

"That's enough time to pack, ain't it?"

"You really want to get rid of me, don't you?"

"You've already left me, Orpha. I'd rather think of you in California than here."

14

Nothing is so dear as what you're about to leave. I had never had California fever. I liked snow and wind and thunderstorms. I hadn't longed to go where it was always summer, where oranges and lemons and apricots grew instead of apples and pears and cherries. We weren't dust-bowl country. We weren't blowing away. Crops weren't

213

bringing the money they once had, but California was no exception. Joe wrote that they were burning oranges in California to keep from flooding the market.

I spent that last ten days like someone under a death sentence: someone saying good-bye to life. I went to the Dudley farm, of course. I touched the table where Lon and I had studied, the bed where we had slept, the stone that marked the place where Lon's bones lay. I sat on the front porch, where I was still able to see— or perhaps only imagine—the faded spot from which Lon's blood had been scrubbed. There the last of the living Lon had spilled, there he had spoken his last words.

Ebon came to talk to me about the furnishings I wanted shipped on to California, including the swinging lamp.

"Everyone in California has electricity," said Ebon.

"I want it for its looks. The grafting table, too. Don't tell me no one in California grafts. You know why I want it."

"I know."

"Can you run two farms?"

"Nettie'll help."

"She'll run you, too, if you don't watch out."

"I'm willing."

"You won't be another Lon with her?"

"That's all gone, long ago. It was gone the night you married Jake. Couldn't you tell?"

"It wasn't a good time for me to notice anything like that."

Ebon left me alone on the porch. He knew why I was there.

Tickets for November 11 must surely have been by chance? Who knew and remembered that date? How many years ago? Ten? I put my palms on the porch floorboards where Lon's blood had fallen. Farewell to Lon, farewell to youth.

IX
JOE

1

"I'll miss you," Mama said at the station, "but it will be a happy lonesome. You'll be with Joe and you'll be away from here."

The whistle you hear in the train that is bearing you away has not the sad sound of the whistle you hear as you lie in your bed at home. In your bed that whistle says, "Farewell, far away, gone forever." In your bed on the train, it says, "Here we come, here we come."

We boarded the train laden, even though the bulk of our belongings was in the baggage car: two trunks and Pussy in a box with cat-sized portholes. Mama had packed two baskets of food. That food lasted until we reached New Mexico. The prices in the dining car made me willing to fast. I would no more have entered the club car than I would have gone into a saloon. We were traveling coach, there was no air conditioning, and soot blew in the open windows.

At night from our berth we watched the East become the West. We kept the curtains open and saw movies enacted just for us. At one stop, a cat came calmly out of the station and waited until she was given an expected handout by the brakeman. A soldier home from some war (where were we fighting in 1932?) was hugged to death by a large family. A lone man put a wreath on a coffin before it was loaded into a baggage car. We spent four hours in the station in Chicago. At midnight, perhaps in Missouri, a bride and groom were showered with rice by their friends and were so taken up with saying farewell to a crying mother, they almost missed the train. The conductor yanked them up the steps just in time. In New Mexico at a whistle stop I bought us a Mexican flapjack called a "tortilla" and for Wanda a beaded Indian headband.

"When we get to California," she said, "I'll find an eagle feather to put in it and be a real Indian."

"You're already a Kickapoo."

"What's a Kickapoo?"

"Mama's papoose."

On the last night we were determined to sleep so we'd be fresh for Joe and California. We didn't sleep. The great white snow peaks reared up as sleep-disturbing as a shout.

"It's like the ground trying to hit us," said Wanda.

"It's the world trying to push people off."

"Is it California yet?"

"Not till tomorrow."

"Will Uncle Joe meet us?"

"He said he'd be there with bells on."

2

He was there, though when he saw us, I think he didn't feel like ringing any bells. It was one of those late November days when the temperature in Los Angeles reaches ninety and a Santa Ana wind has taken every bit of moisture out of the air.

Joe was in his shirt sleeves. So was everyone else, except for women who were in sleeveless dresses. To me they looked like people who had heard a fire siren and had rushed outside without bothering to put on street clothes.

Wanda and I were dressed for travel, winter travel: wool dresses, heavy wool coats, gloves, and cloches—fashionable then, though ours were bought for warmth, not fashion, since they could be pulled down over the ears.

What was wrong with me? I had Joe's word that California was the land of eternal summer. Did I think it was a myth? So there we were, Joe's relatives from back east, looking like Eskimos, Eskimos with two battered trunks, two lunch baskets, and a squalling cat.

If he was taken aback at our appearance, he didn't show it: hugs and kisses for everybody but the cat.

"Orpha, I told you you'd be in California someday, didn't I? Hello, Wanda. Hello, cat. Take off your coats, everybody, or you'll melt before I get a good look at you. Not you, cat; you'll just have to sweat it out."

If Joe hadn't known us, I might not have recognized him at first sight. In the days of his fever and sickness, Joe had been a slab-sides, his bones so visible you expected to hear them clank as he walked.

A person who loses weight appears to have become more than usually visible. Weight gained is a disguise.

Joe wasn't fat. But he was no longer a thin black-haired rakehell with a consumptive's burning cheeks. He had gone from 135 to 175 pounds, his skin was brown, and his expression was as loving as his words. I had grown accustomed to taking everything with a grain of salt, to expecting nothing and not being disappointed. Here was Joe, who said God had cured him, and something surely had; who said it was eternal summer in California, and if this wasn't summer, it was a furnace; who said he wanted to preach love, and if he could preach love as well as he was practicing it with us, he would be eloquent.

Joe had a little truck he called a "pickup," which easily held all our paraphernalia in the back and the three of us plus Pussy in the front seat.

"Will your cat stay in your arms if you take it out of its cage?"

"Oh, yes," said Wanda, who had been on her knees talking through the portholes to Pussy.

"Better be sure. Once she starts running in this town, she's gone forever. Cat hamburger in two minutes, likely."

Wanda was right. Poor Pussy clung to her like a baby raccoon to its mother. The three of us—four, counting the cat—sat in the front seat jammed tight and sweating. We headed north along what is now Sepulveda. Once outside the city, Joe pulled off the road. "Have a look at the land you have come to," he said. "Land," he called it, not state or county or city.

It had once been that, a land with a flag of its own, a government of its own. It was plain old U.S.A. now, but the mountains and sea hadn't changed since Pio Pico or Bear Flag days. There was no smog in 1932, and because the Santa Ana had been blowing, the air was unusually transparent. To our right were the mountains, to the left the sea. The mountains, in spite of the heat in the valley, already wore their wintertime topping of snow. They were not menacing like those sky-bangers we had seen in the night. They had been devised not to threaten people but as a picturesque background for a palm-tree city. They were stately *and* pretty, like lacy white crocheting around a flat tablecloth. Joe named each peak for us, beginning with the smallest: Lowe, with its observatory; Wilson, with its mountain homes; Baldy, barren and glistening, a mountain's mountain. Wanda and I stared and stared. In the East the earth had its ups and downs. Now here above desert heat snow and only an hour's drive away. "We could bring a truckload of it home in a couple of hours," Joe said.

"Let's go," said Wanda.

"Snow is for mountains, heat is for valleys," said Joe.

"Let's mix them up," said Wanda.

"They won't mix," Joe told her. "They've got it in for each other."

Far, far to the east floated a dreamlike shape, another mountain, Joe said. We had to take his word for it. It was scarcely visible. Between eyeblinks it disappeared. The Spanish had named it for a saint, and that, like many things Spanish, had endured the waves of English-speaking invaders.

South was the Pacific. At sundown it was a stretch of glitter. Catalina rode it like a long gray tanker.

Joe gave us all these peaks, the snow, and the sea like personal gifts from Joseph Chase, Californian, to two poor benighted Easterners. "That's enough time for rubbernecking," he said, and headed his pickup into the San Fernando Valley, where he lived. The valley was one big orchard: peaches and apricots and English walnuts; though walnuts grow in groves, not in orchards, as do olives and oranges. Dates, however, grow in gardens, in neither groves nor orchards.

From that very first night, the California landscape began to speak to me. Perhaps it was because it was Joey's home. Perhaps it had been calling to me for a long time, the way the ocean calls to a prairie boy who, after twenty years, makes his way to the sea and ships, hunting, though he doesn't know it, the thunder of waves he has never seen.

3

We reached Joe's at the beginning of Southern California's short twilight. Joe called his home a bungalow. Back east we would have called it a shack, it was put together with so little regard for weather-proofing. Stained redwood, with a big screened porch for sleeping on summer nights, it didn't look bad.

The house was set in the back yard of a peach grower's place. It had been built for a Japanese couple who worked for the Stand-fields when the Standfield children were young. Standfield, a con-scientious Quaker, gave the place to Joe rent-free in return for a little yard work. Joe, at that time, was finishing his studies at Valencia Park before being recorded as a minister in the Religious Society of Friends.

Perhaps my feeling for trees is the same as my feeling for people. I love individuals but hate crowds. At the back of Joe's bungalow was a pepper tree almost as big as the house itself. A pepper tree is a mass of lacy paper-whispering leaves decorated with clumps of red berries. It is a year-round Christmas tree, more inviting than an evergreen from a dark northen forest. I loved that tree, its look, its sound, and its usefulness. There was a platform in it, built, I sup-pose, for the Standfield children. The platform was large and secure enough to hold me. I often sat on it, feeling like a lace-curtain Irishwoman gazing out through the whispering leaves.

On the evening of our arrival Wanda was up and on it before we got into the house. Food brought her down, and, once fed, her eyes closed. After that the talk started.

Now I reach the troublesome part of this story. I've already written part of it disguised as fiction. It was my first piece of published writing. All names were changed; though Joe, on account of the publicity he had received, was immediately recognized. I wasn't in that story; there was nothing in that novel about the arrival of an Eastern sister or of Joe's life in the Standfields' gardener's cottage. So I am not now duplicating any part of my earlier book. I have not opened that early novel for twenty-five years. Thus, episodes now forty years old will, with the changed perspective time gives, constitute, I hope, an entirely different story. I gave that novel as a title the hero's name *Talbot Ware.*

On my first evening in California, Talbot was not yet dreamed of; I was not yet a writer; Joe was not yet a preacher, except as an unrecorded assistant to a minister of the largest Quaker Meeting in California. That night we were just brother and sister reunited after long separation and with much to talk about; so much, the talk took all night.

I probably would not remember that room at all except that it was so strange to me, a combination of Japanese and early California.

The California touch was the portiere of eucalyptus cups between dining and sitting rooms. There were many such in early California. I doubt that any could now be found except in a museum. The Oriental reminders are still common, wares that can be bought in San Francisco and Los Angeles: a grass rug, teacups without handles, silk hangings embroidered with herons and iris, that fat big-bellied god of good fortune.

A breeze off the ocean stirred the glass pendants of a Japanese wind chime. The Santa Ana had died down, and cool damp air had changed burning desert to cool coastland.

Joe and I sat in wicker rockers pulled close together so that we could hold hands. It was sweet to have my hand held by someone I loved and not feel guilty about it.

Our first talk of course was of Papa and Mama: "Are they well? How hard hit are they by the Depression? What do they think of my change of churches?"

What they thought was what I thought. Why? Born a United Brethren. Become a Presbyterian because of the man whose faith saved his life; that I could understand. But why a Quaker? What I knew of them was next to nothing. Queer people, akin to Shakers or Mennonites, using a locution of their own, wearing clothes unlike those of others, refusing to fight, drink, smoke, hang pictures on their walls, or listen to music. I looked at Joe, this big brown man, one-time invalid, poisoner of a dog-poisoner, girl-chaser.

"Why, Joe?"

"Because I love God."

I didn't yet know it, but Joe could talk about his love of God with less inhibition than most men can talk about their love for their wives. There is an obvious explanation: Joe loved God more than most men love their wives and he was also a better talker than most men, Lon excepted.

"Didn't you love God when you were a United Brethren? Or a Presbyterian?"

"Of course I did. But more things got in the way of pure love there."

"Like what?"

"Getting baptized. Getting confirmed. Loving when the government said to; killing when the government said to."

I understood "killing when the government said to." That was war. What was "loving" on the government's say-so? It was marriage, according to Joe.

"Marriage isn't the government's business or the church's, either."

"Not the church's? How could you get married without a church?"

"All it takes for a marriage is a man, a woman, and God. That's all a church is, anyway. Men and women representing God."

"No women preachers."

"Quakers have them. The Quakers marry when a man and a woman in the sight of God and some relatives, if they want to invite them, say to each other, 'I, Mary, take thee, John.' "

"Is that the way you're going to get married?"

"I won't be getting married."

"You sound like a priest."

"The Catholics have some good ideas. Not getting married if you are going to be a preacher is one of them."

"Paul said, 'It is better to marry than to burn.' "

"Lon taught you a lot, didn't he? Well, I'm not burning. And Paul ought to have known from experience that true God-love doesn't leave room for woman-love. One's a little bonfire, the other's a great sun-blaze."

"Are you a preacher already?" I didn't tell him he sounded like it.

"I haven't been recorded yet."

"Recorded? What does that mean?"

"Churches ordain. That is, you aren't a minister till their ministers or priests certify you. Men do it, not God."

"What does the Quaker church do?"

"Quakers don't have a church. We have a Meeting House, and we're a religious society. If a Quaker feels the call of God to be a minister, the Society records the fact. It's between you and God, and all the Society does is to recognize the call and make a record of it."

"Could I be a recorded minister?"

"If God called you."

"If all a Quaker has to do is say, 'God wants me to preach,' I think you'd get some real nuts."

"We do. That's why I'm going to the Institute. A man ought at least to have studied the Bible and know something about Quakerism before he gets recorded."

"Loving God isn't enough?"

"It's the chief thing. But if a man's going to preach, he's going to talk. And a sermon can't be just love, love, love."

I'd heard sermons that were more and worse but I didn't tell Joey so. "I thought Quakers believed in silent worship."

"In California," Joey said, "they talk."

I was having unspoken thoughts again, not bad ones, not ones I needed to write down in order to rid myself of them. I thought when Joey said that, You have come to the right place.

I couldn't learn all there was to know about Joe and the Institute and Quakers and California in one night, and Joe knew it. It was after midnight when he stopped talking and said, "Say, did we have any supper?"

"I didn't. I don't know about you."

"I laid in a supply. I got to talking and forgot it."

We sat quietly for a minute or two, listening to the wind chimes and the pepper tree's papery rustle—and one other sound.

"What's that?"

"Wanda."

"She snores like a grown woman."

"Wanda," I told Joey, "is worn out with travel and excitement. I never heard her make that sound before."

"Now don't get your dander up," Joe said. "She can snore like a horse for all of me."

"A horse!"

Joe, who had been on his way to the kitchen for our forgotten supper, knelt by my chair. "Look, Sis, I've been waiting for this for years. You're worn out, too. And starved. You'll feel better when you get something in your stomach."

"What's chiefly wrong with me, Joey, is a sick headache."

"You've never outgrown them?"

"I've just grown them bigger and better."

"What happened to you and Jake hasn't helped."

"What happened was good for headaches. A pain in the head helps me forget."

Joe took my hand. "Sis, have you asked God for help?"

"I wouldn't bother Him with a headache."

"Do you like to have headaches?"

"If you ever had one of these, you wouldn't ask that."

"Do you think God wants you to suffer?"

"He can stop it any time He wants to."

224

"Don't talk that way, Orpha."

"Well, He can, can't He?"

"Maybe He has, thousands of times. This time, have the grace to ask Him."

I didn't think He would. I didn't want to undermine Joe's faith by my failure.

Joe said, "I have faith if you don't. If I ask God to take away your pain, He will. Close your eyes."

Joe put his hand on my forehead. I closed my eyes for a second, then opened them. Joe's eyes were closed and he was speaking, though not in words I could hear or to any God in a heaven in the sky. He was speaking to someone close to him, someone toward whom he lifted his radiant face. He saw with eyes closed what I couldn't see with eyes open.

What I saw in Joe's face took my mind completely away from the pain in my head. Nor did Joe ask about it when he opened his eyes; nor did I speak of it. It was not only gone, it was also forgotten.

For a minute or two after he stood, Joe was like a man awake but still remembering a happy dream.

Then he said, "I've got something for you to eat I bet you never tasted before. Salami."

"Never even heard of it. What is it?"

"Wait and see."

4

Joe had written me that he didn't want a wife but did need a housekeeper. No woman with sense would have been willing to marry Joe. He was good, he was loving, he was witty; but he wasn't there, as a husband. A woman for him was just a part of God's world. I can report accurately what Joe did; I can report only what I think he thought. The saints, and I think Joe was one, live in their acts, not in another's words.

As to needing a housekeeper, Joe was absolutely right. He had given up eating cooked meals. He had given up changing the sheets regularly. He washed dishes once a week. Slicing salami and cheese didn't involve pots and pans or even a serving dish. A week's accumulation of dirty dishes was meager. Joe swept when he felt the need of exercise. Litter so thick he stumbled over it did cause him

225

to take the grass rugs out and shake them. His life as a householder was perfectly adjusted to his overwhelming preoccupation. God had lifted him above dust, above taking the eyes out of potatoes before boiling them or of seeing that magazines were stacked.

Clutter probably never hurt anyone, and Joe's diet obviously agreed with him. To his staples of cheese and ready-cooked meats, he added California fruits and nuts. He drank goat milk because someone had given him a goat and she had to be milked. He bought whatever looked appealing and didn't have to be cooked and cost little.

I couldn't change overnight to a diet of Monterey Jack and alligator pears; though Joe told me that in Biblical times holy men had lived in perfect health on a diet of locusts and honey. For Wanda's sake and mine, I served cooked meals. Joe ate hush puppies, dried beef gravy, and soda biscuits with complete calmness. I even tried a puffle on him. From any comment he made, it might have been a locust leg, and possibly was no better.

5

I was busy until Christmastime getting Wanda started to school and trying to fit my Eastern belongings into Joe's house of straw matting and embroidered herons. They did not fit. It was like putting a mouse in a spider web. Only the books looked at home with each other. I had about fifty, most of them chosen and bought by Lon. Joe had at least two hundred, many selected to meet the needs of groups who met at his home: Mexicans learning to speak English; Quakers filling their tanks (in Joe's words) with fuel to keep their Inner Lights burning; pedants wanting more knowledge; admirers of Joe wanting nothing but to be with him as often as possible.

I have called Joe a saint. The term depends, of course, on your view of the meaning of sanctity. I think that it takes more than goodness to make a saint. First of all, a saint has a closer relationship with God than other men. God speaks to him in words the saint can hear and can report to others. The saint is holy because he is in direct touch with holiness. He is lovely because he knows

God, who is Love. Because the saint is at one with God, God's power is in him and he is God's willing instrument. Many saints have died rather than forswear God. I do not call Joe a saint without knowing all of this. Family vanity or personal love play no part in my belief. I have read the lives of Saint Joan, Saint Anthony, Saint Theresa, Saint Thomas More, and many others. I may be wrong, but I am not unknowing.

By Christmas the settling-in was complete. I had made clothes for me and Wanda that suited the California climate, which was, compared with any weather I had known, neither summer nor winter.

Christmas itself was no chore. I use that word on purpose because I think it has become so for many people today. In the home of Joseph Chase, Quaker, Christmas was scarcely noticeable. Joe believed that the celebration of Christ on any particular day, especially on a date as uncertain as that of His birth, encouraged people to forget Him on other days. Christ was for every minute of every life. Sundays, Christmases, Easters, were devices used to justify forgetfulness of Christ on other days. So in Joe's house, there was no Christmas tree, no gifts, no special Christmas "cheer."

I was not then and have never become a Quaker. Not because I believe that the United Brethren have chosen a better religious way than the Friends. I am a United Brethren because I was born and brought up a United Brethren. If I had been brought up a cannibal, I would probably still be one, unless they themselves had expelled me as unworthy. As I have said, I can be left, and have been, but leave I cannot. So my first Christmas in California was after the Quaker fashion, not because of personal conviction, but out of respect for Joe's beliefs.

There were two lapses from Quakerly practice, only one of which Joe knew about. I didn't tell Joe that on Christmas Eve I had filled a stocking of Wanda's with candy: gumdrops, jellybeans, peppermint lozenges. I didn't think Wanda would be a better Christian if she received no candy on Christmas Eve.

My other lapse was perfectly open. I cooked a real Christmas dinner. Not a single item was raw, precooked, or workaday. Joe had invited his Mexican class, or at least the six most faithful members, to have Christmas dinner with us. The festive touch was obvious in what was on the table: roast turkey, candied yams, a plum pudding steamed in punctured Hills Brothers coffee cans. A man who thinks he can digest grasshoppers isn't impressed by turkey, however brown and tasty. He isn't repulsed by it, either. Joe ate his fair share of all. The turkey was paid for by me—and that meant paid for out of Jake's five hundred dollars. Where was Jake having his Christmas dinner? I didn't wish him with us. I did, while Joe returned silent thanks, thank God that I was where I was. And I did pray for Jake's well-being.

6

Joe hoped to be recorded as a minister sometime after the first of the year. I visited some of the classes at the Valencia Park Training School myself. Visited, but did not enroll; I had no intention of studying to become a preacher or a missionary. Since I had difficulty in making changes in my own life, I knew that I was not fitted to tell other people how to change theirs. Joe didn't have that trouble. He had changed himself and for the better. So he had not only the right, but also the duty as a follower of God, who had said, "I will bring the blind by a way they know not. I will make darkness light before them, and crooked things straight."

I heard many returned missionaries speak. The Training School was proud of the number of its former students who were now in Guatemala, China, Cuba, Alaska, bringing the gospel to natives. My memory of the report of the husband and wife home from Alaska no doubt tells more about me than about Valencia Park missionaries. This couple's greatest accomplishment, in their own eyes, lay in their persuading the Eskimos they ministered to to give up reindeer-racing. Or was it elk? The racing, whatever the animal, was evil, because the Eskimos bet on the outcome. At the end of the report by this earnest man and his wife, I felt very sorry for the Eskimos. In my opinion, they would soon find another reason for betting. It was also my belief that a Christian training school should prepare its students for more important work than the separation, during the long Arctic nights, of elk and Eskimo.

For the most part, until the first of the year, I watched the weather change. I had believed with other newcomers from the East that California had no seasons. It was the land of eternal summer; summer may be nice, but an unending summer would be monotonous. Back east we had fall when the leaves change color. Then we had winter—icicles, white snow, and glare-ice. Finally, but very slowly, color again, rising temperatures, and thunderstorms.

In California, rain rings in the seasonal change. Wanda and I had arrived in the midst of a November heat wave; there was a wind that carried sand; you could fry an egg on the sidewalk, or the hood of your car. Then, one night, I don't know whether it was the sound or the smell that awakened me. It was raining! A drumming on the cedar shingles; the smell of a thirsty land drinking. The rainy season had come! In California, there aren't year-long showers and driblets, with occasional cloudbursts. Just the four-month lowering of a crystal curtain of raindrops. And afterward, really during, more colors than Eastern woods lots ever show. The brown foothills turn green. No autumn leaf has as many colors as has a field of lupine, mariposa lilies, mustard, Indian paintbrush, yellow violets, California poppies. Compare the slope of a foothill ablaze with the colors of these flowers with the dying-leaf color of a woods lot. No season? No colors?

I was doing nothing but watch the rain fall, the way I might have watched snow eddies back east, when the President of the Valencia Park Training School, the Reverend J. Purvis Ellsworth, came to call. Wanda was at school. Joe was off in Woolman, where, as assistant to the pastor, he had charge of the young people's meetings.

I asked the Reverend Ellsworth in. He was standing in the rain; like other Californians, he didn't seem to mind it. No galoshes, no umbrella, no raincoat; soaked but happy. The ritual of baptism must have been born in a dry land. Rain in a dry country means life. Baptism, man-made rain, means life everlasting. Quakerism, with its disregard for baptism, got its start in rainy England, where water is nothing but a nuisance.

The Reverend Ellsworth came in and stood, dripping. I got him away from the grass rug. After he had dried off a little, he sat.

J. Purvis Ellsworth did not look like a Quaker; or a preacher of any denomination whatsoever. He was large, slab-sided, red-haired. I had heard him preach and knew that he could do that as well as any milder, smoother-looking man. Better. Accustomed as I was to thinking of Quakers as silent, the Reverend Ellsworth had been a shock. He didn't leap onto the pulpit like a Billy Sunday or wear eye-catching costumes like Aimee. He looked and talked like what he was: an oil driller who had found Jesus Christ and wanted to take the good news of that discovery to the world. He wasn't Joe's equal as a preacher. He had had no education. He was capable of persuading but he couldn't charm. Certainly no one slept while J. Purvis Ellsworth preached. His phrasing was sometimes peculiar. He had been born in Texas; he spoke in a loud ringing heartfelt way. In the Bible, God spoke out of a burning bush. In the pulpit J. Purvis Ellsworth was, with his crest of flaming red hair, the burning bush itself. George Fox, who was himself a bit of a ranter, wouldn't have taken the Reverend Ellsworth's preaching amiss.

"Joe is at Woolman," I said.

"I know that," the Reverend Ellsworth told me. "I've seen you at Meeting. I thought I'd stop by and have a little chat with you. Myrtle would've come, but five kids don't leave her much time for visiting. You're a United Brethren, Joe tells me."

"I am, Reverend Ellsworth."

"Don't call me that. Friends don't take any stock in titles. Not even Mister and Missus. You're Orpha Hesse to me, and I'm Purvis Ellsworth. As a matter of fact, what's the point of the double-barreled handles? If you say Purvis, I'll know who you're talking to. And Orpha ought to do the same for you. Now, I'm not here to talk down the United Brethren. They're fine people. Won't fight any more than we will. Believe in sanctification, the same as we do."

Saying "Purvis" instead of "Reverend Ellsworth" made me gulp a little, but I did it. "Purvis, I've been a United Brethren all my life, but I never have really understood what sanctification means."

Purvis told me about sanctification—and a lot more besides. At the Training School, he said, they preached the "Four-fold Gospel": Salvation, Sanctification, Healing by Faith, and the Second Coming of Christ. Sanctification was being "twice born." The first birth was when you were converted. Then, through the grace of God, you were "sanctified," so faith-filled that sin was no longer possible.

"Is that what sanctified means? Unable to sin?"

"Yes."

"Can't you sin?"

"No. All evil in me, all tendency to evil, was taken from me and nailed to the cross."

"How do you know this is true? Have you ever tried to sin? Maybe you could if you tried."

"Orpha, Orpha, that's flighty. I'm glad Brother Joe can't hear you. After the second birth, you are God-filled. Can you imagine God wanting to try to sin?"

"It's probably sinful even to try to imagine such a thing."

The Reverend Ellsworth nodded. "Now do you understand sanctification, Orpha?"

"How do you know when you're sanctified?"

"Wouldn't you know if God completely filled your heart so that all knowledge of past sin left your heart and—"

"Yes, if that happened, I would know it."

"And if all temptation to sin again was crucified on the cross of Jesus? You'd know that, wouldn't you?"

"If that happened, I wouldn't know myself."

"You wouldn't know your old self, that's all."

"Does Joe believe all of this?"

"Certainly. He's studying to be a preacher, isn't he? No one would be recorded by the Meeting as a preacher who didn't believe in sanctification. Oh, Joe believes, all right. Now I have other calls to make. But let us pray together before I leave."

Purvis got down on his wet knees, leaned on a chair, and prayed. He did not pray in silence, as I had believed Quakers did, but vocally and at length. What he was praying for was a second birth for me. I felt that it wouldn't happen. The person I pitied was Purvis, not me. He might doubt his own sanctification if he wasn't able to bring about through prayer a second birth in me. Wanda came home from school and, bright girl that she was, knelt down by a chair and put her face in her hands.

I wanted to save the Reverend Ellsworth the effort and the disappointment of his praying. I wanted to say, "Don't pray for sanctification for me. It will never happen. I'll always be able to sin." I couldn't do it. It's rude to interrupt a speaker at any time, let alone when he's in the midst of prayer. I was quiet. Purvis prayed on. When he finished, he rose and looked at me very closely. He saw it hadn't happened. I was no more sanctified than before he had prayed. For a minute I think he wished he was back amidst the oil rigs. He put his hands on Wanda's head—she was still kneeling—and said, "God be with both of you till we meet again."

Joe was delighted when he got home to hear that we had been visited by the head of the school he was attending.

"Purvis is a fine man. He was making all kinds of money as a driller before his conversion. He kissed the money good-bye without a thought when the call came to preach. What did you talk about?"

"The Training School."

"Did he tell you he founded it?"

"No. He talked about its beliefs."

"You didn't hear anything new, did you? They're about the same as every other Meeting in Southern California."

"Do they all believe in the Four-Fold Gospel?"

"Is that what Purvis called it? I believe I am saved. I believe Christ will come again. I have to believe in faith healing. It's God's gift, and I have received it. You experienced it yourself."

"What about sanctification? Do you believe in that?"

"Sanctification isn't something you believe in. It's something you experience."

"Have you ever experienced it?"

"No. I pray for it."

"I don't understand it."

"It's not something for the head to understand. It's a soul matter. When you're saved, God forgives your past sins. When you're sanctified, you're filled with the Holy Ghost and the desire to sin leaves you."

"Purvis said that after you were sanctified, you couldn't sin. Don't you think Purvis can sin?"

"I think he might do something that people might call a 'sin'—but that God wouldn't."

"Purvis said that without the second birth and sanctification, no one could be recorded as a minister. Is that true?"

"That's true."

"In two weeks you go before the Elders to ask to be recorded. Will they ask you about sanctification?"

"Yes."

"What if it hasn't happened?"

232

"It's the result of God's grace. It can be the work of a second. It could happen while they're asking me the question."

"What if it didn't happen?"

"I'd tell the truth. It'd be a sin not to."

"Maybe you're already sanctified, Joey, and don't know it."

"Don't joke about this, Orpha. I'm not, and I want to preach. I have to. Pray for me, Sis."

7

I couldn't pray that Joe would be unable to sin; and I couldn't tell him that I couldn't. Not telling—that was a sin in itself. The next two weeks were miserable. My unhappiness could not in any way have equaled Joey's. He, who had been called by God to preach, was in danger of being denied the right to preach. Would he have to believe, as the Elders did, that a God who hadn't taken from him the ability to sin wouldn't approve him as a minister?

Joey didn't complain. He took care of all his duties as assistant to the Woolman pastor. He walked a lot. He prayed a lot. He seemed to have lost the ability to swallow food. He didn't sleep much.

I suffered for Joe. I suffered for myself. I did not believe that human beings should consider themselves incapable of sin; and I could not talk to Joe about this and perhaps make what he longed for more difficult to attain. I tried to keep life normal for Wanda. Joe did, too. He played one-a-cat with us. He tried to hide his loss of appetite from her. He kept himself from falling into overlong reveries of silent prayer at the table.

For the first time since I had been in California, I got out my Unspoken Thoughts book. I had thoughts I couldn't speak to Joe or Wanda that I wanted to get out of my mind. My Unspoken Thoughts were written as statements. Were they really questions? Or prayers? Did I write them expecting to hear a heavenly contradiction if they were untrue?

I wrote: *A man who cannot sin would need to have God's wisdom as well as God's sanctity.*

A man who believes that no act of his can be sinful can become, with a clear conscience, a second Satan.

Have the world's worst men been men who believed that their acts were not sinful?

Did Jesus himself ever say that He could not sin?

Isn't "will not" better than "cannot"?

Why not live day by day? Instead of believing that God has given you a lifetime immunity from sin, why not, with His help, resist sin, temptation by temptation?

Who knows what sin is?

8

In my book *Talbot Ware*, the novel I wrote that was based closely upon Joe's experience, what came next in his life is reported in detail. That book was centered about one person, Talbot Ware; a character representing Orpha Chase and her misadventures played no part in it. Another full account of Joey's meeting with the Board of Elders would be repetitious for readers of *Talbot Ware*.

What happened was this: the Elders—there were women as well as men on the Board—questioned Joe as to his desire to preach, his past, his present beliefs. I could have gone. I didn't. I knew the anguish Joe had experienced during the past two weeks. I knew that it would reach a peak during the inquisition (which it wasn't, of course, though that was how I thought of it). I didn't want to witness the ordeal.

The Meeting was on a Saturday afternoon in mid-January. The rain had stopped, the hills were already green. The crests of Lowe, Wilson, and Baldy glistened with snow. Joe, who had been praying instead of sleeping, thinking instead of eating, had dark circles under his eyes, and his big shoulders had taken a forward bend I had never seen before.

"Pray for me, Orpha," he said again before he left.

I did. Not the prayer that he wanted. Not "Lord, sanctify Joe and make it impossible for him to sin again." I prayed, "Lord, help Joe to do what is right." God knew what that was better than Purvis or the Elders.

Wanda, because it was Saturday, was out of school. She wandered around, aware, in the way she had, that something was wrong. A mother's first duty is to her child. I'd better trust Joe to God and pay some attention to Wanda.

"Let's play jacks, Wanda."

Wanda loved this game and so did I. She could beat me, but just barely.

"What is the matter with Uncle Joe, Mama?"

"Nothing." That was a lie, so I added, "He's worried."

"About being a preacher?"

"Being a preacher doesn't worry him. It's taking the examination beforehand."

"Doesn't he know the answers?"

"Yes."

"Then he's O.K., isn't he?"

"He's O.K."

"Mama, I have a surprise for you. Do you want to see it?"

"Can't wait."

Wanda went into her room and brought out my old long-forgotten switch. I handled it gingerly.

"I thought I left that in Amesville."

"You did. I hid it in my keepsake box."

"Why? Do you like me better when I wear it?"

"No. I thought Papa might come and you would want it."

"Papa isn't coming and I should never have worn it in the first place. It was a lie. Let's burn it."

We did. In the fireplace. It was real hair, and the smell was of a blacksmith shop where horses have had their hooves trimmed and the trimmings have been thrown in the fire. Not a pleasant smell. Hair is too near bones and flesh for that. For some reason, perhaps because of the scented hair ointment I had put on it to give it a sheen, the hair smoldered for a long time.

The scent of burning hair was still in the room when, just at dark, Joe came home.

He did not have to tell me what had happened. He was not sanctified. He could still sin. He had told the truth. He had not become a recorded minister. And he was not unhappy. He was, in fact, radiant.

"Listen, you two," he said. "I was so determined to be whatever Valencia Park and Purvis believed was right, I almost stopped trying to know God's will. It is God's will that I be a man capable of sinning, but not sinning. That is God's will for me."

"And never be able to preach?"

"No, no, I can preach. Quakers in the East don't require sanc-

235

tification. Presbyterians believe you can sin at the drop of a hat."

"Are you going to be a Presbyterian now?"

Joe went leaping around the room. "No, no. Of course not. Say, what smells so funny in here?"

"My hair."

"Did you catch on fire?"

"No. My switch."

"I didn't know you had one."

"I had one. I wore it because Jake didn't like short hair."

"What good did that do? You kept your short hair."

"I hid my bob with it. I looked long-haired. Now I am what I look like."

"Me, too. I look like a man who can sin, don't I?"

"Any minute."

"I won't. God willing, I won't."

"Not sinning isn't much of a career," I said. "A baby is capable of that."

"I told you, I told you! Didn't I? I'm going to preach. That's a career."

"Where? On a street corner like the Salvation Army?"

"That's O.K., too. But I'm not. I've got a Meeting House."

"A church?"

"Not a church, you United Brethren, you. A Meeting House. The first Quakers met out of doors or in each other's homes. I've got a Meeting House—a real house, a real place for meeting. The old one-room schoolhouse out at Ortiz. Seats still in. No pulpit, and I don't want that anyway, but the teacher's platform is still there, and a desk I can bang if I get to feeling emphatic."

"Who'll hear you bang?"

"My congregation, Sis. Not everyone believes in sanctification. McGrew, who owns the land the schoolhouse is on and the one who's loaning it, doesn't. He's got eight kids. Clarence Lindley doesn't. Eula Perry . . ."

"They don't mind that you're not recorded?"

"George Fox wasn't recorded."

"What you're doing is like secession, isn't it?"

"From Valencia Park, maybe. But there won't be any civil war, I can tell you that. Quakers have been having differences of opinion since the beginning. Hicksites. Wilburites. Orthodox. They're all

Quakers, just the same. Orpha, do you know, when they got to that final big question this afternoon, the one I couldn't say yes to, the question I thought maybe a miracle would come in time to save me over? Well, a miracle saved me. They asked the question. I couldn't say yes, but at that very minute I was filled with such a flood of— I don't know what to call it—love? Light? I don't know. Understanding? I knew that I could sin, but with God's help I wouldn't. That was enough to lift me off the ground. I mean it. I jumped for joy. I really did. Maybe they thought they had a Holy Roller on their hands. I didn't roll any, but I did jump and I did praise God."

"Valencia Park was probably glad to get rid of you. A hopping, jumping, shouting Quaker."

"I didn't shout any."

"Just quietly affirmed."

"No wonder they wanted to get rid of you at Fairmont, Sister. You've got a saucy tongue. Do you know what I need? Food! Boy, I don't think I've had a bite for a week. I could eat a whetstone. I could eat a bar of Fels Naphtha soap. In the old days, there was always a chub of salami around the house. That was before I got a housekeeper who believed in cooking."

"Martha's in the kitchen. This is Mary willing to listen to you tell me about sanctification."

"Me for Martha," Joe said, and headed kitchenward.

Wanda was making her specialty, oyster soup. It is easy to make— oysters, milk, a little thickened, butter, salt and pepper; oysters, to Wanda, were the food of tycoons and potentates. Besides, think of eating an animal that could make a pearl. Think of eating anything as plump and slimy as an oyster.

Soup was our whole supper, and for Joe, after a week's fast, probably a good thing. Hungry as he was, the thanks he returned before that meal were neither brief nor silent. What he had to say was spoken to God, not to us; it was a continuing expression of the glory he had felt when it was revealed to him that he would not need to feel himself incapable of sin in order to preach. God, since this revelation came from Him, must have known all about it. It wasn't news to Him. It was news to Joe, though, and he couldn't stop being thankful. I signaled to Wanda to start eating. Wanda, too polite to eat while someone was praying, never lifted a spoon.

9

The Ortiz Schoolhouse had never heard preaching like Joe's. Nor had the San Fernando Valley, Los Angeles, or Southern California. Philadelphia Quakers would have been shocked by what went on; but apart from the manner, the message was wholly of the Religious Society of Friends.

Joe's congregation soon outgrew the small one-room schoolhouse. Of those who attended, not more than half were Quaker. Joe was becoming a California phenomenon along with big trees, Hollywood, and the Rose Parade. He had no pulpit antics. He wore a plain sober-colored suit. His power was as mysterious as Houdini's. Speeches (sermons are speeches suited to Sundays) are made up of words. Read any volume of speeches, including sermons (most, wisely, are never collected), and it is difficult to believe that anyone ever had the patience to sit through them. Words spoken are more than words read. To the spontaneously spoken word is added the sound, the stance, the smell, and the body temperature of a speaking man. If words alone are what you want, don't listen: read.

The sermon has a topic more compelling than that of most speeches. It is saying more than "Vote for me," "Support the bond issue," "Visit New Zealand." It has to do with subjects every human being wonders about: the meaning of life, the inevitability of death, the existence of heaven and hell, the nature of sin and forgiveness.

Is there a God? Did Jesus live? Is death the end? Will I see again those I have loved? What must I do to be saved? Let the words be commonplace, the preacher a stodgy fellow who would look more at home behind a counter than a pulpit: if these are the questions he asks, we will listen to hear his answers.

Joe was not stodgy; his words were not commonplace. Possibly Joe would have been listened to if his message had been "Visit New Zealand." He was easy to look at, big, brown, limber as Fairbanks duelling a villain; sweet-voiced as Burton with a mouthful of Shakespeare. Beyond all that he was, in the pulpit, a man on fire. He did not speak in tongues, but his tongue spoke words and languages he had learned in realms we never visited: realms where all the answers are. Listeners came from as far away as Bakersfield and San Diego. Personal magnetism brings listeners. Mark Twain had it and Will Rogers and James Whitcomb Riley. They had listeners to subjects that were skim milk to Joe's cream: politics,

238

travel, humor, and rhyme. Compare those with "What shall I do to be saved?" Politics, humor, travel, and rhyme don't even try to answer that question. Joey tried.

He preached three-fourths of the Four-Fold Gospel: Salvation, Healing by Faith, the Second Coming of Christ.

Salvation, or conversion, as it was more commonly called, was the goal of most churches in Southern California and elsewhere. The church provided a place of worship for believers. More important, it was a means of bringing nonbelievers to Christ. Services for the purpose of conversion were called "revivals." A revival could be a pretty emotional, noisy affair. There was a good deal of crying, screaming, and shaking. Conversion was contagious, and the sight of one man coming down with it affected others.

Joe wanted to bring men to Christ. A man might be of two minds about sanctification; a man of two minds about conversion didn't belong in the pulpit. Nevertheless, Joe felt that God might be found without too much shouting. His own eloquence, conviction, love, thwarted this belief. Before a sermon of his was finished, worshipers, crying, stumbling, praying, came down front to kneel at the mourner's bench. Friends came with them to join in their prayers that they break through to glory. Husbands and wives were reunited there. Drunks knelt there and said farewell to their bottles. Men made the journey on their knees from the back of the Meeting House to the front. Neighbors, long-time feuders, met there, shook hands, and asked God to forgive them.

I thought of the word Jake had torn from my book and I had burned. Perhaps Jake had influenced me more than I knew. These spasms, while holy, seemed unsuited for a public place. Joe didn't, as some evangelists do, take pride in the number of converts he made. He published no lists, gave out no figures. But he couldn't, like a prissy schoolmarm, urge converts who were coming down front, crying and praying, "Come more quietly."

I went to many of Joe's Meetings. Wanda went with me to the daylight meetings. She was nine years old now, almost ten, large as some twelve-year-olds. She was in the fifth grade, studying fractions and the American Revolution. She knew all there was to know (by human beings) of sanctification, salvation, the Second Coming, and faith healing. She said her prayers as she had been taught to

239

do, but in Meeting and after she was quiet and composed; the commotion of the converted, their tears, confessions, and prayers brought no response from her. What life was like to a ten-year-old in the household of someone who brought about these demonstrations, I don't know. Like living in the house of a magician?

Toward the end of May, at a First Day Meeting—the Quaker term for Sunday worship—Joe was using as his text Matthew 7:7-11. His theme that morning was both spiritual and physical. "Ask, and it shall be given you; seek, and ye shall find; knock, and it shall be opened unto you: For every one that asketh receiveth; and he that seeketh findeth; and to him that knocketh it shall be opened."

Why these texts happened to be the ones that so touched Wanda, I don't know. I could feel her body trembling against mine as Joe at various points in his sermon repeated these texts. "Ask, and it shall be given . . . seek, and ye shall find."

As always in Joe's sermons, the askers and seekers began to go, as the saying was, "up front." Some went alone; some with friends already saved who were praying for them.

Wanda said, "Mama, Jesus wants me to go up front." I thought it unnecessary. I thought she was caught up in the contagion that was affecting others. I was even un-Christian enough to wonder if Wanda's desire was to a degree that of the onlooker who feels left out of the drama being enacted before his eyes. The young girl not only sees Juliet; she wants to be Juliet.

"Oh, Mama," Wanda repeated, "Uncle Joe is calling to me."

"Uncle Joe," I whispered, "is reassuring the unsaved and the afflicted."

Wanda stood, her cheeks covered with tears. "Oh, come with me, Mama."

What could I do? Total strangers were charitable enough to accompany their unsaved brethren to the altar. Wouldn't a mother accompany a daughter, moved by her uncle's preaching, in her search for God? I went, of course. I knelt. I put my arm around Wanda. I listened to Wanda pray. The sermon was continuing and the prayers of those kneeling up front were like the music that in those days accompanied emotional scenes in the movies.

A grandmotherly woman kneeling beside Wanda clasped her closely. "Oh, break through to God, honey, break through. He is waiting for you."

At those words, Wanda said, "I have found Him."

She said no more until we were homeward bound in the runabout that had replaced the pickup.

Then she said, "I have had a call to be a missionary in China."

I had feared that Wanda would be overwrought after her experience at Meeting. How could a ten-year-old hear a call to the foreign mission field? Joe had no such fears. Ten-year-olds wanted to be movie stars, firemen, cowboys, toe dancers. Why not foreign missionaries?

Joe was born to speak out, and look up. He wanted a church service quiet enough to hear him speak. Beyond that he didn't object to a little Amen-ing and Praise-the-Lording. Joe was too early for the "primal scream" therapy; though the tears and groans and hallelujahs he called forth weren't too far removed from that vocalizing.

He wasn't afraid of touch, either. He picked up Wanda, and she was a load, kissed her first on one cheek, then on the other, gave her a little shake, and put her down.

"It's not just talk, you know, Wanda. You've spoken up. You have borne witness. You'll have to be an example now. People will look to you for help."

Poor little Kickapoo, I thought. Ten is too early to start being an example. Wanda was a sturdy ten in every way and she accepted Joe's words as an expression of what she already knew. She was not usually an afternoon napper—but after dinner that Sunday, she curled up on the couch on the sleeping porch and slept. No snoring this time; or if there was, Joe had learned that I was touchy on the subject.

Joe wasn't worried about Wanda and the foreign mission field. Time would take care of that one way or the other. He had a problem, one of his own, one that time was only making worse: healing.

"I can't preach anything less than or different from what I find in the New Testament. I can't find a word there about being unable to sin. And even if it was there, and I didn't experience it, I couldn't preach it. Healing is different. The New Testament is full of it. I don't know how a man can preach and not preach healing."

"He might believe it and preach it and not be able to do it. But that's not you, Joey. You took my headaches away."

"Orpha, for God's sake, I didn't take your headaches away. Jesus did. I had faith that He would. He preached healing. I couldn't have done your headaches as much good as a mustard plaster. If you

241

can't understand that, how can I expect those who know a lot less about the Bible than you do to understand?''

Joe was always inclined to walk about when he talked. It was hard to keep him anchored behind a pulpit. He tramped back and forth in front of me, stopping when he had a question to ask.

"O.K. What's your answer? To tell the truth, I didn't think you had one. I don't have one myself. I'm talking to myself and trying harder than usual to make sense because I have a listener. What am I going to do?''

"Do? Do what you've been doing. You believe in healing and you can heal.''

"I can't. I can't. How many times do I have to tell you? People come to Meeting the way they go to a dentist. 'Stop the pain, Doc.' I don't blame them. I've been sick myself. I would've gone to a witch doctor. But what's happening to the Meeting? We don't have a Meeting for worship any more. We have the Ortiz Phenomenon and his magic act. We have wheelchairs and crutches and tumors and running sores. People don't come to Meeting to find Jesus. They come to get rid of pain.''

"In the Bible people were healed *and* they found Jesus.''

"Find Him? How could they miss Him? He was there. What they see now is the Ortiz Phenomenon. You don't know how that galls me.''

"You could give up healing.''

"I couldn't. You can't shed your faith. You can lose it. But I haven't lost it. I said I believed I could sin. I can. Not a sin like this, though. Let a man suffer and die in order to have quiet Meetings and get rid of that Ortiz nonsense. No, if that's what it takes to be sanctified, I'm sanctified.''

Joe tramped. I was able to keep quiet. Wanda, her nap over, came into the living room. Joe paused mid-stride and picked her up.

"When do we leave?'' he asked.

"Leave?'' Wanda said.

"For China?''

"You believed me, didn't you, Uncle Joe?''

"Of course I did.''

"I have to wait until I grow up.''

"I'll be too old to go with you then.''

Wanda rubbed her cheek against Joe's. "You won't ever be too old, Uncle Joe.''

"Wanda," I said, "you're too big to be making someone hold you."

"Too big and too hot," Joe said, letting her slide to the floor.

Joe didn't say a word to me but on his face there was a glint of something remembered. And where had I heard that tone of voice before? And whose voice?

10

In my novel, the growth of Talbot Ware's church and the moves from the Ortiz Schoolhouse to the unused intermediate building outside Montebello, then to the new Meeting House in Los Angeles are fully reported. This was virtually the same as Joe's progress; in Los Angeles he was still the Ortiz Phenomenon, even after he had moved into the Meeting House, a building that, though not as ornate as hers, held as many worshipers as Aimee Semple McPherson's Temple. There he was, the Reverend Joseph Chase, minister of the Religious Society of Friends. The Valencia Meeting, clinging to their belief in sanctification, never recorded Joe as a minister— and Joe never gave up his conviction that he was capable of sinning. The La Puente Meeting, which had never made sanctification a requirement for its members or preachers, did record Joe.

It was not his finally being recorded, or his eloquence, or his obvious love of God that filled Joe's Meeting House to overflowing: it was the healing. Joe thought, prayed, and wrestled with himself and with God about this. He wanted worshipers at his Meetings, not men and women seeking relief from pain. "I feel like a snake-oil merchant," he told me. "I feel like I give away aspirin."

"Does it matter what you feel?"

"Maybe not. But I'd like to feel miserable for a better reason. I don't cure those people. God does. When they praise me, I feel like a charlatan."

Happenings that were called "miracles"—and seemed miraculous —did occur at Joe's Meetings. I saw some with my own eyes. What else should people expect who worshiped a Man who performed miracles, and prayed to be like Him? A Man who brought the dead to life, who was Himself crucified, buried for three days, and after that broke out of His tomb and lived to walk the earth again. Yet Christians who worshiped Christ the Man of Miracles derided Joe.

They thought fakery of some kind was involved. They believed that ailments that could be psychologically induced—neuralgias, asthmas, headaches, tics—were susceptible of help or cure by Joe telling the sufferers that he had faith that Jesus would heal them. The popular medical term for such patients then was "hysterics."

But healing of the kind I saw, whatever the possible scientific explanations, was hard to accept as anything but the result of profound faith.

As Joe prayed, I saw a girl's leg, so twisted as to be three inches shorter than her normal leg, become by some process straightened. The girl had hardly been able to hobble up front. She walked away at the close of the service with only a slight limp.

The doctor who had treated the girl signed an affidavit attesting to the fact that his former patient, who had not responded to any physical therapy, was now so improved as to be considered recovered. Joe, when he quietly declined to accept the affidavit personally, said, "I pray for healing. I am not the Healer."

11

Joe's new Meeting House in Los Angeles was built in 1938. By this time Joe, though still concerned about the compulsive public rush to healing, had made some decisions as to how to cope with it. First Day Meetings, morning and evening, were Meetings for worship only. This meant that Joe would not speak specifically of healing at those times. This did not mean that people weren't healed. You cannot, Joe could not, preach the gospel of a Healer, of a Man who has practiced healing, without listeners experiencing healing. Nor could Joe persuade men and women who had been rid of afflictions of long standing not to proclaim their joy and thankfulness.

He tried. "For the sake of those who may be hearing the gospel of Jesus Christ for the first time, will those experiencing His grace most fully thank Him in the silence of their hearts?"

This meant in plainer words, "Please try to keep quiet until I have finished my sermon."

He announced that Meetings of prayer for healing would be held on Tuesday, Thursday, and Saturday evenings. He was not sure that this decision was a good one. The result was that there were evidently more people wanting to feel good than to be good. The

Meetings for worship continued to be well attended. The Meetings for healing were overflowing.

He tried to lessen this overcrowding by saying that he would, at his home on Monday and Saturday afternoons, talk with individuals who had made arrangements with him. He would never on these afternoons see more than two or three persons.

Joe preached medicine and surgery. Faith in the power of Jesus to heal did not mean lack of faith in those whose efforts were less spiritual. They also were sons of God.

Joe was in many ways Aimee Semple McPherson's opposite. After her abduction had been proved a hoax, she was never again, in the thirties, as popular as she had been in the twenties. The blazing cross on the Angelus Temple, where she continued to preach the Four Square Gospel, still revolved, shedding a light that, when Joe came to Los Angeles, could be seen twenty-five miles out at sea. Aimee had in her Temple a "miracle room" stacked high with paraphernalia no longer needed by those she had cured: wheelchairs, crutches, trusses, spectacles, canes.

Easterners, who tended to think all Californians weirdos (though most Californians were transplants from the East and the Middle West), linked Aimee and Joe together in their minds. They should not have done so.

Joe founded no new church. His large but plain Meeting House supported no cross, stationary or revolving. He preached in an ordinary business suit. He had no miracle room. He urged those who had been healed to forget their past infirmities and to prove by lives of love and compassion that they had indeed been touched by Jesus. Except for the size of his congregation and the number of persons who had personally sought to exploit their healing, Joe did not provide the papers with headlines like Aimee's. Sex, not healing or numbers of worshipers, is what gives a preacher big black headlines. A thousand discarded crutches would not have given the *Evening Express* or the *Examiner* the headlines Ormiston and Carmel gave Aimee. And there were no Ormistons, male or female, in Joe's life. No one was in a better position than I to know this.

We had moved to a house on the outskirts of Montebello, and continued to live there even after Joe's new Meeting House was built for him in Los Angeles. Our house was peculiar to begin with; the location, as the influx of Okies and Dust Bowlers increased dur-

245

ing the Depression, became even more peculiar. The land on the south side of the road, which ran between Los Angeles and the towns of Orange County, had been dairy country. It still was. A big white barn, with its loft and pulley for storing hay, its ground floor with many stalls, stood near us. The dairy herd had diminished. A gas station, a couple of oil derricks, a half-dozen new but ramshackle houses took up the space where cows had once grazed.

Our house, a raspberry-pink stucco that in the thirties was called "Spanish," had belonged to the dairy manager. The new service station was a little farther away, on the other side of the road. An oil derrick was a quarter of a mile back of the house. Night and day we heard the gulp and thud of its pump lifting oil from the earth—a mother producing the food that the autos speeding toward the beaches and groves of Orange County needed to live.

The house itself had five rooms. The large living room, separated only by an archway from the kitchen, had a "dining alcove," or "breakfast nook." All rooms, with the exception of the bathroom, were separated by arches only. This, too, was thought to be Spanish —and, for all I know, may be. Eucalyptus portieres would have given us some privacy and have lightened the effect of the heavy stucco arches. Eucalyptus trees had been planted as windbreaks on citrus land; on dairy land, with nothing to protect but cows, they let the wind blow. Not that I would have had the patience to string together enough eucalyptus cups to curtain one door, let alone four.

The only tree on the place was a weeping willow, dusty, forlorn, as melancholy to look at as its name. It was unclimbable, did not change color or provide any kind of a harp for the wind to play on. Apart from being green, which did rest the eyes in that bleached country, its only use was for Wanda, as a kind of Kickapoo hogan. Once under the dome of its branches, which touched the ground, she was as safe from prying eyes as in an underground vault. Wanda, at fifteen, was getting a little old for tree houses, but a woman is never too old or too young to relish privacy, and this the weeping willow gave her.

Joe, I think, would have been happy in a tent. He did notice and rejoice in the location of the raspberry stucco. It was in the midst of everything. Except for a Ferris wheel and a delicatessen, I don't know what could have been added.

"Orpha," he said, "we are at the center of the world." That was a fact, and the center every day was becoming more crowded. Joe didn't care. Joe was a man in love. The fact that he was in love with God didn't make him much different from a man in love with a mortal. He was in love and his love was returned. Because of this, everyone, pumpers from oil wells, milkers from the dairy barns, me and Wanda, had a kind of dearness and radiance we would not otherwise have had.

Joe came home from his Meetings and preachings and praying bone tired, took off his coat, snapped his suspenders, drank a cup of black coffee, and made merry. Strange phrase? There is no other for it. How could a man be so lucky, he often asked me. Given three months to live, healed by faith, led to God, then given the power to lead others to Him. Men in the backwoods were soberer on sour mash than Joe on the love of God.

It could have rubbed some the wrong way. A man in love, bubbling with praise of his beloved, can be tiresome. His beloved, it is plain to everyone else, is no prize. Besides, the lover wants you to appreciate, not to share, his dear one. Joe was another kind of lover: he was happiest when others shared his love of God.

X
MARIE

1

It was October, month of opals and topazes. The ruby blaze of July had faded. The long drought of summer would soon be broken by the first rains. It was like finding a living spring after a long walk in the desert.

"I can feel the rain coming," Joe said. He was stretched out on the davenport, finishing his coffee.

"How?" asked Wanda, hoping, I think, that God had whispered a forecast to him.

"By my suspenders. They lose their snap when there's moisture in the air."

He twanged them to show us the difference. It was true. They had lost their crisp crackle.

"It's the way you do it," said Wanda.

"Try it yourself," Joe told her.

Wanda leaned down, lifted a suspender as far as she could, then let it fall back. Nothing but a soggy plop.

"Satisfied," asked Joe, "that it's the weather?"

At that minute there was a splatter of big raindrops against the west windows.

"Me and my magic suspenders," said Joe.

"You shouldn't joke that way, Uncle Joe."

"Look who's with us tonight," said Joe. "Wanda, the returned missionary. She was last known to smile in 1910."

"I wasn't even born then."

"Talk that way and no one will ever guess it."

Wanda had missionary nights and Scarlett O'Hara nights. She was reading *Gone With the Wind*, and she alternated evenings of saving China with evenings of saving the South. In appearance she was nearer the Chinese than Scarlett. I am judging, of course, by Vivien Leigh in the movie—which hadn't at that time even been made. Wanda was stalwart and stocky. Her life was in her face and her dark eyes. She was built for stoop labor, close to the ground, with a waist so sturdy it wouldn't snap with bending; not for stamping a high-arched foot on the veranda at Tara. Like all fifteen-year-olds (and many of us later), she had more than one self, and she liked to give them all a try. Joe preferred Scarlett Wanda to Wanda the Chinese missionary. He heard enough preaching, his own and that of others, without hearing more when he got home. Besides, Scarlett Wanda could be shut up. Shutting up missionary Wanda, particularly if you had yourself brought her to that dedicated state, was less seemly. The rain itself, so longed for and needed, took Wanda away from both China and Tara. She went out onto the fake balcony of the raspberry stucco to let "the cleansing rain," she said, "bounce off her tongue."

"I approve," said Joe. "It's a needed ritual."

Joe had another cup of coffee. How a man as constantly keyed up as he was could handle so much that was stimulating, I don't know. Perhaps, I thought, nothing could hurt Joe.

"Orpha," Joe said, "I've let you in for something tonight."

"Are they coming here or am I going there?"

"They're coming here. I know it's my night off. But the Griswolds are in trouble and I told them I'd see them here. Then later I remembered that Ministry and Oversight meets tonight, and we're in trouble, too. Nice trouble, but trouble—what's the best use of the money we're taking in? All you have to do with the Griswolds is listen to them—and apologize for me. Don't let Wanda preach them a sermon if you can help it. Tell them I'll see them on Saturday, same time."

Joe left. Wanda went to bed with *Gone With the Wind*. I listened to the drumbeat of the rain; no shower, but a real change-of-season downpour brought about by the veering of the moisture-laden winds.

The Griswolds arrived when they said they would: 8:30. They were a married couple in their thirties. Burt Griswold had a dark, seamed face and eyes that asked questions. At a time when few people were making money, he was. He owned auto-parts stores in Long Beach, San Diego, Bakersfield, and Sacramento. He bought old or wrecked cars, salvaged their usable parts, and sold them to persons unable to buy new cars and struggling by the use of replacements to keep their old cars running.

"My customers wish," he said, "they had your husband's power and could restore their machines by prayer."

"Joe is my brother, not my husband," I said, "and he does not pray for cars."

"Why not? I'd miss my car a lot more—"

"Burt," said his wife, whose name was Marie, "let's not talk about cars. That's not what we're here for."

"Sure," said Burt. "You tell her what we're here for."

"You can do it a lot better than I can."

I didn't know what their errand was. Had I known, my feeling about them would have been different. Marie Griswold was as blond as her husband was dark. She sat perfectly still, but in spite of the lack of any visible movement, a deep tremor registered on my internal seismograph. Nothing but will power was keeping her teeth from chattering.

"It's this way, Miss Chase—"

"Mrs. Hesse."

"You're married?"

"I was."

"California's where you belong, in that case," said Burt.

"You wanted to see Joe?"

"Marie does. She wanted me to take her to Missouri. There's a man there—"

"A clinic," Marie said.

"That's what he calls it. A man and his nurse, as far as I can find out."

"A doctor," Marie said.

"He calls himself an M.D. But he didn't get his degree from any sawbones college. Not that I hold that against him. He's onto something the sawbones haven't discovered yet, and naturally they want to shoot him down. Marie heard about him from a friend and she said, 'What's the point getting a part of myself amputated when there's a man who can remove the source of the trouble and leave me the way God made me?' This was before she heard about the Reverend Chase."

I didn't yet know what ailed Marie. She was the one who saw that I didn't know what they were talking about.

"I have a lump in my breast," Marie said, cupping her left breast gently. "Nothing but a little tiny lump the size of a walnut. But do you know what the doctor wanted to do? Take off the entire breast. Not just the lump."

"And surgery frightens her," Burt said. "So I set my foot down. No one's going to mutilate Marie as long as I'm around to protect her. She heard of this Missouri clinic where they put a poultice of some kind on the breast. Out comes the cancer like the core out of a boil. The breast heals and the woman is left the shape God made her. Before we could leave for Missouri, Marie heard of the Reverend Chase, who just prays them away. A poultice beats a knife, and a prayer beats a poultice. Wouldn't you say so, Mrs. Hesse?"

It wasn't my place to say anything, except "Joe will see you Saturday night."

I didn't like Burt Griswold. Where I had been brought up, men didn't talk about their wives' breasts, except possibly to doctors. There was something casual, almost flippant, in the way Burt Griswold spoke of his wife's problem, oblivious to her tension and fear.

"Well, what do you say, Mrs. Hesse?" Burt repeated. "A prayer beats a poultice, don't it?" Burt Griswold, though asking for prayer, didn't seem very religious.

"It depends upon what you're praying for, I suppose."

"What does that mean?"

I wasn't sure enough to answer.

"My brother asked me to make his excuses for his not being here. He'll see you Saturday at the same time. I shouldn't try to speak for him."

2

It was strange that the Griswolds should be the first persons I wrote about in my new notebooks, since, as it turned out, they had so much to do with Joe's subsequent life. My thoughts about them, while unspoken, were not hidden, neither under a table nor deep in my mind. I talked with Joe about the Griswolds, and while I think he never opened my notebooks, he was free to do so—and knew it.

It was midnight before Joe got home. He had been so taken up with the meeting of Ministry and Oversight that by now he had forgotten his date with the Griswolds. I had something ready for him to eat. For the most part Joe ate little and didn't care what that little was. He did have a few preferences. He was crazy about tomatoes. If he had lived in the era of the Bloody Mary, he would have become addicted because of the tomato juice, not the gin. He liked tomatoes in any form, peeled, unpeeled, cooked, raw. On this rainy October night I gave him a favorite, a dish called "Escalloped Tomatoes." It was hearty; plenty of small pieces of home-baked bread, butter, and, of all things, sugar. With it Joe drank his usual black coffee.

"How was Ministry and Oversight?" I asked.

"Out of their minds. They wanted to give me a raise in salary."

"I hope you let them. Wanda needs something besides my castoffs. I'd like to buy some real strawberry jam for a change, not pink applesauce with alfalfa seeds."

"They raised me fifty dollars."

"Three hundred and fifty now!"

"I feel guilty."

"Don't. You work eighteen hours a day."

"I'd do it for nothing."

"You can't. You're stuck with me and Wanda. My old bloomers hang down to Wanda's ankles. Alfalfa seeds hurt my stomach. And wait until you hear about the Griswolds. They'll add another two hours a day to your work and make you feel less guilty."

"The Griswolds?" Joe asked.

"The people you had a date to meet tonight."

"Did they come?"

"They did."

"What did they want?"

"Mrs. Griswold would like to live a little longer. And she doesn't want to be mutilated by surgery."

"Mutilated? Who's threatening to mutilate her?"

"In the Griswolds' opinion, the doctor who will remove her breast in order to save her from dying of cancer."

"That's not called 'mutilation.' "

"You talk to the Griswolds. Anyway, she had that all figured out till he heard of you. He was going to take his wife to Missouri, where they take out cancers with poultices. He asked me if I didn't think prayer beat poultices."

"What did you tell him?"

"Nothing. I told him you would see him Saturday night, same time. Would you pray for her?"

"Of course. But not until they understood that everything hinges on God's will. Jesus heals. But Jesus died suffering on the cross because it was God's will."

When Joe began to talk of God's will, he was talking theology, and I was not equipped to understand Joe on theology. He was a college graduate and a seminary student. All I knew of man's relationship with God was "Be good. Do good." And I had failed in both. I had been taught, as Joe had, that it was a Christian's duty to learn the will of God. But never as Joe, a Quaker, had that God's will was to be found not in rules and Bible verses, but in direct communication with Him. It might be God's will for a man to suffer—and die. In his suffering a man might discover God's will for himself—and only through suffering. That was news to me.

"How can you pray for healing with this belief in suffering?"

"I know God heals. I have faith. I also pray, 'Thy will be done.' "

"I don't think Mrs. Griswold cares so much about God's will. What she cares about is her shape."

"God may, too," Joes said. "After all, He made her."

Talk like that shocked me. I was a United Brethren, not a seminarian able to communicate with God.

"Your God sounds like a man," I said.

This shocked me, too. *I* sounded as if Joe and I worshiped different Gods.

"He *was* a man for about thirty years, you know."

I backed away from that subject. Joe was so close to God he could laugh and joke about religious subjects. I couldn't.

"I wish Mama and Papa were here to see your new Meeting House and hear you preach."

"They're going to. That's one of the reasons Wanda will have to put up with old bloomers for a while longer. I'm saving the money for their fare."

They didn't get to California until the time of Joe's trial.

3

I began writing *Talbot Ware* at the same time that Joe began seeing the Griswolds. *Talbot Ware* was to be the life story of Joseph

Chase, with enough that was purely fictional included to preserve, I thought, Joe's privacy. I had noted in my novel-reading that when a man of God, a priest or a minister, falls in love, his emotions are of far more interest to the reader than are those of the unordained. This is particularly true when the lover is breaking his vows. Then, what in the story of a well driller or shoe clerk would be an amorous adventure becomes a struggle between good and evil. Talbot Ware had taken no vows of celibacy, except to himself. These he *had* taken, however; and when he fell in love, the reader's interest would, I thought, be heightened.

Otherwise the story was to be a straightforward account that paralleled Joe's life, a young man sick unto death, healed by prayer, who when cured became a preacher and what is known as a faith healer.

When the trial, unexpected when I started writing, exploded upon Joe, it had to be included. In it, in brief, were the justifications of Joe's ministry. And out of it, and the novel that included it, came changes in my life and Wanda's. And this is my life I am writing now, not Joe's.

4

Joe met with the Griswolds on Saturday at our place as he had promised. I was never with Joe on such occasions. My presence, I believed, would have been as out of place as a third person in a confessional. And such meetings with Joe were rather like a confession, I imagined. The confessor did not say, "Father, I have sinned," but "Father, I hurt."

On Saturday evening, Wanda and I went to the movies. Movies were not thought of highly by either Quakers or United Brethren. An occasional movie might be edifying as well as entertaining. If we kept in mind that what we were seeing was a made-up story, not a shred of truth necessarily in it, we were free to go. Wanda and I saw *Captains Courageous*. It was both entertaining and edifying, so no harm done in that line. But it was difficult to remember that it was a story. It seemed truer than happenings Wanda and I read about every day in the Los Angeles *Express*.

Wanda was at the age and of the temperament to become the heroine—or hero—of any play or movie she saw. She was Spencer Tracy, the hero, himself, as we drove home from the show; she didn't want any conversation that shattered this image of herself. So we came home without talking. Wanda went off to her bed with a nautical gait, forgetting her usual good night to Joe.

"How did it go, Joe?" I asked.

"Fine."

"Did you talk to them about God's will?"

"I did. They have great faith."

"Did you talk to them about poultices?"

"I think the word was mentioned."

"Do you want some coffee, Joe?"

"I do. I need it. Anything to go with it?"

"Raisin pie?"

After I gave him the pie and the coffee, I, too, went to bed: Orpha Hesse, widow, grass widow, alone in the world, I thought; while Joe communes with God and Wanda rides the briny deep with her hero.

5

The Griswolds were at Meeting every Sunday. Joe had evidently converted both. I avoided them, except to nod. I didn't believe the feelings Burt Griswold aroused in me were suitable for a meeting of Christians. That Joe didn't feel as I did was a small splinter between us. "Love your neighbor as yourself."

The first time I saw the Griswolds had been on a rainy October evening. It was raining again five months later when Marie came to call—on me, not Joe.

There is a difference in California between an October rain and a March rain. In October, California has been waiting for rain and welcomes it the way the Valencia Park Training School welcomed sanctification. "Will it never come?" we say in October. In March, after a long rainy season, we ask, "Will it never stop?" The dust has been laid, the tumbleweeds are sodden, dry arroyos are rumbling with water—who needs any more rain?

Marie, without phoning, came in the midst of a rain that had become as constant as air. She, a native of Iowa, unlike Californians, was wearing a raincoat.

"Excuse me," Marie said, "for dropping in this way. I was near here and I suddenly wanted to talk to you. Just you, not the Reverend Joe."

"I'm alone," I told her. "Joe is at church and Wanda is at school."

I helped her off with her raincoat and hung it in the kitchen where it could drip on the linoleum. When I came back to the living room, I said, without thinking what meaning my words might have for a woman who had cancer, "You've lost weight, Marie."

"No, no," she said. "My weight stays constant. People forget from one time to the next how heavy I am."

Not trying to cover up my mistake, if I had made one, but telling the truth, I said, "It's the same with me. One month away from friends and they all say, 'My, but you've lost weight.' And I haven't lost a pound. The only way I can explain it is that I've got a fat personality. They remember me fat and are surprised to see me svelte."

That made Marie laugh. "Do you think I have a fat personality?"

"I don't know you well to enough to say."

"I want to know you better. That's why I'm here. I've got a lot to thank you for."

"Thank me?"

"Without what you said, Burt might not have been willing to see your brother."

"I didn't say a persuasive word. Joe's the one to thank."

"Oh, he is. He is. He has changed all of our lives, mine especially. When I came here, all I wanted was to be well again. I never once thought or cared about God's will for me. Now that's what I care about most. And my caring about that has made my whole family happier."

I watched Marie as she sat in the old Dudley rocker, reminding me of that poor golden-haired child of twenty-five years ago who sat naked in another rocker saying, "She wouldn't let him do it." That poor girl had never heard that God's will might include suffering.

The rain continued. Marie rocked very gently. "I *am* thinner," she said. "You were right."

"I could be mistaken."

"No, no. You saw right. Could I talk to you privately?"

"We are private. We're the only ones in the house."

"Talk to you without your ever telling your brother, I mean."

"Of course. Women have troubles of all kinds it's none of a man's business to know anything about."

"This is Joe's business."

"Well, you should talk to Joe, then."

"I can't. I can't even talk to you about it unless I have your word you won't tell Joe."

"If it's Joe's business, it's my duty to tell Joe, isn't it?"

"If you think so, I won't say anything."

Either way Joe was not going to know anything about it. "Who will it help, then, for me to know?"

"Me, me," Marie cried. She got out of her rocker, came and sat on the hassock by my side. She put her hands on my lap and looked up into my face. "Who else can I talk to? My mother is in Iowa."

I was far from old enough to be Marie's mother. I thought I might even be younger than she. She put her head in my lap, and I could no more resist patting her dry brittley hair than I could deny a cat a caress.

"If you have to tell Joe, I can keep quiet. I thought you might be able to listen and not tell."

"I can listen. And not tell."

"I am going to die."

It was news to me and not news. I could feel death in the texture of her hair and the tightness and color of the skin over her cheekbones. What was there to say? "I am sorry." "Perhaps you are mistaken." "You are going to your reward." I said nothing. I stroked.

Marie stood. "It's not my imagination."

"Why don't you tell Joe? He's not vain. *He* doesn't heal. He knows that not everyone he prays for gets well."

"I know that. But I do believe what he preaches, that suffering is God's will for some. It's God's will for me, and I accept it. And I'm not going to ask Joe to suffer with me."

"Have an operation. It may not be too late. Joe believes in operations."

"I don't want to. I am perfectly happy. If it's God's will that I suffer, I'm willing."

"You must be suffering now. Doesn't Burt notice?"

"I have pain pills."

"Joe'll have to know, sooner or later."

"But you aren't going to tell him?"

"No. I promised you."

"And I'm not going to."

"But Joe . . ."

"You promised."

"I'll keep my promise. I don't understand why, though."

"If you were closer to your brother and God, you would. It's not just Joe—it's the people who depend on him. If he had to watch me dying, what would it do to his faith in the power of his prayers?"

"Nothing. His faith doesn't need to be bolstered up by a lie."

"You promised me."

I kept my promise. I didn't tell Joe about Marie's concern for him, her fervent wish not to shake his faith or cause him pain. Nor could I reveal her confidences about Burt, startled as I was by some of them. These were her secrets with God, and I, as confidant, could give her the gift of comfort if silence was included. I prayed that she would find mercy, and I forgetfulness.

6

Joe certainly never knew that Marie was dying. But Griswold must certainly have known. The funeral was at the Meeting House and the service was the one Joe had established some time before. It differed from the conventional in two main ways.

The casket with the dead body was not at the front of the church, as is usual, but at the back of the room. Joe did not once mention Marie Griswold in his sermon. Instead, he dwelt on the beliefs that had sustained her and should sustain us all. Joe's funeral practice, which emphasized not the dead body but the truths by which the man or woman had lived, became known as the Ceremony of Life. It was used when Joe himself died. His body lay at the back of the Meeting House. No words of Joe's were voiced; only the eternal truths of his master Jesus Christ.

Marie's father and mother, Mr. and Mrs. Sam Shields, of Muscatine, Iowa, had come west for their daughter's funeral. They did not sit with their son-in-law. They took no comfort, it seemed to me, in a funeral service in which their daughter's name was never mentioned and her body was placed out of the sight of those who had gathered to mourn her.

I cried. So did Wanda. I didn't see tears on the faces of anyone else. Mr. and Mrs. Shields sat with dry flinty faces. Burt's face was a mask. Joe's congregation, true believers, did not feel that it became Christians who worshiped God to mourn the departure of one of their brethren to live forever with God and His Son.

I, though, could have mounted that pulpit and said a few words

261

about Marie Shields Griswold. I did not do so, of course. Nor did I, unless I am doing so now, put this into any book of Unspoken Thoughts.

"Take notice, you mourners," I would have said, "of the bravery of a girl whose name was Shields and who offered up her body as a shield to protect those she loved. She protected her husband. She might have lived had she been willing to save her life by submitting to knives that would change the body her husband desired.

"She loved her minister and she believed with him that it is sometimes God's will that we suffer. So she suffered, rather than bring Reverend Chase news she thought might disturb his ministry.

"Marie is dead. She died for the happiness of others. I think she was mistaken in what she did. She wasn't mistaken in being willing to suffer for love. That is the sermon she preached—with her poor body. Let us all listen."

I didn't say a word of this. All I did was cry. When the funeral service was concluded, I went to Mr. and Mrs. Shields. They were strangers in the community, and someone, I thought, should tell them that Marie was loved and would be missed. I wasn't permitted to do so.

When I held out my hand and said, "I am the Reverend Joseph Chase's sister," they looked at my hand as if wondering how any one of the Chase family could have so human-appearing an appendage. That one look was all I got. Or that anyone else got. The Shieldses left the Meeting House very quickly, not even pausing to touch the box that held the body of their daughter.

7

I couldn't get the Shieldses' stricken faces out of my mind. They had come half across the continent to say farewell to their only daughter, and at the funeral, which would, they thought, provide them with their last and only chance to do so, they had not even been permitted to see her face. The daughter, so dear to them, had not been eulogized, her favorite hymns had not been sung, her courage had not been mentioned. They, accustomed to more orthodox burial services, had every right to feel that the man who had failed to cure their daughter had also slighted her in her death.

I loved Marie. Not only for herself but because of the regard she had for Joe. I believed that she would want me to go to her parents, to explain to them as best I could Joe's belief in the healing power of Jesus and, if I could, comfort them.

The Shieldses were staying at Marie's home. I went there the day after the funeral. Mrs. Shields, still grim and red-eyed, met me at the door. For a minute I thought she wouldn't let me in.

"I was Marie's friend," I said. "I would like to talk to you about her. I admired her very much."

"Come in," said Mrs. Shields, without any hospitality in her voice or friendliness in her face.

The room I entered reminded me of Marie. It was the room of a woman who loved her home and who, with time on her hands as she was dying, had labored to embellish it. Tidies had been crocheted for the chair backs, velveteen covers quilted for the hassocks. Nowadays, when we admire the bare and the spare, Marie's living room would look very fussy to us. Marie, heading, and she knew it, for the eternally bare and spare, had wanted to leave behind for Burt a coziness that would remind him of her.

Before I had a chance to tell Mrs. Shields that I felt her daughter's presence in the room, Mr. Shields, with Burt on his heels, came stomping into the room from the kitchen.

"What's the woman doing here?" he asked.

"She's the preacher's sister, Sam," Mrs. Shields said, as if her husband didn't know it.

"I know *who* she is. But don't call that man a preacher. I've known too many good reverends to call that shyster a preacher. The preachers I knew preached the gospel and let the doctors practice medicine."

"Shyster," I repeated, shocked.

"Get her out of here," Sam commanded his wife. "I told you not to let either of those two or any of the people they've hoodwinked in here. The least I can do for my dead daughter is not hobnob with those responsible for her death."

Mrs. Shields said, "Sam, Marie wouldn't like to hear you talking this way. Whatever caused her death, she died a Christian. And Christians forgive."

Burt, who had listened in silence, broke in before Sam could berate Joe any more. "Sam, you'll have to accept the fact that Marie was the one that came to the Reverend, not the other way around. She had this deathly fear of the surgeon's knife. She'd try anything before she'd submit to that."

"I'm not blaming you, Burt, any more than I'm blaming Marie. You let her do what she was determined to do. But you didn't tell her—the way this so-called Reverend did—that you could cure her with a little prayer and laying on of hands."

"Joe never laid on hands," I said.

"Maybe he should have. What's it matter? My girl's dead."

"Sam," said Mrs. Shields, "Jesus Christ healed His believers."

This made Sam tense with rage. "Martha, don't belittle our Saviour by mentioning Him in the same breath with one of these publicity-seeking, money-grubbing, Bible-thumping so-called faith healers. They are covering the country like locusts. That man is responsible for my daughter's death and he'll pay for it, if it's my last act on earth. The Reverend claims the Lord tells him what to do. Well, the Lord's told me that it's my duty to see that Chase pays for Marie's death before he sends other people to their graves by keeping them from seeing a doctor. You tell the Reverend that, miss."

"Mrs.," I said.

"Tell the Reverend, Mrs.," said Sam.

I didn't. There was no point telling Joe that somebody's relative blamed him because a person he had prayed for hadn't recovered. He knew that had happened before and would keep on happening. And it would never in this world stop him from believing that Jesus could heal, or keep him from praying that Jesus would.

8

When a Mr. Eldon McRae called one morning asking if he could come out that afternoon to chat with me, I said yes. Many people, timid about talking directly with Joe, asked to talk with me—as a kind of practice session before moving upward to Joe.

Mr. McRae had a pleasant voice. He was, he said, in the District Attorney's office, and there were matters he hoped I could give him some information about. Because of Joe, I had talked with all kinds of people: reporters, the sick, relatives of the sick, alcoholics, the newly saved. A man from the D.A.'s office, though I wasn't very sure of a D.A.'s function, let alone the function of one of his assistants, was pretty sure to be a normal county official of some sort. And this, Mr. McRae was.

Wanda was at school. Joe was preaching at a Quarterly Meeting in Kern County. When I opened the front door, I saw a man who looked a good deal like my father, plumper, balder, and better dressed.

No one could have been more polite. He complimented me on my house, said we needed rain, asked me if I liked Los Angeles.

Then he asked me the question he had come out to ask, though I didn't realize it at the time.

"Were you a friend of Marie Griswold's?"

"More an acquaintance, though I certainly liked her."

"How long did you know her?"

"About six or seven months, I guess."

"How did you come to make her acquaintance? Was she a member of your brother's congregation?

"Not at first."

"What came first?"

"Marie, Mrs. Griswold, and her husband, Burt, had a date to talk to Joe. Joe had to be away so they talked to me instead."

"What did they talk about?"

It was at this point that it struck me that this was no ordinary conversation. Here was a man, an official of some sort, interested in only one subject: the Griswolds. And he was interested in the Griswolds not because of me, I was sure, but because of Joe. I began to feel uneasy in my conversation with Mr. McRae. I answered all of his questions honestly, but with less freedom than I had had when I had thought that our only purpose was in talking about a woman we had both liked.

"We talked about Marie's health."

"Wasn't this a rather unusual subject for people who had never met before?"

"How do you mean, unusual?"

"Well, we've just met. Wouldn't you be surprised if I started telling you about some ailment of mine?"

"I wouldn't if Joe had been the person you wanted to see in the first place."

"So that's how it was."

"Of course. Marie was sick. She had heard that Joe could heal the sick by prayer. Joe wouldn't like to hear me say that. He prayed, Jesus healed."

"But you said they didn't live in Los Angeles."

"People have heard about Joe in distant places. He's had letters from New Zealand. And Africa."

"So the Griswolds came to see your brother because of Marie's sickness."

"Yes."

"And she died in spite of his prayers."

"She knew she might."

"How do you know that?"

"Joe doesn't promise healing to anyone. I know that. Besides, Marie knew she wasn't getting better."

"How do you know that?"

"She told me."

"Why didn't she go to a doctor then? If prayer wasn't helping."

"She wanted to show her faith."

"In your brother?"

"In Jesus and in my brother as His disciple."

"And she was willing to die for her faith?"

"I can't answer for a dead woman. She had faith and she did die. I was a friend just a few months. Talk to people who knew her better. Her parents. They're still here in town. Her husband."

"I have, Mrs. Hesse. I'm sorry if I've upset you. There've been complaints come to our office and we've had to look into the matter."

I didn't understand what he called the "matter." Joe's praying? Marie's dying? I didn't want to know. I didn't want to be mixed up with killing or dying. What Lon had done had been enough to last me for a lifetime. And ignorant though I was of the law and of district attorneys and their duties, I didn't need to be told that Eldon McRae, the District Attorney's man, was saying in a roundabout way, or trying to get me to say, that except for coming to Joe instead of going to a doctor, Marie might still be alive.

Joe got home from the Quarterly Meeting in Kern County late, but I had waited up for him. I had hot coffee and warm gingerbread with lemon sauce ready for him. He'd eaten in Bakersfield, but that was four hours ago, and he had preached. And Joe always said that he was a hungry talker. Wanda was already in bed.

266

Feed the inner man at Quarterly Meeting. Feed the flesh here. "Boy, does that smell good," he said.

I let Joe have a cup of coffee and his first piece of gingerbread before I told him about Eldon McRae's call. Joe was as calm as if I'd told him that Mama had dropped in for a visit.

"Don't you care that these things are being said about you?"

"I care that McRae came here and got you wrought up. There's no way under heaven I can do the work I've been called to do and not be criticized. I accept that. It's part of the yoke I put on."

"It makes me mad. This man sounded as if he had some official right to make you account for what you do."

"He has. And if you're going to get mad, you'd better save your temper for what's to come."

"More questions?"

"More. And from McRae's boss himself. Fred Benson."

"I thought Fred was your friend?"

"He is. But Fred's got his job to do, the same as I have. And he'd better do it good, right now, because he's up for election."

"What is Fred's job?"

"Orpha, sometimes I think you don't live in this world. As District Attorney, Fred's job is to bring lawbreakers to justice."

"I haven't broken any law."

Joe laughed. He had a big laugh. It came out of the same voice box that permitted him, before loudspeakers had been invented, to make himself heard by a thousand people. No one would have thought, hearing that laugh, that Joe was a man who had just been told that the District Attorney's office was interested in him. Or who knew far more about that interest than I did. Before he could tell me about that, Wanda, awakened by Joe's laugh, came blinking into the room. When she saw the gingerbread, she said, "Mama, I'm hungry"; as if it was hunger that had awakened her.

"You take after your uncle Joe, don't you, pet?" said Joe.

"Everyone says so."

Joe laughed again. "Gingerbread for two, Orpha. One milk, one coffee."

"Coming up," said I.

While they were eating, I went out onto the porch. The September air said exactly what McRae had said: "We need rain." It wasn't an overpoweringly hot night, as September nights can be in Los Angeles. But it had been a warm day and no breeze had

267

come inland off the ocean to cool and refresh us. A first-quarter moon had gone down, and the stars were bright as little brush fires. It was a waiting season, summer past, but what would make this a fact was yet to come.

Joe and Wanda had finished their gingerbread when I went in. Joe said, "Wanda, that ought to hold you from hunger's pangs for another hour or two."

"Uncle Joe," Wanda said, "I want to say my good-night prayers."

"Didn't you say them when you went to bed?"

"Of course. But I feel like praying again."

"That's fine. You run right upstairs and pray."

"I want you to hear me, Uncle Joe."

"God's the One to hear you. You run right upstairs and talk to Him. I want to talk to your mother."

Wanda knew better than to argue with Joe, especially on the subject of prayer, on which he, not she, was the authority.

When she left, Joe said, "Fred's coming out to see me."

"Officially?"

"Friendly, too, I hope. It's called 'preliminary investigation'; nothing formal. He's had a lot of complaints. Not that he hasn't had them before."

"Complaints about what?"

"Me."

"When did preaching become illegal?"

"It isn't the preaching. It's the healing."

"And the dying."

"And the dying. How did you know?"

"I went to see Marie's folks. Her father hates you."

"Why didn't you tell me?"

"Would it have done any good?"

"No, it wouldn't. You did the right thing, Orpha."

"He's the one that's got Fred to come out to see you."

"Fred's a friend of mine."

"He's a lawyer, isn't he?"

Joe, as if he hadn't a trouble in the world, laughed that big loving laugh again. "Orpha, you're still a backwoods girl, aren't you?"

He put his arm around me and walked me through the door I hadn't closed out onto the front porch. This was unusual in Joe. We weren't a family of claspers or huggers. If we had been, perhaps

I wouldn't have been so swept off my feet by the touch of Lon and Tom. Perhaps I wouldn't have been such a cat lover or so eager to hold Wanda in my arms if I had found affectionate touch as a girl in my family. I don't know. Perhaps the same need drove Joe to God.

Out on the porch Joe threw up his arms to the sky. "Oh, Orpha, do we have eyes because there are stars to see? Or did the stars, shining down on blind faces, breed eyes?"

"You talk like that to the District Attorney, Joe, and he'll send you to an insane asylum, not a jail."

"Not Fred. He knows I'm crazy but harmless."

Joe didn't, like Wanda, want an audience to hear him pray. He stepped away from me, clasped his hands, lifted his head, and prayed silently.

I did the same.

I came home on a Saturday afternoon from taking Wanda to a combined swimming lesson and Camp Fire Girls meeting to find Fred Benson and Joe in the living room. Both were drinking iced coffee. The heat still held. I was inclined to get as far away from that conversation as possible. I didn't want to hear more of Sam Shields's hatred of Joe.

Joe, for whatever reason, wanted me to stay, chiefly, I think, so that I would see that Fred Benson wasn't an ogre. He wasn't. He was physically a cross between the village blacksmith and Abraham Lincoln. Heavier set than Abraham, sharper featured than the blacksmith; but with some of the force—and humanity, too—we associate with both men.

"Fred, this is my sister, Orpha. She keeps house for me."

"Glad to meet you, Orpha. I've known your brother for some time."

"Always for bad reasons," Joe said.

"No, no. My wife goes to your church—Meeting, you call it? She hasn't joined yet, but I hear plenty of good from her. If everybody was like Iva, there'd be no reason to call a grand jury."

"Sam Shields isn't everybody."

"Now, Orpha."

"Let her alone, Joe. Do you want a sister who doesn't care whether you're called up before a grand jury or not? You're right, Orpha. Sam Shields isn't everybody. But that old farmer has got just about everybody aroused. There've been complaints before, but nothing substantial when looked into. Doctors, who don't want anybody cured of anything except by a man with an M.D. after his name. Old-line church people, who think the church is stepping out of line if it pays attention to anything but its members' souls. There was even a wife who wanted Joe banned from preaching and praying because her husband, after a couple of sessions with Joe, stopped being an invalid, began wearing the pants again, and was too feisty for the wife to handle. Oh, there've been all kinds. You wouldn't believe the number of people who object to something as seemingly intended for good as asking the Lord for help. And Shields has them all roused up now, what with that son-in-law of his able to substantiate some of Sam's claims.

"I've looked into and dismissed complaints before. I can't do that with this. This will have to go before a grand jury. They're the ones who will decide about the complaint that Shields has sworn out."

"Decide what?" I asked.

"Whether to indict Joe, to bind him over for trial."

"Trial for what?"

"Well, I can tell you, Orpha, what Shields hopes. He hopes the grand jury will say, 'This man should go on trial for manslaughter.' "

That word awakened even the calm Joe. "Manslaughter!"

Joe went out onto the porch with Fred Benson. I stayed inside. I didn't want to hear any more of what Joe's "friend" had to say.

When Joe came back in, he said, "Don't look so downcast, Orpha. Grand juries fail to indict more often than they indict."

"What does that mean?"

"It means they say, 'There's no reason to try this man.' "

"You think that will happen?"

"I do."

It didn't.

Grand-jury members are required by law not to divulge what goes on in their meetings. Before Joe's encounter with such a group, I took for granted that men and women investigating the possibility of a crime wouldn't break any law themselves. I know a lot more about the law and lawyers now than I did then. I wouldn't say now that the first thing a few jurors are bound to do is to leak a few facts to wife or boyfriend. I would now say that it's done. When someone—a juror, possibly, although she never hinted about who she was—phoned me, my first impulse was to hang up. Otherwise I'd be a partner in lawbreaking. I didn't hang up. I listened.

What I heard was that every man who had an axe to grind against Joe was there grinding it. There wasn't a doubt in the world but that the jury would indict and that Joe would be brought to trial for manslaughter.

"Get your brother a lawyer and get him quick," the lady lawbreaker told me. "He's going to need one."

I didn't tell Joe about the phone call. I did ask him what would happen if the grand jury indicted him.

"I'd be tried."

"Like Aaron Burr," said Wanda, who rather relished the idea that history was being enacted in her own home.

"Wanda, the dishes are still on the table." The idea of a trial fascinated Wanda and the dishes went to the kitchen almost as slowly as if under their own power.

"Tried. For causing Marie Griswold's death. Benson said manslaughter."

"I didn't cause her death. I prayed for her healing."

"I know that. But if there is a trial, you'll need a lawyer to say that's what you did."

"There won't be a trial. If there is, I can say so myself."

"Me, too," said Wanda, carrying plates one at a time to the kitchen. "I'll bear witness for you, Uncle Joe."

"At the rate you're going," Joe said, "you won't even be there. You'll still be clearing the table."

9

If the wind hadn't been blowing, perhaps I wouldn't have gone. No, that isn't true. I wouldn't have gone so soon is more accurate. It was a Thursday or Friday morning, near the end of the week, anyway. I awakened to noise. The casement windows, opened because of the heat, were creaking back and forth on the rods that held them open. The heat hadn't lessened. The wind that was blowing was a Santa Ana, that great blast of hot air that the desert exhales over the irrigated valleys to let them know who's master.

Most people hated the Santa Ana. It dried their skin, frizzled their hair, and rasped their nerves. A wind, they thought, should be cooling, even cold. There was something evil about a hot, sand-laden wind. I loved it. Maybe I'm torpid; maybe I need a wind to lean against—or to contend with. I reasoned, if reasoning is what was involved, that static air able to move with the force of a Santa Ana puts motionless people to shame. I would not be motionless.

I had worried night and day since the call from the grand-jury woman. There was no use imploring Joe to do what my caller had urged: get a lawyer. Hiring a lawyer was, in Joe's eyes, an admission of guilt. If you weren't guilty, your acts would speak for you. If guilty, you probably needed a lawyer to bluster or blarney a court into letting you off as easy as possible. Also, Quakers who didn't believe in fighting didn't believe in legal fighting, either. Accused and accuser should meet and settle their differences like Christian brothers.

The sight of Sam Shields's face had convinced me that whatever *he* was, he didn't consider Joe a Christian, let alone a brother. I knew that the mind behind Burt Griswold's hard eyes would care nothing for truth. Joe needed a lawyer; and if he had one, I would have to get him.

The choice wasn't hard. I knew only one lawyer: Ralph Navarro, who was the counselor for the Mexican boys' club Joe had over to dinner now and then. Joe and Ralph were good friends. Joe told Ralph, who was a Catholic, that Catholic saints, communicating directly with God without the help of any priestly intermediary, were on their way to becoming good Quakers. This made Ralph, who was an easy laugher for all that he had a stern Spanish con-quistador look, laugh. They agreed, too, that a priest didn't have time, with a wife and children, for looking after his flock. Ralph was, I judged, far from a priest; with a wife and child dead with Joe's disease, the two were especially able to understand each other.

On that dry, hot, windy morning, as soon as Joe was off to his office and Wanda to school, I called Ralph Navarro. I knew well enough that Ralph Navarro was one of the best-known lawyers in Los Angeles; I had heard Joe say, even though he had refused to listen to me, that "if I was ever faced with the gallows, Ralph Navarro is the man I'd want by my side."

Ralph's secretary answered the phone. I didn't know then that a busy lawyer's days are parceled out, hours, even minutes at a time, for months ahead.

I was told that Mr. Navarro was in conference. "I must speak to him. A man's life is at stake."

"Who is calling, please?"

"I am calling for the Reverend Joseph Chase."

The next voice I heard was Ralph's. "Orpha?"

"Yes, Mr. Navarro. Joe's in trouble."

"I've heard about it. Can you meet me for lunch? Are you downtown now?"

"I am."

"Do you know where the Biltmore is?"

"Of course. Right across from Pershing Square."

"Meet me in the lobby at 12:30. Can you do that?"

"Of course I can."

I didn't know it then, but Ralph had walked out on a luncheon of importance to talk to me about Joe. I told him what I'd heard from my anonymous phone caller. He asked me to repeat the conversation verbatim. No, he said, there wasn't enough there to move to set aside an indictment. Besides, he had heard more. I told him what Mr. Shields had said when I had called on him and his wife.

"Shields is a vindictive man, but Griswold is the most dangerous witness."

"Can't you go there and stop them from saying these things? You know they aren't true."

"Orpha, the only persons permitted in a grand-jury room are the District Attorney, the witnesses, and the jurors."

"Is there any way you could be a witness?"

"Not a chance. Don't worry. If this matter comes to trial, I'll have my say. Fred's been a pretty honest D.A. He's up for election now and will be pushing hard. But we've locked horns before, and I haven't lost yet. I don't expect to this time."

"You're saying you'll be Joe's lawyer?"

"That's what I'm saying."

"Beginning this minute?"

"No use jumping the gun. They haven't indicted yet. But the minute they do, you let me know."

"How will I know?"

"There'll be a man at the house to arrest Joe."

"Arrest? Like a criminal?"

"Like a man accused and indicted. Unless he's tried and con-

273

victed, he's no criminal. You let me know and we'll see he isn't treated like one."

I drove home slowly. Santa Anas often die down in the afternoon, then gust again at night. There was no letup in the heat. I thought that I had done the right thing. Joe asked no questions. Wanda was full of school happenings. Perhaps it was my imagination. Both looked at me, I thought, as if they knew I was hiding something from them.

The phone lady was right: Joe was indicted for manslaughter. Ralph was right: an officer came to the house to take Joe before a magistrate, where he would be charged with manslaughter. I, right or wrong, had called Ralph the minute I heard the news of the indictment and the nature of the charge. Joe, though he wasn't faced with the gallows, proved the truth of what he had declared earlier, that Ralph was the man he'd want by his side in time of trouble. Ralph, as his lawyer, was by his side when he was arraigned. And Ralph was the man who saw to it that Joe was released on his own recognizance.

I can't remember all the legal footwork that preceded the trial, the choice of jurors, number of witnesses called, and like matters. I don't *have* to remember. I have access to a verbatim report of every word said at that trial and could put it all down here if I wanted to. I don't want to. This is my life story, not Joe's, not Fred Benson's, not Ralph's, not Wanda's. Certainly I was a part of the trial. I spoke in it. Certainly I was body and soul with Joe in what could put an end to the life he valued most—not on the gallows, but in the pulpit. My life's accomplishments can't hold a candle to Joe's. But his life has been told, more than once. I'm the only one who's going to tell of my life. Joe will have to play second fiddle here and he'd be the first to urge me to tell it that way.

10

While we waited for the trial, Wanda started her junior year in high school. Joe carried on his ministry as usual. I had my book to work on. When I started *Talbot Ware,* I had intended, as I've

274

said, to tell the story of a hell-raising young man, sick unto death, cured by faith, who became himself a minister and faith healer. I certainly had no idea that he would ever be tried for homicide. I knew, since this was Joe's story (except for the fictional romance, which I inserted in the first version and later removed), that the trial, no matter what its outcome, not only was a part of Joe's life, but also had to be included.

Someplace in the genes of anyone attempting to tell a story, whether with pen on paper or with tongue at the supper table, is the knowledge that listeners' or readers' attention must be caught in the wonderment of "How is it all going to come out?" I was glad to have the story, trial or no trial, to work on. It did not keep me from worrying about the outcome, but it kept me busy. As a writer, I should have tried to talk with the Shieldses and Burt Griswold. Several notebooks of Unspoken Thoughts didn't make Montebello, California (or even me), regard me as a writer. There I was, the sister of the indicted minister; any running around with pencil and pen getting statements from Joe's accusers would not have been suitable. Maybe not even possible. It is unlikely that persons who thought Joe guilty as accused would want to say anything to his sister.

It was suitable for me to talk with Joe's lawyer. Ralph knew a good deal about evangelists, faith healing, and, of course, jury trials. By chance, he had been one of Aimee's lawyers when she stood trial after her pretended abduction.

Ralph had been born in Mexico. Some long-ago Spanish hidalgo had left an imprint sterner and more commanding on his countenance than that on the round-faced, smiling Indian-Mexicans who were pouring across the Mexican border into California.

Ralph didn't underestimate either Fred Benson's ability or Sam Shields's determination.

"I would never have taken this case if I had thought for a minute Joe was capable of the crime they're accusing him of. Or that Burt wasn't."

"Do you really think Burt wanted his wife to die?"

"What do you think Marie was trying to tell you in that last conversation?"

I don't know whether Ralph's ability to see into the nature and motives of people had come to him through his long experience with the law or was something he had been born with. A combination of both, I am now inclined to think.

"Do you really think Burt wanted his wife to die?" I repeated.

"I do."

"Did he believe that Joe would be willing to let her die for twenty thousand dollars?"

"He didn't think Joe would. That's why he gave it to the church, not Joe. That way, Burt would look like a church-loving man. And any doubts Joe had would be put to sleep."

"Doubts about what?"

"Burt's motives."

"Joe never supposed he had any motives except to have his wife healed."

"You did, though."

"I never thought he wanted Marie to die. The most I thought was that he wanted to find a way for her to be healed without being —disfigured."

"Losing her breast."

"Yes."

"If your brother hadn't told Mrs. Griswold that it was God's will for some of us to suffer, his case would be much simpler."

"We all suffer. It must be God's will."

"We don't all claim to be able to put an end to suffering."

"Joe doesn't claim that. He tells everyone Jesus does the healing."

"O.K., O.K. But in one breath he tells that poor woman Jesus will heal her. And in the next, he tells her that it is God's will that some of us should suffer. What is this unhappy woman, in love with the man who is talking to her—"

"In love with Joe?"

"Don't think you're the only woman who can fall in love."

"But Marie was married to Burt."

"I can't think of a better reason for falling in love with Joe. So here is holy Joe, never suspecting Burt's motives. And here is love-lorn Marie determined to accept, without complaining, God's will for her to suffer without accusing the preacher she loves of failing to cure her."

"Do you really think that is the way it was?"

"Right now, that's what I think. But I haven't started digging yet. And convincing a jury may be another story entirely. It would be easier if your brother wasn't a Quaker. Those people set themselves up to be so almighty pure and above reproach, it does the ordinary sinner good to see one take a fall."

"You kept Aimee out of jail."

"Aimee was never in danger of jail. Any high-school debater could've kept Aimee out of jail. All she was accused of was a few nights in Carmel with a boyfriend. That was a nice human thing to do. She shouldn't have messed it up with that story of a desert abduction."

"Joe would never do a thing like that."

"Worse luck for him—and Marie. If he'd spend a week in Hawaii now and then and less time preaching what doesn't make sense— a combination of faith healing and suffering through God's will —Marie might be alive. And Joe certainly wouldn't be standing trial. I don't understand these Quakers. A religion has got to have some rules. Quakers want to play it by ear—and God doesn't whisper the same message in every Quaker ear."

"Is this the message God whispered in your ear?"

Ralph Navarro clapped his brown hands together. "By God, I think you're on the way to becoming a Jesuit. And if you are, you wouldn't tell anyone what God said."

XI
REUNION

1

Ralph Navarro was right about the woman he was talking to then. He could not be expected to see the woman she was to become: a writer. I think he would now have the insight to understand that telling others what God whispers to them is a writer's obsession: often a puny God, whispering into a tin ear. Writers tell us what they hear, and in doing so paint their own dream pictures. Where did Emily Brontë's demon lovers and Ethel Dell's sheiks come from? Not from the lives they lived, but from the dreams they dreamed and the voices they and no one else heard. Out of the lives they lived came only pallid curates and impecunious relatives.

At the time of Joe's trial, I had the simple task, I thought, of telling the life story of Joseph Chase. His life as a boy had been fascinating to me, daring and tough, tender and sympathetic. His sickness, cure, and conversion were a mystery I wanted to explore.

I was well into the story of Joe's life in the month before the trial started; which was also the month when Mama and Papa arrived. Members of the Meeting came out to our house every evening in that month to pray, to plan, to meditate. I was lucky to have solitary work to which I could in all conscience retire.

I was happy to see Mama and Papa. My parents looked as they always had to me: elderly. Papa, like a statesman-farmer. Mama, like a schoolmarm who had strayed into the kitchen en route to a rights-for-women platform. Parents and teachers, who look old to the young from the beginning, don't look much older twenty years later. The young, in ten years, change unbelievably for parents and teachers.

Joe, who had left home a thin, pinch-faced young invalid, was now a man, a sinewy brown California preacher who talked to thousands on First Day; and had conversations with God he wasn't bashful about reporting. I could see my parents trying to envision in their minds the changes, year by year, that had transformed harum-

281

scarum Joe Chase to the Reverend Joseph Chase, and thus make him more recognizably their son. They wouldn't have changed him in any way. They rejoiced in his health, admired the graying of his black curls, marveled at the power of his ministerial oratory. This Joe Chase was a fine man. Was he at one time their farm-boy son? He was as strange to them as Cinderella had been to her mother and sisters at the ball. They talked to him a lot about the past. They remembered the same animals, storms, crops, neighbors. They were surely related. They were somewhat embarrassed by the almost loose way Joe had of talking of God and Jesus. Joe wouldn't, it appeared, have turned a hair to see Them there or to hear Them speak.

Mama *was* taken aback by Joe.

"I count myself a religious person," Mama told me, "and I'm not going to fault anyone, least of all my son, for putting religious talk into his everyday conversation."

"Joe doesn't count himself a religious person," I told Mama.

"What!" she exclaimed. I hurried on to explain the difference in Joe's mind between being religious and being spiritual. "Religions are man-made, Joe says. What is spiritual is the result of the in-dwelling spirit of God. It has nothing to do with churches, or creeds, or ceremonies."

"Is that what the Quakers believe?"

"That's what they believe here in Southern California."

"That church, east or west, never did rank very high in my opinion."

"It does with Joe. And he's studied religions a lot more than you and I have."

"I grant Quakerism's better than nothing," Mama said doubtfully.

Wanda, even more than Joe, had changed in my parents' eyes. While older, Joe had not gone from boyhood to manhood since last they had seen him. Wanda, when last they saw her, was a child, a chunky, good-sized, outspoken child, it is true. Now she was a sexy young lady. They didn't remember what a few years will do to a nine-year-old—in any climate. They attributed the change to the tropical California sun and to our nearness to Hollywood. They didn't approve, or at least Mama didn't, either of Joe's familiarity with God or of Wanda's breasts, so outthrust even the most modest male eyes couldn't miss them. There was nothing self-consciously sexy about Wanda. She was still Kickapoo-shaped, sturdy rather than curvy, the baby fat gone, with no wasp waist or delicate sloping shoulders as replacements. You couldn't count Wanda's ribs, or her eyelashes, either; too many lashes and the ribs too well covered. She was big-eyed, big-breasted, big-hearted. I loved her. There was no one, not even Joe, I could talk to so easily. ("Who does she look like?" I was sometimes asked. "Her father," I would answer, and no one had the nerve to ask, "Which husband?")

"You'd better watch that girl with Joe," Mama told me.

Mama could have been present in the Garden when the Serpent put the apple in Eve's hand; and while Mama did have other thoughts, none bulked as large in her mind as sex and the way un- principled women often used it.

"Mama, Joe is as pledged to celibacy as any priest."

"It's a pledge a good many priests fail to keep."

"Wanda's my daughter."

"She's got Matthews blood. It's bad blood."

2

I sat on the front porch with Papa while we listened to the passing cars and the distant thud of an oil pump.

"This is a far cry from Amesville," he said.

"Do you like California?"

"I can't see California for thinking about Joe. How did the boy ever get himself into such a mess?"

"By praying, I reckon."

"This is no time for joking, Orpha."

"I'm far from joking. That's the one and only reason he's being tried. He prayed that Marie Griswold be cured of her cancer. She wasn't cured. She died. Joe is really being prosecuted for practicing medicine without a license."

"It won't end that way."

"I don't understand you."

"Joe is accused of manslaughter. Half the parents in the world would be in jail if praying for their children's health was called 'doctoring without a license.' They aren't because no one gave them twenty thousand dollars to pray."

"Joe wasn't paid twenty thousand to pray. He never saw the money."

"He should have. And it should've made him suspicious. Just because Roosevelt is passing government money around like water don't mean a seller of used-car parts got hold of twenty thousand in any legal way. Joe's still a socialist, I suppose? Share and share alike? Well, he and Roosevelt likely see eye to eye. But it'll take F. D. R. himself to get him out of this jam. And I doubt that prayer is Franklin's long suit."

Papa hated Roosevelt almost more than he loved Joey—but not quite. Papa was a good old Republican farmer and he tended to believe that every setback, personal or national, stemmed from Roosevelt policies. It was Roosevelt and socialism that had caused Joey to be so careless about the sources of the money his church received.

"Oh, Orphy," he said, and there were tears in his eyes, "where did your mother and I fail you children?"

I knew what he meant about me. The two marriages. But Joe?

"Joe's a fine man," I said. "He had the will to get well and the brains to get educated and the heart to find God. And you and Mama should be proud of him every minute. He does heal people. I've seen them. He cured my headaches."

"Ah, well," said Papa, his cheek still streaked with tears. "That pain was all in your head."

Papa was no jokester. This attempt to be funny while his heart ached touched me, so I went to him and clasped him—something I had been too timid to do when young.

"It'll turn out all right. You wait and see. God won't desert His own."

"His only begotten Son got crucified."

I stood back from Papa to look at his face. There were no tears now, only a sternness I didn't remember ever seeing before. While Joe had been finding God, had Papa been losing Him?

It was nearer Halloween than Thanksgiving, nearer jack-o'-lanterns than pumpkin pies. In spite of this, Wanda and I made a supper to celebrate the folks' arrival as near a Thanksgiving feast as we could. By Thanksgiving Joe might be in jail. We might not all be together again for a long time.

Papa and Mama had dropped Joe off at the Meeting House; then, in his car they had gone on to explore Hollywood and Beverly Hills. There were street maps telling tourists where the stars lived.

California traffic alarmed my father, but he was a good driver, steadfast and not easily buffaloed.

I had at first planned a traditional California dinner—Mexican food: tamale pie, guacamole, refried beans, flan. Fortunately, I gave it up. Later, when I did make a tamale pie, it was not relished. I prepared, instead, the food all of us had grown up with: chicken and dressing, two kinds of potatoes, milk gravy, creamed peas, two kinds of pie, pumpkin and mince.

They were all late getting home for dinner. Joe had been meeting with Ralph Navarro and his Ministry and Oversight board. No one else in that group had a Thanksgiving dinner awaiting them. So they took their time. Papa and Mama were sure they had seen Errol Flynn watering his front lawn. Despite the delay, the food had not been harmed.

Joe had never been more loving, never more confident. He asked Papa to return thanks when we sat down to the table. "If I did it, Pa, we might never get to the food." Even so, Joe added a postscript to Papa's prayer. "Thank Thee, dear Lord, for Thy everlasting love and for bringing five people who love each other together. May we never forget that we live in the bounty of Thy gift of life and that we are Thy children and brothers of Thy son, Jesus Christ. Amen."

I had put all the food on the table, but Joe, in the warmth and exuberance of his feeling, served, scooping out mounds of potatoes and inquiring, "Dark meat or white?" like a devoted butler. When not carrying food, he was son, brother, and uncle, hugging and kissing.

"You don't know how I've longed for this day."

"I once had visions of you being a lawyer, Joseph," Mama said. "It never crossed my mind you'd need one."

"It crossed mine," Papa said.

"God has sent me the best."

This kind of talk grated on Mama's ears. Not that she didn't believe that God had His finger in every pie. Obvious facts didn't need much talking about. If she heard Papa declaring, "My wife is the light of my life and the ornament of my hearth," she'd start looking for the other woman.

It didn't occur to me then—it does now—that the five of us seated at that out-of-season Thanksgiving table constituted what was typical of Southern California. Not a native child of the Golden West among us.

A woman, twice married, husbands departed, and hopeful now of finding herself—not a husband.

A Midwestern couple, Roosevelt-hating, God-fearing, churchgoing, Republican-voting: the real backbone of Southern California.

Girl, born out of wedlock (bastard in the sociology textbooks); pure product of California sunshine (beach or desert), California poppies and Hollywood, beholding eyes would affirm.

Joe, most typical Californian of all, a man come to the state (the one-lung state) in his youth for his health. Product of the great California school system, and possessing that talent more admired in California than anywhere else: a talent for public performance. Joe's talent was for preaching the gospel, a gospel somewhat esoteric. Why would Californians who divorce, make sexy movies, build tract houses, kill each other by speeding on their freeways, produce and drink wine, take to a man preaching conversion, faith healing, and the Second Coming? Perhaps they feel the need of God more than most. Uprooted, far from home, divorced, lonesome, doing what they had been taught as young people was wrong, they long to be loved and forgiven. Perhaps they found it was easier to follow a man who looked like a young Ronald Colman and preached like a holy Clarence Darrow than some bland plump-jowled chicken-fed pulpiteer. Joe, whether because of his long sickness or his youthful skirmishes with girls, looked like a man who had sinned, suffered, and repented; and for those reasons could supposedly understand the plight of others who had trod that same painful path.

"Joe," Mama said, "you haven't had a word to say about the meeting of your lawyer and the church members. What went on? What was their opinion? Did they reach any conclusions?"

"They did," said Joe. "But let's not talk about it. This is homecoming day. There'll be plenty of time to talk about the trial later."

"It's wrong for them to try you, Uncle Joe. They try criminals. Some Thanksgiving!" Wanda said, and began to cry. To muffle her sobs, she wrapped her big napkin, which had belonged to Lon's mother, about her head.

Some Thanksgiving was right. Only Papa and Joe ate any pie. Wanda, her napkin still wrapped around her head, went to her room to cry.

286

"Orpha," said Mama, "you're going to have to watch that girl."

"I'll talk to Wanda later," Joe told me.

"I don't know what you can say."

The three of us sat for a long time, silent. Mama, without a word, began to clear the table. Once she was in the kitchen, Joe said, "Don't think that I don't take that woman's death to heart."

"A preacher takes risks he can't foresee," Papa said, trying to ease Joe's pain.

"I can't stop preaching the Scripture," said Joe, "trial or no trial."

I left Joe and Papa at the table and went to Wanda's room. Usually, following an outburst of that kind, Wanda, like someone who has had too much to drink, went sound asleep. She did have on her nightgown, but she was on top of the covers, propped up against the bed's headboard.

"You made quite a fuss, Wanda. Do you think Joe's done something wrong?"

"Maybe."

"Do you think Uncle Joe took money from a man in return for trying to make sure the wife died?"

"Of course not. He couldn't do that. I didn't mean that. Only, how can Uncle Joe believe that God wants people to suffer? Or think that God speaks to him? I am going to stop being a Christian. I think Uncle Joe's dangerous. Some people could say what he says and no one would pay any attention. But whatever Uncle Joe says, you believe. If I'm not a Christian, it'll be easier to doubt him."

Wanda weighed almost as much as I did, but she still sat on my lap. "I think it's too hard to be a Christian, Mama. I'll try to be good and sensible, but I'm not going to get carried away again by anyone who says he hears the voice of God."

Wanda reminded me of myself, after Lon's death. I, too, was going to be good and sensible. Not get carried away. Be ruled by my head, not my heart. That rational girl married Jake Hesse.

3

Joe's raspberry-colored stucco house of uncurtained arches, one bathroom, and three bedrooms was not big enough for five people. I gave my room to Papa and Mama while they were there, and slept with Wanda. I had lost the ability to sleep with anyone—or with anyone as warm and spread-eagled as Wanda. At the end of a week my parents found a two-room-and-kitchenette apartment on what was still called "Normal Hill" because the old Normal School had been located there. I had expected my mother, accustomed to a large farmhouse and the duties of feeding chickens, gathering and selling eggs, making buttter, to be bored and unhappy in two box-like rooms not far from the heart of a sprawling city. Instead, she loved it. We are attached to the homes we have and the occupations that keep us employed, not because we love them, but because we aren't bold enough to experiment with any other. We are too adaptable for our own good. We are farmers and teachers and writers by chance, not choice. Mama had been a housewife because she had married a farmer-nurseryman; the wife of such a man kept house.

In her two-room apartment, which she could keep spotless with one hour's work a day, and with a city library only three blocks distant, Mama's career as a housewife was over. She read. She brought home books on subjects she had never heard of before. She attended night classes, learned to cook Mexican and understand the differences between the teaching of Buddha and Confucius. In short, she became a Californian—and a Southern Californian, who, as a person more recently uprooted than his northern brethren, hunts replacements more avidly.

The Depression was not yet over, but for people who had been as thrifty as the Chases, it was a blessing. Their days of moneymaking were finished, but what they had saved went far: more carrots for a dime than they could eat in a week; round steak, twenty-five cents a pound. And at a cafeteria, with which Los Angeles was well populated, they had good meals and the pleasure of "eating out" for thirty-five cents.

A library is not the solace for an outdoor man it is for an indoor woman. Griffith Park was in the city but far from urban. Tramping there, Papa met a man who was beating the Depression—or at least coping with it—by raising rabbits. People who could not afford beef could still afford rabbits, and the man who raised them sold not only their flesh but also their fur. Rabbit-raising was not permitted within Los Angeles city limits. This man lived out east of Montebello. Papa accepted the invitation to visit with a double purpose

—to inspect rabbit-raising and to drop in on his children. The outcome of the inspection was that Papa became a partner of the rabbit raiser, a man with the unlikely name of Tennessee Overturff. In this partnership, Papa made an even more unusual discovery than had Mama. She had become a housekeeper through marriage. Papa had been a farmer-nurseryman by choice, not marriage. Now he discovered that he preferred working with animals to working with plants. Ask any cattleman whether he would rather ride cattle or seed the harvest grain. A rabbit is not a cow and a hutch is not a corral. The same difference is there, however. Don't ask me how either is able to kill, let alone chomp down with his teeth, on animals they have nurtured.

So there we were: five Southern Californians. Mother, attending night classes and studying Oriental religions. Father, switched from Rome Beauties to rabbits. Daughter, trying to become a writer. Granddaughter, trying to become an unbeliever. Son, California's, possibly the nation's, best-known evangelist and faith healer, facing the accusation of having caused a young woman's death by persuading her to rely on prayer instead of medical treatment.

Did California cause any of this? No, though it does seem to draw to it people with unusual inclinations.

4

With Papa and Mama out of the house, Wanda in school, Joe busier than ever before, I wrote six hours a day. Papa, whose rabbit operation was located in what was then called "the Whittier Narrows," often stopped in to see me on his way home to his Normal Hill apartment. What I wanted to do, with both Mama and Joe absent, was to prod Papa into talking about the young Joe, the Joe I had been too young to assess or evaluate.

November, in the old days before smog in California and before the rainy season had really started, could be bell-clear, tawny and crimson at sundown, poinsettias beginning to bloom, and geraniums still as red as in July.

On such an evening, Papa stopped in with a dressed rabbit (as far as the rabbit is concerned, this means undressed—no fur, no head, no guts, no feet) in a paper bag. I cooked the poor creatures he brought to me; they were tastier than chicken, but I kept them out of the sight of Pussy's offspring; to a cat (even to me), they looked like skinned cats.

Papa and I stood on the front porch admiring the sunset. The clouds had opened up on the western horizon as if melted by sun heat; the sun itself appeared visibly afire. Through the cloud opening, Catalina was a gray hump on the water like some basking Pacific sea monster.

"Nothing like this to be seen in Amesville," Papa said.

Papa had made a California discovery: Congoin. Congoin was the name given for some reason to maté by the company distributing it; maté was "the tea of the gauchos." Congoin, people said, accounted for the endurance and virility of the South American cowboys. A pot of Congoin, a twist of dried meat, and the gaucho could ride all day without hunger or fatigue. Congoin had no caffeine in it, and hence did not interfere with sleep. Joe scorned it. Sleep was nothing he cared about.

Papa and I, sleepers, by choice, drank either Congoin or sassafras tea in the evening. Mama had brought me a big aromatic bag of sassafras bark when she came west.

It was Congoin that evening for Papa and me. We sat facing each other in the breakfast nook, our cups of pale-green gaucho tea on the table.

"I wish you'd tell me more about Joe when he was a little boy."

Papa, who knew the reason for my question, wasn't eager to answer it. "Fools' faces are seen in public places," he said. "I'm not enthusiastic about your making a public exhibit of Joe."

There was very little I could do that would make Joe any more public than he was at that minute. I didn't remind Papa of this.

"Joe won't be called Joe in this story. It's the story of a man named Talbot Ware. Things happen to him that never happened to Joe—or to anybody else as far as I know. Joe'll be disguised completely."

"Is the trial going into your book?" The trial was two weeks away.

"Yes," I said.

"No point your trying to disguise anything or anybody after the trial. How many preachers in the United States have ever been tried on charges of this kind?"

"Readers will think I read about the Chase case and livened up my story a little by attributing some of what happened in it to Talbot Ware."

Papa was not a snorter, nor a harrumpher. He did make a sound of disbelief deep in his throat.

"I'll miss my guess if they don't do the opposite. Say, 'This is Joe Chase disguised as Talbot Ware.' "

"The trial isn't what I want to talk about, Papa. And who knows what will happen in it, anyway? It's Joe as a little boy. You knew him before I did. Did you ever think he'd be a preacher?"

"Joe, a preacher? He was scallywag. You know that."

"Lots of scallywags have been converted and become preachers. Was there anything about Joe when he was little that made you think he would be a preacher someday?"

"Well, he was a great talker. And he could charm a bird out of a tree. Those two don't add up to the ministry. Though they're no drawback. What I thought he'd be was a politician. Joe was no great hand at plowing or milking the cows. He went to church because he had to."

"What caused the change?"

"Blessed if I know. What changed you?"

"From what to what?"

"Good schoolmarm to, first, the wife of a crazy man, then the wife of a fussbudget shoe salesman."

"You never said a word to me against either one."

"They were O.K. as far as any dealings I had with them. As for living with either one—no, no."

"They were the ones that asked me."

Papa reached across the table and took my hand. "Orpha, I think you always underrated yourself and I think I know the reason why."

I had never kissed or been kissed by Papa; never had my hand held, my shoulder patted—or, for that matter, my bottom spanked. We had hardly ever touched. I had felt less guilty committing adultery with Tom than I did holding hands with my father. If Jake had found Tom and me in bed together, I would have been sorry about being caught, but I wouldn't have felt dirty or abnormal, as I would had Mama come in the door and found me sitting in the breakfast nook holding hands with my father.

Papa recognized my uneasiness. He squeezed my hand and let go of it.

291

"I don't worry about Joe. His path is settled. You're the one who's drifting. No husband, no children."

"Wanda's my child."

"That girl'll be married before you can say boo."

"Wanda doesn't even keep steady company with anyone, let alone talk about marriage."

"She's your child in that. She won't waste time on courtship. She'll up and marry the way you did. No, I don't worry about Wanda or Joe. It's you, buried here like some old priest's half-nun housekeeper."

"I like keeping house for Joe."

"That's a job for some widow of sixty, not for a girl of thirty."

"I haven't been a girl of thirty for some time, Papa. You know that."

"You won't stop being a girl for me as long as you live, Orpha. And you're a better-looking girl now than you were when you were kicking piepans twenty years ago. Try to remember that."

Wanda's school bus dropped her off before Papa left. Milk was her drink, not sassafras tea or Congoin. She joined us at the table.

"Grandpa, are you saved?"

"I've always thought so."

"Can you hear God talking to you?"

"No."

"How do you know what to do then?"

"I read the Bible and pray."

"Do you think Joe hears God?"

"I do."

"It would be better if he didn't, wouldn't it?"

"Easier for him, maybe. Not better."

"I wouldn't want to hear God speak to me."

"Feeling the way you do, Wanda, I don't think you have to worry."

When Papa left, I went out onto the porch with him. The sunset had burned away to a few somber clouds, rust-colored at their edges. Catalina had disappeared. The usual evening breeze off the ocean was blowing inland.

"We live in a good land," Papa said. "Misfortune brought us here, but the land itself is a blessing."

292

I didn't want my father to think that I had drawn away from his touch. I put my arms around him as if we were parting forever.

"Good-bye, Papa. I'll remember what you said about piepans."

When I went inside, Wanda had taken the rabbit out of its sack. She was holding it by its hind legs, like a doctor with a newborn babe.

"Do you want to eat this?" she asked.

"Not very much."

"I'd like to bury it. I don't think I'll ever eat meat again."

"Wanda, I don't think I can keep up with your resolves. Are you still working on not being a Christian?"

"I will be a Christian like Grandpa. Read the Bible and pray. But I'm not going to hear voices or tell people they have to suffer. I don't want to eat this poor little animal. I'd like to bury it as an offering."

"Cook it and you'll have a burnt offering."

"I'll do it for you and Uncle Joe. I'd like to bury its bones afterward with a marker for me."

"What do you plan to put on the marker?"

"God is love."

"What do we give Joe for supper?"

"Tomato gravy, creamed peas, biscuits, hot gingerbread with lemon sauce. I'll cook the rabbit, but I won't eat it."

"Bury it uncooked if you want to."

Wanda kissed me. "It has suffered enough."

Wanda was in the kitchen cooking when Joe came home.

"What's that you're drinking? Pa's virility tea?"

"Congoin."

"Is the kettle on? I'll have a cup."

"Not coffee?"

"Virility tea."

"Has it been a bad day?"

"Not especially."

"Here's your Congoin. Are you giving up coffee?"

"Never. But whatever there is in this that gives gauchos their endurance, I thought I could use tonight. Give Pa my thanks."

"He was here on the way home. With a rabbit."

"Good. A little meat wouldn't hurt me, either."

"Wanda has buried it."

"Buried it! What was wrong with it?"

"Not a thing. Except it was dead. Wanda's gone back to being a Christian again. Not your kind. Papa's kind. She wanted to mark the occasion with a sacrifice of some kind."

"Who was to be the sacrifice? Me? I don't get any supper?"

"Oh, yes, you do. Tomato gravy and biscuits. You wouldn't have wanted that rabbit if you'd seen it. It was a pitiful sight. Wanda feels like she's saved its life by not cooking it. It's buried with a marker, 'God is love.' "

Joe finished his second cup. "Do you ever wish you'd never taken on the raising of that girl?"

"Never. I have doubts about everything else. Not her. Joe, I tried to get Papa to talk about you when you were little. The whole idea of a book about you upsets him. If he had his way, there wouldn't be a biography or autobiography in the world. He thinks it's boastful, talking about yourself or your family. He thinks what you do should speak for itself."

"It's going to—loud and clear—in a month or so."

"He thinks that shouldn't ever be mentioned."

"If you write about me, it'll have to be. But I can't say I'm crazy about playing Johnson to your Boswell, either."

"Except for Boswell, who'd know about Johnson today?"

"I bet that doesn't cut much ice with Johnson today."

"I bet it does with Boswell. Joe, I thought when I was asking Papa about you, why not ask Joe himself."

"What did you ask him?"

"If he ever thought you'd be a preacher."

"What did he say?"

"He said no. He said you were a young scallywag."

"I can't deny that. But, inside me, I was hunting for something. Scallywagging was just busywork. I didn't know what I was hunting for. I did know I had an amount of love and praise in me that chasing girls didn't take care of. Someplace at the center of the world was a radiance. I wanted to be there. I wanted to be a part of that shining."

"When you were a little boy?"

"What's little?"

"Twelve or thirteen."

"That was when I began yearning for the light."

"You went to church every Sunday."

"Church? What's church? An organization. A ceremony. A religion. I wanted an indwelling Christ. I wanted something I had never heard of. How did I find Him? Sickness. Suffering. God's will. A follower of a man of God. A healing."

Joe wasn't telling me what I needed to know any more than Papa had. What did he *do* when he was scallywagging? What did he *do* when he was hunting for the radiance?

Wanda came in to set the table for supper.

"Uncle Joe," she said, "I'm going to be an old-time Christian like Grandpa."

"That's the way I started," Joe told her.

"They won't put her on the stand, will they?" I asked Joe when Wanda went back to the kitchen.

"Surely not. She never even talked with Marie. Marie herself's the one I wish could talk."

"You don't take the credit when people get well, do you? Well, don't take the blame when they die."

XII
TRIAL

1

As I've said, much of the trial detail is reported in *Talbot Ware*. Writers often tell the same story over and over again; new locations, characters with new names, but the same old story. Since I wasn't even a character in the book (at that time I shared Papa's feeling about revealing myself), I am not selling secondhand goods as new when I report my actual participation in the trial.

The trial was by jury and there was a hassle of a week or more between Navarro and Benson on the acceptability of jurors. Ralph was convinced that persons with church connections of some kind would understand and sympathize more with what Joe had done and was doing than those who did not believe in God, let alone believe in the ability of God to heal.

Benson reversed the strategy and tried to keep church members off the jury. Both lawyers were mistaken. News accounts after the trial indicated that the three or four churchgoers on the jury were supporters neither of Joe nor of faith healing. They were supporters of their own churches and they did not relish the large number of worshipers and the sums of money that had been lured away from them by Joe and what they considered his publicity-seeking.

The courthouse was crowded with spectators. Long before the doors opened, a line stretching from the courthouse stairs a couple of blocks down the street had formed. Many were members of Joe's Meeting. An equal number had come simply to see the show; not believers, not churchgoers; curiosity seekers to watch the spectacle of the downfall of a preacher, the exposé of a hypocrite.

Joe rode with Ralph to the courthouse. I went with Wanda and my parents. Papa and Mama couldn't have been much more downcast had they been going to Joey's funeral. Back where we came from, "They took him to court over it" was often as much of a condemnation as a verdict of guilty. "Not guilty" frequently meant no more than that a good lawyer had done wonders with a jury. "They took him to court over it" said, even if the jury's verdict was "innocent," "Where there's smoke, there's bound to be fire."

I didn't share my parents' old-fashioned backwoods notion. Knowing that Joe was innocent, I was enough of a Californian to think that all the publicity he was getting might do him and his Meeting good. Papa and Mama were in some ways more Quakerly than Joe himself. They believed that if you had a light, modesty required that a bushel should immediately be put over it. What they would have done in the time of a man like Jesus, I don't know. That walking on water and blasting of fig trees would surely have seemed to them exhibitionist; the show-off stunts of a man most certainly not a good, reliable, voting Republican.

I had never been in a courtroom before. In some ways it reminded me of a church. The jury could have been the choir. The judge could have been the preacher. Joe and Ralph at one table, below Judge and jury, Fred Benson and his assistants at another, could have been seekers at the mourner's bench. It was even churchlike in the requirement that every witness place his hand on a Bible before he spoke and swear to tell the truth. (Not Joe, of course; as a Quaker, he was permitted to affirm.) This swearing on the Bible actually went beyond what happens in church, where persons testify without ever touching a Bible.

Judge Maxwell had a fine face, worthy of any pulpit. If Benson had been, as he declared when he visited us, Joe's friend, it didn't show now. He had no smiles for anyone, let alone Joe. Ralph did not have Benson's expression of eagerness to attack; but there was a calm assurance there that would make any reasonable attacker think twice before striking.

Joe was himself, even able to smile at Mama, who sat beside me. Because of the crowded courtroom, we had been separated from Wanda and Papa, who were someplace behind us.

When Benson made his opening statement, telling the jury why Joe had been indicted and of what he was accused—manslaughter—I could feel Mama shake with anger. "The accused," said Benson, "by claiming that he could by prayer cure Marie Griswold of the cancer that subsequently caused her death, prevented her from having the relatively simple operation which has saved the lives of many other women afflicted in the same manner. He is thus as much the cause of her death as if he had forcibly restrained her from seeking medical help. Words can be as destructive as bullets, when used by an eloquent man, convinced of his own powers. Let this eloquent man tell a pious, God-fearing woman that he is an instrument of God, and what chance does this woman, already weak with her sickness, have to seek recommended medical help?"

Benson had more to say. If I hadn't held onto her arm, Mama would, I feared, rise to her feet and throw the D.A.'s words back into his teeth.

The D.A. called a number of preliminary witnesses: a surgeon who testified as to the number of women with cancer of the breast who had been saved by surgery; the parents of a child who had died in spite of Joe's prayers.

Marie's father, who was probably even more anxious to have his say than Mama, was at last given his chance by Benson.

"What is your relationship to the deceased?"

"I am her father."

"Was she a church member?"

"Her whole life."

"When did you first see the Reverend Joseph Chase?"

"At Marie's funeral."

"This was the last time you saw your daughter?"

"I was not permitted to see her then."

"Why not?"

"No one was permitted to see her. She was, at least I was told she was, put into a plain box, not a regular coffin, which was placed at the back of what they call 'the Meeting House'; not up front, as in a regular funeral."

"Was your daughter's funeral otherwise 'regular'?"

"It was not. My daughter's name was never spoken. Not a word was said praising her or sorrowing for her death. It was like somebody wanted to forget she had died—and why."

"Somebody?"

"Holy Joe," shouted Sam Shields, pointing at Joe. "Holy Joe, that's who wanted to forget why she died."

Ralph was on his feet; his icy voice carried far. "Need I state my objection, Your Honor?"

Maxwell pounded on his desk with the gavel until the room was utterly still. "Order in the court. Mr. Prosecutor, let this be the only time I need admonish you to restrain your witness from name-calling. And no more leading questions."

Benson's tongue could be oily as well as sharp. "Your Honor," he said, "please remember that my witness is a bereaved father faced with the man he has reason to believe caused his daughter's death."

"Mr. Benson, as you know, this jury is here to answer that question. Let's have no more surmises by you or by your witness."

"I apologize to the Court. Your witness, Mr. Navarro," Benson said.

It was all Benson wanted to hear, but Ralph had a question or two he wanted answered.

"Mr. Shields," he asked, "did you inquire as to whether the manner of your daughter's funeral was any different from the manner of other funerals held in that Meeting House?"

"I did not."

"Why not?"

"I'm new here."

"You don't know anyone who has attended the Meetings of Reverend Chase?"

Mr. Shields did not reply.

"Your son-in-law had been in attendance at those Meetings for six months. Isn't that true?"

Mr. Shields remained silent.

Judge Maxwell said, "Answer the question, Mr. Shields."

Ralph shook his head. "Let him step down, Your Honor. He is a father in deep sorrow. I wouldn't want to add to his pain."

2

While the trial lasted, Joe stayed in town at the home of his lawyer. In my opinion, he did so less because of any need for further consultation with Ralph than because of a desire not to have to listen to his family discuss his trial. My parents, with Joe away, were staying out at Montebello with me.

The trial was in its second week before Benson called Burt Griswold to the stand. Marie's father had been angry, distraught, accusing. Since he had not seen his daughter for more than a year and

302

had never seen Joe at all until his daughter's funeral, what he had to say actually had very little to do with the issue at stake, specifically: Was Joseph Chase guilty of manslaughter? His daughter had died and her father wanted to blame someone.

Burt Griswold had pertinent facts. If Joe was to be convicted as accused, Griswold was the one who could do it. He was totally unlike his father-in-law, the feisty farmer. Grave, sorrowful, dignified. Also handsome.

He was sworn in and identified himself.

"Mr. Griswold, how long were you married to Marie Griswold?"

"Twenty years."

"How old was she when she died?"

"Thirty-six."

"How long had she known she had this tumor?"

"Two years."

"How did she obtain this knowledge?"

"A doctor's examination."

"What was the doctor's recommendation?"

"An immediate operation."

"Why was this not done?"

"My wife was inordinately afraid of the knife. Particularly used as it would have to be used in her case."

"Did she prefer to die rather than risk an operation?"

"No, no. But there are many new ways of treating cancer. Marie heard of a clinic in Missouri that removes surface cancers of the kind she had with herb poultices. I was ready to let someone else look after my business while I took Marie to Missouri. I wasn't very enthusiastic about herb poultices myself, but if you had seen that girl—"

"You mean your wife?"

"Yes, my wife, Marie. She was always a girl to me. If you had seen her relief when I found out about this clinic, you would understand why I was willing to drop my work to go with her to Missouri."

"Did you go?"

"No. Before the time came to leave for that trip, Marie had heard of the miracles of healing being credited to the Reverend Chase."

"Was your wife a churchgoing woman?"

"She was. She was more than that. She didn't just go to church. She believed in what she heard preached there."

303

"Were you also a churchgoer?"

"I was. Where my wife went, I went. Though I was never the believer she was."

"Did your wife have a meeting with the Reverend Chase about her tumor?"

"She did. We did. She wouldn't go without me."

"Where was this meeting held?"

"In the Reverend's study at his home."

"What did the Reverend Chase say to your wife?"

"He said that Jesus had told his disciples to go forth and heal. That he was one of the Lord's disciples and that he like the other disciples had been given by the Lord the power to heal. He showed us some before and after pictures of patients healed by prayer and faith."

"Was there any laying on of hands?"

"No, sir. No hanky-panky of that kind. Marie wouldn't have permitted that sort of thing, let alone me. Just faith and prayer would heal her."

"And you believed this?"

"She did."

"And you?"

"I had my doubts. I said, 'Why not pray and have the operation, too?' To her, that was like saying she didn't have faith in the power of the Lord. And she had faith."

"And faith in the power of the Reverend Chase?"

"That, too. And he was going to save her from those terrible knives. To her, he was just like an angel with a gift from heaven."

"So you went along with her in her faith-healing belief?"

"I did. Look, I'd been married to that girl for twenty years. Whatever it was in my power to give her, I always gave her. I wasn't going to make her give up her faith in her religion, be maimed by those knives, and like as not die anyway."

"Did you warn her of this possibility?"

"Certainly not."

"Did the Reverend Chase warn her?"

"He did not. He told her there was nothing to fear."

"In your hearing?"

"In my hearing."

"What exactly to the best of your recollection were his words?"

"He said, 'Marie, the Lord can make you whole. He made you the woman you are now. Have faith that the Father who made you in the beginning can save and preserve you now. What can men do to equal Him?' "

"By 'men,' he meant doctors?"

"He did."

Ralph rose. "Objection. That is supposition."

The Judge said, "Sustained. Mr. Benson, no more tricks. The jury is instructed to disregard the reference to doctors."

"You attended church with Marie?"

"I did. I gave her all the comfort I could."

"You made a donation to the Reverend Chase's church?"

"I did. At Marie's request. She wanted to help the work the Reverend Chase was doing in any way she could."

"What was the amount of your contribution?"

"Twenty thousand dollars."

"These are hard times. That was a considerable contribution."

"I'm not a poor man. It was not an excessive sacrifice and it gave my poor wife so much happiness to help someone she thought was helping her."

"But who killed her?"

"*Mr. Benson,*" thundered Judge Maxwell, "*you are in contempt. I will deal with that later. You will now conduct yourself strictly according to proper procedure—or I will ask for your replacement. The jury will totally disregard the District Attorney's last question and draw no inference from it. Continue, Mr. Benson, if you feel you are able.*"

Benson paused, then asked Griswold, "What, provided you heard him speak, did your wife's physician say in regard to her condition and his prognosis of it?"

"The doctor who examined Marie said that the removal of her tumor would require a simple operation and would cure all her troubles."

"And to your knowledge the Reverend Chase promised her a cure through prayer and thus prevented her having this operation?"

"He did."

"Your witness, Mr. Navarro."

Ralph left Joe's side and advanced to face Griswold. He carried what appeared to be a folded newspaper.

"Mr. Griswold, there are a number of questions I want to ask you.

305

And will ask you later. At this point, may I congratulate you on the absolute truth of your statement that you are not a poor man."

Griswold appeared confused. His inclination was to deny everything the Defense Attorney said. Nothing, on the surface, was apparently condemnatory in the Defense Attorney's agreeing with a statement of his own.

"Mr. Griswold, I believe that one of your used-parts stores is located in Sacramento. Is that correct?"

"That's right."

"Yuba City is a nearby town?"

"If you could call fifty miles nearby."

"I want to be accurate, as I am sure you do. Let's say 'not distant.' Is that better?"

"I don't care what you call it."

"Near enough at least so that you had some customers from Yuba City?"

"I wasn't in all my stores all of the time."

"But you were in Sacramento occasionally?"

"Like as not."

"Often enough so that you got acquainted with a Mr. and Mrs. Robert Leach? Customer of yours?"

"I don't remember the names of all my customers."

"Of course not. I have an item here that may help you remember the Leaches. It is from the July 18, 1938, issue of the Yuba City Courier. By the way, can you recall the date of your wife's first visit to the doctor who diagnosed her trouble and advised an operation?"

"No, I can't. I'm not a lawyer who goes around with his pockets stuffed with dates and reminders."

"Quite so. Well, I am a lawyer who does have his pocket stuffed with dates and reminders."

Navarro took a small sheet of white paper from a pocket and read from it. "Dr. Raymond Burkett, on April 10, 1938, diagnosed the lump in Marie Griswold's breast as cancerous and advised an operation."

"How do you know that?"

"Dr. Burkett. He is prepared to testify if you doubt that date."

Benson addressed Judge Maxwell. "Your Honor, I do not see the point of all this unnecessary time-wasting chatter. Is the defense counsel attempting to confuse the witness—or the jury?"

Navarro spoke to the Judge. "The meaning of this chatter will soon be made clear to all, Your Honor. First of all, the District Attorney directed his questions to establish that Mr. Griswold had been for twenty years a loving and devoted husband of his late wife." Ralph turned to Griswold. "That is true, isn't it, Mr. Griswold?"

"Marie is the one who could tell you. Whatever that girl wanted, I wanted."

"Always, Mr. Griswold?"

"We disagreed about trifles. What couple doesn't?"

"Did your wife consider Eloise Leach a trifle?"

"I am not going to try to put words into the mouth of my dead wife."

"That's commendable, Mr. Griswold. I wouldn't want you to do that. Let's talk about known facts. We have a record here of what Robert Leach thought of you. On July 18, 1938, the Yuba City *Courier* reports, and I read from that paper, 'Yesterday Burt Griswold was found guilty of alienating the affections of Robert Leach's wife Eloise and was ordered by the court to pay the complainant $25,000.' Is that true, Mr. Griswold?"

"It's a long time ago."

"Is it true, Mr. Griswold?"

"It's what the paper says."

"Is this the same Burt Griswold whose chief desire in life was to protect and cherish his wife? Who never looked at another woman?"

"I object, Your Honor," said Benson.

"Objection sustained," said Judge Maxwell.

We—Papa, Mama, Wanda, and I—went home as soon as Court was adjourned. Joe hugged Mama before he left with Ralph. "There's nothing to worry about, Mama."

She wasn't convinced. Neither were the rest of us. We spent a miserable evening, unable to decide whether it was better to stay up and worry together or to go to bed and, sleepless, worry alone. No one was hungry. No one could read. Wanda couldn't study. I was particularly nervous because I knew that Ralph intended to call me to the witness stand the next day. He had tried to bolster my spirits by telling me, as Joe had told Mama, "There's nothing to worry about. I'll ask you a few simple questions. All you need to do is to answer them truthfully."

"What if I can't remember?"

"Tell the truth. Say you don't remember."

Mama was convinced that within a week Joe would be in jail. "If a man like that Griswold can sit up there and tell lie after lie about Joe, how's the jury to know any different?"

"Ralph Navarro knows the difference. He'll let them know," said Papa.

"How?" asked Mama. "He can't just say, 'You liar, you.' "

"No, he can't. And he won't. You saw what he did today. The jury knows now that Burt wasn't the devoted husband he was making out to be. And he didn't have to call him a liar, either. And I'll miss my guess if the jury didn't note that it was less than four months after his trial up north that he was recommending poultices for Marie instead of an operation."

"He did it for her sake, he says."

" 'He says.' The whole drift of what Navarro was doing today was to show the jury that you couldn't put any faith in anything that man had to say. If you didn't get that, it's a good thing for Joe you aren't on the jury."

"I didn't miss it all. But proving Burt Griswold's a scoundrel doesn't clear Joe of what he's accused of."

"The trial isn't over yet, not by a long shot," Papa said.

"I wish Joe was here," Mama said. "What's he avoiding us for?"

"Ralph Navarro's got to know the ins and outs of every move Joe's ever made. By the time this trial's over, he'll know more about Joe than we do."

"I know what Joe would want us to do if he were here," Wanda said.

"What?" I asked.

"Pray," said Wanda.

For once in her life, Mama agreed one hundred percent with Wanda.

I was the first witness called next morning. Because I wasn't a Quaker, I swore with my hand on a Bible to tell the truth, the whole truth, and nothing but the truth. I was determined to do so, although I hoped that what I was saying would help Joe.

Ralph spent a short time inquiring about my acquaintanceship with the Griswolds, how I had been the first to see them when they came seeking help from Joe. I told him that I had often seen them at

Meeting after they had accepted Joe's ministry, and later I had met with Marie.

"When was the last time you saw Marie Griswold?" Ralph asked.

"About three months before her death."

"What was the purpose of her visit?"

"She said she liked me. She liked to talk to me, needed to talk to me as a friend."

"Can you remember anything specifically she had to say that day?"

"I can. First of all, she wanted to tell me that Joe's prayers weren't curing her. She wanted to show me her breast."

"Did you look?"

"No. I'd seen that sight before. It's terrible."

"What was her general appearance?"

"Sick, very sick. I told her she must go to see my brother."

"What was her reply to that?"

"She said she wouldn't. That my brother had told her that suffering was a part of life. That Jesus Himself suffered on the cross. She said she didn't want her failure to recover to be a setback to my brother in his holy work. She made me promise not to tell my brother."

"Did you keep your promise?"

"I did."

"Was that the end of your conversation?"

"No. She had other things to tell me."

"Will you please describe them."

"She asked me not to tell that, either."

"You took an oath a few minutes ago, Mrs. Hesse, to tell the truth, the whole truth, and nothing but the truth. You haven't forgotten that, have you?"

"No."

"What else did Marie Griswold tell you?"

"She told me that she was not and had never been afraid of having an operation. She did not want me to think she was so childish and weak-kneed."

"Why didn't she have the operation then?"

"Her husband. She said she was afraid she would lose him completely if she went against his wishes."

"His wishes?"

"That she—well, the way she put it was, 'didn't remain a whole woman.'"

309

"In other words, not have a breast amputated?"

"That's what she meant."

"Then she didn't believe in faith healing?"

"Oh, yes, she believed. But she was willing to try those poultices to please her husband, too."

"Did she criticize her husband to you?"

"Oh, no! She loved him very much."

"I am sure she did. Thank you, Mrs. Hesse. Your witness."

The District Attorney called me by my first name, as if we were old friends.

"Orpha, you have a very good memory and have brought out some pertinent facts. Who else was present during this conversation?"

"No one. It was a private conversation between Marie and me."

"There was no other witness?"

"I told you, Marie was there."

"So you did. Your only witness, then, is a dead woman. That'll be all, Orpha."

The District Attorney turned toward the table where he had been sitting. I rose to resume my seat. At that moment, Wanda stood and began to move toward the front of the room.

"That is wrong, Mr. Benson. I was a witness and I am not dead."

The Court, eager to laugh at something and with very little so far to laugh at, laughed.

Ralph turned to Judge Maxwell. "Your Honor, may I have a word with this young woman?"

"I will give you five minutes, Mr. Navarro, unless you request a recess for cause."

Ralph motioned Wanda to him and they spoke together in voices that did not carry. Turning from Wanda, Ralph addressed Judge Maxwell. "I have an unexpected witness, Your Honor. I'd like to put her on the stand."

"Swear her," Maxwell said.

Wanda, who a good deal of the time considered herself a Quaker, asked to be excused from swearing. Having affirmed, she seated herself in the witness chair. She was wearing schoolgirl clothes, including bobby sox, but, with the exception of Joe himself, was the calmest-appearing person in the courtroom.

"What's she doing up there?" Mama whispered.

"I don't know."

"She wants attention."

If she did, she got it.

Questioned by Ralph, Wanda identified herself.

"You say you were a witness of the conversation between your mother and Marie Griswold?"

"I do."

"Your mother has just testified that she and Marie Griswold were alone."

"That's what she thought."

"Please explain how you were there but invisible."

"I was sneaky. They were in the living room when I got home from school. I came in the back door as usual. Then I heard voices in the living room, so I sat down in the dining room."

"Could you hear through a closed door?"

"There isn't any door between the living room and dining room. Just an archway. I could hear perfectly."

"Are you accustomed to eavesdropping in this way?"

"I told you I was sneaky. If grownups know you are around, they don't say anything very interesting."

"Did you hear anything very interesting that afternoon?"

"I did."

"Tell the Court what you heard."

"I heard this woman—"

"Mrs. Griswold?"

"Mrs. Griswold, yes. Well, she said that though Uncle Joe had prayed for her, she was getting worse."

"What did your mother say to that?"

"She said she should tell Uncle Joe. Mrs. Griswold said she wouldn't. She said she wouldn't have an operation, either, because her husband didn't like women without breasts."

"Did she want her husband to like her?"

"Oh, yes. She said she would rather die than have her husband not like her. She didn't use those words exactly, but that's what she meant."

"Mrs. Griswold *is* dead, you know."

"She was kind of romantic, wasn't she, dying for love, like Juliet?"

Burt Griswold, Fred Benson, and Mama were all on the verge of apoplexy. One more word from Wanda would have resulted, I'm

311

sure, in an outburst of some kind from one or the other. Ralph didn't permit another word.

"That will be all, Wanda. Your witness, Mr. Prosecutor."

Mr. Prosecutor didn't want the witness.

3

Our drive home was silent. Our evening was silent. I was downcast because I had had to break my word to Marie. Mama was mad at Wanda, confessing in public that she was a sneak and an eavesdropper and referring to breasts as if they were as common as fingers or toes. Wanda's feelings were hurt by Mama's criticism; and by her own recognition that the picture she had painted of herself as a witness wasn't very flattering.

Only Papa, less self-centered than we were, thought about Joe. "All this trial has done so far is prove that Griswold's a skunk. What's *he* being tried for? Skunkism? If so, the trial 'bout as well end now. Every man on the jury would vote 'Guilty' to that charge. So where does that leave Joe? Manslaughter's even worse when the victim is the wife of a skunk. If the boy told that poor woman that she could be healed by faith and prayer, and because of that she didn't have the operation she needed, Navarro's going to have to come up with something more than running down Griswold."

Wanda, though abashed by what she had revealed about herself, was young enough to feel hungry. Without a word to us, she went to the kitchen and in minutes produced her old stand-by for important occasions: oyster soup. We didn't know we were hungry until we began eating. We didn't know until we had finished how much of our distress had been physical—hunger and weariness.

Joe was the first witness called by Navarro next morning.

As a sister, I was too close to Joe to see him accurately. He had a face an advertiser would like to use in a cigarette or beer ad. Strong, handsome, but good; so that a potential purchaser would think, If a man like that uses that brand, I'd like to try it myself.

How many ministers do you know whose face would sell anything you had to pay money for? This may be saying more that is detrimental to us than to ministers.

Joe was placed under oath and took the stand. While he did not face the crowded courtroom with the same dedication with which he faced his congregation, he did appear eager to talk.

There was no Joe-ing of his witness by Ralph; it was Reverend Chase all the way.

"Reverend Chase, you understand clearly what the charge against you is?"

"I do."

"Will you tell us what, as you understand it, this charge is?"

"It is charged that I, by telling Marie Griswold that the lump in her breast that had been diagnosed as cancer could be cured by faith and prayer, prevented her from having the operation that would have saved her life."

"Did you do this?"

"I did not."

"There have been reports in the papers of some hundreds of persons who claim to have been cured of their afflictions by you. Do you deny that these cures took place?"

"I do not deny the cures. I deny that they were my cures."

"To whom do you attribute them?"

"To Jesus Christ. And to the faith and prayers of the ailing."

"Did Marie Griswold come to see you?"

"She and her husband did."

"What did they want?"

"Her husband did most of the talking. Because of his wife's fear of surgery, he hoped for what he called 'faith healing.' "

"Did you promise her such healing?"

"I did not."

"Was anyone present during your talks with Marie Griswold?"

"Her husband."

"You have heard your sister's testimony, Reverend Chase. Did your sister tell you of her last talk with Marie Griswold?"

"She did not."

"When did you last see Marie Griswold?"

"After her talk with my sister."

"Your sister has testified that she promised not to tell you what Mrs. Griswold had told her."

"I heard her testimony."

"What did Marie Griswold have to say to you?"

"Exactly what she told my sister."

"And your reply?"

"I repeated what I had told her when first I talked with her."

"Which was?"

"Jesus heals. He does not, however, condemn the healing of the surgeon or the doctor. They, too, are God's children and there is that of God in every man."

"Mrs. Griswold's husband was with her at the time of this visit?"

"No, she was alone."

"Reverend Chase, why do you think that Marie Griswold asked your sister to keep the information she gave her from you, then came to you with it?"

"Her pain had become more intense."

"What was your advice?"

"Call a doctor. Preferably the one who had first diagnosed her trouble, and make an appointment."

"What was Marie's reply?"

"She was afraid that I would be distressed by her lack of faith in Jesus and the power of prayer."

"She then left your office?"

"No. She did not leave until I had her permission to call Dr. Burkett and make an appointment for her."

"Which you did later?"

"Which I did then, with Marie listening."

"Your witness, Counselor."

Benson bristled up to Joe like a man who has endured more than is humanly reasonable.

"Marie Griswold visited your office alone?"

"She did."

"Your secretary was, I suppose, present."

"It was after hours. My secretary had gone home. Marie and I were alone."

"Another of these conversations believed to be private. Where was Wanda?"

Benson enacted a player in a drama where an expected actor does not come in on cue. The courtroom gave Benson the laugh he had been asking for.

Judge Maxwell gaveled for silence. "The Bench is unable to see anything very funny in the death of a woman, or the trial of a man accused of being responsible for her death. Proceed, please."

"I've finished with this witness," Benson said.

314

"You may step down," the Judge directed Joe. "Mr. Navarro, will you please continue."

"My next witness is Dr. Burkett. Dr. Burkett, will you please take the stand?"

After Dr. Burkett was sworn and had identified himself as the physician who had first examined Marie, Ralph began his questioning.

"You have heard the Reverend Chase's statement that he phoned you asking for an appointment with Marie Griswold. Do you remember any such call?"

"I do."

"Did you take the call yourself?"

"I did."

"Isn't that unusual?"

"It is. But as the Reverend has said, it was after hours: my nurse and secretary had both left. So I took the call myself."

"Do you remember what was said?"

"I do. But if I didn't, the content of the call is here."

Dr. Burkett held up a black appointment book. "The Reverend recalled Marie Griswold to my mind. He said that she had been coming to him hoping that by faith and prayer her cancer would be cured. She had concealed from him, up to that time, that her condition was worsening. She was in his office at that minute and had consented that he arrange for an examination and treatment by me. Here is my appointment book. You can read date, time, and name for yourself."

Ralph took the book and read, " 'Marie Griswold—14th at 3 p.m.' Is that correct?"

"It is."

"You then saw Marie Griswold?"

"I did not. Please read the words under that date. Notice they are not my handwriting. My secretary took that call."

Ralph again read: " 'Mr. Griswold canceled his wife's date. She is feeling better.' "

At that minute, Sam Shields, who had noticeably avoided his son-in-law since Ralph's revelation of the Yuba City–Sacramento incident, stood, pointed his finger at his son-in-law, and screamed, "You killed my daughter! You killed my daughter!"

Judge Maxwell gaveled for silence. "Restrain that man," he di-

rected the bailiff. Restraint wasn't necessary. Mrs. Shields, her hand
on his arm, had persuaded her husband, whose intention, it appeared, had been to by-pass the Court and take care of justice himself, to return to his seat.

Judge Maxwell, when the courtroom had recovered from the
shock of Sam Shields's outburst, announced that he was adjourning
Court until two that afternoon.

"Meanwhile," said he, "I direct the District Attorney and Counselor Navarro to meet with me in chambers."

When the Court reconvened, Judge Maxwell announced that,
with the District Attorney and the Defense Attorney's approval, he
was directing a verdict of not guilty as charged in the matter of the
Reverend Joseph Chase.

4

There was relief among the Chase family, but no wild rejoicing.
There was to be a public service of prayer and thanksgiving that
night at the Meeting House. Jubilation would be expressed there.
We, the family, just wanted to sit down quietly together and thank
God that it was all over. The wear and tear of the proceedings
showed more in my parents' faces than on Joe's. The lines that had
always run down the middle of Papa's cheeks had deepened. Mama
had pursed her lips so often listening to Burt Griswold's horrible
lies that she had permanently crinkled her upper lip. Joe was unchanged. If he believed that it was God's will for some of us to
suffer (and he did), he didn't believe that it was God's will for him,
at least not then.

We did not leave the courtroom until four. The services at the
Meeting House were to begin at seven. Everyone was hungry and
no one, certainly not I, wanted to go all the way home to Montebello to cook. Papa had the solution. Food and, at the same time,
something he had long wanted to do: go to a Chinese restaurant.
He would take us all. The rabbit business hadn't made him a tycoon, but he had enough spare change in his pocket to finance a
Chinese meal.

A strange place to eat seemed appropriate after the strange experience we had had: son-brother-uncle on trial for having prayed a young woman to her death.

Only Mama objected. "Who knows what goes into Chinese food?"

"The Chinese," Joe told her. "And it must be good. Look how many million Chinese there are."

"I'll tell you something that doesn't go into them," Papa said. "Rabbit." He gave Wanda's ear a tweak. "That'll suit you, won't it, Wanda?"

Someone—it had to be Joe—had told Papa about Wanda's sacrificial rabbit.

Joe had been in Chinese restaurants before. For the rest of us, it was as strange as a trip to Peking or Hong Kong. The waiters wore Chinese robes, with slippers that whispered mysteriously on the floor. The lights came from candles, set deep in globes the color of cabbages or eggplants. None of us, without Joe's help, would have known what to order; rice and chop suey were the only Chinese dishes we knew about, and chop suey was not on the Mandarin's menu.

It was an odd time of the day to be eating, too late for lunch, too early for dinner. We were almost alone in the quiet dining room. What we talked of was not the trial, over and done with and the sooner forgotten the better, but back home. Back home where the snow was already falling, the persimmons were ripening, the corn had been cut and shocked.

Back home! In California, eating Chinese food, back home was where none of us would ever go again—though none of us knew it. It was a bad time to try to sell our back-east farms. Ebon and Nettie were living at the Dudley place and running the other two farms. Not making a fortune, but keeping the farms up and sending enough to California to keep us all from starving, together with Joe's salary and Papa's rabbits.

The fortune cookies were the part of the meal everyone enjoyed most. It was like having a book you could eat. I remember mine, Wanda's, and Joe's. I was old enough to have known that you don't stop living at fifty. Nevertheless, I thought that Wanda, Joe, and I were the ones whose fortunes would have the longest commitment.

My fortune read (I still have it): "An admirer is concealing his affection for you." I loved that. I believed it. I hoped it was Ralph,

317

but doubted it. There was no indication that he was an admirer, let alone that he was concealing any affection for me.

Wanda's message was from an Oriental with an X-ray eye. "Neither the highest mountain nor the deepest river will keep you from what you want." I believed that. That was my Kickapoo. What would she want? Her wants were changing. Whatever they were, would she get them?

Joe's fortune was the sad one, worse because it was so believable. Joe laughed it off. He pretended, or perhaps believed, that it had reference to what had just happened. "These things," he told us, "are baked, written, and put together months ago."

The fortune read, "When suffering comes, you have the heart to endure it."

"The suffering came," he said. "I endured it. Confucius say, 'Good boy. Inscrutable Quaker.'"

Joe ate his fortune cookie, rolled the slip of paper it had held into a wad, and flipped it like a spitball in my direction. It landed in my cup of tea. I took it out; I still have it. "Confucius say," I told Joe, "'Do not swallow everything that lands in thy cup.'"

5

People who think Quakers are meek, silent, and undemonstrative don't know Quakers—or California. Quakers weren't Puritans. The Puritans hanged Quakers. California Quakers weren't Philadelphians, who never tolled a bell or wore a wedding ring. They weren't Middle Westerners, who forbade novel-reading and thought organ music erotic.

Most people don't know about, let alone remember, Quaker maidens who threw off their clothes in Oxford, England, to demonstrate that before God they had nothing to hide. They have never heard of James Naylor, who rode an ass into London accompanied by Quaker ladies on foot hallelujahing and waving palm leaves. George Fox, father of them all, stood silent for two hours before a crowd of two thousand gathered to hear him speak. He then spoke for three hours. When he finished, he said to a friend, "I famished them for words."

Because I had learned these things and many more in the time

I lived with Joe, I did not find the crowd that met Joe when he appeared at the Meeting House at seven un-Quakerly. I was surprised that Joe's trial had attracted so many persons and that its outcome was causing so much rejoicing.

The Los Angeles *Times* reported that five thousand people had gathered to welcome the return of their pastor and to celebrate the trial's outcome. That was only the beginning of the *Times*'s story. The Meeting that began at seven lasted until midnight. Joe's talk was short. The remainder of the time was taken up by individual testimony and a subsequent flood of healing and conversion—usually in that order. The *Times*'s headline was QUAKERS REALLY QUAKE. Since that is how the Society of Friends got their nickname in the first place, this was hardly news.

This was almost forty years before Kathryn Kuhlman's listeners were falling to the floor unconscious at the sound of her voice. It was before Oral Roberts; before the P.T.L. Club and their hundred-million-dollar receipts, and Billy Graham and his twenty million dollars. It was a time when twenty thousand was a sum capable of making people think that skulduggery must be involved somewhere. Nineteen-thirty-nine was years before the organization known as Women Aglow, the primal scream, and transcendental meditation—though the Quakers in some respects had it both ways; they valued silence and meditation (less in California than elsewhere) from the beginning, and some of the sounds to be heard at a Quaker protracted meeting were pretty primal. It was a better or worse time, but it was a time less accustomed than this to the kind of response that his congregation gave Joe on the evening of his trial.

Papa and Mama, tired, amazed, and proud, drove off to their Normal Hill apartment as soon as the Meeting was over. Wanda and I were ready for bed. Joe wasn't. He wanted, of all things, to stop at Marie Griswold's grave. We would pass the cemetery where she was buried on our way home.

"If she had not died, none of these things would have come to pass."

By "these things" he meant the conversions, the healings, the coming together of thousands in the Christian fellowship we had just witnessed. Marie's death and the trial her death had occasioned were responsible for these happenings.

319

"She suffered for all of us."

There were cemeteries on each side of the highway—it wasn't yet a freeway—as you left Los Angeles headed for the towns of Orange and San Diego counties. Marie Griswold was buried in the cemetery on the right as we drove toward Montebello.

Joe didn't expect, or perhaps even want, Wanda or me to go with him.

"I'll only be gone a minute," he told us. "Take a snooze, Wanda. Tomorrow's a school day for you."

Joe was gone half an hour. During the whole of the trial, he had been cheerful. His face, when he returned, had changed. He was with us, he drove us home, but his mind was elsewhere.

6

We had a real California Christmas celebration: a picnic dinner in Westlake Park, with one of Papa's rabbits in a pie called "chicken" —for Wanda's sake.

Though the services at the Meeting House had not changed—the birth of the historical Jesus was as nothing compared with the continued life of the Eternal Jesus in the human heart—nothing since the trial had ever been the same there. The congregation had doubled. The collection had tripled. The twenty thousand dollars, which had been returned to Griswold, had been replaced twice over by individual donations. And the greatest change of all was the widespread regard for Joseph Chase.

The rapid acceptance of a novel by an unknown writer was the result in large part of this public interest in Joe. While who Joe was surely had something to do with the book's publication, what Joe did before I mailed the manuscript may have had even more influence.

Joe never read the whole book. He would, if I asked, read a few pages to check for me the accuracy of some fact or interpretation.

"The more this thing is one-hundred-percent correct," Joe said, "the less I like to read it. It upsets me. It's like looking into a mirror and seeing yourself reflected there as you were years ago."

In February, after the trial, Wanda, who was taking a commercial course in high school, typed the last page of *Talbot Ware* for me. Four hundred and sixteen pages. I asked Joe, before I sent it off, to look through the pages on the chance that he might spot something he objected to or that was unsound.

Joe read here and there, then said, "You've really worked on this, haven't you?"

"More than a year."

"Why?"

"I'm not sure. I like to write. I wanted to tell Talbot Ware's story. I thought he was a good man, maybe a great one. I wanted people to know about him."

Joe put the manuscript back in the box I intended to send it off in.

"How do you know where to send it?"

"I don't. It's guesswork. I'm sending it to the publisher of a writer I like to read. If they publish what I like to read, maybe they'll want to publish what I write."

Joe shook his head. "I wouldn't count on it."

"I don't."

Before Joe put the lid back on the box, he put his hand, palm down, on the front page. It was a gesture I had seen him make with invalids when praying for them. His fingers had the same upcurve as when resting on a man's shoulder or a child's head.

When he opened his eyes, he said, "It may have a chance."

Did Joe's blessing do it? Would any book about a man who had received as much publicity as Joe have been published? Was there a hunger at that time for the life story of a good man? Hitler was at work in Germany. Czechoslovakia had been swallowed. Lindbergh and Henry Ford had been given Nazi medals. The cyclotron, the device that would split the atom and make the destruction of Hiroshima possible, had been developed. Three thousand Americans had been in Spain fighting the Fascists. In America a poll showed that we favored neutrality. England was at bay, and the rest of the world was on the threshold of Hitler's war; Americans didn't know it. We did know something was wrong. Was this one of the reasons people wanted to read about a good man, whose worst fault since his own cure and conversion had been to pray for the health of a woman who had died in spite of his prayers?

These are speculations. Whatever the reasons, the book was accepted. An advance payment of seven hundred and fifty dollars, the largest single sum any one of us had ever held in his hand, was sent me. Four months after publication, the book was bought for a movie. For this I was paid seventeen thousand five hundred dollars, which I and the publisher shared half and half. We were all rich.

I didn't see how a movie could be made from the book. I needn't have worried. The producer saw. The trial was dramatized. Joe's romance, which I had first fabricated, then omitted, was concocted once again, with added embellishments. A moviemaker can do this. The events of a book he buys aren't history to him. He isn't dealing with the assassination of Lincoln or of Kennedy. If he thinks a better movie would result if the assassin had escaped, then been brought to trial for attempted murder, that's the way he'd concoct the movie if he could get away with it. Joe was more real to me than Kennedy or Lincoln. He wasn't that real to producer-director Oscar Ronson; but Joe was well enough known to prevent Ronson from changing his story as much as Ronson's cinematic instincts may have suggested.

Ronson, experienced with authors, didn't ask me to have a hand in the scriptwriting. He did ask me to be a technical adviser at seventy-five dollars a week. My duties, as he explained them, would be ones I could handle. Tell him as much as I could about Joe's birthplace and parents. Be more explicit than I had in the book about Joe's illness. Keep everyone straight about who Quakers were and what they had done. I was no expert on Quakers, but Joe was. With Joe helping me, Ronson would have two workers for the price of one.

7

It was midwinter, which is spring in California, foothills blazing with mustard and lupine and Indian paintbrushes, when all of this was settled. The trial was more than a year past. Joe's congregation continued to grow, and people listened to him on the radio. Joe was an old Californian by now, but look what had happened to us newcomers! Mama, a student of Oriental philosophy who met with people who held hands at the beginning of a meal and, after a period of silence, all said "oomm" together. Papa, with his partner, had started making (and selling) something they called "Bunny Burgers"—a terrible thing to happen to a rabbit. (I never tasted one, but I was told that they were better than hamburgers, twice as large and twice as cheap.) And here I was, a published author and an employed technical adviser. To celebrate, we all met for supper at our house. Even Wanda, who could usually be counted on to cook, was too excited to stay put in the kitchen. She was having her first technical, prearranged date, with a boy who phoned her a week ahead of time, had a car, and was bringing her a gardenia corsage. The occasion was the Junior-Senior Ball at Montebello High School.

XIII
GREG

1

Before I started work, Mr. Ronson asked me to talk with him about the picture.

"I know something about Quaker standards," he said. "I admire Quakers. Otherwise I wouldn't be making this picture. Now obviously we're not going to have a cast of Quakers."

"I'm not a Quaker," I said.

Mr. Ronson was surprised and perhaps disappointed. Had he hired the wrong technical adviser?

"From your book—" he began.

"I'm a United Brethren. But I've lived with Joe for so long and attended so many Quaker Meetings, I probably know more about Quakers at this point than I do about the Brethren."

Mr. Ronson had never heard of the Brethren.

"Are they a regular church?"

"Oh, yes. They and the Quakers have many of the same beliefs."

"In that case, I'll go on with what I had to say. It has to do with the actor we've hired to play your brother. My thought had been that since your brother—"

I interrupted Mr. Ronson again. "Talbot Ware is not my brother."

Mr. Ronson was a genial man. If for some reason I wanted to pretend that I was writing fiction, not biography, he wasn't going to argue with me.

"I know that. Their careers are nevertheless somewhat the same. I was going to say that it would be better not to have the usual Hollywood playboy taking the part of Talbot. It would jar on people. Have you seen *Gone With the Wind?*"

"No."

"I wish you had. Look what they did there. Every female star in Hollywood wanted the part of Scarlett. They gave it to an unknown British actress—unknown to us, that is. She was perfect for the role.

327

Ran away with the picture. My idea is we should do the same. Stars like Errol Flynn or Clark Gable don't fit your brother. Don't fit Talbot, I mean. The thing to do is discover a male Vivien Leigh. And I think I've done it. A good actor, but not well known. Gregory McGovern. That's the matter I wanted to speak to you about. Gregory's been divorced. His wife divorced him because he was living with another woman. That broke up long ago, and none of this was ever well known. I just wanted you to hear this from me. I didn't want you to think I was trying to run in some highflier to play your brother. Play Talbot, I mean. Gregory's been hunting for something. He thought women were the answer. Maybe it was God. He's got the look of a searcher on his face. That's the look Talbot needs. I wanted you to know about him before you heard from someone else and was shocked."

I didn't know what to say to Mr. Ronson. Did he think all the sin in the world was corralled in Hollywood? I thought that he was right in his idea that an unknown actor would be better for the part than some man we could not disassociate from his past record. But that he believed he had to prepare me for the fact that an actor had been divorced! Had to sell me on him; not because he was a good actor, but because he had not led a guiltless life! What kind of a puritanical backwoods ninny did he think I was? Did he think that where I came from all unmarried people were virgins and all married couples faithful? We had myths about Hollywood in Amesville. I didn't know Hollywood had myths about us.

"I am interested in the actor's ability, not his matrimonial record," I said.

Mr. Ronson was amused, perhaps pleased. "I didn't know you were so professional."

"I'm not professional. I'm not Pollyanna, either."

"Rebecca of Sunnybrook Farm?"

"Anne of Green Gables."

"I'm sorry. I know what you think of your brother. What the world thinks of him, in fact. I wanted you to understand it wasn't our intention to tear down his image in any way."

"It wasn't Joe I was worrying about. I was worrying about myself."

"Yourself? Why, I was just giving you credit for being your brother's sister, raised in the same way."

"Joe is a saint. I'm not. I've had two husbands. The first one killed a man, then committed suicide. The second packed up and left me. We're divorced. You don't want to hear all about my life and I don't want to tell you. But I'm a grown woman, not a child, I'm not a Quaker, or even a very good United Brethren. I do know Joe's life and I do know what it was like back east—and that's what you want, isn't it?"

Mr. Ronson gazed at me, trying, it appeared, to see in my face traces of these events.

"That's what we want. Maybe your brother would be willing to talk with us."

"He won't. He'll talk to me, but he said he couldn't be hired to come onto the movie set or to talk to anyone about it. As far as he's concerned, this is a story about a man named Talbot Ware. Joe has his hands full with his own work. Talbot Ware is your job. And I am your helper, if you still want me."

"I still want you. And I want you to talk to Gregory."

I never had the confidence that causes a woman to wonder if the man she is to meet will be attractive. What I always wondered was: Will I be a disappointment to the man? I no longer had my girlhood illusion that men liked manly girls, though I never learned to pretend a fragility or incompetence I didn't possess. My piepan-kicking days were long past. What that exercise had been expected to accomplish—that is, impress a man—I still wanted to do.

Now I used my head instead of my legs. I tried to be knowledgeable, informed, quick-witted. I had come to understand that all else aside, it wasn't very tactful or kind to beat a man at his game, or what he thinks is. I didn't yet understand that though I had changed the equipment, I hadn't changed the game. I had no wish to compete or excel, only to demonstrate an ability that would make me agreeable to men.

What Greg McGovern thought of me as a woman didn't matter. I wasn't worried about that. He was ten years younger than I, a movie star, or would be if Talbot Ware was a success. He was accustomed to associating with glamorous actresses. What I was concerned about with him was my job. One of my chief duties, Mr. Ronson had told me, would be to help Greg "get inside" my brother's personality. To do this, I didn't need to look glamorous myself or to know anything about the history of the movies. All I needed to do was to help Greg understand a man like Joe; help him to walk and talk, to preach and pray like him, a man backwoods-born, but college-educated.

The matter of how Joe walked or talked didn't strike me as being of any great importance. What was important for the actor who played Talbot would be an ability to suggest a young man who had been a teen-age rascal, a young man dying, a born-again Christian, and finally an inspirer of wonder-working faith. It was a difficult role, and Gregory McGovern had his work cut out for him.

Mr. Ronson arranged for Gregory McGovern to come out to Montebello to talk to me. I had never seen the actor on the screen or even his picture in a movie magazine. I somehow had the idea that he had been chosen for the part because Mr. Ronson saw in him some likeness to Joe.

2

The man who came to the door that April afternoon was not in the least like Joe. That is most of what I remember of Greg's appearance on our first meeting. I wonder now that he made so small an impression on me. There were two reasons, I suppose. First, I was deeply concerned with adequately doing my job as a technical adviser. What could I tell this young man that would help him play the part of Joe? Second, he *was* a movie actor, and movie actors were not, I thought, completely real, normal beings. They were more like department-store models, manufactured to display certain wares.

In spite of these preconceptions, I do remember certain impressions. Not only did Greg not look like Joe, but also he didn't even look like a movie actor. He wasn't handsome, he wasn't large and muscular; he looked like a man in his thirties. Talk with glamorous stars hadn't made him glib. He knew he was supposed to be instructed, and I knew that I was supposed to instruct. Neither knew how to begin. I sat in the old Dudley rocker. He sat on the new California chesterfield.

"Have you heard my brother preach?" I asked.

"Oh, yes."

"Do you think you can do that?"

"Oh, yes."

"What makes you think so?" This wasn't a very polite question. I wasn't Ronson interviewing an applicant for the job. It was better, I believed, than to sit silently rocking.

"This," said Greg.

He stood, walked across the room. It was Joe's walk, exaggerated just enough so that I was able to see, as I had never been able before, what made Joe's walk so peculiarly his. In the days I had wanted to be manly in order to endear myself to the boys, I had practiced Joe's walk without success. It was a natural progress: water flowing, arrow traveling. This Greg had. When he reached the fireplace, Greg turned, said, "Let us pray."

He didn't have Joe's voice. What he had was sincerity and conviction. God, I suppose, could tell that he was an actor playacting. I couldn't. It was lucky that Wanda was still at school. She would have accepted China once again as her destiny.

"Well?" asked Greg the actor, not the preacher, when he had finished.

"Did you make up that prayer as you went along?"

"Make it up? No, it's part of the script. I read the same lines when I tried out for the part."

"Then you didn't believe what you were saying?"

"I believed it when I was saying it. If I really believed it, I'd have to start preaching."

"If you were playing a man who murdered his mother, could you say to her, 'You dirty old hag, I've wanted to do this for a long, long time'? And mean it?"

"I didn't say I could play every part in the world."

Greg had one of Joe's characteristics. He was a walkie-talkie. For conversational purposes, it would be better to take a stroll with him. How I could help him play Joe, I didn't know. He was already able to reveal aspects of Joe to me more clearly than I had ever seen them in Joe myself. Since I couldn't tell this man anything about Joe, I asked him about himself.

"How did you happen to become an actor? Were there actors in your family?"

"Farmers. Nothing but farmers. Down in Riverside County."

"How did you find out you could act?"

"High school. I was a nothing in high school. I mean, I didn't know who I was. Then I got a part in a play."

"What play?"

"You wouldn't know it. The high-school English teacher wrote it. All about Ramona and Alessandro. I was Alessandro."

"You don't look very much like an Indian."

"I don't look very much like your brother, either."

"You pray like him. And walk like him."

"I walked and talked like an Indian when I was an Indian. I had an identity then. I knew who I was. I was an Indian in love with Ramona."

"Who are you when you aren't acting?"

"What makes you think I'm not acting now?"

"If this a play, what's its name?"

"Greg and Orpha."

"You may know your part, I don't know mine."

"You're a writer. Isn't it the same for you? If you wore a very big label saying 'Orpha,' you wouldn't have been able to spend so many hours being Talbot Ware. It's the same with me. My own label isn't very strong. A play's my fairy godmother. It waves a wand that takes me out of the cinders."

"It's not the same for me. I'm not nobody trying to be somebody by writing about Joe. I'm a lot of people. Maybe not the mother-murderer: I think I ought to be able to be her. Writing is about the whole world, and murder is there. You ought to be able to act that part if you're going to be a great actor."

"Be a great actor? That ambition is the end of good acting. Be Joe Chase, if I can."

"Talbot Ware."

"O.K., Talbot Ware. But mix him up with ambition, and good-bye preacher."

"You and Joe have something in common."

"Preachers are actors?"

"No, no. What I meant was you're both country boys."

"Different country. You ever been to Riverside County?"

"Orange County. Los Angeles County."

"It's a different world where I come from. Desert and mountains. Sagebrush and cactus and palm trees. And tumbleweeds. Oh, God, tumbleweeds! How can a man love trees who's ever seen a tumbleweed? A tree sprinkles down acorns or pine cones. Then it stands there, taking no more responsibility. Suck up water, make sap, make leaves, shed leaves. A tumbleweed gives its all. It's the Jesus Christ of plants. Breaks loose, travels spreading the gospel. Then dies."

"Spreading the gospel of tumbleweed?"

"What else? You ever see one?"

"Of course."

"Like all Easterners, you think it's dry, dusty, has no flower. Also peculiar. Goes rolling around the country like it's alive."

"I was born in the East. But I'm a Westerner. You were born on a farm. I don't call you a farmer because of that."

"I work at being an actor. Do you work at being a Westerner?"

"I don't have to. It comes natural. I'm a tumbleweed that has rolled home."

Greg stopped his circling of the room, sat once again on the chesterfield.

"Say, what are we talking about?"

"Ourselves, I reckon. Mr. Ronson wanted me to help you play Joe. You're already more Joe than I ever knew, so that subject's out. What's left?"

"More than tumbleweeds. How long you been out here?"

"Almost ten years."

"You're an old maid?"

"No. Widow. And grass widow."

"What's 'grass widow' mean?"

"Where I come from, it means having a live ex-husband."

"We're in the same boat. Makes you feel like a failure, doesn't it?"

"Not me. Makes me feel like a success. I'd hate myself if I'd kept on with that life."

"So you walked out?"

"No, he did. But he wouldn't have, if I'd done what he asked."

"Ten years alone."

"I've got a daughter. And living with Joe is far from being alone."

"Aren't you lonesome at night?"

"Not for Jake."

"O.K., Tumbleweed. It's none of my business."

"That's right. I'm hired to advise you, not vice versa."

Wanda came home early because she knew a movie actor was going to be at the house.

"Hi, Kickapoo," I said. "This is Gregory McGovern, the man who's going to play Talbot Ware."

Greg rose, said, "How, Kickapoo. I'm Geronimo."

"My name's Wanda," Wanda said, rebuking me. "I have a picture of you. Will you autograph it?"

"You have made my day, Wanda."

"Where'd you find his picture, Wanda?"

"In a movie magazine."

Greg held Wanda's pen poised above the picture. "For Tumble-weed's daughter, with love from Geronimo."

"Sign your real name," Wanda asked.

"Best wishes to Wanda. Gregory McGovern."

Wanda sat down, gazing at the picture as if it were of greater consequence than the man himself. Perhaps it was. She could show it to her friends. It was indisputable evidence that she had seen the actor and talked with him.

There was more to being a technical adviser than talking to the star. I was expected to show up on the set every day. They depended on me for reliable information about life thirty-five years ago on a back-east farm. There hadn't been much I could tell Greg about being Talbot-Joe. There was a great deal I could tell Mr. Ronson, the costume and set designers, and even the scriptwriters, about how people lived at the turn of the century.

They thought that trays of drying fruit looked farmlike and back-easty. Apples and corn, yes. Apricots and figs, no. They thought that a little farm boy should wear overalls. Not then in southern Indiana and Kentucky: what that boy wore was knee-length pants over which hung a skirt-jacket of the same material. Luckily I had a snapshot of Joe in just such an outfit; otherwise little Gary Gaines, hired to play Talbot as a child, would have resigned rather than appear in such a sissy getup.

The moviemakers could not believe that in 1910 families were still looking at stereopticon views and showing their picture albums to guests. Brady had been making pictures as early as the Civil War. In 1910 was the Kodak craze just hitting farm families? Yes, it was. Women on the farm did not wear the form-fitting basques that movie Westerns had accustomed audiences to expect. My mother wore a kind of Mother Hubbard, cinched in at the waist by the broad strings of a voluminous gingham apron. In 1910 breasts had not yet become public.

With World War II about to erupt, World War I seemed a century ago. Surely Mr. Ware could say of Talbot, racketing around, "How you gonna keep them down on the farm?" No, not in 1910, he couldn't.

Mr. Ronson did more than support me. He offered reasons for sticking close to the facts that had never occurred to me.

To the man who had to remove "How you gonna keep them down on the farm" from the script, he said, "Because there's so much in this story that's strange, we've got to be more careful than usual to keep everything else a hundred-percent believable. When you've got a twisted leg coming straight in a church meeting and a woman choosing death because she thinks it's God's will, everything else has got to be the way people remember it. Or if they don't remember, believe it to have been."

3

So I was right; and as technical adviser I had to be right. As a woman, being an authority on what had happened thirty-five years ago made me appear to others, I was afraid, almost half a century old. That wasn't the way I felt. I hadn't felt so young since we had put on the play of the crusaders at Fairmont School.

The story of a good man is never as engrossing as that of a villain. The trial was a godsend to Ronson, as was the lure of the fictitious woman who would have taken Talbot away from his calling. Ronson's job, and mine to a much lesser degree, was to make a picture so appealing that it would bring in paying customers by the thousands. This was child's play compared with real marriage and death, with real divorce and religion; and I was childish enough to enjoy it.

I taught poor little Gary Gaines how to play a farm boy. Gary was nine years old, but small enough to play a six-year-old. He was unhappy to begin with about his size, and further humiliated by the outfit he had to wear—nothing more than a dress, in his opinion. Those little shorts that peeked out from under the dress had as well, he thought, have been a diaper. He moped around out of sight as much as possible and, far from giving the impression of a fun-loving little rascal, appeared to have been from the cradle a good gray parson with a mean streak.

I didn't do it for the movie, though it helped the movie. I did it for the boy's sake, he was so miserable, and for my own pleasure. I taught Gary how to play what Joe and I called "mumbletypeg." Mumbletypeg was played with a jackknife, two blades open. The knife was given a toss onto firm earth or a good-sized board, the object being to drive the blades or blade into the earth or board so that the knife stood upright instead of falling flat. Upright on one blade counted five points; on two, one point.

It wasn't really a dangerous game, though those sharp blades made it seem so; and since players sat opposite each other, a too enthusiastic toss might actually have wounded an opponent. We used the very jackknife Joe and I had used as children. Gary and I had an audience when we played. This was good for Gary. Size didn't have any part in this game, and Gary was much better at mumbletypeg than I. With success, he began to act like a boy instead of a pint-sized preacher.

One of the persons who came to watch us was Greg. I wondered how I could have been so blind to his looks when I first saw him. Not that I thought him plain then and now found him handsome. I hadn't seen him at all that first time, except to notice that he didn't look like Joe. Mumbletypeg wasn't nearly as absorbing as talk about the role he was to play. And now I used my eyes, especially when he said to me, "Mind if I play with Gary for a minute?"

I didn't mind at all. I gave Greg my place, thinking, This won't be as easy as preaching or walking, Greg. I was wrong. It was easy for him. He beat Gary a couple of times, then was too kindhearted to continue doing so.

Everyone knows Gregory McGovern now. Not everyone remembers him as he was thirty-five years ago, though he has the kind of face that has weathered well. The square-faced boys with the big jaws have the bone structure that is a natural encouragement for jowls. The bones in Greg's face, more delicate, ran to nose, forehead, and high cheekbones. He played mumbletypeg with his whole face: entire dramas of defeat, surprise, and pride were enacted there. I saw then how he would be able to play Joe young and foolhardy, Joe middle-aged and God-touched.

What you observe in another person tells you something about yourself—if you're interested enough in yourself to note it. I was. I had broken free of my bondage to wheat-haired, tall, heavy-thighed men. Beauty may be in the eye of the observer; the eyes of this observer had been incapable of reflecting much diversity in beauty. I was also free of my bondage to reason. Reason would have told me, "He's a good and kindhearted mumbletypeg player; he is also a semi-successful actor; most important of all, he is ten years younger than you. Forget him."

I would have forgotten him, I think, if he hadn't handed me a note after he'd finished his game with Gary. Words I read always impress me more than words I hear. You have a chance to dream about, exaggerate, add to the written word. With the spoken word, you're mixed up with a live speaker, too busy thinking of a reply, to meditate or dream. It was Lon's remark written on my composition that had kept me awake nights imagining. It was Jake blaming and destroying words who alienated me.

Greg handed me a sheet of lined paper torn from a notebook.

"Read this," he said. "No, not now. When you get home. It's something I'd like you to know. I already told you I need to have lines written for me. Nobody wrote these for me, so I had to write them myself. I know them by heart. It'd be like playacting for me to say them. Read them when you get home."

I was embarrassed. It was like playacting right then. I could imagine a scene in a play like that, but I had never expected to be handed such a note in real life. I put the folded sheet in my purse as quickly and carelessly as if it had been an overparking notice found under my windshield wiper.

"O.K.," I said. "I'll read it at home."

Greg handed me Joe's jackknife, which he still held. "Challenge you to a game someday."

"You're too good for me," I said.

4

When I became a technical adviser, I also became a car owner, a yellow Dodge convertible with red leather upholstery. I remembered when Ebon had said that Ford, by abandoning his all-black cars, would have troubles. He hadn't, Dodge hadn't; and here I was driving the brightest possible combination of colors, far from the buggies and spring wagons of Bigger Township.

I had no inclination to read Greg's note before I got home—and not much inclination then. Delay breeds fear. I thought it might be a message saying, "I am sorry to tell you that I have informed Mr. Ronson that you have not been helpful as a technical adviser. I know that you have tried, and I give you credit for that. Mr. Ronson should have employed someone with more, or at least some, experience with moviemaking. Sincerely, Greg McGovern."

I went in the house, Wanda and Joe not yet home, sat down in the crying chair, picked up the latest of Pussy's descendants, a beautiful cat with a California name—Honcho. Jake would have approved the change in name. Fact, not delicacy, had caused it. Honcho was too obviously male to be called "Pussy."

I weighed Greg's note and thought again it might be critical. Why didn't I wad it up and throw it in the wastepaper basket, or burn it à la Jake? I had been hired by Ronson, not Greg McGovern. My contract didn't require me to please every living soul connected with *Talbot Ware*.

Of course I was interested in whatever Greg had to say. So, rocking, Honcho as heavy on my lap as a lump of warm lead, I read. "Dear Orpha:

"Forgive me for not using your full name. I've been doing some reading about Quakers and find they don't Mister and Missus each other. Since I'm going to be playing a Quaker, maybe I'd better start talking like one.

"What I want to talk about is your book, *Talbot Ware*. I don't want to downgrade anyone else on the lot, but if anyone, including Ronson, has ever read anything but the script, I'll eat my hat. My Quaker hat, which is pretty good-sized, as you know.

"That book made me laugh and cry. That book is about your brother. He couldn't have written it, though. It had to be written by someone who stood outside Joe Chase, saw his good and his bad, his strangeness and his holiness, and loved him.

"I don't know who I became reading that book, Joe Chase (saint, his sister says) or the sister who saw, loved, and wrote. I'm certainly more like Joe in most ways (subtract the saintliness) that I am like the writer. Anyway, I wanted you to know that I read the book. It made me laugh and cry. I lived it. Because I am to be the writer's brother, and because I lived with the writer's book for a couple of evenings, I think I can sign myself yours,

"With love, Greg"

Honcho, stroked till the sparks flew, jumped off my lap and lay at my feet with a cat's slow tail ripple, which says, "What goes here?"

I wasn't sure myself. Except for one thing: the book had been read and liked. Greg was right. On the set, no one spoke of the book. Joe had refused to read it. Wanda had typed it and, for all she had ever said, those four hundred and sixteen pages had been only a million or two punches on a keyboard. Some editor had liked what he read, or the book would never have been published.

Liking of the book certainly pleased me. It was nothing to the effect "Yours, with love" had on me. Back in Bigger Township, no letters except those between parents and children, husbands and wives, or lovers on the verge of marriage were so signed. Lon did say, "Your loving husband." Jake said, "As ever." Papa signed his letters, "Your affectionate Dad." Mama wrote, "Lovingly, Mother."

Hollywood wasn't Bigger Township. People parting for the day kissed. Strangers called each other "darling," and "Yours, with love" from a Hollywoodite might mean just as much and just as little as "Yours sincerely" meant elsewhere: a way to end a letter and no guarantee whatsoever that every word was gospel truth.

I was still in my rocker, note in hand, when Wanda returned from school. She came by school bus and her hours were more dependable than Joe's, who came whenever the Lord, the afflicted, and Ministry and Oversight woke up to the fact that the poor man had to eat as well as pray. This was no hardship for Joe, who was no more bound to schedules than the Old Testament locust eaters. It would have been an inconvenience for a maker of soufflés and omelets. Stewed tomatoes, however, stayed much the same; if their fifteen-minute cooking time ran to an hour, no harm was done.

Wanda picked Honcho up from the floor as if he were an abused and battered child.

"Poor old Honcho," she said.

"He jumped out of my lap of his own accord just a minute ago."

"Any mail for me?"

There never was any mail for Wanda; she was eighteen and hadn't stopped hoping. Perhaps there would be a letter saying, "We are pleased to inform you that you have been awarded the Singer Sewing Machine Prize for the best-dressed teen-ager of the year."

Why scorn the hopeful? Look at the prize I had just received. "Your book made me laugh and cry. Yours, with love." Acclaim, understanding, love, unasked for, unexpected, all declared on a sheet

339

of binder paper, National Brand 45-491. I handed the sheet to Wanda. Let her see what the novel she had typed meant to someone else.

What the words said meant less to her than who they were from.

"May I have this to put in my McGovern scrapbook?"

"I didn't know you had a McGovern scrapbook."

"I started one when I got Greg's autographed picture. Look, I'll show you."

The book she brought from her room was the standard-sized product used by high-school girls for football programs, report cards, snapshots. Wanda's book didn't have any such collection. Its title, printed in black crayon, was on the outside: The Book of Gregory McGovern, Actor. And that is what it was. There was not a picture or a line of print in the book that did not relate to Gregory McGovern. Some of it had to do with Greg before he became an actor: information I knew nothing about and would have had no idea where to find. The high-school baseball team he had played on, the high-school sweetheart he had married and been divorced from.

"Where did you get all this stuff?"

"Some of it I wrote for. Some of it I found in stores that keep old movie magazines."

"Why?"

"It's a hobby."

"Like stamps?"

"Stamps aren't human. And they don't become famous."

"Do you think Greg'll be famous?"

"It's a gamble," Wanda, already California-wise, said. "He'll have to have the break of a few good pictures."

"Like *Talbot Ware*?"

"That's a start. May I have his note for my scrapbook?"

I didn't want to part with it. And I didn't want to tell Wanda I didn't want to. "Wait till I show it to Joe."

"It's a very kind note. Most boys don't write such notes to their mothers."

"Mothers! Boys! He's twenty-nine years old."

"You're ten years older."

"I am. You're over ten years younger. Do you feel like his daughter?"

"No, Mama. I don't feel like anybody's daughter but yours."

Wanda gave Honcho a flip, brought the note to me, and gave me the hug habitual to the twenty years that separated us—or, more truly, joined us. "I'm proud of you, Mama. I ought to make a scrapbook about you, too."

Joe, when I showed him the note, said, "That boy's got some line, hasn't he?"

"What do you mean, 'line,' Joe?"

"When it comes to sweet-talking the author of the book, he knows how to do it."

"You don't think he meant it?"

It wasn't in Joe to say something wounding. "Oh, sure, he meant it."

It wasn't in Joe to salve your feelings by saying what he didn't believe. Still, I felt some salve in that statement.

I handed the note to Wanda. "Put it in your scrapbook, Wanda. It's handwritten and shows his good-heartedness."

5

Before Wanda could get the note pasted down, I borrowed it back. I didn't need to lie about my reason for doing so. Wanda took for granted that I wanted to read it through again before answering it. I wanted to read it through, period. Again and again. Laughter and tears and love. Written words send me to dreaming in a way spoken words never do. For one thing, the eye can inspect written words over and over; the words the ear hears no longer exist. They are nothing but memories; and everyone knows that memories can distort. Even the way Greg formed his letters came to have meaning. His was not the neat spare little hand of a bookkeeper. Oh, no. It was clear and plain, and at the same time wild and free.

For two days I did my housework, gave what technical advice I was asked for. I was truly present in none of this. I was living in a dream. On the evening of the third day, the phone rang and all of my belief in the power of the written word as compared with the spoken went up in smoke. For the first half of the conversation, belief was intact. The speaker was Greg, telling me that he wouldn't be needed on the lot the next day. I didn't know why he should be telling me. I worked day in and day out, no matter what actors showed up. Then, all at once, with no more said, I moved out of my dream into real life, where I was madly in love. I knew that phrase, of course; until that moment I had never known its meaning. Mad meant crazy, out of one's mind, with no thought of what is rational, Godly, appropriate. I knew at once what had happened. I was in love, and when this takes place, matters that would once have troubled you are insignificant. Ten years older. A bad example to Wanda. A millstone around Joe's neck as a preacher: his sister and housekeeper taking up with a movie actor! I knew all of this, and wasn't troubled. What troubled me wasn't what Joe or Wanda or the congregation might think of me. Nothing mattered but what Greg thought. My madness hadn't separated me from a belief of the time and place in which I was brought up: that a woman ruins her chances with a man if she is forward with him. Half a man's pleasure is taken away from him if he is pursued. No matter what she feels, the woman who falls in love with a man must appear to retreat. I was madly in love, but not mad enough to forget for a minute this fact.

All this took place in my mind between one sentence of Greg's and the next. What he said next might have been the words of a mind reader. "Orpha, I've been talking to Ronson. He says you'd do the picture more good to spend the day with me tomorrow telling me about Joe's sickness than teaching Gary any more mumbletypeg."

"I wasn't going to teach him any more. He's better than I am, already."

"I was just kidding. How about the day with me?"

"Here?"

"No. Out in the sagebrush country. See a tumbleweed tumble. How'd you like that, Tumbleweed?"

"Where you were born?"

"Right. Hemet."

"That's a long trip, isn't it?"

"A couple of hours. We'll stop at the Mission Inn for lunch. It's high time you discovered that there's more to California than Orange and Los Angeles counties. Will you go?"

"Of course. I'd love to. What time?"

"Ten o'clock. Wear something cool. It heats up early out that way."

"Of course, I'd love to" didn't sound very reluctant. There wasn't much hint of "Catch me if you can" in it. But it was at least an answer to an invitation, not an invitation.

342

6

It was still April. As we drove southeast we went from spring to summer.

"Aren't you glad I told you to wear something light?"

I was. I was glad for every word he said, though I tried to hide it. We drove through the Santa Ana Canyon; there was still water in the river in those days, and I knew a bliss beyond that of twilight or firelight, beyond the sight of a room gleaming after the dance of my housekeeping zeal. This was the response of life to life; not to objects or visual effects. We drove through the canyon named for the Mexican general, I in my white dress, half chambray, half lace-insertion, expecting nothing, glorying in what was.

I think I may have felt the same way with Lon. I was too young and inexperienced then to know in the beginning what I felt or to give it a name; and what you can't name doesn't truly exist. Remember Helen Keller in the movie tasting and feeling water? The beauty and splendor of water didn't truly exist for her until she had a name for it: water. The name for what I felt was love. I needed that word in order to characterize the nature of what was happening to me. Otherwise I might have believed I was having some kind of an unusual, but pleasant, fit: a smile that extended the length of my body.

Neither Greg nor I felt any need to talk, though we did talk: about the scenery, my dress, the movie, and Greg's early life, not Joe's.

We drove past the stumpy base of Old Saddleback, whose outline was clear on Santa Ana days in Montebello. We saw where the Santa Ana was being changed from a river to a bed of sand by the first of the irrigation canals that robbed it of its water. We went past the Sherman Institute, where Indians were being taught to say farewell to wigwams and firewater.

"My wife was an Indian," Gregory said, "like Kickapoo."

"Kickapoo hasn't any Indian blood. That's just a nickname."

"Where'd she get those looks?"

"I don't know. Not from any Indian."

"Not from you?"

"She's not my daughter."

"Your husband's?"

"No. A foundling who needed a home. Why did you leave your wife?"

343

"I didn't. She left me. She was a Soboba, and when we were in high school, she liked me, because I was white, I guess. After we were married, she disliked me for the same reason. She said I looked washed-out. Compared with Eloy Souza, I did. Hey, let's cut this out."

"You started it."

"O.K. I'll stop it. Oh, God, I'm glad you could come with me today."

"Why today?"

"Any day."

I did the first touching. This was wrong in more ways than one. Morally, to begin with, though morals weren't what I was worried about then. It was wrong if I wanted Gregory McGovern to love me. And I did. I put my hand on his bare arm; he was driving in his shirt sleeves with the sleeves rolled back. Greg could drive with one hand. He could have put the arm I touched around me if he had wanted to. He wanted something better: to put two arms around me. We were driving east on that divided road outside Riverside that was arched over at that time by two rows of great gnarled pepper trees. Greg turned out from under the lacy fernlike shadows of these trees onto a dirt lane leading to someone's grove or grainfield on the slope above us. There he parked.

"There he parked." How many love stories, marriages, seductions start that way. "There he parked." There we parked and Gregory put both arms around me. Reading words, hearing words, may seem at the time all the happiness a heart can hold. The heart can hold much more. These are only a preparation for touch. It isn't true, but at that minute, a lifetime without words did not seem to be much of a deprivation.

Greg said, "Let's get out and walk around."

It was a good idea. What we had to walk around in was an olive grove. Olive trees produced a fare for sophisticates; and apart from their fruit, olive-tree leaves, which are bicolored, one side gray, one side green, give those who walk beneath them a kaleidoscope roof of changing colors.

I stood apart from Greg for a while, watching this wash of colors; and also letting my heart slow down to a more normal beat. Greg, for whatever purpose, also walked a few tree rows away from me. As he did so, I saw that his walk, so much like Joe's, was not an imitation. It was Greg's own walk. Had I fallen in love with Greg because he was like Joe? I didn't think so. Girls, they say, pick out husbands who resemble their fathers. I hadn't picked out Greg because he was a second Joe.

I gained a lot of knowledge in that olive grove. First, that Greg *was* in some ways another Joe. Second, that, once you love, differences in age disappear. Disappeared for me, that is. I think perhaps for Greg they did not. Love made me as young as Greg or younger. Perhaps every woman is seventeen when loved. She is what she feels then, which is not only young but timeless. Crow's-feet and laugh lines are gone—to her. Being loved makes a woman lovable, which is better than being beautiful.

We got to Riverside Inn for a late lunch; we ate and talked for so long we never, that day, made the trip to Greg's birthplace.

It was nearer evening than noon when we left the Inn. Outside, the sun, low in the west, was turning snow-covered Mount Tahquitz into a strawberry sundae. "My folks lived at the foot of that mountain," Greg said. "I've climbed it dozens of times. Do you like mountains?"

"I was made for them," I answered.

I was exuberant, made for whatever was sky-piercing and out of the ordinary. "A sky is wasted," I said, "without a mountain to threaten to pierce it."

"No mountains where you came from, were there?"

"We called them mountains. They were foothills, really. Little mounds of earth. How could we tell, never having seen the real thing, that they weren't mountains?"

"Imagination?"

"Some, maybe. Not I. I never imagined anything like a mountain till I saw one."

We drove home slowly. The shallow Santa Ana flowed pink over its white sands. I could not make up my mind whether it was better to sit close enough to Greg to touch him or far enough away so that I could see his face. The madly in love want all senses involved at once. It can't be done. Touch is able to fool the other four into thinking that they are not being neglected.

Greg walked me to my door, where we parted like actor and technical adviser.

Wanda greeted us. "Did you get me some pictures?"

"Never got to Hemet."

345

"What happened?"

"Spent too much time eating lunch," said Greg.

"What did you eat?"

"Damned if I know," said Greg, and hurried to his car before he had to face more questions.

<h1 style="text-align:center">7</h1>

Joe was in his bedroom-study working on a sermon.

"Nice day?"

"Beautiful."

"Think you'll make a preacher of him?"

"He's a good actor. He can be anything."

Wanda had dinner ready. Macaroni and cheese and coleslaw. "How could Greg forget in four hours what he ate for lunch?"

"I don't know. Ask him."

"Do you remember?"

"Of course. A chicken tamale."

It was a chicken something. Madness in love carries you unconcerned toward the loved one. The return is something else. Oh, Wanda, dear one, who is the mother and who is the daughter in this establishment? My cats taken care of, supper cooked, while I am frisking around in an olive grove.

I gave Wanda a hug. "Dear daughter, I'd be lost without you."

We had to urge Joe to get him to the table. The grace he returned was not silent. When he prayed, I heard Greg's voice. I didn't want to lose Joe's voice. He had weathered so much; sick and far from home; never able to attain sanctification; accused of causing a young woman's death. Weathered them all, safe now. Joe believed that it was God's will that some should suffer; perhaps that he should suffer. Was it God's will that I add to his suffering? "What kind of a man of God," they would ask, "is he, with a fornicating, moviemaking sister?" I prayed that I should not be the cause of his suffering. All I did to prevent it was to be wary and secretive. The job I held and my age were a protection. My work required that, day in and day out, I be near, if not with, Greg. Joe, who had been able for the love of God to live celibate, took for granted that I, after my two sorry marriages, would welcome celibacy also. The trouble was, I did not have a heart as open to God as Joe's. Or a heart big enough for Him and Greg.

Nowadays children know that sex has once (at least) played some part in their parents' lives. Long past, probably; pitiful, with frames and dispositions so little suited for amorousness, grotesque to imagine, let alone catch sight of such old coots naked in bed together.

Children from a sheltered life in the backwoods where Wanda and I were born didn't connect their parents with sex—or themselves, either, if they were churchgoing girls like Wanda. Wanda attributed to me and Greg, as we all do to others, more or less, something of the same nature she felt. She admired Greg. She had a crush on him. He was a movie star, handsome, funny, courteous. I helped her collect pictures and printed items when I could find them for her scrapbook. I took her with me to the studio, where she could really talk with her hero. By a stroke of good luck, since she had an expressive as well as a striking face, Ronson decided, I suppose, because he thought it would please me and Joe, to cast Wanda as one of the persons cured by faith. Oh, Kickapoo, how proud you were then, and I also.

I was torn two ways: don't hurt Joe or Wanda; don't let your concern for them keep you from being with Greg when you can. I was happy that complications on the set prevented me from brooding twenty-four hours a day on my problem.

The scriptwriter, who had been requested to add some new scenes and to alter some dialogue, resigned. At my suggestion, Ralph Navarro came over to have a look at the courtroom procedure. No one was going to question what went on at a religious revival. Persons there, it was widely believed, were more or less out of their minds anyway. What went on in a court was a different matter: the law, not God, was in control there.

After Ralph had advised, changed, corrected, we had some food in the studio commissary. Greg took Wanda home.

"Will anyone be interested in the story of a preacher?" I asked Ralph.

"The hero of the best-selling story in the world was a preacher."

"Do you think Joe's a hero?"

"Not exactly. But he's more of a hero than a home-run king or a wrong-way flier. What everyone's interested in—me, too—is the ten-thousand-year-old question: Is there any meaning in our life here on earth? Any more meaning than in the lives of buzzards, catfish, and coyotes? We live, spawn, eat, and die. Is that it? We long to believe there is more. That someone cares. That there is purpose in our living and in our living according to a gospel. Here is a man who believes he has an answer to those questions. The drawing power isn't Joe; it's the story. I hope your contract gives you a percentage of the profits. You've got a good man playing the part of Joe. He believes in whatever he's doing. He's God's man in this picture."

"Not outside the picture?"

"Well, no. Who is?"

"Joe," I said.

8

Greg and Wanda weren't home yet when I got there.

"What can be keeping them?" I asked Joe.

"Over at Papa's Bunny Burger stand, maybe."

"Should we go ahead and eat?"

"Of course. If they've had a wreck, our starving won't help any. I guarantee they haven't. They're young, they're hungry. They're both actors, with a lot to talk about. She and Greg have a lot in common."

"A schoolgirl and a married man?"

"He's not married now any more than you are. You put the percolator on and I'll get supper. What kept you so late?"

"Talking to Ralph Navarro."

"He got a part now, too?"

"Of course not. He's there to advise about the trial scenes."

"Lord God!"

"You'd agree with him. He says your being the main character won't cut any ice. It's what the movie's about that matters."

"What's he think it's about?'

"Is there a God? Can we and should we work for a Kingdom of God here on earth?"

"Isn't that what your book's about?"

"It's about you. Since that's what you believe, I suppose he's right."

"Orpha, I'll never read it, but I may turn out to be your biggest fan."

We were in the midst of supper when Greg and Wanda came in.

"Eat," Joe urged. He had prepared his favorite variation of the tomato dish: basically, tomatoes, bread crumbs, butter, but with the addition of any other chopped-up green vegetables around the house —zucchini, eggplant, onion, parsley. A real vegetable mulligan stew. Joe was proud of it. At Joe's invitation, Wanda and Greg filled soup plates with the concoction and joined us at the table.

"Haven't you had anything to eat yet?" I asked.

"Oh, yes," Wanda said, "but a long time ago. And nothing as good as this."

I was jealous, an emotion more shameful than anger or lust or greed. Jealousy doesn't want anyone else to have what you have. At the minute I hadn't reached the point of pain because Greg had chosen to be with Wanda when he could have been with me. I was jealous because they were young and I wasn't; because they could eat one meal at six o'clock and sit down and eat another at eight. I was unable to stay at the table and listen to their banter. I went to the kitchen for more coffee for Joe. Wanda joined me.

"Don't worry about my classes tomorrow, Mama. I won't do a thing but study tonight, I promise you."

I took Joe his coffee, thinking that I deserved pity and that Joe should notice that I had been ignored by Greg. At the same time I was determined, whatever I deserved, not to let anyone know what I felt. I would not go to the porch with Greg to say good night. After all, he was not my guest. Let Wanda say the farewells.

Greg put an end to nonsense of that kind.

"Good night, Wanda. Good night, Joe. Orpha, it's still early. Take a little spin with me and tell me what Navarro had to say about the court scene."

I wanted to say, "No. You could've stayed and heard Ralph himself." That didn't make sense, since I intended to go with him and the purpose of the drive wasn't quarreling. If it had been, it would have been hard to get started after Greg's first remark once we were in his car.

"Orpha, in addition to everything else, you've been a wonderful mother. I'd know that girl was your daughter anywhere. She talks like you, thinks like you, laughs like you. A girl has to really love

349

her mother to adopt all of her mother's ways. I was proud of you all over again when I saw what you'd done for Wanda."

"With Wanda."

"For, with, together, in spite of, because of. It was like being with you as a kid instead of a woman."

"Which do you like best, kid or woman?"

"Woman. Wanda's a scrapbook lover, a kid. You don't love me in any scrapbook way, do you, Orpha?"

"No, Greg."

The jealousy was gone. Wanda was my daughter; because she was an intelligent, well-behaved girl, he loved me the more. He loved me for the way I had brought up my daughter.

"Want any more to eat, Orpha?"

"Eat!"

"Well, they say, like mother like daughter, and I tell you that child of yours is an empty pit."

"Oh, Greg, I love you. I love you because you're sweet to Wanda."

"I'm sweet on you. That's what counts."

I was happy. I had forgiven myself for my jealousy. It was disgusting that I had ever felt it. If Wanda was like me, was I going to be like my mother? Jealous of my own daughter? I would prove to myself that I had cleansed myself of that slime by encouraging Wanda to be with Greg when she could.

"When," Greg asked, "are we going to make it to Hemet? Don't you want to see the desk with my initials carved on it at Fruitvale? We've got to go soon if we want to see the tumbleweeds tumble. That was a fine olive grove. I know better. When?"

"Let's keep going right now and never stop."

"All the way to Mexico. That's the direction we're headed."

"All the way!"

"Olive groves without end?"

"Never-ending olive groves."

There was a lot of talk like that. We never got to Hemet. Many olive groves, many tumbleweeds, but never the carved initials or the house where he was born and his parents still lived.

It was lucky for me that I had some other occupation than watching Greg perform, and publicly doting on him. In addition to being technical adviser, I had the job of house-moving. Joe had finally listened to the members of the Meeting who urged him to move out of his inadequate, ugly, and now unpleasantly situated raspberry home in Montebello into a suitable parsonage nearer the Meeting House in Los Angeles. The parsonage they chose was in San Marino and actually nearer Pasadena than Los Angeles. Three or four miles of travel on the new highways was nothing; and in any case nearer than Montebello. Joe had come to see or had been made to see that he was guilty of a kind of reverse vanity—proud to let everyone know that he was so humble and unostentatious that he could live in a stucco box set amidst abandoned dairy barns and new hamburger stands without complaint.

"Has this place seemed so awful to you, Orpha?"

"It has seemed like home to me. But apart from how it looks, it isn't big enough or near enough for the people who want to see you and the people you ought to see."

"If anyone thinks this is down-at-the-heels, they ought to see the Ortiz place. We made it serve its purpose, didn't we?"

I knew what he meant. There was honor in enduring, pleasure in making-do. We liked a wind to lean against. We were good at living in spite of. We had been stoics a long time before we became Christians. The house in San Marino was nothing for a stoic to take pride in: unless what he really pined for was a cabin at Walden; not this shingled redwood mansion of ten rooms, three fireplaces, and two and one-half bathrooms.

The moving-in was left to me and it was quite a job. In addition to changing houses, I had my work at the studio. These jobs kept me from being with Greg as much as I wanted; they also prevented me from being downcast when I wasn't with him.

The filming dragged on, with many reversals, firings, and rewritings. I had some pride when dialogue from the book replaced dialogue of the three or four writers who finally had a hand in the script.

The delay was all to the good for the producer. Joe's reputation, which had at first been somewhat bizarre, with the variety and number of his healings, had become, at the time of his trial, shady. This all passed away.

Everyone was far too busy to pay much heed to me and Greg; and we took care that there was very little to pay heed to. We didn't dine out, go to motels; or even find pleasure in olive groves. Greg had an apartment of his own at Pacific Palisades, and I could drive there quickly and easily the infrequent times when we were both free.

I had choked down my foolish jealousy of Wanda. And Greg took Wanda to games and movies, but not when we could find time to be alone together. A father couldn't be kinder to her, I thought. Certainly not her own father.

It was a time of happiness—not complete. I knew that what I was doing was wrong; that I endangered Joe's career, was not the mother Wanda deserved, or the woman God admired. I had the foolish, though I didn't see it as such then, belief that Greg and I would soon be married. What we were indulging in was what already had come to be known as "premarital sex." This was different from "living in sin." "Premarital sex" merely meant that acts marriage sanctioned were not being postponed until marriage. "Living in sin" meant that the value of marriage had pretty well been lost sight of. "What can marriage give us," the couple living in sin asked, "that we don't already have?"

Marriage, I still believed, could give Greg and me a great deal.

My hand hadn't been asked; and I was brought up in the era when girls were taught that the surest way to discourage a man from proposing was to make motions in that direction herself. No, that was the second surest way to discourage a man. The surest way was what I had so enthusiastically done: give the man what he should believe he could have only by marriage. "Why marry," we believed the suitor asked himself, "when all this is mine for the taking?" Since I had made the worst mistake of all, I was resolute in avoiding the second. I never asked, "When?" or "Why not?" about marriage.

The furniture, pictures, knickknacks, clocks, footstools, hooked rugs, crazy quilts that came from the farms back east, which had been sold, were more than our new home and my parents' apartment together could hold. It was Mama's intention never again to be burdened as a caretaker of household effects. She was a liberated woman before that phrase was invented, emancipated while others still clung to their chains.

Not I. I loved furniture. Greg did not say to me, "With this ring I thee wed." After a fashion, I said to Greg, "With this furniture I thee wed," and brought what I fancied a dowry to his apartment. We may not have had a wedding. We did have a home—or what looked like a home to me. Drop-leaf cherry table, walnut secretary, cross-stitched lilies and crosses on canvas surrounding "God Bless This Home," the whole framed with what appeared to be carved acorns and wheat heads.

I never spent a single night surrounded by that back-east furniture with the Pacific sounding in my ears. I counted the ticks of the clock I had heard from my childhood; never before had they gone so fast. "Five o'clock already. I don't believe it," I'd say to Greg. It was a dependable clock, and I did believe it and would be home in time to have supper with, if not to cook it for, Wanda. Joe, never busier, not only with the Meetings and people who needed his counseling and prayers, was often absent. He was also wanted on radio and could hardly say no to invitations that would permit a hundred thousand instead of a single thousand to hear his message of love and hope. He looked worn and fagged to me; the skin taut and bright across his cheekbones as in his old T.B. days.

"Poor Greg," I told Joe, "is going to have to go on a diet if he's going to play you at this stage of your career."

"Let them hire an emaciated middle-aged man whose shoulders are bent with the woes of the world. Spare Greg the dieting."

"You know what this movie might do, Joe? It might carry your beliefs to more people than you have ever been able to do yourself."

"It might. There was a Man I've read about who, except for what I've read, I might never have known. The movie is just a modern form of Scripture."

"But the movie is about you."

"You know better than that."

"Joe."

"Yes, Sis."

"Take care of yourself. Man cannot live by tomatoes alone."

Joe gave me a bone-cracking hug. "That feel weak and feeble to you?"

It didn't. It did feel feverish.

10

I had one last object, at least I told myself it was the last, to take to Greg's place: a slender hall mirror, a snow scene painted on the top fourth of the glass, with hooks on each side at the bottom where you could hang your coat and hat, then slick up your hair before entering the parlor. Greg's empty little foyer was made for just such a piece of furniture. I entered with my key and before going into the living room tried out the looks of the hall mirror in Greg's foyer; also my own looks in the mirror.

"Come on in," a woman's voice called. "I've been expecting you."

Who could be there? Some of Greg's family down from Hemet? I had, insofar as I knew, the only key besides his own and the cleaning lady's to Greg's apartment. She did her work in the morning.

I didn't answer until I stepped into the living room and saw who had called to me. It was Cherry Holman, the young woman who played the girl who had tempted Talbot Ware to forget his vow to give his life to God and run away with her instead. She was the ideal girl to do it, not much older than Wanda, blond and slender but younger-looking. By fourteen, Wanda had had the look of a mature woman, almost of a mother, a woman born to take care of a man's needs. Cherry had the look of a woman who wanted a man to take care of her needs. And with that child's frame and woman's figure, a man would want to.

"Hello, Cherry," I said. "How did you get in here?"

"With my key, Orpha," Cherry said, holding up a duplicate of my key, on a key ring the shape of a heart—which was something I didn't have.

"Why haven't I ever run into you before?"

"I stay away in the afternoons."

"What's the key for then?"

"Nights."

"Why are you here now?"

"We were bound to run into each other sooner or later. Greg told me to come over and have a talk with you."

"Did he tell you what to say?"

"Greg doesn't tell me what to say."

"He knew what you would say, though."

"I don't know that he did. What do you think he wanted me to say?"

I was tongue-tied for a long moment. Then: "I guess he'd expect you to say, 'I sleep with Greg McGovern. He loves me. Stop bothering him. Stop bringing him crazy furniture. You wrote a book with a good part in it for him. He's grateful. He's shown his gratitude. Let him alone now.' "

"You poor sad woman," said Cherry. "Sit down."

Cherry had been on the sofa, feet up, reclining. She stood, took my hand, led me to the sofa. "Sit down. Rest. Don't you love Greg? He wouldn't say anything like that in a million years. He knows I wouldn't say that in a million years."

"What would you say?"

"The truth. You're not the only woman in Greg's life. And I'm not. Face it. Accept it. Like it—or leave him. You're pretty lucky he liked you at all."

"You mean my age?"

"You're old enough to be my mother."

"That's true."

"Here I am telling you the facts of life. Not the other way around."

"Some people are slow learners."

"You've learned something. What're you going to do about it?"

"Cry, I reckon."

"You didn't ever think he'd marry you, did you?"

"I hoped."

"You poor loner!"

"I'm not a loner. I've been married twice."

"What ails you? You determined to pick out a loser for a husband?" Cherry patted my shoulder in the way I did to console a downcast Wanda. Something really does ail me, I thought. Women who ought to be mad at me, want to pull my hair out and curse me, treat me instead like long-lost sisters or mothers. They feel sorry for me. They tell me about their cross-eyed babies. They take me to a mirror so that I can see that we look like sisters. No one considers me a threat.

Cherry, who thinks I am old enough to be her mother, and I am, has more right to console me than most.

"At your age," she began, and I cut her short.

"I know something about your age, because I've been there. But you don't know a thing about being my age. Sam Johnson married Tetty when she was twenty years older than he was, loved her all of his life. Disraeli's wife, Mary Ann, was still older, and Dizzy worshiped her. Age doesn't mean everything!"

"Oh, fuck that kind of talk, Orpha," Cherry said. "I don't know who those guys were, but I bet they weren't handsome or young or actors. Were they?"

"No, they weren't."

"O.K. Forget that kind of kidding yourself then. You love Greg. Do you think if you weren't the author of that book, you'd be in here this afternoon?"

"I respect Greg. Maybe you don't. I don't think he'd make love to someone just to bolster his career."

"The hell he wouldn't. Not that he'd be conscious of it. But he's one of those guys with balls filled with ambition. He doesn't know himself what gives him a hard on. And don't blame him for it. That's the way he's made. Just be thankful he is that way, since you love him. Otherwise, believe me—and I've known Greg longer than you have—he would never have given you a second look."

Cherry was sitting in a parlor armchair that had belonged to Mama. It had never heard such talk before. Furniture lives longer than people. It's a pity we have never taught it to converse. The stories sofas could tell would outsell the most pornographic pens now at work. Think of the time wasted on dolphins when the best they can do is report enemy submarines! The sofa knows all about grandparents.

I knew Cherry was telling the truth. I had known it all the time. I had listened to my body and hung up the receiver on my brain. Cherry, as she looked at me, reminded me of someone. Does everyone we have ever known, if we live long enough, appear to us again with other names and in other guises? Sometimes looking the same? Sometimes of a different appearance? Saying what we remember having heard before?

Cherry was Marie: a much younger, much prettier Marie, but saying what Marie had said, though certainly not in Marie's words: "Suffering is sometimes God's will." I put out my hand. Cherry's hair was as dry and brittle as Marie's; for a different reason, though: bleaching, not sickness.

"I'm going now," Cherry said.

"Isn't Greg expecting you?"

"He is. It's good for people to have a few little surprises now and then."

"I'm supposed to be home cooking supper."

"Good for your family to have a few surprises, too. Wanda can cook, can't she?"

"She can. How did you know?"

"Greg."

It was one of those out-of-this-world, whatever that means, twilights California can have in September. California's hottest days always come in September. This hadn't been one of them. It had been eighty at the most. The trees around Greg's apartment were what they should be: not maples and elms and sycamores ("Through the sycamores the candlelight is gleaming on the banks of the Wabash far away") planted by homesick Easterners. Instead, they were the trees of California, brought in from elsewhere, it is true, but with no nostalgia dripping from their branches. They filled the room with California scents: more eucalyptus than anything else, a touch of pepper. There was a clash of palm fronds on the evening breeze that poured in off the Pacific.

The day was dying: as if, had it been asked, it would have been against it. If dying had to be done, the sun was going down quietly; there was no blaze of glory to celebrate nightfall: nothing that the Spanish call an "African sunset," a black-and-red conflagration. Day was dying with a whimper, not a bang, a few sad wisps of pink out toward Catalina. The sea was sending its surf against the shore in a whisper, decently subdued, aware of the hour and the coming of darkness.

I lay on the sofa, my hand on the chair that had come out of old times and had traveled from far places. I felt at that minute as if I might never move or speak again.

A sad, sad sundown. Should I go home? Never see Greg again? Never speak to Joe or Wanda of having known him? Stay? Tell Greg I would never see him again? I felt like I've read that people feel after a bullet has hit them. Stunned, but not in real pain. The pain comes later.

I felt part of the sofa, the chair, the sunset. I had the smell of eucalyptus oil and ocean brine. I felt the way the dead feel after they have said good-bye to their own life and have become part of the life of the universe. Or that's the way I thought I felt.

Greg came in, said, "Tumbleweed, I didn't expect to find you here," and I was alive again.

357

"I should have gone, I suppose."

"Why? Why? It's good to have you here at this hour. We haven't seen many sunsets together."

"This is a kind of pitiful one."

"It goes down in more ways than one. Cherry was here?"

"Yes."

Greg came to me, lifted my head and shoulders so that I lay with my head in his lap when he sat down.

"She's not a bad girl."

"I know it."

"She knows I love you."

"We didn't talk about that."

"What did you talk about?"

"That you would never marry me."

"Want me to tell you something? I'll marry someone as near like you as I can find."

I didn't say, "Why look for a replica?" I didn't want to mention age. I didn't say anything to him about Tetty or Mary Ann. For one thing, when I was with Greg, we were of an age. Why remind him of the difference?

There was no difference of any kind. Cherry's words didn't change the feel of Greg's hands or the warmth of his body. The body's language is stronger than sounds shaped by the tongue and teeth.

"You've still got make-up on, Boy."

"I did have. Now it's on you."

"What part were you playing today?"

"Holy Joe."

"I know that. What age?"

"Getting well. Getting religion."

"You are pretty brown for that stage."

"For you, too?"

"Just right. Always."

Greg helped me dress. He always did. A strong man, tender.

"Stand up there, against the wall," Greg said. The wall faced the windows and the windows faced the street lamp, whose light, leaf-shaped, came in through acacia trees. I had on a green dress, and Greg said, "Maybe you're a dryad, not a tumbleweed, after all, Tumbleweed."

Greg and I, both as uneducated as rabbits—if education is what you get in a school—were readers. "A tumbleweed tumbles for fun. A dryad running away from a man became a tree."

"You're not running?"

"I haven't."

"You don't feel demeaned?"

For a second I didn't understand him. Demeaned? Besmirched, after what I had learned from Cherry—and what had happened in spite of that. I had forgotten Cherry. "We were one," I said.

"Let me tell you something, Tumbleweed. You've had two husbands. Compared with me, you've lived in a nunnery. You read of these women whose husbands have two or three wives? And they know it and put up with it? Know why? When a woman loves a man, nothing separates them as long as he doesn't repudiate her."

He snapped the last snap of my dress. "What a final sound that has."

"Final for today. I want to get home before Wanda starts calling the police."

"She's a practical little soul, isn't she?" Greg asked.

I still didn't like to talk about Wanda to Greg. "I need to get home in time to fix Joe's gargle, too."

"Remember," said Greg, "you have never been repudiated."

It was a kiss that threatened never to stop. I stopped it, ran to my car, and drove slowly home.

11

I headed away from the beach toward the mountains; not much traffic in either direction. An evening of a lugubrious sunset now had a rain-ring around the moon. Showers were promised before morning. I felt the glory that always followed being with Greg; though words had been said that let some of the glory seep away. "Demean." Demean was one of the words. Should I have felt "demeaned"? Would a good woman have felt "demeaned," and was Greg disgusted with me because apparently I didn't care how many women he had had, just so long as I was one of them?

The other word was "repudiate." I was not repudiated and had not been; why should that reassurance dissipate the glory? In a way, that was like a man's telling his wife, "I haven't divorced you, have I?" Reassuring, but with not the warm loving ring of "You are my dear sweet darling" or "Never leave me." I did not feel demeaned. I had not been repudiated.

I drove so slowly, Wanda could have roused the entire police force of Los Angeles, Hollywood, and San Marino. Joe's raw throat, before I got home, without my honey-and-glycerine gargle, could have closed permanently.

There was one thing I would in the future do. Lack of repudiation was not enough for me. I would never again ask for it. All invitations, advances, proposals, must come from Greg. I would be there. I would not run or turn into a tree. I would say yes and not feel demeaned. If asked, I would come. If touched, I would respond. When the phone rang, I would put the receiver to my ear. If he wrote, I would read his letter. None of these things would I initiate myself.

Joe was in pain when I returned; he'd been drinking hot tomato juice, too acid to soothe his throat.

"Isn't Wanda with you?" he said in his fading voice.

"With me? No. I haven't seen Wanda since she left for school this morning. Hasn't she called? Isn't there a note?"

"Don't worry. It's not late. She's a young lady now. She doesn't have to check with Mama if she wants to be out until ten. You're late yourself, Sis. Big stuff at the studio?"

"No. I stopped to talk with Greg."

"I don't like to think about that fellow. Being me. You know what it's like? It's like having your shadow begin to speak. Want to know something else? I'm never going to see that picture. It would give me the willies. I feel like one-half of Siamese twins as it is—and I used to be a whole man."

"You let me write the book."

"That was just words. I never thought it would be published, let alone become a movie."

Joe's voice had gone from creaking to croaking. "Don't say another word until you gargle," I told him. "Do you have to go out tonight?"

"I ought to, but I'm—"

"Hush. You don't have to. So don't."

The warm gargle helped, and not talking helped; not talking was not Joe's long suit. He was born to spread the news. "Did I tell you —" he began.

"No, and not now. Try listening. You be the listener." Joe cupped a hand to an ear like a listener learning the art.

"Joe, you should see a doctor. You don't want to end up like Mama, flannel soaked with turpentine wrapped around your neck every night."

"There are worse ways for necks."

"Why, sure. The guillotine."

"I'm not joking. I've seen a doctor."

"When?"

"A couple of months ago."

"What did he say?"

"The old complaint."

"Not T.B.?"

"That's right."

"I didn't know that you could have T.B. of the throat."

"You can have T.B. of anything. The eyeballs, the bladder, the skin. Tuberculosis is tubercle bacilli gnawing away at some part of you. When they gnaw on the lungs, you can hemorrhage and bleed to death very quickly. That's an easy way, or at least fast way, to go."

"What can you do for your throat?"

"Stop talking, for one thing. They call it 'going on silence' in the sans. Rest. Eat."

"You haven't done any of those things."

"I eat."

"Tomatoes!"

"I pray."

"Are you better or worse?"

"Worse."

And I had been moaning over such words as "demean" and "repudiate." Joe had had the words "die" and "preach no more" to think about. How could brother and sister lead lives so separate? I with my body-glorying and he with his body-fading? Did he think he had been repudiated by God?

"You remember that young woman Marie? I told her that God healed. She accepted that. She also accepted something else I told her and that I believe at this minute. We cannot know God's will for us; and we must accept that suffering is sometimes His will. Look what happened to His own Son."

361

Joe was whispering now, not following any doctor's orders, with a throat that obviously required more lubricating.

Death is the final repudiation. When life leaves you, the best lover you've ever had, then you are truly demeaned. I got Joe another glass of warm gargle and emptied his basin. He was in the crying chair, and I sat on the floor beside him and held his hot, thin hand.

I leaned my head against Joe's knee. I had come from the imitation brother to the real one.

Joe said, "As it must to all."

"You fought it down once. It isn't fair for you to have to do it twice."

"Tell Job that."

"This isn't the Old Testament."

"What makes you think life's better now?"

"Have you told Mama and Papa?"

"No."

"The Meeting?"

"No."

"What do you plan to do?"

"Preach for as long as I can, then stop. Then become a part of the Kingdom I've spent so many years talking about."

"Do you want to die, Joe?"

"No, but I've never expected to avoid it."

"You're not afraid to die?"

"When you come to Meeting, what do you do there, Orpha? Have you ever listened to what's said there? By me?"

"Of course."

"Don't 'of course' me. You couldn't have listened and ask that question."

Joe may not have felt sorry for himself. I felt sorry for myself. "I'll be so alone, Joe."

"You've got Wanda."

"She'll be marrying and making a home of her own."

"Let's hope so. Orpha, do you know what would taste good to me? Would please the doctor and you, too, I hope; you're so good at it. A fine slippery omelet that slides down without chewing or swallowing. I may be willing to die. The roads are filled with drivers willing to die, and I bet nine-tenths of them would please God more by staying on their side of the line. I'm not asking to die. I'm willing, but not asking. Meanwhile, an omelet."

Wanda came in before Joe had finished, and I made her an omelet, too. I was going to help Joe to bed, lay out his pajamas, put a glass of gargle on his bedside table. Joe wouldn't have it.

"I've got a lame throat. There's nothing wrong with my legs. You better take care of Wanda. She's a sleepy-looking girl and she has no excuse for not going to school tomorrow."

12

When I was a girl, a room like Wanda's would have seemed to me made for Princess Elizabeth: ruffled chintz curtains, a bamboo desk, a hope chest, a full-length mirror, a radio. I don't think it struck Wanda as being in any way out of the ordinary. Wanda was as calm about what she did have as what she didn't have. She didn't live in her possessions or her lack of them.

Where did she live? With me, certainly in the early days—my helper in every way, false hair, cats, cooking. If there was less closeness now, who was to blame? Her mother, with her love affairs, certainly; not daughter, with her dates—though possibly a daughter with dates is happy to have a mother with an absorbing occupation of her own.

I wanted to tell Wanda about Joe. Not that she needed to know or that he wanted her to know. It was I who needed Wanda's sympathy and understanding.

I stretched out on top of Wanda's flowered ruffles.

"Are you sick, Mama?" she asked.

"Tired, Kickapoo. Sad."

"Mama, why do you call me Kickapoo? I'm not Indian, am I?"

"You know you're not. Except that every last one of us may have a drop of Indian blood. And it would probably be a good thing."

"But why do you call me Kickapoo?"

"When you were put into my arms, you had what I thought was an Indian look, dark and quiet and calm."

"I'm glad you didn't call me Apache or Sioux."

"They were fighter Indians. Kickapoo sounded to me like an Indian lollipop. Something lovable and sweet."

"Who put me in your arms?"

"Your uncle."

"Where was my mother?"

"Off getting married."

"Didn't she want me?"

"She did. The man she was marrying didn't."

"Didn't my father want me?"

"He was married to someone else."

"So I'm a bastard."

"Half of the world may be. How can we know? Or about Indian blood. It's not where we came from that matters; it's who we are."

"So I'm a bastard. I've got bad blood. It explains a lot of things."

"It doesn't explain anything. You're a wonderful girl. I don't know how I could have lived without you. I should have talked with you about these things long ago. Maybe I did it for my own sake. Vanity. I wanted to think, and I wanted you to think, that you were my own child. Though I knew you knew the difference. Perhaps it had to do with sex. In the backwoods, sex was not a nice subject to talk about."

"Kids talk about it."

"Perform it, too?"

"Not me."

"I know that, Kickapoo. I know that, Kickapoo. I don't know how I got started on this. I wanted to talk to you about Joe."

"Is something wrong with Uncle Joe?"

"He doesn't think of if that way."

"Has he lost his faith?"

"He'd think that was worse than death. Uncle Joe is dying."

"Does he want to die?"

"He doesn't want to die. If it's God's will, he's willing."

"We will pray for him."

"I have. Joe thinks his work here is finished. He thinks God is calling him home."

"What is his trouble?"

"The old sickness."

"Uncle Joe can't leave. He won't die."

"His words will live on, that's true."

"He will live on in Greg. Greg is so much like him. Whenever people see and hear Greg, it will be like Joe never left."

"He can walk like him, talk like him, sound like him when he preaches. He can never be Joe."

"Do you want to sleep with me tonight, Mama?"

"No. I'd keep you awake. I'll tumble and toss."

The newish moon was low in the west before I went to bed. I looked in on Joe. He was stretched straight out, sleeping soundly. I touched him gently. Before his fever had gone down, he had thrown back his covers. I pulled them up, covering his pajama top, which was already wet with the consumptive's night sweat. He had used all of his gargle. I fixed him a fresh glass. I closed his Bible. He would read no more that night.

I went to what had been intended as a maid's room, but was now called "the cat room." Two of Pussy's descendants, when they weren't prowling, slept there: Private Eye and Honcho. Neither was prowling that night.

In my own room, I watched the moon, still shaped like a canoe, launching itself onto, or into, the Pacific. A brother was dying. A daughter, without any explanation, stayed out until all hours. And what tore my heart? Not dying brother, not straying daughter. A gallivanting actor who had told me that whales could not live in sardine cans. Dying, straying—my pain was for Greg. Greg, who had given me as a gift of love the assurance that he had never repudiated me. Not that he never would.

Not that he never would. I undressed. I lay on my two pillows and said my nightly prayers. The moon-canoe had sunk. I prayed upward, as is no longer the custom. I was thankful, I was compassionate. Save Joe. Protect Wanda. That was my minute's prayer. My hour's prayer was, "Oh, let Greg love me forever."

I slept, I finally slept.

Wanda decided to go to secretarial school. Joe, with his worsening throat, his mounting fever and lessening pounds, continued to preach. I did not falter as a technical adviser. I saw Greg. There was no way that I, with my work, and he, with his, could avoid seeing each other. Seeing is nothing without touch and the right words. "Hello." "How's it coming?" "Take care." What are they? They are repudiation, when they are spoken by a lover.

At night I waited for the phone call. Among the letters I looked for his handwriting. At the studio or on location, I hoped for the glance, the handclasp that would say, "For your sake, I am wary, but nothing has changed."

Love, unrequited, hurts the body as much as tubercle bacilli hurt the lungs. As the weeks passed, at that point where the throat ceases to be throat and becomes chest, a heavy stone lodged and grew in size. It had nothing to do with any biological illness. It was no sympathetic imitation of Joe's ailment. It was sorrow. It was tears, congealed, hardened, and unshed. It was a sob I couldn't utter. This stone at the bottom of my throat in no way hampered speech or action. It made all speech appear to me useless. It is called, nowadays, "depression."

And all this sorrow, if that is the name for it, because one layabout actor had decided not to lay about with me. While near at hand were real causes for tears. Joe, with a throat almost gone, staggered through his work as pastor. Wanda, at eighteen, had discovered what most girls discover at fifteen: boys. She was dignified about it, but what with my work, my concern for Joe, my own heartbreak, I didn't have time to talk with Wanda—as I should have.

Joe had seen a doctor. He knew what was advised. He could not follow that advice, which was, in effect: Stop preaching. He could no more stop preaching than a soldier who has enlisted for the duration can follow the advice of someone who says, "Boy, if you want to be alive tomorrow, withdraw from this encounter." Joe could not withdraw.

His increasing frailness was noticed. Because his devotion and vehemence did not decrease, his frailness was overlooked. Besides his doctor, Wanda and I alone knew what was the trouble.

"Tell them," I urged him. "Let them see what a man can do in spite of pain."

"Boast a little?" Joe asked.

He was joking, but the joke covered a declaration.

"Is there vanity in it? You, who have healed so many, reluctant to tell the congregation that you can't heal yourself?"

"I never healed anyone. God did."

"You are remembering Marie."

"I haven't forgotten her. She suffered and kept her mouth shut."

Joe was in bed with Private Eye, the tabby-striped tom, at his feet. Private Eye had a bloody slash from some challenging tom.

"Private Eye and I are laying up for repairs," Joe said. "You go to Meeting tomorrow. If anyone asks, say I'm under the weather. Meeting's in charge of the Christian Endeavor kids, so I won't be needed."

I put my hand on Joe's forehead.

"Now don't go fooling around with my temperature. Don't you know what a temp's for? To kill the bugs. They hate heat."

I leaned over and kissed Joe.

"You shouldn't do that. These bugs are always on the lookout for a new victim."

He was wan, bone-white. His great fever showed in the glitter of his eyes. Their brightness and his smile would have fooled anyone who didn't know his history. I knew. It broke my heart. I was able to cry. I thought, These warm tears will melt the stone in my throat. They did not. When I left Joe, the tears dried, the stone with its choking weight returned. How could this be? A flurry of easeful tears for a dear brother dying; and the tombstone heaviness of granite in my throat for a man known less than a year? We cannot escape ourselves. I was not a Joe, able to forget my body in the ecstasy of union with God. My body had been entered and not by the Holy Spirit.

In bed, I no longer thought of Joe. I didn't wonder where Wanda was. My whole concern was Greg, Greg. I even considered getting in my car and driving to his apartment. What if I found a woman there? Someone would then be repudiated.

13

I went to Meeting the next morning as Joe had asked me to. Joe was almost voiceless. Wanda pleaded for another hour of sleep.

The Christian Endeavor Young People had a service that would have astounded—astounded? horrified—early Philadelphia Quakers. There was a choir in robes that would have done credit to any papal nuncio. The singers were not as active as Elvis or Tom Jones, though they were far from stationary. They sang the revival songs that had accompanied Americans on their westward march across the continent.

> "Calling to-day, calling to-day.
> Why from the sunshine
> Of love wilt thou stray,
> Farther and farther away?"

The young people were earnest and devoted. Their faces gleamed with sincerity and love. Today they would be called "Jesus freaks."

367

It was not freakish some thirty or so years ago to go to church and sing hymns of praise.

The preaching service, with a half-dozen of the young people speaking, was actually nearer an early Quaker service. The young people, they were sixteen or younger, were articulate and sincere. Joe would have been proud of them. They were products of his preaching and teaching, the results of his love for them and for Jesus.

They didn't mention Joe; not a word about "our absent pastor," "our dear leader," "our ailing friend in Jesus." Singing and preaching as if they had been born with these gifts and owed none of their ability to Joe's example. It is not unusual for a member of a Quaker congregation to rise to his feet and speak. It is expected. In the early days there were no Quaker ministers routinely delivering sixty-minute sermons at every First Day Meeting. The members of the congregation, moved by the Spirit, spoke individually.

I was moved. By the Spirit? I don't know. No, I do know. Not by the Spirit, but by anger, by rebellion, and by pity. The great Meeting House would not have been standing or filled except for Joe. And no one spoke his name, let alone prayed for his well-being.

Members of the congregation, testifying, usually spoke from their seats. I rose and walked to the pulpit from which Joe spoke—and below which had clustered the hundreds who had knelt there seeking conversion or healing or both. I was speaking about Joe. I also felt that I was speaking for Joe—or at least taking his place; even though I did what he did not want done. I told the congregation of his sickness.

"Dear friends in Jesus," I began, "dear friends of your pastor, Joseph Chase. I am here to tell you something which, if Joe had his way, you would never know. I am perhaps failing him in making this disclosure. Worse than that, I may be ignoring the will of God in telling you what my brother had decided to keep secret.

"Many of you have been healed by Jesus through my brother's prayers. Many of you, perhaps all, not only heard about his trial but also were present during the hearings. You know what the accusation was—that Joe had told a woman who had come to him seeking healing that it was God's will that some must suffer. And that she, accepting this, had accepted her suffering and death without one word of complaint. She was afraid that an outcry on her part would disturb her pastor's work of healing and saving.

368

"Joe believed what he told this woman. He believes it about himself now.

"Most of you know that Joe, when young, was sick for a long time with consumption. He has now had a recurrence of that disease —located in the throat, not the lungs. He has seen a doctor. This is something that no operation or radiation or medicine can cure. Perhaps complete rest, complete silence, cleaner, drier air.

"This would mean that Joe would have to give up his calling to preach, or, if he recovered, forgo preaching to the people he has loved and worked with for so long. He will not do this. He will leave all in God's hands.

"He did not intend that you should know any of this. I didn't know that I would speak to you of it when I came here today. I hope I have not betrayed him or that this knowledge will in any way undermine your belief in the gospel he has preached or the Christ who heals and saves."

I did not want to cry in public. What I had done was bad enough —given away my brother's secret. I didn't want to speak like a sister already bereaved.

"Let us sing," I called to the leader of the young people's choir. "Let us sing 'Blessed assurance, Jesus is mine. Oh, what a foretaste of joy divine.' "

For the duration of the song, the congregation was able to restrain itself. When the singing finished, John Chisolm, the Christian Endeavor adult leader, came to the pulpit. I retired to a chair behind him. Chisolm was a gaunt-faced, black-haired, spare, broad-shouldered man. The pulpit, which came up to my shoulders, reached only to his waist. I had never heard him speak in Meeting before. He was no screamer. He didn't need to be. His voice was resonant and carrying. Its vibrations lifted the hair at the back of my neck— that or his message.

"I have often asked myself," he said, "where was Lazarus when Jesus hung from the cross? Where was the daughter of Jarius? Where were the paralytic, the blind, the hemorrhaging He had cured? At His feet, praying? Bathing Him with their faith and tears? No, they were where we are. Comfortable, happy, listening to songs, enjoying the well-being and salvation His belief and prayers had brought them.

"Is this what we should be doing? True, Joseph Chase asks no more than Jesus Christ for the prayers of his followers. He, too, says,

369

'Thy will be done,' and is willing to accept suffering and death as the price of salvation for others.

"This does not mean that every man, woman, and child here should not at this minute be kneeling, praying that it be the will of God to restore our brother to health."

Then John Chisolm stepped from behind the pulpit, knelt beside it, and prayed: "God in heaven, hear our prayers."

With these words, the entire congregation knelt. In that Meeting House, from a little after one until almost six, praying did not cease. Occasionally one person prayed alone; more often the entire building swelled with the combined entreating and praising voices of many. For short intervals a silence even more moving than prayer filled the room. Vocal prayer was the voice of humans speaking to God. Silence was God's reply.

It was still September, once again tumbleweed time. We were on standard time, and at six in September, unless man has tinkered with the clocks, daylight is fading. John Chisolm dismissed the gathering with the prayer of parting. We left cleansed by our five hours of concern for another and communion with God.

I drove homeward north toward the mountain peaks, which were rosy-purple as plums in the fading light. I had betrayed Joe, but my Judas kiss might mean life instead of death. I had perhaps a false concept: that the force of a large number praying could be compared in power to that of an army to a single man. Surely a great wave cresting has more strength than the trickle of a stream. I let myself hope.

My parents' car was in the driveway when I reached home—my father already in the car, waiting for my mother, still in the house.

"I'm sorry I missed you, Papa."

"You shouldn't have left your brother."

"He's not worse?"

"No, no. But he needs someone to look after him."

"I left Wanda here. I went to church. Joe asked me to."

"Church till dark?"

"It was an afternoon prayer meeting—for Joe. I thought Wanda would take care of Joe."

"Wanda went for a ride with that actor fellow."

"The one who's playing Joe?"

"That's the one."

370

"I was a Mary this afternoon, not a Martha. Praying, not housekeeping," I told Papa.

"Well, Jesus wasn't sick when he praised Mary instead of Martha," Papa reminded me.

"Joe isn't better at all?"

"Not that I could see. Here's your mother. Ask her."

"Orpha," Mama said, "if you can't arrange to be home more regularly with Joe, hire someone."

"I was depending on Wanda."

"How many times do I have to tell you that girl is not dependable? I'll be glad to come over and spell you. I know that with your job on the picture and housekeeping, you don't have much time or energy left for nursing. Joe's my boy. I'd like to help take care of him."

"Joe's not usually as sick as he was today. This is the first time he's ever missed a First Day Meeting."

It was now too dark to see Mama's face. Someone in the house—it had to be Joe—turned on the porch light and by it I saw the tear streaks on her cheeks. "Joe does not expect to be better," she said.

14

Inside, Joe, looking much better than he had when I left that morning for Meeting, was eating Mama's elaborate version of Wanda's oyster soup—chopped celery and parsley afloat in the creamy dish.

"Let me fetch you a bowl, Sis."

Joe's voice was low, but out of his decision, I thought, to spare it rather than out of pain.

"I'm not hungry," I said.

"That was some Meeting you've been attending."

"It became an old-fashioned protracted Meeting before the afternoon was over."

I was of two minds—ten minds—as to whether I should tell Joe what I had done; and what had followed the telling. I decided to tell him. He would hear sooner or later, anyway. Better from my own lips.

"Joe, at Meeting this morning I told the congregation of your sickness."

"I asked you not to."

"In spite of that, I did."

"Why?"

"I thought they should know of the sacrifice you were making to carry on your ministry."

"Sacrifice? It's my joy, my health, my salvation."

"Health?"

"I'm not talking about this damned consumptive flesh of mine. It was born to die. Its time isn't long. I'm talking about my soul. My heart."

He was talking about the absence of what choked me.

"After I told them about you, no one would leave. Children, old people. Everyone stayed all afternoon. And prayed for your health."

"God bless them. He will. But their prayers will not be answered. Get me some more soup, Sis. Eat a bite with me."

I refilled Joe's bowl and got a bowl for myself.

"I have never been happier," said Joe.

"I have. I was your Judas this morning. I betrayed you."

"Will the Los Angeles County Sheriff be out to arrest me—cart me off to a Pilate?"

"It was your secret."

"It could not have been much longer. I'm not done for yet. You'll have to sit through more sermons and prayers before the year is over."

"If a doctor told you he could cure you, would you accept the cure?"

"I would. Unless I received a message I haven't received yet— that my death would do more to speed the Kingdom than my life. Now, don't take on. Boys all over the world—soldiers—are willing to die for poorer causes. Look at Germany now. Look at what I've been spared."

"Did you ever think we'd have a talk like this?"

"Not like this. I thought you'd come to California and we'd talk."

Joe took his bowl and mine to the kitchen. He was stronger. His shoulders were less stooped, his step more energetic.

"I'm going to my room," he said. "I have to speak in Whittier tomorrow. I need to do a little planning."

"Do you feel up to it?"

"I do now."

When Joe left, I went outside. A quarter-moon was falling into the sea. The night was unusually still. The garden had been planted by its original owners with California plants. I walked among poppies, manzanita, smoke trees. Pio Pico would have felt at home there. I did not at that minute know where my home was. I knew where I felt most at home—with Greg. Home was with him. What the moon did, whether the wind blew off the sea or rested, whether the plants were yuccas or pawpaws—even, oh, God, whether my brother lived or died—seemed of little consequence. Whether my daughter roamed or stayed lovingly at home did not disturb me. Except . . . except. With whom did she roam? And the concern here was not for her, as it should have been, but for myself.

I walked that yard, chewed a bay leaf, stripped a toyon branch of its berries, stayed clear of cactus. Who was I? I was all that was behind me. I had built myself. I was a part of all I had loved. And hated? If Lon walked beside me, had never left me, would I be another woman entirely? A cat came to brush at my ankles. Private Eye? Honcho? I picked it up and it rode between my crooked arm and shoulder. The need to caress, to fondle, doesn't fade with age. (Ending my thirties, I thought I had entered age.)

Joe's light was still on. Carrying the cat—it had turned out to be Honcho—I went into his room. He was in his pajamas at his trestle table, reading the Bible and taking notes.

"Hail, Witch of Endor," he said.

Honcho jumped to his lap. "Hail, Wizard. When did Wanda leave?"

"Sometime around twelve."

"With Greg?"

"Yes."

"What do you think of that?"

"What's 'that'? Greg? Or Wanda's stepping out?"

"Greg."

"You probably know him better than I do." Joe's word was "probably." His look left that word out.

I answered the look. "I do."

It's a strange fact. I had been able to talk with Joe of death, his death. Yet I couldn't talk with him of love, my love. Is death more Christian than sex? Saints die but do not copulate. Had the early church fathers been mistaken when they attributed the birth of Jesus to a virgin? As if holiness is born of virginity and sex is the source of sin? Is this the reason I could talk with Joe about sickness and death, and couldn't talk with him about love and the body's flowering? It is decent and suitable, though sorrowful, to die? Making love is indecent and should be kept secret?

I wanted to take Joe's hand, say, "Joe, you cured my headaches. Please ask God to take the stone out of my throat. Joe, it is there because I have been repudiated. It is there because I have been demeaned. Or have I? Is it wrong to be loved by a man who loves other women? Is sex like religion? Must you love only one person at a time? What if Wanda has fallen in love with Greg? What shall I tell her?"

None of this was said to Joe. He had his own death to face, and I could not add to that weight by asking him to assume my burden. Whether out of love of Joe or shamefacedness in letting him know the life I had led, I kept silent.

The paper next morning made any talk I might have had with Joe about my anguish seem trivial. A "faith healer," the *Examiner's* term, who had healed hundreds, was himself stricken. His congregation, which had not suspected his illness, had learned of his sickness through a talk by his sister. "After the disclosure of his affliction, which is judged to be terminal if he does not give up preaching and move to a healthier climate, the entire congregation spent the afternoon in prayer for their ailing pastor.

"The shooting of a movie purportedly based on the life of the Reverend Joseph Chase, although the hero in this script is named Talbot Ware, is nearing conclusion. The condition of the Reverend Chase and the effect of the prayers of his flock upon his health are not expected to subtract from the interest of audiences in this film.

"The Reverend Chase's role in the film is being played by Gregory McGovern, recent star of the radio series *Undercover Agent.*

"McGovern and the Reverend Chase's ward, Wanda Dudley, a teen-ager, have been seen together recently."

Joe had read the article before I got up. When I put breakfast on the table, he handed the paper to me. "Read this," he said.

"Do you mind?" I asked when I finished.

"Why should I? A preacher is sick. His people pray for him. Nothing shameful about that, either. It'll be a godsend to your movie people."

"How? In what way?"

"Didn't Lon ever tell you about the appeal of the biter bit?"

"Never. What does that mean?"

"It means that the one who has been the do-er gets done. In this case, the pray-er gets prayed for; the healer has lost his health. In football they call it a turnover. Twice as many people will want to see your movie now."

"What about what it says about Wanda?"

"She isn't the first girl who's stepped out with a movie star. It won't hurt her any."

"It hurts me."

"You knew she'd marry and leave you someday."

"I didn't know she'd marry Greg."

"So far as I know, he hasn't asked her."

"He won't. He doesn't care about marriage. He's an irresponsible man."

"How do you know?"

I still couldn't tell him. "I know."

Joe asked no questions. "Men can change. At Greg's age I would've been a disaster as a husband."

"You didn't want to be a husband then."

"Maybe Greg doesn't, either."

"Should I warn her?"

"I'd wait until I had more reason than now."

XIV
HOMECOMING

1

Joe was amused by the celerity with which the picture was being finished. He understood quite well the motive. "With me alive," he said, "it's an open-ended story. It's a Chinese box inside a Chinese box. The trial seems the end. The jury says innocent. The audience, reading the papers, knows better. The big trial is yet to come. The hero faces death. Well, I think I'll make it. I don't mean live, but refrain from dying until they finish the picture."

Joe kept his word. All shooting was finished. All actors, unless they were called back for some retakes, were through. It was then Joe, weak, steadily worsening, home almost all the time, received the phone call from Wanda. "Uncle Joe, Greg McGovern and I were married this morning in Reno. Give Mama my love. I'll talk to her when we come back from our honeymoon."

Joe pushed the buzzer in his room which rang both in the kitchen and in my room. He had no strength to waste making unnecessary trips; and no voice except a whisper, which he saved for a crisis.

Joe was dressed. He always dressed. By "dressed," I don't mean wearing a coat and tie. I mean slacks and a soft flannel shirt and shoes, not bedroom slippers. He was stretched out on his bed, supported in a half-upright position by three pillows stacked stair-step fashion. There was a table by one side of his bed with phone, radio, books, pen and paper. He handed me a sheet of notepaper on which he had written Wanda's message.

I read it. I sat in the chair near the foot of Joe's bed, from which visitors could face the man they had come to see. That message from Wanda written in Joe's tall spider-hand took away all hope. Had the woman Greg married not been my own daughter, I might still have hoped; and still have suffered. I might, had he married another woman, have believed what Greg had told me before: "You are not repudiated." And I might have been eager for Greg to prove it, and to prove also that sharing with another was not demeaning. But with Kickapoo? Oh, no, no.

I could not (had it been possible) have consciously hurt Kickapoo. And she, by some mysterious faculty still not understood by me, had been able to set me free. The stone was no longer in my throat. I have heard it said by a man who believed that he was drowning, going down for the third time, that a great calm came over him as it appeared that he was to be separated forever from life. When he lost hope, he lost pain and fear.

Joe, because I was silent, did not know what I felt. Or did he? What he said, and he made the effort of two words, might have meant one of two things, or possibly both.

"Don't grieve," he whispered.

"Don't grieve because you have lost the man you loved" or "Don't grieve because your daughter has married a man who will break her heart"?

I wasn't grieving for either reason. I had yet to reach the point of worrying about the life that lay ahead for Wanda. I was rejoicing, with tears, it is true, because of my unexpected deliverance. I was going down for the third time, and the prospect was peaceful.

2

Joe, as if he, too, was on contract to Ronson Films, stayed alive until after the picture's first showing. Neither Joe nor I attended the premiere.

The movie was a great success. The reviews in the morning papers praised the actors, the story, and the man on whose life the story was based. "This picture is timely," Marvin Millar wrote. "We all, whether we knew it or not, have been, in this era of violence, hungry for the story of a good man. Joseph Chase, the minister on whose life this film is based, is dying. No similarity between his life and that of the Man he calls Master has been or should have been made in the picture. Nevertheless, the audience, along with this reviewer, felt that Talbot Ware would have been willing to give his life if he had believed that by doing so he could further the Kingdom of God on earth."

Joe had enough voice to say, "Burn that trash."

"I will. I will see first what is said about Greg."

"Burn it."

I did. But not before I read, "Gregory McGovern, known up

to this time as a radio sleuth, proves himself a real actor. If he wants to change professions, his portrayal of a faith-healer evangelist is so convincing he will be able to find a pulpit any time."

3

Joe didn't want a nurse, nor did I want him to have one. Consumption is a wasting disease; it weakens, it kills; but it is not an instrument of torture. Emily Brontë died of tuberculosis standing before a mirror combing her hair. Katherine Mansfield went to a party, came home, ran up a flight of stairs, and died. Keats said to his friend and nurse, Joseph Severn, "I'll die easy, Severn." And he did.

Joe, unlike these others who died of his sickness, thought of death less as a farewell to earth than a journey to God. He, who had been a follower of Jesus, was going to join his brother.

All of this made Joe an easy patient to care for: the flesh failing, but not tortured; death less an anguished farewell to earth than the advent of what had long been anticipated. Nursing someone you care for, like writing or love-making, demands concentration; and concentration, where the whole person is undistracted by more than one concern, frees and liberates. There is no outside world. So, I was content taking care of Joe; and Joe was content. It was Joe's ease that was responsible for mine.

Sometimes Joe's voice returned. When it did, we talked of old times, when we were children back east. I was never a doll lover, but someone, taking for granted that little girls liked dolls, had given me a big sprawly rag doll. She was named Mary Ann; Raggedy Ann was the name, I think, of most rag dolls. Not mine.

"Joe, do you remember when you held poor Mary Ann by one leg and swung her round and round, banging her head against the red-hot heater so I could smell her burning?"

"Scorching," said Joe.

"Scorching," I agreed. "Why did you do it?"

"I liked to hear you howl."

"If I had been quiet, would you have done it?"

"Likely not."

"That's the only cruel thing I remember your ever doing."

"To you, maybe."

Joe, in the time between supper and bedtime, had in the days of his health usually been at meetings of one kind or another; now he liked, if able to escape from his bedroom, to lie on the sofa in the living room. The sofa faced the fireplace, and in a rainy January, a fire always burned there. I sat on the floor beside the sofa; Joe's arm of almost fleshless bone lay across my shoulders.

"That's orange wood," Joe said.

"Back east, what would we be burning?"

"Oak. Hickory. Pine."

Both of us, at the same moment, felt cold air on our shoulders, as if talking of the East had brought its climate as well as its wood back to us. There had been no knock. It was the sound of the front door being closed that caused me to turn. There, coatless as usual, a big shawl over her head and shoulders, was our Kickapoo. She ran to us, dropping the shawl as she came.

"Forgive me, forgive me," she said.

"For what?" I asked.

"For getting married without telling you."

"Why did you?"

"I thought you might say no."

"You're eighteen. We couldn't stop you."

"I thought you wouldn't like it."

I didn't ask why she thought that. I was afraid she knew.

"No one is happy when children leave home," Joe said.

"Uncle Joe, Uncle Joe, you can talk." Wanda dropped to her knees, put her cheek to Joe's, and cradled him in her arms. "You're the best father I ever had."

Joe motioned her away. "I'm catching," he said.

For whatever reason, Wanda didn't feel as free to clasp me and kiss me as she had Joe. She took both of my hands and said, "Mama, Mama. We're going to Arizona on location. I came to get the rest of my clothes."

"Except for clothes, wouldn't you have come to see us?"

"Yes, I would have. There's another reason I'm here. Can I have Honcho for my own cat? When we come home?"

Then Wanda laughed and hugged me as she had Joe.

"Welcome home, Wanda. I'm not catching."

I went with Wanda to her old room to help her choose the clothes

382

she'd need in Arizona. We were neither good choosers. It is easier just to take all.

"Mama, I know about Greg."

I held my breath. She did not say, "About you and Greg."

"I know about Greg and other women."

"How do you know?"

"He told me. He's very honest. There have been other women. He didn't say it might not happen again. But he will never repudiate me."

I didn't intend to say a word or make a sound. Evidently I did.

"I know," Wanda said. "You think I don't know what I'm talking about. I don't, if you mean experience. I know something, though, with all of my heart. And that is, what counts in love is not your head. I don't care what Greg does . . . no, I care. I mean, whatever he does, rob a bank, make love to another woman, I am his wife, and I belong to him. It will always be that way. Nothing will ever change that."

"I hope so."

Wanda gave me a mothering look. "Jake was enough to make you doubt every man on earth. Kicking cats and making you wear that false hair. Why did you marry him?"

"I was using my head. . . ."

"Poor Mama. Is Uncle Joe worse?"

"Yes."

"He won't get better?"

"That's what the doctors say."

"He's cured so many people."

"God has."

"But not Joe?"

"No."

"I don't understand God."

"Joe is about the only one I know who does."

"Is it all right if I talk to him some more?"

"It's all right for you to talk. Don't try to get him to talk. I'll finish your packing. I'll probably get things wrong. That way, you won't have to blame yourself."

Clothes represent occasions: women's clothes, anyway. I chose Wanda's high-school graduation dress, swimming suit for Newport,

383

dancing leotards. I folded a life. In some ways Wanda's leaving was a more sorrowful dying than Joe's. I don't mean that Joe was more eager to leave than Wanda; only that I anticipated a more peaceful afterlife for Joe than for Wanda.

Joe had Jesus' word for what lay ahead; Wanda had nothing but Greg's. "You will not be repudiated." Wanda, inexperienced, believed that she needed no more assurance from Greg than that she would never be repudiated. Should I tell her? What could I tell her?

"It is not as easy as you think, Wanda."

"What makes you think so, Mama?"

"Greg told me the same thing."

"Oh, no, Mama."

"Oh, yes, Kickapoo."

"Did Greg make love to you?"

"Yes, Kickapoo."

"Why did you let him?"

"I was in love with him."

"Did he repudiate you?"

"If repudiated means cast me off, no. But I felt demeaned just the same."

What would be gained from telling her any of these truths? Apart from confessing to her the life I had lived, did I really want to ruin her marriage? Maybe she had a strength I hadn't. Maybe, maybe. Separated from Greg, would Wanda probably have found and married a less talented scoundrel? If loving more than one woman constitutes rascality, Greg didn't have any corner on that market. Nor any man.

I cried as I packed. I packed and cried.

All is chance. Wanda perhaps not more so than a child engendered by the union of spermatozoa and ovum in my own body. Wanda had come to us because of Lon; not in the way usual for man and wife, but still our child.

I had finished packing by the time Wanda returned. "Uncle Joe is asleep," she said. "He went to sleep before I had a chance to say good-bye."

"I'll tell him. Or you can, when you come back."

"Do you want me to come back?"

"Of course. There's an old saying, 'Sons marry off, but daughters marry on.' "

"What does that mean?"

"Sons attach themselves to their wives' families. Daughters never leave home."

"Is that what you want?"

"Yes." Wanda, not as tall as I, leaned her head against my shoulder and hugged me. "Greg's going to be a big star. There'll be starlets and travel and God knows what else. You've got a hard row to hoe. Do you think you can make it?"

"I can make it. I didn't think going to China would be easy."

"Is Greg your China now?"

"No, no. I'm not going to try to change Greg. I meant I don't give up easy."

I said good-bye to Wanda in what had been her own room. I didn't want to watch her carry her bags to the car and drive away.

Every arrival foretells a leave-taking; every birth a death. Yet each death and departure comes to us as a surprise, a sorrow never anticipated. Life is a long series of farewells; only the circumstances should surprise us.

I did not go downstairs until I had washed my face and combed my hair. Joe was awake then.

"We'll miss her," he said. "But we'll bear up."

4

Joe's death, like Keats's, might prove to be easy. His dying, like Keats's, was long drawn out. In April I overheard by chance his whispered prayer. "Take me home, Father, take me home."

5

In April, Joe had for a short time, a week perhaps, a flare-up of health. He could speak; he could stand with the meagerest support. I had seen enough miracles in Joe's life to think that this might be another.

Joe was torn by this terrible time in the world. Men were marching, nations were falling, blood was flowing. America faced enemies across the two oceans that no longer seemed a moat against threat and attack.

Yet the kingdom Joe believed in and preached was the Kingdom of God, not a kingdom spread by tank and gas chamber and saturation bombing.

"What is all the healing in the world worth," Joe asked me, "if the healed take their strength and their well-being and use it to slaughter their fellow men? I had as well be working in a munitions factory. They'll give me an office in the War Department with a weekly allotment of able-bodied fighters to produce."

"You could heal only women," I suggested.

"Oh, Jesus Christ. Oh, Holy Moses in a haymow. In the Kingdom of God, dear Orpha, there are only human beings. No, no. Where I made my mistake was in failing to preach that the purpose of well-being was to advance the Kingdom of God. No other purpose. Not just to feel good. Rinky-dinky, on your toes. I don't preach pain. But if I have helped the ailing to regain their strength, which they will then use to kill their fellow men—also women and children—I have been God's enemy. I have betrayed Jesus Christ. My God, my God, forgive me."

Joe, who had been with me in the living room, said, "I must pray."

He went to his room a steady upright walk with a little help now and then from a handhold on a chair back. He was in his room perhaps an hour. When he returned his face was illuminated. At first I thought that the light from the sun setting in a cloudless sky was the cause of all that glow. It was not. It was Joe transfigured by an inner light.

"It has come. It has come," he said.

At first I thought he meant death, the return he had asked for to his Father. Death was far from his mind.

"It has come. It has come," he repeated. "Sanctification. The second birth. I was not yet ready for it. I can now sin no longer."

Joe saw something on my face that made him laugh. "Oh, old cynic," he said. "Oh, backwoods sexpot. You think that because sickness prevents me from lechery, I am freed from sin. Oh, Orpha, there is more sin in malice and hatred, and in the slaughter that goes on in Europe now, than in all the sex in the world. Let every soldier throw away his musket and top a woman: the Kingdom of God is nearer those rutting men and women than it is the killers."

Joe sat down, panting a little. He may have been sanctified. He was not cured. "Orpha, I am going to preach Sunday."

"Are you able?"

"I can do it."

I let it be known.

6

What Joe's congregation, what the people of Los Angeles, expected, I don't know. A miracle of some kind? In any case, out of curiosity or love of the man, their preacher, or love of the Savior whose gospel he had preached, they were there. More had come than the Meeting House could hold. The building used for Christian Endeavor and young people's Sunday school was also filled. Joe could not be seen there, but his voice by means of loudspeakers could be heard there.

I no more than his congregation could foresee the outcome of Joe's rising from what the doctor called his deathbed. Winged chariots I did not expect. Nor did I expect any sudden transformation of this wan fleshless man into the burly rubicund Joe of former years. Enough had taken place before my eyes for me to know something unexpected could happen.

I drove Joe to the Meeting. Increase in weight wasn't the miracle. His clothes hung on him. There was a change. He needed no help of chair or cane or shoulder to get there. On the way to Meeting he sat upright, his face alive with the impatience and enthusiasm of a man who has something to say and resents postponement.

The people awaiting Joe had had an inspiration: they would welcome him, not by sitting on their benches while he walked to the pulpit; they would and they did stand on each side of the sidewalk down which he had to proceed from parking lot to Meeting House.

Joe seated himself behind the pulpit. Those who had come to hear him speak took their places in the vast auditorium. Singing, which was customary, was omitted. No opening prayer was made. Nothing, it had been decided, should take precedence over the word of their pastor.

Joe rose, a gaunt man, great eyes ablaze in his ravaged face but with a clear strong voice, forceful, eloquent gestures, and a posture no disease, it appeared, would ever change.

Joe's sermon has appeared too many times in Quaker anthologies for me to repeat it here. Because its phrasing is that we use today, it is perhaps better known than Penn's "Fruits of Solitude" or Woolman's "Journal." I have this day reread that sermon. It is not, on the page, as moving as it was when spoken in Los Angeles that April morning more than thirty years ago. Part of its impact was the result of the speaker's earnest eloquence. Joe appeared to be saying, "Today in one sermon, I condense for you all I have been saying, or have been trying to say, these past years. This Meeting and I, your minister, have received acclaim because of the healing that has taken place here. Healing has taken place. We would not have been walking in the footsteps of our Lord and Savior Jesus Christ if we had failed to believe in and hence, through faith, to have received the healing He Himself bestowed upon His followers.

"If I or you, or newspapers or radios, have made it appear that this is no more than some kind of a religious health spa, all of us, and I most of all, have sinned.

"My message today is, and has been, however obscured before: the Kingdom of God is coming, and our duty and opportunity as children of God is to speed its arrival. What characterizes the Kingdom of God? The love of God and the love of your neighbor. Where these two emotions are felt, and lives reflect them, the Kingdom of God exists.

"Terrible times are upon us. They already spread across Europe and the Pacific. We are called Friends. You cannot, bearing that name, pick up a sword and slay your neighbor. You cannot, as a son of God, attack your blood brother."

There was more to the sermon. Joe, never a speaker who found it easy to speak without moving about, came out from behind the pulpit for the final minute or two of his sermon. He stood in front of the pulpit; actually, though those unaware of the extent of his illness didn't know it, supporting himself against its homey California fumed oak.

As he spoke his final sentences, Joe spread his arms, body upright, arms horizontal. His last words once again were of the Kingdom, of love of God and love of neighbor. If he was a sick man, his face didn't show it. Instead, it was illuminated with the radiance of a man experiencing the love of which he spoke.

His sermon finished, Joe moved lightly and quickly, without the support he was accustomed to need at home, to the minister's armchair behind the pulpit.

The audience was silent: there was not an amen or a prayer, no praise God or hallelujah. A few did kneel at their seats, silent, faces buried in their arms. Joe's words, his tone, his expression had spoken to them as a message for which he was just the mouthpiece. Its source was elsewhere. God's Son had spoken to them.

It was not seemly for a congregation to rise until their minister, with a word of blessing and benediction, dismissed them. Joe did not rise. After some minutes' wait, not impatient for his words, still lost in their spell, John Chisolm went from his place on the dais to Joe. Joe, behind the pulpit, could not be seen by those of us sitting below him.

Then, John Chisolm, taking his place behind the pulpit, said, "Joseph Chase, our beloved minister, has gone to join his Father."

7

Joe's funeral service was like Marie Griswold's. The mortal flesh, which had served as a dwelling place for Joe Chase's immortal spirit, was ignored. Joe's body, in an unornamented pine box, had been placed on trestles at the back of the Meeting House. The box might have contained songbooks, or cushions for weak backs. There was nothing about it to indicate that it held what had been a man.

Joe's name was never once spoken by those who were in charge of the funeral service. This was Joe's desire and, in the funerals of others, his practice. This was not an occasion for weeping over flesh that no longer lived; it was the right moment to celebrate the beliefs and principles by which the man had lived. Joe's funeral service was simply a continuation by more than one speaker of Joe's final sermon: We are here to further the establishment on earth of the Kingdom of God.

Though the words spoken were those Joe himself would have chosen, I paid less attention to them than Joe would have approved. I thought about Joe. For me, living, as I was, with Joey while yet he was alive, the services for Joey, dead, ended without my knowledge.

My mother, who had been sitting beside me, roused me. "Orpha, it's over. The people will be at the parsonage before you are if you don't get home."

I got to my feet. Everyone was invited (it was now four o'clock) to the parsonage for a cup of tea or coffee, a Quakerly wake. There was no—and this was Joe's wish—graveyard ceremony. The body had served its purpose. Its disposal, where or how, was of no consequence. Remember the life lived, not the body decaying.

As I left the Meeting House, Ralph Navarro touched my arm. "Your brother left a message with me for you. He said it was a birthday present."

"Birthday! My birthday is in July, not April."

"He knew you would say that. 'Tell her it's my birthday I'm celebrating, not hers.'"

"Joe's birthday is—"

"His birthday—" Ralph could not bring himself to say "in heaven"—"elsewhere."

Mama was tugging at my arm. "Orpha, this is a serious occasion. You should be at the house to greet people."

"Come to the house, Mr. Navarro. It won't be like the funeral service. Everybody will talk of Joey there."

8

Ralph Navarro was well known because of his defense of Joe at the trial. At the parsonage, the silence about Joe at the Meeting House was made up for. Everyone remembered the extraordinary greeting Joe had received when, helped by Ralph, he had been acquitted at his trial. "Were you ever in doubt as to the outcome of the trial?" Navarro was asked.

"Never," said he. "The innocent are sometimes hanged and the guilty go scot-free. But neither the law nor the country is yet in such bad shape that prayer has become a felony."

More than half of those who had come to laugh and cry, to praise Joe and to say that it was improbable that any of us would ever see his like again, were still present when Ralph said to me, "Could we go to Joe's study? I have a date at seven. These people are set to talk about Joe until midnight."

In Joe's study, Ralph said, "It's a simple matter. The gift Joe has for you is the house where he lived when you and your daughter first came to California. Now, don't worry about the money. The owner, who is an admirer of Joe's, practically gave it to him. You don't have to live there if you don't want to. You can't stay on here at the parsonage, of course. And Joe hoped that if you owned that house, you might not feel any need to join your parents. He says you and he have talked about that before."

"I loved that place. I could have bought it, though."

"Would you have thought of it?"

"I suppose not. I'm a drifter, I'm afraid. I take what comes."

"Well, this house has come. You don't have to make any decision right now. Or this week, even. You can rent it, sell it, live in it. Joe's memory was that you had loved it and it gave him pleasure to think that he could provide for you the place where the three of you had been happy together. By the way, where is Wanda? I haven't seen her today."

"She's on location with her husband."

"California has been good to you and Wanda. She marries a movie star; you write a book that becomes a movie."

"California wasn't good to Joe."

"I think he'd argue with you about that. California can't cure all diseases. But before he died, it made him the foremost evangelist in the country. People converted and cured by his ministry. Joe would have counted that a greater boon than a long life."

"It will be lonely without him."

"Pick up your pen, girl. Tell it all to a piece of paper."

"I've said it all about Joe."

"I didn't mean write more about Joe. More about people like Joe."

"There aren't any more like Joe."

"Joe would be the first one to tell you you were wrong. Not duplicates, God, no. But with the same goals he had."

"I don't know them."

"Then search for them. Don't let Joe blind you to lesser men. And women."

"The failures? I'm one; I promise you that's a subject I'll never touch."

"O.K., O.K. I've got to run. I'll see you at the end of the week about the house. Joe was a fine man. He lived his death. Talk of dying with your boots on. You and I saw that happen."

I saw Ralph to the door. The April twilight had turned into a clear April night. Many stars. Orion halfway up the sky. A touch of warm dryness as a Santa Ana began to play about with its gift of desert warmth.

Twenty or thirty people remained. They had not missed me. Without Joe, the house was empty. Could a person's life be told by the houses he had lived in? Were they symbols? The outward and visible indications of their inhabitants? This was not even Joe's house. It was the church's, and had been built to serve the church's purpose. Big enough to accommodate the Ministry and Oversight board when they met; plain, certainly, but with a certain elegance, the home God's servant deserved.

I had never felt at home in the parsonage. I was not born, evidently, to be a servant in the house of the Lord. In what house had I felt at home? Lon's house was his mother's—except for the grafting table and our bed. Jake's? Better a servant in the house of the Lord than a dissembling handmaiden in a house of puffles. Mama's home? No more mine than Wesley was.

Joe hadn't cared where he lived. His home was elsewhere. He was just a sojourner on earth. Joe saw my need, as he had seen my pain; the one he supplied, the other he took away.

Oh, Pepper Tree House! It had been built to let the earth in, not exclude it. Other houses were stockades, made to repulse the enemy earth: keep out the cold, keep out the sun, keep out the wind, keep out the scent of dirt and flowers and weeds and trees. Pepper Tree House had been built to let as much of the earth as possible in, while still protecting you. And even with door and windows tightly closed, earth and its flowering were inside with you.

The thought of the home, my home that awaited me, made me smile and cry. Joe's friends understood the tears, not the smile. I explained it to them.

They loved Joe all the more when they heard my story.

"When do you leave?"

"As soon as possible. This place is too big for me. The house Joe bought was the first place we lived in after Wanda and I came to California. We were very happy there."

"I haven't seen Wanda today. Where is she?"

"Off on location with her husband, making a picture."

"You haven't cast her off for marrying an actor?"

"Of course not."

9

Joe's friends, Papa, Ralph Navarro helped me move.

"You won't regret this," Ralph said. "You don't have much of a house, in my opinion, but Los Angeles is in for a boom. Chicken coops will soon sell like castles."

"Not my chicken coop. This is for me."

The house was much as we'd left it. Either it hadn't been lived in or it had been well taken care of by those who had lived there. I had been afraid either that I had romanticized its straw mats and eucalyptus portieres, or that, though I hadn't, they had been misused or even destroyed during our absence. It was like being able to dream a beautiful dream the second time. Nothing had changed: the pepper-tree rustle, the earth smell of the grass rugs, the swim of the fish-shaped shadows of eucalyptus leaves across the matting.

I don't like change. That is the reason why when I have to endure change, I work so furiously to obliterate all signs that there has been any. At the end of the second day, all the gear of moving was, if not properly stored, at least out of sight. I sat down at dusk with a cup of Papa's virility tea. I missed Joe, with his black coffee. The cats, seeing that something was being passed from hand to mouth, stayed close. Neither tom wanted or needed virility tea. I sat in the crying rocker that had accompanied us on all our moves. The front door was open. The red sky promised heat the next day. Iris and stock were blooming. I was a woman nearly forty, alone with my tea and my cats. "Rocker, rock my pain away."

I had never in my life been alone before. I had been Wesley Chase's girl and Alonzo Dudley's wife and a widow with a hired-man helper. I had been the wife of Jacob Hesse, the unfaithful wife of this man who had made a writer of me by refusing to hear me talk. I had been the paramour of my own daughter's husband.

I was, without doubt, the product of the life I had lived. There was no reason why this product had to rewalk the paths by which it had arrived, alone, to rocker, cats, and Congoin.

I was not long alone. While I was getting my second cup of tea,

Wanda arrived. When I returned to the living room, there she was, with Honcho in her arms. I put down my cup. She put down her cat.

"Mama, Mama." Always a strong clasper, Wanda held me very tight.

"Wanda, are you all right? Is something wrong?"

For a minute or two, still holding me tight, Wanda said nothing. Then she loosened me and backed away.

There were tears in her eyes. "How can you ask that when Uncle Joe's dead?"

"With you, I mean."

"I'm fine. Really fine. The reason I came was to get Honcho. You said I could have him. Remember?"

"Of course you can have him. Are you settled so he'll have a good home?"

"Settled as can be. A nice apartment on Los Feliz. Honcho will love it."

Wanda picked up the gray cat, Siamese blood in it from somewhere, so that his eyes were a little crossed. Wanda buried her chin in his heavy fur, stroked him, cuddled him, rocked him back and forth in her arms.

"We will never be separated, will we, Honcho?"

Wanda really had come to get Honcho, not to greet me or to say a last good-bye to her uncle Joe.

Children like animals because they are more nearly their size than are adults. Old people cherish animals because they have lost anyone to caress; and the hand, still hungry for response, takes what it can get. But a young woman, newly married, lavishing so many kisses and hugs on a cat?

Wanda and I were still shy with one another. I with good reason; she for whatever reasons she might have. I watched her go to her car, still clasping and nuzzling Honcho: a lost friend, newly found and faithful.

My Congoin was cold. I drank it anyway.

The red sky had faded, the fire had left nothing but ashes. I walked outside, learning the trees over again by the feel of their leaves in my hand and their scent when I crushed them in my nose.

I went inside and measured by the pedometer of my own stepping the dimensions of what Ralph had called my chicken coop. It was my castle. I stepped where Joe and Wanda before me had stepped. That was a past time. This was a now. I must live in it.

I sat at the table, relic of my first days of learning. It was equipped, as always, with pen and paper: memorial to Lon, who didn't believe in letting words race through the mind unrecorded. What companion did I have now but paper? And Private Eye, who knew only the language of hands, not lips.

I wrote a title, *Pepper Tree House*. In it would go, in it did go, the story of a family as courageous in its own way as Joe. Not a word of the life I had really lived. No guns were fired, no vows broken, no dogs poisoned in that book. Or in the sixteen novels that followed it.

XV
EVENTIDE

So I emerge from the closet of unmerited piety. This is the life I really lived. As are also, in their own way, the lives of all those women imagined by me. Their virtues were mine before I bestowed them as a gift on fictional characters. Mine in my imagination, anyway, I mean.

I had thought of it often before. I thought of it again with the air of evening skimming in off the channel through the lanai where I sat. I had watched Molokai, the big land-colored island, become at sunset the color of a threatening rain cloud. My thought once again was of Tom, good Irishman, who had cried because Nora and I had been unmoved by Lindbergh's flight and its meaning. Tom would smile now if he could know that I had come to live on the very island Lindbergh had chosen for his last resting place.

When I read that Lindbergh had chosen to be buried in Hawaii on the island of Maui, I marveled. So far from home! Ralph had not yet made me understand that for some men, the world is their home; they can choose islands or lagoons or Beverly Hills, as women (this woman) chose houses. We haven't been called "house" wives for nothing. When I moved into Pepper Tree House, I never expected to leave it. I had a deep longing to be faithful to something. In loving Pepper Tree House, I was being faithful not only to a house, but also to a past. Its rooms spoke to me with the voices of those who had once spoken there: voices of Papa and Mama; Wanda and Joe; dear durable Pussy, and, after her death, her offspring.

Faithfulness to the past can be a kind of death aboveground. Writing of the past is a resurrection; the past then lives in your words and you are free. *Pepper Tree House,* the novel, except for the house itself, was wordbuilt, a work of the imagination. That novel did not free men. Ralph did. He made it possible for me to leave that house and the past it represented.

It was time, God knows, at forty to learn the difference between love and "being in love." Why was I such a late learner? If this whole book hasn't answered that question, a sentence can't do it now. Perhaps without Ralph, I would never have learned it. If Lon had lived, such learning would not have been necessary.

I have been blessed with a long life. I have been given enough time to learn, first with a man like Jake, that the mind should not be trusted with decisions that involve the body. The body, too, must speak. And body-speak, in acts that involve the body, is a better basis for unions that involve the body than the message brought by all the gray cells in the cranium clanging together in approbation.

So Ralph came to Pepper Tree House: to talk of the deed for the property, of Joe's accomplishments, and to drink Papa's virility tea, for which he had a taste. By the time he said "Marry me," I knew the difference between love and "falling in love." I dishonored neither Lon nor Ralph by thinking Ralph an older Lon. They were individuals, would have liked each other; and Ralph, a steadfast Catholic, in a sense, does represent a Lon successful in his effort to shed his unbelief.

Loving, not being in love, I was ready, when Ralph, no longer attracted by the hurly-burly of the California courts, accepted the offer of the University of Hawaii to teach in its law school. I was ready to leave not only the house we lived in, but also the homeland itself.

Home, when you grow big enough to accept it, is not Bigger Township or Fairmont School, or Pepper Tree House or Los Feliz Boulevard. It is the sand and sky, the sun and stars, the wind and sea of the whole earth we live on; the planet we call "home." Lindbergh knew that. So did Ralph. Because of Ralph, I have been learning it.

I had been waiting all day for Ralph's return. Usually I do not wait. Oh, as the day ends I listen for the sound of his car; but day long I keep house, write, taste the wind, watch the sea colors change. That day I hadn't written a word or flicked a dustcloth. I couldn't have said how many colors the sea had been since Ralph left that morning. He had had a day for reading the five hundred and sixty-five pages I had put into his hands. What would he say?

The first book I wrote had been of Joe. *Pepper Tree House* had followed. After that, I had tried to fight free of the past by living in book after book elsewhere. That morning I had put into Ralph's hands the past itself, my past, nothing evaded or disguised. The real way to exorcise the past, I had decided, was not to run away from it, into imagined experiences among imagined persons. Instead, in a burst of truthtelling, I put the whole tangled bit into words; words that will live outside me.

I had not put the big cardboard box containing the typed manuscript into Ralph's hands with any idea of making revelations to him about myself. He knew me pretty well, I thought. What I wanted was the opinion of a man of taste and intelligence concerning the book as narrative. Was it readable? Were there omissions, repetitions, contradictions?

Waiting for news that concerns you is always better endured when moving. The lethal arrow finds the sitting duck more easily than the bird on the wing. The sun was down. The mynah birds no longer hunted for the crumbs I had thrown out earlier. I left the lanai, walked the length of the long book-lined hallway off which the bedrooms opened.

The books at the far end of the hall were the few that had belonged to my parents. Next to them were Lon's and mine. Crowding the shelves from floor to ceiling were the books that had been Joe's. The books I had bought when I began to make money, together with Ralph's, spilled over onto shelves in our bedroom.

It was the books, as I walked between them, touched them, that made me aware of what I had not thought of before: what I had put into Ralph's hands was something more than a sheaf of sentences, chapters, and sections. I had given him a woman's life, his wife's life. Most of it he of course already knew. But never before had it been put to him, not just baldly, but as a writer puts it, striving to make the reader despise the cowardice, recoil from the nastiness, observe the ugliness. Life does not specify and label as writing does. And love, being a part of life, knows how to live with life. Can it live with writing? When it is faced with a bill of particulars?

In the sudden understanding of what my book had been saying to Ralph, even that trivial unlovely phrase of a childhood school ground frightened me. Could a man love a woman who had once been called an "army mule"? Ralph had at least been kept in ignorance of that bit of ugly truth.

I didn't hear Ralph drive in. He called to me from the lanai. I came out of the darkness to the last shimmer of light, which, with the sea and our garden touching, is a double twilight: sky light falling downward, reflected water light ascending.

"Where are you?" Ralph called. "I thought you'd be anxiously waiting."

I had been anxiously waiting; the anxiety I'd felt had been, to judge from Ralph's face, uncalled for. He was smiling. The dark face, Iberian or Indian, small-boned nose and eyes of more importance than jaws or cheeks, ages far more beautifully than the Teutonic or Anglo-Saxon face. Ralph's white hair made his bronze skin glow—or perhaps it was the other way around—bronze skin made the white hair shine.

As I faced him, Ralph lifted and thumped the cardboard package of typed pages onto the glass-topped table.

"You wanted me to read this, didn't you?"

I nodded. "What do you think?"

"So far, so good."

"So far, so good?"

"Remember, I'm just a reader now. All I know is what I read in these pages. You do intend this for publication, don't you?"

"Ralph!"

"O.K. As a reader, I think some thirty or so years have gone by. Did Orpha die at Pepper Tree House? That's the last we hear of her. Who's been writing her books all these years? Is this a posthumous publication?"

"Posthumous!"

"Maybe Wanda, using Orpha's name, wrote them."

"Wanda!"

"Well, what did happen to Wanda? I liked what I read about that girl. Married an actor, borrowed a cat. Then no more Kickapoo."

"This is Orpha's story, not Wanda's."

"Then Orpha should have told us less about Wanda."

"I thought I told enough for the reader to know that Wanda would endure—and, with Greg for a husband, would have need to. Oh, Wanda's strong; she loves on. She was never repudiated. She felt demeaned and hid it. It's all there."

"How about Greg?"

"The whole world knows about Greg. He had the universal face. On it the world sees the emotions it wonders about."

"Then there's me. What happened to me? I drink virility tea and take off?"

"Oh, Ralph, you're the next book: 'The Man I Really Loved.' "

Ralph laughed. Laughing changes Ralph's face. The lawyer, the judge, the teacher, the hidalgo disappear. The man who is left is the man I married. The man I married clasped me, certainly not like a writer, not even like a wife of thirty-five years. Clasped me with what his face promised: ardor.

"O.K. That takes care of me. Now, what about you?"

"Me? After five hundred pages, you ask that?"

"I am the reader now, asking the writer a question. That's legitimate, isn't it? What happened to you after you left Pepper Tree House?"

"It's in the book."

"Married. A short horse and soon curried, I think your mother used to say."

"What happened to me, Ralph, is what happened to Joe. That's in the book, too. You remember what Joe said before he died?"

"I remember."

"I say the same thing, though for different reasons. After all the pain and stupidity and cruelty in my life, I found that love sanctifies."

Ralph turned me so that together we faced Molokai, now only a deeper darkness in the dusk. The wind off the sea was as sweet as if blown across a field of flowers.

"Also, I've been lucky."

"Lucky?"

"Fortunate. Blessed. There's nothing wrong with lucky, though. Lindbergh was lucky. They called him 'Lucky Lindy.' "

"Luck wasn't what Lindbergh flew on. The wings that carried him were faith and endurance."

"And a good plane."

"That wasn't luck, either. Lindy helped plan it."

"Never argue with a lawyer."

"There have been times when I thought you'd never learn that."

I rubbed my cheek against Ralph's evening stubble. "How did the two of us ever get here? Ever find each other in the first place?"

"Providence," said Ralph, "and a good woman's pertinacity."

"Pertinacity." That was a lawyer's word for mulishness. I accepted that. But "good" after what I had feared Ralph had seen in those five hundred pages made me cry.

403

Ralph took my tears onto his own face. "Cry for joy," he said. "Look, there are lights on Molokai, and far off across the water Lahina begins to shine. We're home. You endured and got your work done. Tumbleweed, tumble no more."